W9-BUJ-807

THE FORGETTING TIME

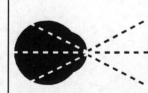

This Large Print Book carries the
Seal of Approval of N.A.V.H.

THE FORGETTING TIME

SHARON GUSKIN

THORNDIKE PRESS
A part of Gale, Cengage Learning

GALE
CENGAGE Learning·

Farmington Hills, Mich • San Francisco • New York • Waterville, Maine
Meriden, Conn • Mason, Ohio • Chicago

GALE
CENGAGE Learning®

Copyright © 2016 by Sharon Guskin.
Grateful acknowledgment is made for permission to reproduce from the following: *Life Before Life: Children's Memories of Previous Lives.* Copyright © 2005 by Jim B. Tucker, M. D. Reprinted by permission of St. Martin's Press. All right reserved.
Thorndike Press, a part of Gale, Cengage Learning.

Thorndike Press® Large Print Core.
The text of this Large Print edition is unabridged.
Other aspects of the book may vary from the original edition.
Set in 16 pt. Plantin.

LIBRARY OF CONGRESS CATALOGING-IN-PUBLICATION DATA

Names: Guskin, Sharon, author.
Title: The forgetting time / by Sharon Guskin.
Description: Waterville, Maine : Thorndike Press, 2016. | © 2016 Series: Thorndike Press large print core
Identifiers: LCCN 2015048595 | ISBN 9781410487360 (hardback) | ISBN 1410487369 (hardcover)
Subjects: LCSH: Parent and child—Fiction. | Large type books. | BISAC: FICTION / Literary.
Classification: LCC PS3607.U66 F67 2016b | DDC 813/.6—dc23
LC record available at http://lccn.loc.gov/2015048595

Published in 2016 by arrangement with Flatiron Books, a division of Holtzbrinck Publishers, LLC, c/o St. Martin's Press, LLC

Printed in Mexico
1 2 3 4 5 6 7 20 19 18 17 16

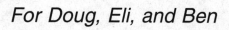

For Doug, Eli, and Ben

ONE

On the eve of her thirty-ninth birthday, on the bleakest day of the worst February in memory, Janie made what would turn out to be the pivotal decision of her life: she decided to take a vacation.

Trinidad was not the best choice, maybe; if she was going that far she should really have gone to Tobago or Venezuela, but she liked the sound of it, Trin-i-dad, its musicality like a promise. She bought the cheapest ticket she could find and got there just as the carnival revelers were all going home, the gutters filled with the most beautiful trash she'd ever seen. The streets were empty, people sleeping off the party. The cleanup crew moved slowly, in a contented, underwater shuffle. She'd scooped up handfuls of confetti and stray glittery feathers and plastic jewelry from the curb and stuffed them in her pockets, trying to absorb frivolity by osmosis.

There was a wedding going on in her hotel, an American woman marrying a Trinidadian man, and most of the guests were there for it. She watched them circling one another, the aunts and uncles and cousins wilting in the heat, their cheeks daubed with a smear of red sunburn that made them seem happier than they were, and the bemused Trinis, who were always in groups, laughing and talking in fast Trini slang.

The humidity was intense, but the warm embrace of the sea made up for it, like a consolation prize for the loveless. The beach was exactly like its picture, all palm trees and blue water and green hills, with sand-flies that brushed and stung your ankles to remind you that it was real, and little shacks planted here and there that sold bake 'n' shark — deep-fried shark in a pocket of fried fresh dough that tasted better than anything she'd ever eaten. The hotel shower sometimes had hot water and sometimes cold and sometimes it had no water at all.

The days passed easily. She lay on the beach with the kind of glossy magazine she never usually allowed herself, soaking in the sun on her legs and the spray of the sea. It had been such a long winter, snowstorms falling one after the other like a series of calamities that New York was ill prepared to meet. She had been assigned the bathrooms of a museum her firm was designing, and often she had fallen asleep at her desk, dreaming of blue tiles, or taken a car home after midnight to her silent apartment, collapsing into bed before she could wonder how her life had turned out this way.

She turned thirty-nine on her second-to-last night in Trinidad. She sat by herself at the bar on the veranda, listening to the rehearsal dinner in the open banquet hall next door. She was happy to have avoided the requisite "birthday brunch" back home, those throngs of friends with their husbands and children and their enthusiastic cards assuring her that "This is the year!"

The year for *what*? she'd always wanted to ask.

She knew what they meant, though: the year for a man. It seemed unlikely. Since her mother had died, she hadn't had the heart to go on dates the two of them couldn't analyze afterward, moment by moment, over the phone; those endless, necessary conversations that sometimes went on longer than the dates themselves. Men had always come and gone in her life; she'd felt them slipping away months before they actually did. Her mom, though, had always

9

been there, her love as basic and necessary as gravity, until one day she wasn't.

Now Janie ordered a drink and glanced at the bar menu, choosing the goat curry because she'd never had it before.

"You sure about that?" the barman said. He was a boy, really, no more than twenty, with a slim body and huge, laughing eyes. "It's spicy."

"I can take it," she said, smiling at him, wondering if she might pull an adventure out of her hat on her next-to-last night, and what it would be like to touch another body again. But the boy simply nodded and brought her the dish a short time later, not even watching to see how she fared with it.

The goat curry roared in her mouth.

"I'm impressed. I don't think I could eat that stuff," remarked the man sitting two seats down from her. He was somewhere in the midst of middle age, a bust of a man, all chest and shoulders, with a ring of blond, bristling hair circling his head like the laurels of Julius Caesar and a boxer's nose beneath bold, undefeated eyes. He was the only other guest that wasn't with the wedding party. She'd seen him around the hotel and on the beach and had been uninspired by his business magazines, his wedding ring.

She nodded back at him and took an

10

especially large spoonful of curry, feeling the heat oozing from every pore.

"Is it good?"

"It is, actually," she admitted, "in a crazy, burn-your-mouth-out kind of way." She took a sip of the rum and Coke she'd ordered; it was cold and startling after all that fire.

"Yeah?" He looked from her plate to her face. The tops of his cheeks and his head were bright pink, as if he'd flown right up to the sun and gotten away with it. "Mind if I have a taste?"

She stared at him, a bit nonplussed, and shrugged. What the hell.

"Be my guest."

He moved quickly over to the seat next to hers. He picked up her spoon and she watched as it hovered over her plate and then dove down and scooped a mouthful of her curry, depositing it between his lips.

"Jee-sus," he said. He downed a glass of water. "Jee-sus Christ." But he was laughing as he said it, and his brown eyes were admiring her frankly over the rim of his water glass. He'd probably noticed her smiling at the bar boy and decided she was up for something.

But was she? She looked at him and saw it all instantaneously: the interest in his eyes, the smooth, easy way he moved his left hand slightly behind the roti basket, temporarily obscuring the finger with the wedding ring.

He was in Port of Spain on business, a corporate man who had done something lucrative with a franchise, and he'd decided to give himself a little "vacay" to celebrate the deal. He said it like that, "Vacay," and she had to stifle a wince — who said things like that? No one she knew. He was from Houston, where she'd never been and had never felt the need to go. He had a white gold Rolex watch on his tanned wrist, the first one she'd ever seen up close. When she told him, he took it off and put it on her own small moist one, and the thing dangled there, heavy and sparkling. She liked the feel of it, liked its strangeness on the same freckled hand she'd always had, liked watching it hover like a diamond helicopter over her goat curry. "It looks good on you," he said, and he glanced up from her wrist to her face with such directness of intent that she blushed and handed him back the watch. What was she doing?

"I guess I should get going." Her words sounded reluctant even to her own ears.

"Stay and talk with me some more." His voice had a note of pleading in it, but his eyes remained bold. "Come on. I haven't had a decent conversation in a week. And you're so . . ."

"I'm so . . . what?"

"Unusual." He flashed a smile at her then, the ingratiating grin of a man who knew how and when to use his charms, a tool in that arsenal that nevertheless flared, as he looked at her, like metal in the sun, shining with something genuine — real affection coming right at her in a blast of heat.

"Oh, I'm very usual."

"No." He considered her. "Where are you from?"

She took another sip of her drink; it fuzzed her edges a bit. "Oh, who cares about that?" Her lips were cool and burning.

"I do." Another grin: quick, engaging. There and gone. But . . . *effective.*

"Okay, then I live in New York."

"But you're not a New Yorker originally." He said it as a statement of fact.

She bristled. "Why? You think I'm not tough enough to be a New Yorker?"

She felt his eyes lingering on her face and tried to withhold any evidence of the rising warmth in her cheeks. "You're tough, all right," he drawled, "but your vulnerability is showing. That's not a New York trait."

Her vulnerability was showing? This was news to her. She wanted to ask where, so

13

she could tuck it back where it belonged.

"So?" He leaned closer to her. He smelled like coconut sun lotion and curry and sweat. "Where are you really from?"

It was a tricky question. She usually demurred. The Midwest, she'd say. Or: Wisconsin, because she'd spent the longest time there, if you included college. She hadn't been back, though, since.

She never told anyone the truth. Except, for some reason, now. "I'm not from anywhere."

He shifted in his seat, frowning. "What do you mean? Where'd you grow up?"

"I don't —" She shook her head. "You don't want to hear about all this."

"I'm listening."

She glanced up at him. He was. He was listening.

But *listening* was not the word. Or maybe it was: a word usually used passively, suggesting a kind of muted receptiveness, the acceptance of the sound that comes from another person, *I hear you,* whereas what he was doing now with her felt shockingly muscular and intimate: listening with force, the way animals listen to survive in the woods.

"Well . . ." She took a breath. "My dad had one of those regional sales jobs where

14

they kept moving us around. Four years here, two years there. Michigan, Massachusetts, Washington State, Wisconsin. It was just the three of us. Then he kind of . . . kept on moving — I don't know where he went. Someplace without us. My mom and I lived in Wisconsin until I was out of college and then she moved to New Jersey until she died." It still felt strange to say it; she tried to look away from his intent eyes, but it was impossible. "Anyway, then I moved to New York, because most people there don't belong anywhere, either. So I have no particular allegiance to any place. I'm from nowhere. Isn't that funny?"

She shrugged. The words had bubbled up from inside of her. She hadn't really meant to say them.

"It sounds pretty fucking lonely," he said, still frowning, and the word was like a tiny toothpick pricking that soft part of her she hadn't meant to show. "Don't you have family somewhere?"

"Well, there's an aunt in Hawaii, but —" What was she doing? Why was she saying this to him? She stopped talking, appalled. She shook her head. "I don't do this. I'm sorry."

"But we haven't done anything," he said. There was no mistaking the wolfish shadow

15

that crossed his face. A line from Shake-speare came to her, something her mother used to whisper to Janie when they passed teenage boys at the mall: *"Yond Cassius has a lean and hungry look."* Her mother was always saying things like that.

"I mean," Janie stammered, "I don't talk like this. I don't know why I'm telling you this now. It must be the rum."

"Why shouldn't you tell me?"

She glanced at him. She couldn't believe she had opened herself up to him — that she was falling under the admittedly consid-erable charms of this businessman from Houston who wore a wedding ring.

"Well, you're a —"

"A what?"

A stranger. But that sounded too child-like. She grabbed the first word she could think of: "A Republican?" She laughed lightly, trying to make a joke out of it. She didn't even know if it was true.

Irritation spread like brushfire across his face.

"And that makes me what? Some kind of philistine?"

"What? No. Not at all."

"You think that, though. I can see it plain as day on your face." He was sitting up straight now. "You think we don't feel the same things you do?" His brown eyes, which had been so admiring, bore into her with a kind of wounded fury.

"Can we go back to talking about the curry?"

"You think we don't get our hearts broken, or break down crying when our children are born, or wonder about our place in the grand scheme of things?"

"Okay, okay. I get it. You bleed when pricked." He was still staring at her. *"'If you prick us, do we not bleed?'* It's from the *Merchant of —*"

"*Do* you get it, Shylock? Do you, really? 'Cause I'm not so sure you do."

"Watch who you're calling Shylock."

"Okay. Shylock."

"Hey."

"Whatever you say, Shylock."

"Hey!" They were grinning at each other now.

"So." She glanced at him sideways. "Children, huh?"

He waved away the question with one large, pink hand.

"Anyway," she added, "what's it matter what I think about anything?"

"Of course, it matters."

"Does it? Why?"

"Because you're smart, and you're a human being, and you're here right now at this moment and we're having this conversation," he said, leaning toward her earnestly and touching her lightly on the knee in a way that should have been slimy by any rights but wasn't. She felt a tremor pass through her quickly, outrunning her will to squelch it.

She looked down at her ravaged plate.

He probably lived in a McMansion and had three kids and a wife who played tennis, she thought.

She'd known men like this, of course, but she'd never flirted with one before — a country club man, a man who had a gift for sales. And women. At the same time she could feel that there was something else in him that drew her — it was in the quickness of his glance and the volatility of his emotions and the sense she had that there were thoughts blowing through him at a million miles a minute.

"Listen. I'm going to check out the Asa Wright Nature Centre tomorrow," he said. "Want to come along?"

"What's that?"

He jiggled his leg impatiently. "It's a *nature center.*"

"Is it far?"

He shrugged. "I'm renting a motorcycle."

18

"I don't know."

"Suit yourself." He signaled for the check. She felt his energy swiftly changing course, pulling away; she wanted it back.

"All right," she said. "Why not?"

The center was hours away, but she didn't mind. She clung tightly to his back on the motorcycle and reveled in the speed, taking in the lushness of the landscape and the chaotic tumble of the towns, the new concrete houses abutting ramshackly wooden ones, their metal roofs shining side by side in the sun. They got there by midday and, having settled into a companionable silence, followed a tour guide through the rain forest, giggling at the names of the birds he pointed out: the bananaquit and oilbirds, the bearded bellbird and blue-crowned motmot, the squirrel cuckoo and boat-billed flycatcher. An ease had set in by the time they were having high tea on the wide veranda of the former plantation house, watching the copper-rumped hummingbirds hover at the feeders dangling from the porch: four, five, six hummingbirds bobbing and whirring in the air, like a magic trick.

"It feels so colonial," Janie said, leaning back into her wicker chair.

"The good old days, huh?" He squinted

at her inscrutably.

"You're being facetious, right?"

"I don't know. They were good for some people." He kept his face blank for a moment, then burst out laughing. "What kind of an asshole do you think I am? I was a Rhodes Scholar, you know." He said it lightly, but she knew he was trying to impress her. And had succeeded.

"You were?"

He nodded slowly, his quick eyes filling up with bemusement.

"Got me a master's in eco-no-mics from Bal-li-ol College. Oxford, England." He spread out the syllables, playing the rube.

He wanted a laugh and she gave it to him. "So shouldn't you be teaching at Harvard or something?"

"For one thing, I make about twenty times what I'd make teaching, even at Harvard. And I'm not beholden to anyone. Not some head of the department, or president of the university, or spoiled-ass son of a major donor." He shook his head.

"Lone wolf, huh?"

He faux-pouted. "Lonely wolf."

They laughed together. Complicit laughter. She felt something between her shoulders loosening, a muscle she'd mistaken for bone, and a lightness came over her. Her scone crumbled to pieces in her hands and she licked the stray bits on her fingertips.

"You are just too fucking cute," he said.

"Cute." She made a face.

He recalibrated quickly. "Beautiful."

"Right."

"No, really."

She shrugged.

"You don't know, do you?" He shook his head. "You know a lot of things, but you don't know that."

She cast about for something sardonic to say and decided instead on the truth.

"No," she admitted, sighing, "I don't. Sadly. 'Cause now —" She was going to say that she was almost forty and fast on the road to losing whatever it was she'd had, she was all but ready to point out the three gray hairs and the deepening wrinkle between her eyebrows, but he waved all that away with a hand.

"You could be a hundred years old and still be beautiful," he said, as if he meant it, and she couldn't help it, it was *such* a good line — she smiled at him, soaking it all up with a queasy feeling that she was being swept along toward a shore she hadn't envisioned and needed to do some serious paddling in the other direction if she wanted to get home safe.

21

She held tightly to his waist again on the way back. It was too loud for either of them to say anything, for which she was grateful, no decisions to be made, nothing to worry over, only the palm trees and tin roofs spinning out behind her, the wind whipping her hair across her face and the warm body close to hers; this moment, then the next. Happiness began to burble in the base of her spine and rise, giddily, up her body. So this was what it was like: the present moment. She felt it like a revelation.

And wasn't this what she'd been after — this *lightness* that came galloping through, grabbing you by the waist and hauling you along with it? How could you not surrender yourself to it, even if you knew you'd end up sitting bruised in the dirt? She supposed there must be another way to experience that breathless rush of being alive — something inward, perhaps? — but she didn't know what it was or how to get there on her own.

Then the ride was over, and they were standing there awkwardly, outside the hotel. It was late; they were tired. Her hair was coated with grime from the wind. A bumpy moment, and nothing to speed them over it. I should go inside and pack, she thought, but the wedding reception was going on in

22

the banquet hall, and now they could hear the steel pan drums starting up, the sound rippling out across the night, carrying its own distinct, watery beat — drums invented years ago from the discarded cans of the oil companies, music from garbage. Who was she to resist? The humid air cradled her body like a large damp hand. "Want to go for a walk?" They said it both at the same time, as if it was meant to be.

Trouble, trouble, trouble, she said to herself as they walked, but his hand was warm in hers and she thought maybe she'd give herself this. Maybe it was all right. The wife was probably one of those women with hard, perfect faces, blond hair that gleamed around huge diamond studs. She wore short white skirts and flirted with the tennis instructor. So why should Janie care? But, no, that wasn't right, was it? This man's eyes were warm, genuine, even, if you can be calculating and genuine at the same time, which maybe you couldn't be. And he liked her, Janie, with her imperfect face, her pretty blue eyes and slightly hooked nose and curly hair. So probably — probably the wife was lovely. She had long, swinging brown hair and kind eyes. She used to be a teacher but stayed home now, caring for the little ones, patient and gentle and too smart for the brutality of that life, it was sucking the lifeblood out of her and yet feeding her at the same time — she was loving, that's what it was, this man was well loved (something in the relaxed way he moved, the shine on his face) and right now the wife was sleeping with all of their little ones in their big bed because it was easier that way, and she liked the warmth of their small bodies nestled against her, and she missed him so very much, and maybe she thought that sometimes on those long, long trips he was up to something but she trusted him because she wanted to because he had that boldness in his eyes, that life —

Why do this to herself? Can't she let herself have anything?

He was pointing out the shells scattered across the beach while she was stuck there in her thoughts.

She nodded absently.

"No, look," he said, taking her head in his big warm hands and pointing it toward the shore. "You need to look."

The shells were scuttling across the beach to the water, as if the sea was drawing them in with the power of its charm.

"But — how?"

"Sand crabs," he said. His hands were still

on her face, so it wasn't hard for him to turn it toward him and kiss her once, twice, only twice, she was thinking, just a little taste and then they'd turn right back, but then he kissed her a third time and this time she felt all of her hunger rise up like a perfumed plume of smoke from a genie that had been locked in a bottle for a hundred years, encircling this man she barely knew — though her body knew him, it wrapped itself around him fiercely and kissed him as if he was the dearest of the dear. Their defenses fell away, like their clothes. And maybe it was some uncanny combination of chemicals triggering pheromones, and maybe they'd been lovers back among the pharaohs and had just now found each other, and who knew why, really? Who fucking knew?

"Jee-sus," he said. He pulled back from her a little, and she was pleased to see that all the confidence was rubbed clean away from his face and he was as stunned by it as she was — by the force of this passion that had no business being there but was there just the same, shocking the bejesus out of both of them, as if some Ouija board hijinks at a slumber party had summoned an actual ghost.

To have sex on the beach (Wasn't that a

drink? Was this really her life, a cheesy cocktail?) with a man she didn't know, who fooled around with women, without using a condom, was a very, very, very bad idea. But her body didn't think so. And she'd never surrendered fully to anything in her life and perhaps it was time. She could hear the steel pan drums ringing like metallic bubbles loop de looping in the air, and the happy shouts of the revelers who were dancing, and the laughter of the bride and groom who were dancing, too, under that high, thatched roof. And she was almost forty and might never marry. And there was that lovely wife sleeping in that big bed with all those rosy-cheeked children and she had no one she was going back to, no house and no children and no husband, there was no one to love her at all except this warm body with its quick steady heartbeats and its burning life force. It was as if the page she'd been living on had been suddenly ripped from the binding, and she was on the loose side now, the torn, free side, fluttering down to the sandy shore, the moon rearing up high overhead.

When their bodies had had their fill at last they clung to each other on the beach, gasping.

"You . . ." He shook his head, smiling

26

wonderingly, those alive and admiring eyes taking in her white, sand-abraded body glowing on the beach. He didn't finish the thought; he stopped himself before finishing, having had an adult lifetime of just such discipline, and she didn't know what it was he was going to say about her, though she knew she'd have the rest of her life to consider the possibilities. She had a sudden impulse to tell him something — to tell him everything, all her secrets, quickly, now, before the warmth began to fade, in the hope that there might be something she could continue to hang on to, a connection she might keep —

Keep? She almost laughed at herself. Even with the present moment grinning in her face, she couldn't help turning the other way.

The end unraveled quickly. She was still processing what had happened, still replaying it in her mind as they walked slowly back to the hotel in silence, side by side, his hand touching her lightly on her back as they walked in a gesture that was part caress and part moving her onward.

"Guess this is it, then." He stood outside his door. "It was a real pleasure spending time with you."

His face was appropriately tender and

somber, but she could feel the wind in him kicking up, this urgency running through him that was the opposite of what was running through her, and knew without saying anything that her desire to entangle and to linger had no chance against his need to get the hell out of the hallway and back on his own again.

"Should we . . . exchange e-mail or something? Hey, you ever come to New York on business?" She tried to keep her voice light, but he looked at her sadly.

She bit her lip.

"All right, then," she said. She could do this. She did do this. He leaned down and kissed her, a dry husbandly kiss that still took away a tiny part of her.

She didn't know his last name. She realized that later. She hadn't needed to know, the limits of the thing being so clear that they hardly needed to be described. She'd wished, later, though, that she had it — not for the birth certificate, nor through any wish to reach out to him and complicate his life, but simply for the story itself, so that she could say to Noah someday, "One night I met this man, and it was the most beautiful night that ever was. And his name was ___"

Jeff. Jeff Something.

But maybe she had wanted it that way. Maybe she had planned it that way. Because there was no finding Jeff Something from Houston, and it had only bound Noah to her more closely, made him even more hers.

TWO

"But I'm not finished." These were the words that popped unbidden out of Jerome Anderson's mouth when the neurologist told him his life was functionally over.

"Of course not. Mr. Anderson, this is by no means a death sentence."

He hadn't meant his life, though; he'd meant his work. Which was his life, when you got right down to it.

"It's Doctor Anderson," he said. He quieted his panic by watching the neurologist sitting across the table, her elegant hands fumbling as she proceeded to tell him about his illness.

In the year since his wife had died, every woman he had met was simply Not Sheila, end of story. But suddenly he became aware again of the details that belonged only to living women: the way the doctor's eyes were moistened slightly in sympathy, the rising and falling of the soft curves he could only barely make out under the white coat as she breathed. He saw the sunlight pooling on her glossy black hair as she sat at her desk, inhaled her smell of antibacterial soap mixed with something light, familiar — the citrusy scent of perfume.

Something stirred inside of him as he looked at her, as if he was waking up from a long nap. Now? Really? Well, nobody ever said the mind was simple, or the body, either. And together they could certainly get up to some mischief. That was fodder for a study. Do patients facing serious impairment or death find their sexual organs aroused? He should shoot Clark an e-mail about it; he'd been doing some interesting studies on the mind-body connection. They could call it "An Inquiry into Eros/Thanatos."

"Dr. Anderson?"

The desk clock was ticking, and beneath that, he could hear the breathing of the two of them.

"Dr. Anderson. Do you understand what I've been telling you?"

Breathing, a word that inhaled and exhaled. Lose a word like that, and you lose everything.

"Dr. —"

"Do I understand? Yes, I'm not that far

31

gone. Yet. It seems I can still decode basic sentence structures." He felt his voice beginning to slip from his control, checked it with difficulty.

"Are you all right?"

He felt his pulse. Seemed normal, but he didn't trust it. "May I borrow your stethoscope?"

"Excuse me?"

"I want to check my heart rate. See how I'm really doing." He smiled, which cost him something, a mustering of flagging resources. "Please. I'll give it right back." He winked. What the hell. She was going to call psych on him any minute now. "Promise."

She pulled the stethoscope from her long neck and handed it to him. Her eyes were baffled, alert. Did this wracked being still have a spark of mojo left? He glimpsed himself in the reflection of the window behind her, barely visible against the blazing metal of cars in the parking lot: was that hollow-cheeked apparition really his face? He had never cared much about his looks, aside from knowing that they had sometimes helped him with the subjects in his work, yet now he felt the loss with a pang. He still had his hair, though the curls women used to like were long gone.

The stethoscope smelled faintly like her. He realized why the perfume was familiar to him. It was something Sheila used to wear when they went someplace nice for dinner. Probably he had bought it for her. He had no idea what it was; she'd always written down what she'd wanted and he'd dutifully given it for Christmas and birthdays, never paying attention to the details, his mind on other things.

Heart rate was a bit high, if not as rapid as he had supposed.

Sheila would have laughed at him, *Come on now, stop examining yourself and just feel it, will you?* — the way she'd laughed at him on their wedding night (was it forty-four years ago already?) when he had battered her with questions, midcoitus, *"and this feels good, like this? But this, right here, this doesn't?"* in his eagerness to figure out what worked, his curiosity egging him on, as strong as the desire itself. And what was so wrong with that? Sex, like death, was important, and yet why did no one seem to care enough to ask the questions that mattered? Kinsey did, and Kübler-Ross (and he had, too, or had tried), but they were rare and often faced the hostility of a pea-brained, backward-looking scientific establishment . . . *Let it go, Jer,* he heard Sheila say.

Just let it go.

He should have been embarrassed — his bride laughing at him on his wedding night, the stuff of comedy — but it merely confirmed to him the wisdom of the choice he'd made. She laughed because she understood what kind of animal he was, she accepted his need to know along with the rest of him, that whole human fleshsack of quirks and failings.

"Dr. Anderson." The doctor had come around the desk, placed her hand on his arm. That was something he'd never thought of, years ago, when he'd been a resident delivering bad news: the power of touch. He could feel the faint pressure of her nails through the cotton of his shirt. He began to sweat at the thought that she was going to take her hand off, so he pulled his arm away roughly, noting the startled instinctive frown as she processed the rejection. She retreated behind her desk, her diplomas on either side of her: staunch little soldiers in their Latin uniforms. "Are you all right? Can I answer any questions?"

He forced his mind back to what she had been telling him. Back to the moment when she had said that word: aphasia. A word like a pretty girl in a summer dress wielding a dagger aimed at his heart.

34

Aphasia, from the Greek word *Aphatos,* meaning: speechless.

"The prognosis is definite?'

A cart rolled through the hallway outside the room, liquids in glasses tinkling.

"The prognosis is definite."

Surely there were other questions.

"I'm not sure I understand. I didn't have brain trauma, or a stroke."

"This is a rarer form of aphasia. Primary progressive aphasia is a progressive type of dementia affecting the brain's language center."

Dementia. Now that was a word he would happily lose.

"Like —" He forced himself to say it. "Alzheimer's?" Did he study this in med school? Was it significant that he didn't remember?

"PPA is a language disorder, but yes. You might say they were cousins."

"What a family." He laughed.

"Dr. Anderson?" The neurologist was looking at him as if he was unhinged.

"Relax, Dr. Rothenberg. I'm fine. Just — processing, as they say. My life, after all . . ." He sighed. "Such as it was. *'For in that sleep of death what dreams may come / When we have shuffled off this mortal coil / Must give us pause.'* " He smiled at her, but her expression was unchanged. "Oh, good grief, woman, don't look so alarmed — don't they teach Shakespeare at Yale anymore?"

He yanked off the stethoscope, handing it to her. You see what I have to lose? He raged inwardly. Things I never thought I'd lose. Is there life after Shakespeare? Now that is a question worth asking.

Is there life after work?

But he wasn't *finished.*

"Perhaps you'd like to talk to someone — there's a social worker — or, if you prefer, a psychiatrist —"

"I am a psychiatrist."

"Dr. Anderson. Listen to me." He noted, but could not feel, the concern in her eyes. "Many people with primary progressive aphasia continue to take care of themselves for six or seven years. More, in some cases. And yours is in the very early stages."

"So I'll be able to feed myself and — wipe myself and all of that? For years to come?"

"Most likely."

"Just not be able to talk. Or read. Or communicate in any way with the rest of mankind."

"The disease is progressive, as I've indicated. Eventually, yes, verbal and written communication will become extremely difficult. But cases vary widely. In many

36

instances, the impairments progress quite gradually."

"Until?"

"Parkinson's-like symptoms can develop, along with decline in memory, judgment, mobility, et cetera." She paused. "This can often impact life expectancy."

"Time frame?" The two words were all he could manage.

"The conventional wisdom is seven to ten years from diagnosis to death. But there are some recent studies that —"

"And the treatment?"

She paused again.

"There is no treatment for PPA at this point in time."

"Ah. I understand. Well, thank God it isn't a death sentence."

So this is what it felt like. He'd always wondered; he knew what it was like to be on the other side of the desk. So many years ago now, those months they made the psych residents give out the most severe diagnoses, said it was "practice," though sadism was more like it. He remembered the hand-trembling anxiety of entering that room where the patient waited (hands in your pockets, that was his mantra back then: hands in your pockets, voice calm, a mask of professionalism that fooled nobody); then the wild relief when it was done. They'd kept a bottle of vodka under the sink in the psych bathroom for such occasions.

This doctor now, this cutting-edge neurologist they'd sent him to (coiffed, polished — her makeup itself a kind of bravado) must've delivered a good dozen of these a month (it was one of her specialties, after all) and still looked peaked around the edges. He hoped there was a bottle of something for her somewhere, when this was done.

"Dr. Anderson —"

"Jerry."

"Is there anyone we can call for you? A child, perhaps? A sibling? Or — a wife?"

He met her gaze. "I'm alone."

"Oh." The sympathy in her eyes was unbearable.

He took it all in and rejected it at the same time. He wasn't finished. He would not let himself be finished. It was still possible to get the book done. He would write quickly; that's all he'd do. He could finish in a year or two, before simple nouns and then language itself became alien to him.

He had known he was getting tired. He had thought that was what it was. Why he couldn't find the right words for things, sometimes, even though he knew he knew them. They wouldn't come out of his mouth or roll off his pen, and he thought it was because of the exhaustion. He was not getting younger and had always worked long hours. Or perhaps he had picked up a strain of something on his last trip to India, so he went for a checkup, and one thing led to another, one doctor led to another, and he wasn't afraid. He was a man who didn't fear death and had never let pain slow him down, a man who had survived hepatitis and malaria and could work straight through lesser illnesses and barely take notice of them, so there was nothing to be afraid of — and yet somehow he had ended up here, on the edge of this cliff. But not over it, not yet.

So many words. Oh, he wasn't ready to give up any of them. He loved them all. *Shakespeare. Saltshaker. Sheila.*

What would Sheila say to him if she were here? She'd always been smarter than he was, though people laughed when he'd said it — the kindergarten teacher smarter than the psychiatrist? But people were idiots, really; they saw the blond poof of her hair and his degrees, whereas anyone with even half a brain could see how shrewd she was, how much she understood, how much she let herself know.

If Sheila were here —

But was she? Could she be visiting him, in his time of need? Her scent was here. He had no particular experience with spirits, but he didn't disbelieve in them, either; it was a subject for which insufficient data existed, despite some valiant efforts here and there, Ducasse's Butler case, for instance, or Myers's Cheltenham ghost, not to mention the early-nineteenth-century studies of mediums by William James and his ilk.

He closed his eyes for a moment and tried to feel her presence. He felt, or wanted, something. A stirring. *Oh, Sheil.*

"Jerry." Dr. Rothenberg's voice was low. "I really think you ought to talk to someone."

He opened his eyes. "Please don't call psych. I'm all right. Really."

"Okay," she said softly.

They sat for a moment in silence, looking across the desk at each other, as if they were on opposite sides of a raging river. What strange creatures other human beings are, he thought. It's amazing anyone ever connects.

Enough. He leaned forward, caught his breath. "Are we done, then?" Consider it a favor, he thought. You are hereby released

40

from the cockeyed attentions of a disinte-
grating man.

"Do you have any more questions? Anything else about . . . the course of the
disease?"

What did she want from him? A wave of
panic overcame him suddenly. He gripped
the sides of his chair, and could see her relax
at last at this sign of weakness. He forced
himself to release it.

"Nothing you can answer. Nothing that
won't be answered soon enough." He was
able to stand without wobbling. Gave her a
little salute.

He watched her watching him as he gathered his briefcase and his jacket, could see
the discomfort her confusion caused her.
All in all, this was not the reaction she'd
expected.

Let that be a lesson for you, he thought as
he closed the door behind him and leaned
against the wall, trying to catch his breath
in the too bright, fluorescent corridor, amid
the rolling, unstoppable roar of the well and
the sick. Never expect.

It had been the lesson of his life.

THREE

Janie kneeled on the pink tile in her best black dress and tried to quiet her mind. Dirty bathwater oozed across the floor, dampening the knees of her stockings, spotting her velvet hem. She'd always liked the dress because its high waist was sympathetic to her figure, and the velvet gave it a festive, bohemian air, but now, streaked as it was with egg yolk and bubbly patches of shampoo that shone like spittle, it had transformed into her most opulent rag.

She pulled herself to her feet, glanced in the mirror.

She was a mess, all right. Her mascara blackened the area under her eyes like a football player; her eye shadow left sparkly bronze streaks across her temples; and her left ear was bleeding. Her hair still looked good, though, billowing and curling around her face as if it hadn't gotten the message.

Serves her right for thinking she could

take a night off from Noah.

And she had been so excited, too.

Janie had known it was probably irrational to get worked up about a date with someone she hadn't actually met. But she liked Bob's photo, his open face and kind, squinting eyes, and she liked his humorous voice on the phone, the way it vibrated deep within her body, waking it up. They had talked for over an hour, delighted to discover so many things in common: they had both grown up in the Midwest and made their way to New York after college; they were the only offspring of formidable mothers; they were decent-looking socially competent people, surprised to find themselves single in the city they loved. They couldn't help but wonder (they didn't say it but it was there, in the reverberation of their voices, in their easy laughs) if all that yearning might be ending very soon.

And they were going to dinner! Dinner was unambiguously auspicious.

All she had to do was get through the day. It was a trying morning, more couples therapy than architecture, as Mr. and Mrs. Ferdinand dithered about whether the third bedroom was an exercise room or a man cave, and the Williamses confessed at the last moment that they wanted to cut the baby's room in half since, actually, they'd need two master bedrooms instead of one, which was fine; she didn't care if they slept together or not, only why couldn't they have told her before she'd finalized the plans? Throughout the day, in between these meetings, she'd found herself checking her phone as Bob texted her in thrilling bursts "Can't wait!" She imagined him (Was he tall or short? Probably tall . . .) sitting in his cubicle (or wherever programmers worked) perking up when his phone buzzed with her response "Me 2!" — the two of them texting away like a couple of teenagers, getting through their day like this, for everybody needed something, didn't they, to pull them through?

And, to be honest, she was looking forward to a night away from Noah. She hadn't had a date in almost a year. The dinner with Bob had inspired her, reminding her that she was not living the life she'd planned.

The sacrifices of the single mom had been her mother's refrain throughout her childhood, delivered always with the same ever-so-slightly rueful smile, as if giving up the rest of your life was the price you had to pay for the only thing that mattered. Try as she might, it was impossible for Janie to imagine her mother other than she was: her nurse's uniform neatly pressed and tightly belted, her white shoes and bobbed pewter hair, her sharp, knowing blue eyes untouched by time or makeup or any palpable regret (she didn't believe in it).

You didn't mess with Ruthie Zimmerman. Even the surgeons she worked with seemed a little afraid of her, wincing nervously when she and Janie ran into them in the supermarket and Ruth's eyes followed an unmistakable path from her own vegetable-and-tofu-laden cart to their six-packs of beer and packages of bacon and chips. Nor could you ever envision her going on a date or sleeping in anything besides her plaid flannel pj's.

When Janie decided to have Noah, she'd been determined that she would do things differently. Which was probably why she had stuck to her plan that night, even when things started to go so palpably awry.

She'd arrived ten minutes early at Noah's school and spent the time alternately checking for texts from Bob and spying on Noah through the window in the Fours room. The other children were doing something that involved gluing blue-painted macaroni on paper plates while her son, as usual, stood right by Sondra's side, tossing a Play-Doh ball from hand to hand as he watched her supervise. Janie quelled a spike of jealousy; from his first day at preschool, Noah had been inexplicably attached to the serene Jamaican teacher, trailing her like a puppy. If only he had liked any one of his sitters half as much, it would have made going out so much easier. . . .

Marissa, the head teacher, a woman brimming with natural cheer or caffeination, spotted her at the window and waved her arms as if she were marshaling an airplane, mouthing *Can we talk?*

Janie sighed — again? — and plopped on the bench in the hallway under a row of construction-paper jack-o'-lanterns.

"How's it going with the hand-washing? Any progress?" Marissa flashed an encouraging smile.

"A little," she said, which was a lie, but better, she thought, than "Not at all."

" 'Cause he had to skip art again today."

"That's too bad." Janie shrugged in a way she hoped didn't denigrate the macaroni project. "He seems okay with it, though."

"And he's getting a little . . ." She scrunched her nose, too polite to go further. Just say it, Janie thought. Dirty. Her son was dirty. His every exposed bit of skin was either sticky or smudged with ink or chalk or glue. There was a red smudge from a

46

Magic Marker that had been on his neck for at least two weeks now. She'd done her best with wipes and coated his hands and wrists with hand sanitizer, which seemed to seal in the grit, as if she had laminated him.

Some kids couldn't stop washing their hands; hers wouldn't go near a drop of water without a battle. Thank god he hadn't hit puberty yet and started to stink, or he'd be like the homeless man in the subway you could smell coming from the next car over.

"And, um, we're cooking. Tomorrow? Blueberry muffins? I'd hate for him to miss that!"

"I'll talk to him."

"Good. Because —" Marissa cocked her head, her brown eyes welling with concern.

"What?"

The teacher shook her head. "It'd be nice for him, that's all."

It's only muffins, Janie thought, but didn't say. She stood up; she could see Noah through the little window. He was in the dress-up area, helping Sondra pick up hats. She playfully dropped a fedora on his head, and Janie winced. He looked adorable, but the last thing they needed right now was head lice.

Take off the hat, Noah, she silently willed him.

But Marissa's voice was chattering in her ear. "And, listen. . . . Can you ask him not to talk about Voldemort so much in class? It's disturbing to some of the other kids."

"Okay." *Take. It. Off.* "Who's Voldemort?"

"From the Harry Potter books? I mean, I totally understand if you want to read those books to him, I love them, too, it's just that . . . I mean, Noah's advanced, of course, but they aren't really appropriate for the other children."

Janie sighed. They were always making the wrong assumptions when it came to her son. He had a miraculous brain that picked up information seemingly from the air — some stray comment he had heard once, perhaps, who knew? — but they always tried to make it mean something else.

"Noah doesn't know anything about Harry Potter. I've never even read the books myself. And I would never let him watch those movies. Perhaps another child here told him about them, one with an older sibling?"

"But —" The teacher's brown eyes blinked. She opened her mouth again to say something and then seemed to reconsider. "Well, listen, just tell him to lay off the dark stuff, okay? Thanks so much —" she said, opening the door to a mosh pit of four-year-olds covered with blue paint and macaroni.

Janie stood in the doorway, waiting until Noah spotted her.

Ah, this was always the best moment of her day: the way he lit up when he caught sight of her, that crooked, face-splitting grin as he tumbled forward, taking a running leap across the room and hurling himself into her arms. He wrapped his legs around her waist like a monkey and placed his forehead right against hers, looking at her with a merry gravity all his own, as if to say, Oh, yes, I remember *you*. It was her mother's eyes looking back at her, and her own eyes, too, a clear blue that looked quite nice thank-you-very-much on her own face, but on Noah, surrounded by the profusion of blond ringlets, took on another dimension entirely, so that people always did a little double take upon looking at him as if ethereal beauty, located in a boy child, was some kind of trick.

His capacity for joy always stunned her, something he taught her merely by looking in her face.

Now she stepped outside with Noah into the darkening October afternoon and felt the world telescoping momentarily to the small figure bouncing on his toes beside her. They walked hand in hand beneath the trees, rows of brownstones flanking the sidewalks as far as they could see.

The phone buzzed in her pocket, bringing her back, suddenly, to Bob, that invisible collection of traits (deep voice; delighted laugh) that hadn't yet knitted together into a whole human being.

"Feel like I know u already. Weird?"

"No!" she texted. "Same here!" (Was this true? Maybe.) Should she xo? Or was that too forward? She settled for a single x. He responded immediately: "XXX!"

Oh! She felt a current of heat run through her body, as if she'd swum into a warm patch in a cold lake.

They walked by the café on their corner, and the scent drew her in; she decided to fortify herself for the conversation ahead. She pulled Noah inside.

"Where we going, Mommy-Mom?"

"I just want a coffee. I'll be quick."

"Mom, if you drink coffee now you'll be up 'til dawn."

She laughed; it was like something a grown-up might say. "You're right, Noey. I'll have a decaf. Okay?"

"And can I have a decaf corn muffin?"

"All right." It was too close to his dinner-time, of course, but what the hell?

"And a decaf smoothie?"

50

She ruffled his hair. "Decaf water for you, my friend."

The coffee was fragrant as they finally settled down with their bounty on their stoop. The sun was setting beyond the buildings. The light, rosy and tender, brought out the blush in the brick town houses and the brownstones, glancing on the loosening leaves of the trees. The gas lamp out front was flickering. It had been the deciding factor convincing her to rent the place, despite the fact that it was expensive, on the garden level, and had no direct sunlight. But the mahogany woodwork inside and the pleasant hedges and gas lamp out front made her feel cozy, as if she and Noah could burrow together there safely, apart from the world, apart from time. She hadn't counted on the fact that the always-flickering flame out the front window would catch her gaze at odd times during the day and reflect itself in the back kitchen windows at night, making her startle more than once with the feeling that the house was on fire.

She cleaned Noah's grimy hands with an antibacterial wipe and handed him his muffin.

"You know, they're making muffins tomorrow in school. How about it?"

51

He took a bite, triggering a cascade of crumbs.

"Will I have to wash up after?"

"Well, cooking is messy. There is flour and raw eggs. . . ."

"Oh." He licked his fingers. "Then, no."

"We can't keep doing it this way forever, bug."

"Why not?"

She didn't bother answering him — they'd been around and around this, and she had other things she needed to say.

"Hey." She nudged him gently.

He was busy, working away at his corn muffin. How could she have let him order that? The thing was enormous. "Listen, I'm going out tonight."

He stared at her. He put down the muffin. "No, you're not."

She took a deep breath. "I'm sorry, kiddo."

A wild light shone in his eyes. "But I don't want you to go."

"I know, but Mommy has to go out sometimes, Noah."

"So take me with you."

"I can't."

"Why not?"

Because it wouldn't kill Mommy to get laid at least once before you go off to college. "It's a grown-up thing."

52

He blitzed her with a desperate, crooked smile. "But I'm precocious."

"Good try, buddy, but no. It'll be fine. You like Annie. Remember? She came over to Mommy's office last weekend and played Legos with you?"

"What if I have a nightmare?"

She'd considered this. His nightmares were frequent. He'd had one once while she was out networking at an industry event; she'd returned to find him glassy-eyed and shaking in front of a Dora the Explorer video while the sitter (who had seemed so high-spirited! Who had brought homemade brownies!) lifted a few fingers in a limp wave from where she lay, haggard and shell-shocked, on the couch. That one had never come back, either.

"Then Annie will wake you up and hug you and call Mommy. But you won't."

"What if I have an asthma attack?"

"Then Annie will give you your nebulizer and I'll come home right away. But you haven't had one in a long time."

"Please don't go." But his voice wavered, as if he knew the jig was up.

She was already dressed, fussing with her hair while half-following a YouTube video of a giggling teenager showing the correct way to put on eye shadow — which was surprisingly helpful, actually — when she heard Noah's high voice summoning her from the living room.

"Mommy-Mom! Come here!"

Was SpongeBob over already? Didn't they play those shows in an endless loop?

She padded to the room in black stockinged feet. All was as she'd left it, the bowl of baby carrots untouched on the leather coffee table, SpongeBob bellowing as he ambled on his weird bowlegs across the screen, but Noah was nowhere in sight. Something flashed in the pass-through to the kitchen. Was it the reflection of the flickering gas lamp?

"Hey, look at this!"

It wasn't the flickering gas lamp.

As she rounded the corner and caught a glimpse of him, standing by the kitchen counter next to an open carton of organic omega-3-enhanced brown eggs, smashing one after the other over his springy blond head, she felt the night slipping away from her.

No; she wouldn't let it. Anger rose from nowhere: her life, her life, her only life, and couldn't she have a little bit of fun, just one night? Was that really too much to ask?

"See, Mommy?" he said, sweetly enough,

but there was no mistaking the willfulness glowing on his face. "I'm making egg-Noah. Get it? Like eggnog?"

How did he even know what eggnog was? Why did he always know things that nobody had told him about?

"Watch." He picked up another egg, swung his arm back, and hurled it at the center of the wall, whooping as it splattered. "Fastball!"

"What is *wrong* with you?" she said.

He flinched and dropped the egg in his other hand.

She tried to modulate her voice. "Why would you do such a thing?"

"I don't know." He seemed a bit frightened.

She tried to calm herself. "You're going to have to take a bath now. You know that, right?"

He shuddered at the word. Egg was rolling down his face, oozing into the hollow of his neck. "Don't go," he said, blue eyes nailing her to the wall with his need.

He was no fool. He had calculated that the thing he hated most in the world was worth tolerating in order to keep her home. He had wanted her there that much. Could Bob, who had never even met her, compete with that?

No, no, no; she would go! For god's sake: it was enough! She wouldn't succumb to this kind of blackmail, especially from a child! She was the adult, after all — wasn't that what they always said in her single moms' group? You make the rules. You need to hold firm, especially because you're the only adult. You're not doing them any favors by giving in.

She lifted him in her arms (he was light; he was only a baby, her boy, only four). She carried him into the bathroom and held his squirming body tightly in her arms as she turned on the water faucet and checked the temperature.

He was writhing and screeching like a trapped animal. She stepped to the edge of the bathtub and placed him on the bath mat (legs sliding, arms flailing), somehow managing to pull off his clothes and flip on the shower.

The scream could probably be heard all the way down Eighth Avenue. He fought as if his life depended on it, but she did it, she held him there under the water and squirted shampoo on his head, telling herself again and again that she wasn't torturing anybody, she was only giving her son a very-much-needed washing.

When it was over (a matter of seconds,

though it felt endless) he was lying in a heap on the floor of the bathtub, and she was bleeding. In the midst of the chaos, he had craned his neck and bitten her ear. She tried to wrap him in a towel, but he wrenched away from her, scrambling out of the tub and into his bedroom, skidding on the floor. She took some antibiotic from the medicine cabinet and applied it while she listened to the howls reverberating throughout the house, filling every cell in her body with woe.

She looked in the mirror.

Whatever she was, she was not a woman going out on a first date.

She walked to Noah's room. He was on the floor, naked, rocking, with his knees clasped between his arms — a puddle of a boy, pale skin glimmering in the green light cast by the glow-in-the-dark stars she'd pasted on the ceiling to make the tiny room feel bigger than it was.

"Noey?"

He didn't look at her. He was crying softly into his knees. "I want to go home." It was something he said in times of distress since he was a toddler. It had been his first full sentence. She always answered in the same way: "You are home."

"I want my mama."

57

"I'm here, baby."

He looked away from her. "Not you. I want my other mother."

"I'm your mommy, honey."

He turned. His doleful eyes locked onto hers. "No, you're not."

A chill ran through her. She was aware of herself as if from a distance, standing over this shivering boy under the eerie light of the fake stars. The wood floor was rough beneath her feet, its knots like holes a person could fall through, like falling out of time.

"Yep. Your one and only."

"I want my other one. When is she coming?"

She pulled herself together with an effort. Poor kid, she thought; I'm all you've got. We're all we've got, the two of us. But we'll make it work. I'll do better. I promise. She squatted by his side. "I won't go, okay?"

She'd send Bob an apologetic text, and that would be the end of that. For what could she say? Remember that adorable son I mentioned? Well, he's a little unusual. . . . No, theirs was too fragile a connection to withstand those sorts of complications, and there was always another lonely New York woman waiting in the wings. She'd cancel the sitter and pay her anyway, because it

58

was the last minute and she couldn't afford to lose another one.

"I won't go," she said again. "I'll cancel Annie. I'll stay with you." She was grateful, not for the first time, that no adult was there to witness this weak moment.

But who cared what other people thought? The color rose to Noah's face, a blossoming of pink on clammy skin, and his lopsided grin knocked her sideways, blotted out the room. It was like looking at the sun. Maybe her mother was right after all, she thought. Maybe some forces were too strong to resist.

"C'mere, you goof." She held out her arms, throwing all of it to the wind: the dress, the date, this thrilling night and perhaps all the thrilling nights left to her, a woman aging by the moment, squarely in the middle of her one and only life.

Here, in her arms, was what mattered. She kissed his sweet, damp head. He smelled nice, for once.

He lifted his face. "Is my other mother coming soon?"

FOUR

Anderson opened his eyes and looked around the room in a panic.

His pages. Where were they? What the hell had he done with them?

The room was dim, the air swirling with dust. Boxes half-packed with files flanked every wall, rising up around him as if he'd fallen six feet under instead of drifting off on the cot in his office again. The window was high and narrow, like a slit in a fortress; now it cast a spear of light on the wooden floor and the books piled here and there and the manuscript pages scattered where he'd tossed them angrily the night before. He got up quickly and gathered the pages one by one. When he was finished he sat down again, holding the manuscript in his lap: a bulky thing, like a cat. He straightened the edges with his hands, the ends tickling his palms. It didn't seem like much, this bundle, and yet it contained the sum of his life's work. He set aside the title page and looked at the dedication.

For Sheila

He tried to feel her now, in the room, but couldn't do it; she was fixed to the page like a pinned butterfly. It occurred to him that Sheila's death, which was the worst thing that had ever happened in his life, had not substantively changed the course of his days. On the other hand, in the five years since he'd been diagnosed, the aphasia had nearly ruined him.

He flipped to the first page. Ah, there they were: his words.

Even though it may seem hard to believe, evidence might exist that life after death is actually a reality.

It was irrational to think the sentences might have erased themselves in the night simply because he had dreamed it, yet no more irrational than anything else that had been happening to him. Yesterday he had been on the phone with the librarian of the Society for Scientific Exploration in London, discussing the storage of the files he was donating. He wanted to make sure that even though his office was closing, his research would be accessible to any serious scientists that might find it useful. He wanted to tell her about the new cases out of Norway that Amundson had sent him, to ensure that these would be filed properly, but when he came to the place in the sentence where the name of his old colleague should have come up, the name simply wasn't there.

"The files from up there." That was the mortifying phrase that came out of his mouth instead. Of course, the librarian had been puzzled.

"What do you mean? Up where?"

Anderson saw the fjords and forests and women of Norway. Amundson's face rose in his mind, the bulbous nose and the whiskers on his jowls, the cheery, skeptical, but never cynical eyes.

"The new files on birthmarks, you know."

"Oh. You mean that study from the professor in Sri Lanka?"

"No, no, no." He felt a momentary surge of despair and wanted to hang up the phone, but he took a breath and willed himself to go on. "The new birthmark research, the research from that guy — that guy up there. Up north. You *know* who I *mean*," he snarled at the poor woman. "In Europe. The ice mountains . . . the . . . the *fjords!*"

"Oh. I'll make sure the Amundson studies are filed properly," she said at last, coolly, and he felt a flicker of victory that she now thought him a total asshole instead of mentally impaired.

The week before, he'd pulled *The Tempest* from the shelf in his bedroom and flipped to the end, but when he came to the line *"Our revels now are ended,"* the words seemed to shiver in his mind's grasp, like a moment that was even now passing. How could he not know that word, *revels*? He, who had read and reread this play, this speech, a hundred times? He had to look it up in the damn dictionary. He should copy out his whole library, he thought, until his hands were swollen, copy every last word from every one of his books, so that he would retain a physical memory there in his hands of all those words he couldn't bear to lose.

He leafed through the manuscript in his lap. He'd e-mailed it to his agent, of course (it was no longer a paper world); but he'd also printed it out so he could feel the weight of it. A lifetime of work; the strongest cases, distilled for the populace. Decades of patient labor doing the casework, years of writing draft after draft, shooting for clarity, always clarity. His last chance at making a difference: he'd worked like a maniac for four and a half years to finish it while his mind was still capable, before the fog rolled in. Some days he'd forgotten to eat.

The academic community would always consider Anderson a failure. He knew that. There was a moment, when he had first left his job at the medical school and his colleagues still valued him, when his books had been reviewed: twice by *The Journal of the American Medical Association,* and once in *The Lancet.* But as his colleagues aged they forgot about him, or more accurately they forgot they had respected him once. No one in that world had shown him any attention for decades now. He was famous in the paranormal research community, of course; he was invited to speak everywhere they studied ESP, or near-death experiences, or mediums. But he would never be accepted again by the scientific community, the only community he had ever really belonged to; he had finally given up that battle, decades after Sheila had exhorted him to do so. It was over.

But now he had written something for a different audience: he was aiming for nothing less than the world.

"If people can understand your data —

not academics, I mean *real* people — it might change something for them." Sheila had said this to him more than once, but only gradually had he realized the force of her logic, when she was already fighting the heart disease that would kill her.

When he considered his future readers now, he pictured a man like himself, back before any of this had started, when he was at the medical school. He saw himself on a chilly Friday evening walking back from his office through the square, puzzling over a study on somatic symptom disorders, tempted by the warmth and light of the bookstore. Stepping in for a quick browse, he glances at the books on the table, searching for something to grab his attention — and the book calls out to him. He picks it up and flips it open to the first page. *Even though it may seem hard to believe, evidence might exist that life after death is actually a reality.*

Evidence? he imagined the man thinking to himself. Impossible. But he sits down anyway on a nearby leather chair, and begins to read. . . .

Anderson knew it was a fantasy. But he had been a man like that once. He, too, had needed evidence. And now he could provide it. He could leave his mark. He had felt full of confidence, until yesterday. Until he had talked to his literary agent and found that every publisher had turned him down. When he'd hung up the phone, he kicked the manuscript across the room, scattering pages like ash.

Now he looked at the words again.

Even though it may seem hard to believe, evidence might exist that life after death is actually a reality. . . .

No; he would not let this stop him. He thought of that other Amundson, the Norwegian who had discovered the South Pole, his victory dwarfed by the noble failure of his competitor, Robert Falcon Scott. Scott, who had perished with his men in the frozen tundra. A brave man who had died trying, the cold claiming him toe by toe, foot by foot. Another casualty of the terra nova, the great unknown.

FIVE

She was late.

The day had started badly. Noah had awoken in the night again, upset from a nightmare and drenched with urine from head to toe. She'd tried in the morning to clean his stinky body with wipes as he squirmed and whimpered but finally gave up, dusting him with baby powder and dropping him sulking and emitting an unmistakable litter-box odor at Little Sprouts.

So: she was late. It would have been fine if it hadn't been the Galloways. The Galloway renovation had been one of those jobs in which everything that should have gone one way went the other. They had moved in two weeks ago, and she'd been at the house almost daily since then, including a visit on Thanksgiving morning.

Today they had a checklist. They started with the appliances in the kitchen and ended up in the guest bath.

The three of them stood in the small bathroom, staring at a trickle of water from the expensively tiled shower stall to the new checkerboard floor.

"You see?" Sarah Galloway pointed a shiny red talon at the tiny stream. "It leaks."

Why are you taking showers in the guest bath anyway? she wanted to ask, but didn't. Instead, she popped out her measuring tape and measured the curb of the shower stall, which, as she knew, was standard.

"Hmmm. It's standard width."

"But you SEE the LEAK."

"Yes . . . I was wondering. . . ."

Sarah looked over at Janie with the puzzled-owl expression that Janie had come to understand was a Botoxed frown. "Wondering what?"

"I mean, is this a question of the shower stall or the amount of water? Because if there's a lot of water it might be understandable. . . ." Janie paused and said it all in one quick breath. "Is this the first shower somebody's taken here today or the second? Do you take particularly long showers?"

God, she hated this part of the job. She might as well have asked them if they're having sex in there. And if so, she supposed they ought to have told her, so she could have customized the size. . . .

Frank Galloway cleared his throat. "I think our shower use is pretty, uh, normal —" he started to say, when Janie's phone buzzed in her pocket.

"Just a sec."

She glanced at her cell. *Little Sprouts Day Care.* Oh, for god's sake. "Listen, I'm sorry, I've got to take this. It'll just be a moment." She stepped into the next room. What did the teachers want now? Probably to complain that Noah was smelly today. Which, okay, he was, but —

"This is Miriam Whittaker." The gravelly voice of the preschool director scraped against her ear.

In a second, her breath caught, her knees jellied — is this the moment between before and after, the one everyone feared? The choking on the apple core, the tumble down the stairs? She leaned against the wall. "Is Noah all right?"

"He's fine."

"Oh, thank goodness. Listen, I'm in the middle of a meeting, can I call you back?"

"Miss Zimmerman. This is very serious."

"Oh." The tone was unnerving; she gripped the phone tightly against her ear. "What happened? Did Noah do something?"

The silence that followed bled slowly into her consciousness, telling her everything and nothing she needed to know. She could hear the woman breathing on the other end of the phone, Sarah Galloway clucking quietly but not that quietly to her husband in the bathroom. "Inattentive," she thought she heard.

"Did he cry during naptime? Pull someone's hair? What?"

"Actually, Miss Zimmerman." There was a sharp intake of breath. "This is a conversation we need to have in person."

"I'll be there as soon as I can," Janie said briskly, but her voice wavered, the fear poking through the skin of her professionalism like bone.

The Little Sprouts director was a lion, a witch, and a wardrobe all in one. Built like a box, black clad from her hip-granny spectacles down to her pointy ankle-length boots, Miriam Whittaker wore her hair long, a silvery mane grazing those broad shoulders with unexpected eros, like a middle finger to the vagaries of time. She had been running the school-obsessed neighborhood's premiere preschool for the last fifteen years, and thus had a somewhat outsized sense of her own importance relative to the universe's grand scheme. Janie had always found Ms. Whittaker's imperiousness with grown-ups amusing, sensing through its veil a kind of pathos and scattershot warmth.

Now, though, wedged across from Ms. Whittaker in a little plastic orange chair between the potted plant and the Bookworm poster, Janie saw in the older woman's face something far more disturbing than her usual flashy authority: she saw anxiety. The woman was almost as nervous as she was.

"Thank you for coming in," the other woman said, clearing her throat. "On such short notice."

Janie kept her voice level. "So what's this about?"

A pause ensued, in which Janie tried to keep her breathing as steady as possible, in which she heard every tick of the preschool's beating heart, the sound of a faucet in the art room, a teacher singing *clean-up, clean-up, everybody clean up,* a child somewhere, not hers, screaming.

Ms. Whittaker lifted her head, focusing on a spot slightly to the left of Janie's shoulder. "Noah has been talking to us about guns."

So that's what this was all about? Something Noah had said? But that was easy. She felt the tension in her body begin to relax.

71

"Don't all little boys do that?"

"He's been saying he's played with guns."

"He was probably talking about a Nerf gun," she said, and Ms. Whittaker glanced at her. There was something hard in her eyes.

"A .54-caliber Renegade rifle, is what he said, to be exact. He said the gunpowder smelled like rotten eggs."

She felt a flicker of pride. Her son knew things — this had always been the case with Noah, some quirk in his brain, like the brains of savants, only instead of numerical equations he knew random facts he must have overheard somewhere. Was Einstein's brain like this? Was James Joyce's? Perhaps they, too, had been misunderstood as children. But meanwhile there was the matter of what to say to this woman who sat glowering at her across the table. "I don't know where he gets this stuff, really. I'll tell him not to talk about guns."

"You're trying to tell me you don't know where he used a gun? Or how he knows that it smells like sulfur?"

"He didn't use a gun," she said patiently. "And as for sulfur — I don't know. He says funny things sometimes."

"So you deny it?" She wouldn't look at Janie.

72

"Maybe he saw something on television?"

"He's been watching television, has he?"

Oh, this woman. "He watches Diego and Dora and SpongeBob and baseball games. . . . Maybe they had an ad on ESPN for hunting, or something?"

"There's another thing. Noah has been talking a great deal about the Harry Potter books. Yet according to you, you haven't read them to him or shown him the movies."

"That's true."

"And yet he seems to know them extremely well. He's been going around saying some sort of killing spell."

"Look, it's just how Noah is. He says all kinds of things." She shifted her legs. Her butt was going numb in the tiny chair. She'd cut the Galloway visit short; Mrs. Galloway was probably calling all her friends right this minute to tell everybody she was wrong, she couldn't recommend Jane Zimmerman Architecture after all. She was losing clients because of this nonsense. "So that's why you called me in here from an important business meeting? Because you think my little boy talks too much about guns and Harry Potter?"

"No."

She shuffled some papers on her desk, ran

a knobby, be-ringed hand through her silver hair.

"We were having a discussion about discipline today at school. There was a biting incident . . . but never mind about that. We discussed our rules, how hurting each other is never acceptable. Noah offered — on his own — that he was once under water so long that he blacked out. He actually used the words 'blacked out,' a strange word choice for a four-year-old, wouldn't you think?"

"He said he blacked out?" Janie tried to process it.

"Miss Zimmerman. I'm sorry, but I have to ask you." Her eyes, finally focused on Janie's, were pinpricks of cold fury. "Have you ever held your son's head under water until he passed out?"

"What?" She blinked at the other woman; the words were so terrible and unexpected that it took a moment for her to absorb them. "No! Of course not!"

"You understand why I'm having difficulty believing you."

She couldn't sit in that seat a moment longer. She leaped up and began to pace. "He hates baths. That's probably what it is. I washed his hair. That's my crime."

The woman's silence was contemptuous.

Ms. Whittaker's gaze followed her as she walked back and forth across the room.

"Did Noah say anything else?"

"He said he called out to his mommy but nobody helped him, and he was pushed underwater."

Janie froze. "Pushed under?" she repeated.

Ms. Whittaker nodded curtly. "Please sit down."

She was too baffled to stand any longer. She sunk back into the little chair. "But — nothing like that has ever happened to him. Why would he say that?"

"He said he was pushed underwater," Ms. Whittaker repeated forcefully, "and he couldn't get out."

Understanding washed over Janie at last. "But — that's his dream," she said quickly. "A nightmare he has. That he's stuck underwater and can't get out."

A fragment of the night before came back to her — Noah pummeling her with his hard fists, yelling *Let me out, let me out, let me out!* Their nighttime drama, gone by morning. Remarkable, how completely it dropped out of her consciousness, until the next night. "He's had the same nightmare for years. He's just confused."

She glanced up, but Ms. Whittaker's face was like a heavy metal door. You could bang

75

and bang, but nothing would open it.

"So you must understand my dilemma." Ms. Whittaker spoke slowly.

"*Your* dilemma? No, I don't. I'm sorry."

"Miss Zimmerman. I've spent many years with small children, and in my experience they do not talk about their dreams this way. That sort of — confusion — is not common."

Common, no; nothing about Noah was common, was it? Janie tried to think. It wasn't only that he knew things; it was more than that, wasn't it? When had she first become aware that Noah was different from other children? When had she stopped going to her single moms' group? Somewhere along the line, when discussions had evolved from sleeping through the night and infant gas to baths and preschool there had been one too many moments when she'd looked around after sharing (his nightmares and fears, his long, inexplicable bouts of crying) and seen blank stares instead of nods. It was just part of Noah's uniqueness — that's what she'd always said to herself, only now —

Ms. Whittaker cleared her throat, an awful sound. "A young child with a water phobia talks about being held underwater . . . and clings for dear life to a junior teacher here,

76

sobbing uncontrollably for hours when she's absent —"

"I picked him up at noon that day."

". . . and then the other evidence of a house somehow not quite in order, the fact that the boy smells . . . well, you understand? I have an obligation. His teachers and I have an obligation. . . ." She lifted her head, a flash of silver, a sword, slicing. "To report any sign of child endangerment to child protective services. . . ."

"Protective services?"

The words dropped down into a well without a bottom. She felt a hot, tingling sensation, as if she'd been slapped hard on both cheeks. The Galloways; her financial worries; everything that had cluttered her mind fell away.

"You must be joking."

"I assure you I am not."

It was impossible. Wasn't it? She was a good mother. Wasn't she?

She looked away from her, at the playground out the window, and tried to pull herself together. They couldn't take him away. Could they?

A crow alighted on the swing set, taking her in with its sharp beady eyes. She forced the panic back down her throat with an effort.

"Look," she said, keeping her voice steady. "Have you ever seen a mark of any kind on him? Or any evidence of abuse? I mean, he's a happy kid." And it was true, she thought. She could feel Noah's joy, anyone could. "Talk to his teachers —"

"I have." Ms. Whittaker sighed, rubbing her temples with her fingers. "Believe me, I don't take this lightly. Once you're in the system —"

"Noah's quirky," Janie said suddenly, interrupting her. "He's imaginative." She cast her gaze out the window. The crow ruffled its feathers, cocking its head at her. She turned back into the room and faced her adversary. "He lies."

Ms. Whittaker lifted an eyebrow. "He lies?"

"He makes up stories. Just little things, mostly. Like once, at the petting zoo, he said, 'Grandpa Joe had a pig, remember? It was so loud.' But he doesn't have a grandpa, much less one with a pig. Or in school — one of the teachers said that he told the class about going to the lake house in the summer and how much he loved it there. How he'd jump from the raft into the water. She was proud of him for speaking up at circle time."

"Yes?"

"Well, you see, there isn't any lake house.

And as for swimming . . . I can't even get him to wash his hands." She laughed, a dry sound echoing in the room. "And at night, before he falls asleep, he says he wants to go home and asks when his other mother is coming. That kind of thing."

Ms. Whittaker was staring at her.

"How long has he been talking like this?"

She thought about it. She could hear Noah's toddler voice, that plaintive whine. "I want to go home." Sometimes she'd laugh at him. "You're right here, silly." And before that, when he was a baby, there was a period of time (a blur now, yet agonizing while it was happening) when he would cry for hours, calling "Mama! Mama!" while wriggling in her arms. "I don't know. A while. But don't many children have imaginary friends?"

The director was looking at her speculatively, as at a child who has bungled basic arithmetic. "This is beyond imaginative," she said, and the statement rang in Janie's ears, reverberating in a back room of her mind that had been waiting for it, she realized, for quite some time.

Janie felt all the fight begin to seep out of her. "What are you saying?"

Their eyes met. The hardness was gone; the woman's eyes shone with a sadness Janie had no defense against. "I think you should take Noah to see a psychologist."

Janie looked out the window, as if the crow might think otherwise, but he had gone. "I'll do it right away," she said.

"Good. I have a list you can choose from. I'll e-mail it to you tonight."

"Thank you." She tried to smile. "Noah's been happy here."

"Yes. Well." Ms. Whittaker rubbed her eyes. She looked exhausted, every hair on her silver head a testament to overseeing other people's children. "We'll all be looking forward to his return."

"Return?"

"After he's been in therapy for a while. We'll be in touch before the summer session and reevaluate the situation then. All right?"

"All right," Janie murmured, and stumbled to the door before the woman could say anything else she couldn't bear to hear.

Outside, she sat heavily on a bench among the tiny boots and coats. No call to child services, then; she'd averted that disaster. Her mind went black with relief. And at the far corner of the blackness, flickering like a spark that had gone astray and was beginning to smolder, the anxiety (which had been there all along): what was wrong with Noah?

Six

"APHASIA IN MAURICE RAVEL,"
BULLETIN OF THE LOS ANGELES NEUROLOGICAL SOCIETY

At fifty-eight, Ravel was struck with aphasia, which quelled any further artistic output. Most strikingly, he was able to think musically but unable to express his ideas in either writing or performance. Hemispheric lateralization for verbal (linguistic) and musical thinking offers an explanation for the dissociation of Ravel's ability to conceive and to create . . .

"Jerr!"

Anderson slid his uneaten plate of food over the article he'd been trying to read and glanced up. The man in front of him, a portly fellow with a goatee floating like an island in the center of his chin, was holding his tray aloft and looking down at him inquiringly. It couldn't possibly have been worse.

He had known the medical school cafeteria was probably a bad idea, but he had thought that the collegial buzz of activity, the long walk to the familiar building, might do him some good. Now he nodded at the man and bit into an apple. It felt cold and mealy in his mouth.

"You're here!" the man said. "I was telling Helstrick just the other day I was sure you'd moved to Mumbai, or Colombo." He waved a manicured hand. "Or some such."

"Nope. Still here." Anderson looked up at his colleague and broke into a sweat. He'd known this man for decades but couldn't remember his name.

The man had been a rising star when they were both medical residents, the two of them friends and competitors, talked about in the same breath. They had been in the same institution now for the last twenty years and still both seemed startled at the different directions fate and their interests had taken them. Now the other man was chairman of his department at the medical school and Anderson was . . . Anderson was . . .

Anderson was forcing himself to move over, letting this nameless man take up the space next to him. He marveled at how much compressed energy some bodies had. The steam from his food tickled Anderson's nose. He thought maybe he'd throw up. That would put an end to the meal in a hurry.

"So, where've you been hiding, then? Haven't seen you in months! Did you hear the latest?"

Anderson picked his response carefully. "I doubt it."

"There's talk that Minkowitz is in the running for a — you, know. The *N* word."

"The *N* word?" Anderson stared.

He whispered. "Nobel. Just talk, you know, but —" He shrugged.

"Ah."

"His recent studies have really been groundbreaking. They actually change our current understanding of the brain. We're all very proud."

"Ah," Anderson said again. The man looked at him sideways, and he could tell exactly what he was thinking: you could have been a part of this, you could have done something, if you hadn't swerved so inexplicably. You could have changed lives.

They all thought this, Anderson realized. They always had, but he had been too busy to feel the weight of it. He looked around him now at all his colleagues chatting and chewing, clanking their silverware. Doctors, mostly; cautious, oblivious people. He could sense their aura of smug certainty even in the way they plunged their forks into their baked ziti. He had known some of them for decades and had always thought of this as his community: these strangers whose names he had forgotten, who wanted nothing to do with him.

"So how's the soul business? Discover any new ones lately? Or is it old ones?" The nameless man chuckled to himself. "Actually, I've been meaning to call you. Corinne swears our attic is haunted, I told her she should look you up. 'Jerry'll get to the bottom of it for you,' I said. 'Course, it's probably the squirrels." He winked. A man pleased with himself in every particular. In his surety that his work was valuable and that Anderson's was not.

At another moment in time, Anderson would have nodded, his eyes elsewhere, would have let the other man's mockery fall on the shell of civility he'd had to create around himself. His usual response was to pretend not to hear the humor behind the inquiries, to answer back with an utterly serious discussion of his work, as if his data could possibly interest them, as if he could still change their minds. "Well, actually, I had an interesting case recently in Sri Lanka," he might have said, and talked until he saw their mockery drain out into boredom.

Now, though, he looked right into this familiar, nameless man's small, shiny eyes, and words fell into his head, and he said them: "Fuck you." The most eloquently expressive and pithy sentence he had said in some time.

The man narrowed his eyes. He opened his mouth and closed it. He spooned some soup into his mouth, red splotches rising on his neck and his cheeks. He wiped his lips on his napkin. For a few moments, he said nothing at all. Then:

"Oh, my — is that Ratner? I've been trying to get a hold of him for weeks!" Hoisting the tray scattered with his half-eaten lunch, he scurried away from Anderson's table in search of more favorable climes.

Anderson pulled the Ravel article from beneath his plate, smoothed it, and began reading again. He bent his head low over the text in what he hoped was the universal sign for "bug off." He'd tried three times that week to read it, and had found his mind oddly resistant to completing the task.

. . . Hemispheric lateralization for verbal (linguistic) and musical thinking offers an explanation for the dissociation of Ravel's ability to conceive and to create . . .

Perhaps he was in denial, and that's why he couldn't get through it. Or perhaps the aphasia was interfering with his attempts to understand different aspects of its progression. If he wasn't so frustrated, the irony of it might have tickled him.

Swimming at Saint-Jean-de-Luz, Ravel — an expert swimmer — suddenly found that he could not "coordinate his movements" . . .

Saint-Jean-de-Luz. He'd been to that beach once, years ago, on his honeymoon. He and Sheila had driven down the French coast. He had two weeks off and had promised not to talk about the lab or the rats. Without his usual topics, he had been both flummoxed and free. They ate and spoke of the food; they swam and spoke of the water and the light.

They'd stayed in a large white hotel on the beach. The Grand Hotel Something or Other. Bobbing fishing boats. The light on the water, in the air, bouncing off Sheila's white shoulders. There was nothing like that light, as the painters all knew.

He tried to focus on the words again.

. . . Ravel — an expert swimmer — suddenly found that he could not "coordinate his movements" . . .

What had that been like — that moment when he suddenly found he could not control his own body? Did he think it was the end? Was he flailing, sinking?

Ravel's was a Wernicke's aphasia of moderate intensity. . . . Understanding of language remains much better than oral or written abilities. . . . Musical language is still more impaired . . . with a remarkable discrepancy between loss of musical expression (written or instrumental) and musical thinking, which is comparatively preserved.

A remarkable discrepancy, he thought. They should write that on my tombstone. He made himself go through that paragraph again.

a remarkable discrepancy between loss of musical expression (written or instrumental) and musical thinking, which is comparatively preserved . . .

Which meant — the words finally sinking into Anderson's consciousness, as if he were recognizing words he himself had written — which meant that Ravel could continue to create orchestral works, he could hear them in his head, but he couldn't get them out. He couldn't mark the notes. They were locked inside forever, playing for an audience of one.

In spite of his aphasia, Ravel recognized tunes easily, especially his own compositions, and could readily point out errors of incorrect notes or rhythm. Sound value and note recognition were well preserved. . . . Aphasia made analytic deciphering — sight reading, dictation and note naming — almost impossible, hindered especially by an inability to recall the names of notes just as garden-variety aphasics "forget" the names of common objects. . . .

The sounds in the cafeteria, the rumbling of voices, the ding of the register, the clattering of trays — these sounds slowed down, and underneath them he heard the incessant staccato drumbeat that was his future, coming right at him. Perhaps Ravel had created another masterpiece, a better *Bolero*.

Perhaps he had built it in his mind, bar by bar, and yet found himself unable to write a single note, to mark a single melody. All day long those melodies would loop through his mind, interlocking and separating with a precision only he himself had mastered, and no one knew. All day long, melodies steamed up out of his coffee cup, poured from the faucet into his bath, hot and cold, intertwined and separate: imprisoned, unstoppable.

Wasn't that enough to drive anyone mad?

Wouldn't it have been better if he had died out there in the ocean?

If he hadn't cried out — if they hadn't seen him — he would have started to sink. His limbs would have stopped flailing eventually, the natural impulse to fight easing out of him by the lull of the waves, the glory of the light sifting down through the water. He could have relaxed, then, let his body take him down — take, too, all the unwritten concertos . . . all of them gone, at once.

It wouldn't have taken much, Anderson thought. He could have simply loosened his hold on life. He could have given up.

For a moment, Anderson felt relief flooding through him, cooling his anxious mind. He didn't have to read the article, he thought. He didn't have to do anything.

He could simply let it all go.

But the desire to continue beat on in him, like a boxer who was losing his hold on the floor but couldn't orient himself enough to get the hell out of the ring. He spread out the pages in front of him, focused his mind, and began, again, to read.

SEVEN

The gas lamp flickered in the wet March mess like a beacon of far-off sanity as Janie half-dragged, half-cajoled Noah down the block. He had lost his mitten somewhere along the way and his icy hand clutched hers and pulled her down, like dead weight.

She grabbed a hunk of damp, unexciting mail from the box (more bills and second notices) and shut the door fast against the snow.

Inside, it was warm and almost disturbingly quiet after the rush of the subway and the white noise of the wind. They both stood, adrift, in the room; Noah seemed dazed, subdued. She closed the wooden shutters, trapping them in the yellow half-light of the floor lamp, and settled him on the couch in front of a DVD ("Look, honey, it's Nemo! Your favorite!"), putting his binder of baseball cards in his lap. He'd been like this more and more lately, his jubilance muffled, as if the dour tone of the doctor's office had seeped into his bones. He sat and watched his shows without comment; he didn't want to play or throw a ball around his room.

She couldn't shake the chill; her teeth were still chattering. She'd had such hopes for this one. She'd been sure this would be the doctor who would change everything for them.

She put a kettle on and made tea for herself and butterscotch hot cocoa for Noah, filling the mug with so many marshmallows you could barely see the liquid. She stared for a moment at the tiny confections bobbing cheerfully in the frothy brown like small white teeth, then ducked down beneath the border of the pass-through to the living room, sitting on her haunches, so Noah couldn't see her cry. Pull yourself together, Janie. It was like pushing a yowling cat into a bag, but she did it. She quelled the sobs, let them roil in her stomach, and stood. Out the back window, the snow fell into the yard and kept on falling.

Noah was sitting quietly, watching the movie with his small hands flat on the plastic binder, his blond head tilted back against the couch, when she brought the hot chocolate. The last four months had been trying emotionally and disastrous work-wise, but she had to admit that she'd gotten used to seeing that blond head always bobbing in her peripheral vision, the comfort of knowing he was *right there.* Three nannies and two day care centers had failed to stick, and after the last fiasco (Noah bolting out the door of Natalie's Kids and down Flatbush Avenue, a few feet away from the rushing cars), she had given up and invited him and his latest nanny to play at her office. They sat quietly enough (too quietly!), building things with his Legos while her assistant scowled and drafted and Janie tried to move the projects she still had going a few steps closer to completion.

She sat next to him on the couch, cradling her tea in her hands, trying to get warm. She didn't even mind his scent: that sickly sweet, slightly curdled smell that Noah carried with him wherever he went now.

She supposed Dr. Remson had been kind enough, as well he should be, for three hundred dollars an hour. And he'd taken his time with Noah, with her. But in the end he'd been the same as the rest of them. He'd had no answers for her. He'd cautioned her to wait.

But wait was precisely what she couldn't

do. When she explained this to him, he'd suggested the name of another psychiatrist in case she wanted treatment for herself . . . as if spending more money on more therapy was the only answer he could come up with.

"We've had three months of sessions, now," she said. "And that's all you can say to me? He's having nightmares every night, and crying bouts during the day. And baths are impossible."

Tapping his black leather sneakers on the Persian carpet, thick glasses perched jauntily on his balding head, Dr. Mike Remson didn't look like one of New York City's foremost child psychiatrists, no matter what *New York* magazine had said. He sat there in his leather armchair, fingers tented, furry caterpillar eyebrows rising over guarded, heavy-lidded eyes. Even after answering his questions in session after session, she still had the impression he was trying to decide if she might be the problem after all.

"Noah's beginning to trust me," he said carefully. "To speak more about his fantasies."

"His other mother?" Her hands were clenching and unclenching. She planted them on her knees.

"That, and other things."

"But *why* is he imagining another

95

mother?"

"Often such an imaginative fantasy life is caused by events at home."

"So you say, but we've been over that, there's nothing."

"No exceptional stress?"

She let out a small, hoarse laugh. Nothing you aren't causing, Doctor. "Nothing that predates this situation." The fact was, she was running through her savings. She'd already cashed in her IRA and spent the small inheritance from her mother she'd put aside for Noah's college education. (Her goal now was simply to get him safely to kindergarten.) She'd had to cancel four meetings with prospective clients this month alone because she couldn't take Noah to meetings and site visits, and she didn't have much time anyway, what with all the doctors. She had no work on the horizon, and no way to pay the bills without work, and no answers.

She'd been taking him to other doctors for months: neurologists, psychologists, neuropsychologists. Noah and Janie both hated it, the long subway rides, the endless wait in crowded offices, Noah paging listlessly through *Horton Hatches an Egg* while she did the same with a year-old copy of *Time.* The doctors talked to him, they did

96

tests on his brain, they tested his lungs again (yes, he has asthma; yes, it's mild), then they sent him out to the next room while they talked to her, and in the end she'd been both relieved and frustrated to find they had found nothing and had nothing to offer, except the promise of more tests. And all along she'd been waiting for the sessions with Dr. Remson, who was supposed to be the best.

"I've been to three specialists, two psychologists now, and you. And nobody can tell me anything at all. Nobody will give me even the possibility of a diagnosis."

"The child is four. That's young for an accurate mental health diagnosis."

"Doctor, I can't even bathe my son." The last time she'd tried, a week before, he had worked himself into such a state that he'd triggered an asthma attack.

It had been his first attack in eighteen months. As she'd held the nebulizer to his face, his ragged breaths amplifying in her ears like the sound of failure, she'd made a commitment to herself: she'd stop waiting for him to get better. She'd do whatever it took to help him now.

"Behavior therapy might help —"

"He's done that. It hasn't worked. Nothing's worked. Doctor — please. You've done

97

this for a long time. Haven't you ever seen a case like Noah's?"

"Well." Dr. Remson leaned back, putting his hands on his big corduroy knees. "Perhaps there was one."

"There was a similar case?" Janie held her breath. She couldn't look him in the eyes, focusing instead on the toe of his shoe. Dr. Remson followed her gaze, his brows knit together, the two of them watching his black foot tap tapping against the deep crimson squares on the Persian rug.

"It was during my residency at Bellevue, many years ago. There was a child there who spoke often of something traumatic that had happened to him during a war. He drew violent pictures of bayoneting. Rape."

She shuddered. She could see the drawings as if they were right in front of her, the blood drawn in red crayon, the stick figure with its wide-open mouth.

"He was from a small town in New Jersey, a loving, intact family to all reports. They swore up and down he had never seen any images like the ones he drew. It was very startling. He was only five."

A case like Noah's. The puzzle pieces of Noah finally fitting together, forming a picture. She felt relief, and a chill of foreboding.

"And what was his diagnosis?"

The psychiatrist winced. "He was a bit older than Noah. And still far too young for the diagnosis."

"The diagnosis?"

"Childhood-onset schizophrenia." He pulled his sweater across his belly, as if his words had caused a drop in temperature. "It's rare, of course, in a child this young."

"Schizophrenia?" The word hung high up in the newly cold air for a moment, sparkling like a jagged icicle, before understanding fell. "You think Noah has schizophrenia."

"He's too young, as I said, for a proper diagnosis. But we have to consider it. We can't rule it out." His eyes watched her steadily beneath the heavy lids. "We'll know more with time."

She stared down at the carpet. The crimson pattern was dense, unfathomable, squares within squares within squares.

He paused for a moment. "There is sometimes a genetic component. You said you don't know anything about the father's family?"

She shook her head miserably. After sporadic, nighttime Googling that had gone nowhere for years, she'd been trying more seriously to hunt down Jeff from Houston. The week before, she'd gone one step farther: she'd spent the better part of two days looking through every recorded Rhodes Scholar for the last two decades. She'd focused on every Jeff and Geoffrey, every scholar from Texas and then from every other state, and there was nobody who'd looked even remotely like the man who had told her his name was Jeff. She'd called the hotel in Trinidad, but it was now a Holiday Inn.

So Jeff — if he even was Jeff — had not been a Rhodes Scholar. He probably hadn't been to Oxford. (She'd looked him up at Balliol College, too, and found nothing.) Perhaps he wasn't even a businessman. He'd made it up — but why? She'd thought it had been to impress her, but now she wondered: had he been in the throes of a full-blown psychosis?

Janie felt the doctor's intent gaze hovering above her like some kind of brown furry bat, but she couldn't lift her eyes to meet it. She looked at her knees, clad in their gray tights; they suddenly seemed absurd to her, their grayness, their roundness.

"I know you want answers," Remson was saying. "But this is the best we can do. We can and will reevaluate as the treatment progresses. In the meantime there are various antipsychotic medications we can try.

100

We can put Noah on a very small dose now, if you like. I'll write you a prescription."

The words had been slipping slowly through her mind, as if she were quietly, sleepily freezing to death, but at that word — *medication* — Janie jolted awake.

"Medication?" She lifted her head. "But he's only four!"

The doctor nodded apologetically, lifting the palms of his hands. "The medication may help him to have a more normal life. We'd reevaluate every few months, once we get the dosage right. And, of course, I'll keep seeing him. Twice a week." He pulled a ballpoint pen from a cup on the table beside him and wrote out a script.

He tore the paper off his pad and handed it to her as if this were an everyday thing. His face was awful in its blandness. "Why don't you take some time to process this," he said, "and we'll talk next week." His outstretched hand still had the prescription for the antipsychotic. Janie had a strange, overwhelming desire to crumple it in his face. Instead she grabbed it and shoved it in her pocket.

Now Janie nestled on the sofa by her son, resisting the urge to pull him into her lap and cover his head with kisses. "Doing okay, bug?"

Noah half nodded, his face mustached by cocoa, eyes on the television screen.

Her phone buzzed — but it wasn't the psychiatrist, offering Noah a newly discovered miracle dose of Chinese herbs and omega-3s. It was a text from Bob, of all people, her erstwhile Internet flirtation from months ago.

"Hey! Things any easier? Want to try again?"

She laughed briefly at the poor man's timing, a loud and mirthless sound, like the bark of a depressed seal. Then she shut the phone without responding and sipped her tea. It wasn't doing her any good, though. She needed stronger stuff.

Janie put Noah to bed early that night. He was in a cuddly mood, his arms pulling her head down to kiss him on the lips, his fingers brushing her face in the dark.

"What part of the body is this?" he whispered.

"That's my nose."

"This?"

"That's my ear."

"And this is your noggin."

"Yes. Good night, bug."

" 'Night, Mommy-Mom." He yawned. Then (she'd known it was coming, it was

102

always now, when he was halfway toward sleep already and she thought maybe this time it would be different, maybe this time he wouldn't say it): "I want to go home."

"You are home, sweetie."

"When is my other mother coming?"

"I don't know, bug."

"I miss her." His head was turned into the pillow, away from her. "I really, really miss her." His body began to shake.

Even though it was a delusion, his grief was real. She knew enough of grief to know that. "It hurts, doesn't it?" she said quietly.

He turned toward her, his mouth crumpling. He flung his arms around her and she held his head against her body while he wept and rubbed his nose into her shirt.

"I'm so sorry, honey," she whispered. She stroked his head.

"I miss her so much." He was crying in earnest now, great wheezing sobs that seemed to emerge from his chest fully formed, like tufts of black smoke. Anyone would think this was a brokenhearted child, an abandoned child. Yet she had never once left him overnight. "Make it better, Mommy."

She had no choice in the matter. "I will."

Janie came out of the room sadder than she

remembered being at any time since her mother's death. She brought her computer into the kitchen and pulled out the prescription for risperidone. Then she took out a mug and the bottle of bourbon a client had given her years ago and took a long swig.

The mug had a picture of a kitten chasing a butterfly; it had been a gift from a colleague who thought she had a cat. Tonight it seemed comforting to her, like an optimistic fortune in a fortune cookie that one disbelieved and yet put in one's pocket anyway. The bourbon swirled warmly in her belly, did a misty rain dance around her panicked brain.

She reached over to the computer, opened the search screen.

Impact of antiperspirants.

No.

Impact of antipsychotics in children.

Psychiatrists prescribe the drugs to kids in some cases of serious illness when they think the benefits outweigh the risks. . . . At the same time, reports of deaths and dangerous side effects linked to the drugs are mounting. A USA TODAY study of FDA data collected from 2000 to 2004 shows at least 45 deaths of children in which an atypical antipsychotic was listed in the FDA database as the "primary suspect." There also were 1,328 reports of bad side effects, some of them life threatening.

My god. No.
She clicked out of that page quickly and opened a new one.

On antipsychotics, one loses his sense of self, his mind is fogged, his emotions ruined, his memory lost as a result of the treatment.

She closed the window quickly, tried another window, then another. Opened window after window, each one looking out on some new horror, until the bourbon drained slowly from the bottle into her mug and her eyes felt as if they were bleeding.

She held the liquor in her mouth, feeling it burn her tongue. The kitten on the mug was demonic, or rather, ordinary. At any moment he would pounce and tear the pretty butterfly's blue wings to pieces with his teeth.

She looked up risperidone and skimmed the list of side effects: *drowsiness, dizziness, nausea. . . .* It went on and on. When she was done reading, she felt dizzy, nauseated, agitated, sweaty, itchy, feverish, and fat. Her head was spinning, though it might have been the drink.

You tried so hard to give your kid food that was healthy, she thought. The soy cheese pizza. The organic peas and broccoli and baby carrots. The smoothies. The hormone-free milk. The leafy greens. You kept processed food to a minimum, threw Halloween candy out after a week. Never let him eat the icies they sold in the park, because they had red and yellow dye in them. And then you gave him this?

She grabbed the prescription and crumpled it up, then smoothed it out on the table and stared at it. After a while she got up and put the bottle of bourbon back in the closet.

She thought of calling a friend to come over, to comfort her or dispense much-needed advice, but she couldn't bear to share the diagnosis with anyone, to hear her own panic echoing back to her over the phone.

She'd always thought of herself as a successful person. She'd worked hard, building up her own business from scratch, surviving even in a tough economy; she had raised

Noah on her own, creating a cozy home for the two of them. Now she was failing at the only thing that mattered.

She opened up a new window on her laptop. She stared at the blinking cursor for a moment, then sent out a flare to the gods of the Internet:

Help. She was sure she was not the first, nor the last, person to Google that.

The Beatles, Help, YouTube
The Help, Rated PG-13-Drama. Set in Mississippi during the 1960s, a southern society girl returns from college determined to become a writer, but turns her —
Help.com. I'm a member of the flat earth society and I have to do a presentation of why other people cannot believe that the earth is flat —

She rested her head on the keyboard. Lifted it again. Fingers moving across the mouse pad, talking to the ghost in this machine.

I don't even know what to ask —

How do I ask a girl to homecoming?

My son wants another mother —

Are moms allowed to discipline another's child?

Another life —

The Veronicas — "In Another Life" — Lyrics — YouTube
Another Lifetime, a documentary about reincarnation including free streaming video interviews . . .

Ha: a new age doc. She'd seen way too many of these sorts of documentaries during the last year of her mother's life. Her mother had been a practical woman, with a wide circle of practical friends, but when she got the diagnosis (leukemia, the worst kind), all of that went out the window as far as her friends were concerned. One by one they dropped by with brown powdery packets from Chinese homeopaths, with crystals and documentaries and pamphlets about procedures in Mexico, and Janie and her mother had humored them the best they could. She'd spent hours sitting by her mother's bedside, holding her hand while they watched these films and made fun of them, one after the next, baloney followed by malarkey. Documentaries on channeling spirits, alchemical healing, shamanic drumming. Janie giggled through a scrim of tears as her dying, tough-minded mother used the last of her fierce energy to mock the cheesy graphics, the beaches and rainbows in these films, which offered what they couldn't possibly deliver: hope. It was the best part of the worst days of Janie's life, laughing with her mother over those movies. Somehow, her mother's mockery made Janie believe that she wouldn't need any of those kooky things. She would survive from sheer will and modern medicine. There was another experimental procedure they were trying, better than the one that caused her such painful bloating. It would be enough.

And yes (clicking now on the YouTube link, eager to distract herself from both the horror of the present and the equally unbearable past, to find something to lighten her heavy yet over-bourbonated brain), yes, there it was, on this one, too: that corny shot of the ocean waves. And there was the sun and the waterfall . . . and the flute, of course! — and the same deep-voiced narrator. . . . Was it the same guy? Was that his life's work, narrating new age documentaries?

"A majestic cycle of life and death and life beginning anew, each with its own lessons . . ."

Majestic cycle of life . . .

Oh, her mother would have chuckled at that one. "How about that, Mom?" she said aloud, reciting the words in a faux stentorian voice: "MAJESTIC CYCLE OF LIFE!"

She paused, as if giving her mother time to answer, but there was no one there, as she very well knew.

"In the United States some groundbreaking scientific explorers have been studying reincarnation. . . ."

"EXPLORERS, MOM!" she shouted, aware she was amusing no one, not even the dead, but unable to stop herself from trying. It was that, or start crying, and she knew nothing good would come of that. "They're EXPLORERS!"

"The most well-known of these explorers is Dr. Jerome Anderson —"

"I'll bet your ASS he's a doctor! What's he got, a PhD in Quackery?" She hiccupped, guffawed.

". . . who for many decades has been studying young children who seem to recall details from previous lives. These children, often as young as two or three, talk in specific detail about missing their previous homes and families —"

Janie pressed PAUSE. The room went silent.

Clearly, she had heard it wrong. She went

back a bit.

"Dr. Jerome Anderson, who for many decades has been studying young children who seem to recall details from previous lives. These children, often as young as two or three, talk in specific detail about missing their previous homes and families —"

She pressed PAUSE again, and this time everything paused: the moving images, her mind, her breath, caught half-formed in her chest.

On the screen, she could see the profile of a head that must belong to Dr. Anderson. He had curly black hair and a striking, angular face. He was talking to a little boy who looked South Asian, a boy of three, perhaps, wearing ragged trousers. Behind the boy, a wall of bricks rose up from red mud. The image seemed grainy, as if taken decades earlier. She stared at it until, like anything stared at long enough, it became something else: Man. Boy. Place. Time.

But this was . . . ridiculous.

On the screen, the little boy was facing the grown man. He looked extremely uncomfortable. He probably had dysentery, she thought.

She rewound again.

"Dr. Jerome Anderson, who for many decades has been studying young children

111

who seem to recall details from previous lives . . ."

She *knew* better than this. This was the bourbon, diluting her common sense.

She paused the image.

She had seen firsthand how the manipulative preyed upon the gullible. She knew that there was no end to what desperate people would do. And wasn't that what Janie was now?

Then she heard it.

There was no point going to Noah's room yet, or trying to wake him. She knew the drill. After ten minutes, the whimper would become a shriek, the shriek would turn into words: "Mama, Mama!"

She would find him twisting in the sheets, flailing, screaming. *"Let me out, let me out, let me out!"*

There was nothing worse than watching your own child tumbling down through the darkness and not being able to stop it. Anything was better.

Even drugs? Even *this*? She looked at the image on the screen.

The whimpering was becoming sharper now, the pitch heightening. Soon he would call out for her, and she would go to his side and try, unsuccessfully, to comfort him. Sleeping, drenched in sweat, he would thrash in her arms.

The doctor and the boy were still there, frozen on her computer screen. She picked up the prescription and held it in her open hand.

Somebody tell me what to do, she thought.

She sat at her kitchen table with her laptop, the prescription in her hand, her son crying in his sleep. She stared at the image on the screen, wondering when it would begin to lose its power.

Many of the subjects in our cases are born with birthmarks or birth defects that match wounds on the body of the previous personality, usually fatal wounds. One case that includes both an announcing dream and a birth defect is that of Süleyman Çaper in Turkey. His mother dreamed during her pregnancy that a man she did not recognize told her, "I was killed with a blow from a shovel. I want to stay with you and not anyone else." When Süleyman was born, the back of his skull was partially depressed, and he also had a birthmark there. When he became able to talk, he said that he had been a miller who died when an angry customer hit him on the head. Along with other details, he gave the first name of the miller and the village where he had lived. In fact, an angry customer had killed a miller with that name in that village by hitting him on the back of the head with a shovel.

JIM B. TUCKER, M.D., *LIFE BEFORE LIFE* .

EIGHT

The packing tape yowled in protest. Anderson cut it with his teeth and closed the box, feeling as if the cardboard flaps were shutting above his head. It would be quiet in there, with his life's work.

It had taken him months — pulling out the cases one by one to look through them again had slowed him down considerably — but the Institute was entirely packed up now, ready to be shipped.

Let the next generation of scientific seekers find his work and make of it what they will. He hoped they would. He'd gotten a letter, recently, from a colleague in Sri Lanka, where there were so many cases you could sweep them up like fish in a net.

All that evidence he had compiled. He'd been sure that the editors of the medical journals could not ignore it. As if evidence itself could be indisputable. He had misjudged human nature. He had screwed up by forgetting the human ability to reject anything it wants to — Galileo himself should have taught him that much.

From somewhere far away, or in the room, a phone began to ring.

"But I don't understand. I thought she turned it down. Why does she want to talk?" His literary agent was saying something on the telephone, but it made no sense to him. "Does she want it or doesn't she?"

"She's having second thoughts. She'd want some changes and wants to make sure you're on the same page with that. She's one of the top editors in the field. She has a string of bestsellers under her belt. It's very good news."

The same page, he'd thought. Top in the field. Bestsellers. The lingo was funny to him. He pictured a huge white page slanting up like a mountain, with himself and the editor standing at the top of it, shaking hands. He'd never had to deal with people who were in the business of making money. With the academic press that had published his few books, money had hardly been discussed, but then again, nobody had read those, outside of the small community of like-minded researchers. This, he thought, was another world entirely. Thirty years ago the word *bestsellers* would have made him scoff; now it quickened his breath. How things had changed for him.

The editor got on the phone immediately after her assistant had announced his name.

"I couldn't get this book out of my mind," the editor said. Her voice was sharp and chipper at the same time. A force in the industry, his agent had said, citing a number of successful books he'd never heard of. He tried to imagine her: dark-haired, fervent, with a white, heart-shaped face, a dynamo Snow White wrapping the telephone cord around her fingers as she talked . . . what was he thinking? Nobody had telephone cords anymore. He was sweating like a schoolboy on a first date.

"I think a lot of people will be interested in it. But it does need some work."

"It does?"

"Particularly the American cases."

"The American cases?"

"Yes. They are all so old, in the seventies and eighties, and far less . . . dramatic. It's an American audience, after all. So many of the other cases are set in exotic places, and that's good, but we also need to focus more on the American stories. So people can connect."

He cleared his throat, buying himself time.

"But people can connect," he said slowly, carefully repeating her words like a child learning to speak, or a sixty-eight-year-old losing his vocabulary. "This isn't an American story. It's a —" What was the word he was searching for? Something vast that contained all the planets and solar systems inside it. He couldn't find the word so switched tactics: "It's a story for everyone." Gesturing widely and invisibly with his hands, as if to encompass everything he meant but couldn't say.

"Right. But the only recent American case you have here . . . you know, in which the child remembers being his own great-uncle?"

"Yes."

"Well, the other cases seem stronger somehow."

"Well, of course."

"Why of course?"

"When the subject is a member of the same family you can't really verify the facts in the same way."

"Right. What I mean is, we need one or two strong new cases. American cases. To anchor the book."

"Oh. But —"

"Yes?"

He opened his mouth. The objections rose

within him: *My office is closed. I haven't had a new case in six months. . . . There are not as many strong American cases, anyway. I'm not sure I can even write a cogent sentence, much less a chapter. . . .*

"All right," he said. "That's fine. An American case."

"A strong one. So we're on the same page?"

He stifled a laugh. He was exhilarated, reckless. He was slipping down the mountain now, tumbling, head over heels. "Yes."

Purnima Ekanayake, a girl in Sri Lanka, was born with a group of light-colored birthmarks over the left side of her chest and her lower ribs. She began talking about a previous life when she was between two and a half and three years old, but her parents did not initially pay much attention to her statements. When she was four years old, she saw a television program about the Kelaniya temple, a well-known temple that was 145 miles away, and said that she recognized it. Later, her father, a school principal, and her mother, a teacher, took a group of students to the Kelaniya temple. Purnima went with the group on the visit. While there, she said that she had lived on the other side of the river that flowed beside the temple grounds.

By the time she was six, Purnima had made some twenty statements about the previous life, describing a male incense maker who was killed in a traffic accident. She had mentioned the names of two incense brands, Ambiga and Geta Pichcha. Her parents had never heard of these, and . . . [none of] the shops in their town . . . sold those brands of incense.

A new teacher began working in Purnima's town. He spent his weekends in Kelaniya where his wife lived. Purnima's father told him what Purnima had said, and the teacher decided to check in Kelaniya to see if anyone had died there who matched her statements. The teacher said that Purnima's father gave him the following items to check:

— She had lived on the other side of the river from the Kelaniya temple.

— She had made Ambiga and Geta Pichcha incense sticks.

— She was selling incense sticks on a bicycle.

— She was killed in an accident with a big vehicle.

He then went with his brother-in-law, who did not believe in reincarnation, to see if a person matching those statements could be located. They went to the Kelaniya temple and took a ferry across the river. There, they asked about incense makers and found that three small family incense businesses were in the area. The owner of one of them called his brands Ambiga and Geta Pichcha. His brother-in-law and associate, Jinadasa Perera, had been killed by a bus when he was taking incense sticks to the market on his bicycle two years before Purnima was born.

Purnima's family visited the owner's home soon after. There, Purnima made various comments about family members and their business that were correct, and the family accepted her as being Jinadasa reborn.

JIM B. TUCKER, M.D., *LIFE BEFORE LIFE*

NINE

Janie closed the book in her hand and frowned into the depths of the diner. She was waiting for a man she didn't know, whose work was either mind shattering or total baloney, and who now held Noah's future in the palm of his hand. And she couldn't even get through his book.

She'd tried. The book was a serious-looking thing — she'd had to order it online, since the academic publisher that had put it out twenty years ago was now out of business, and it had cost her fifty-five dollars for the paperback. She'd picked it up again and again over the past two weeks, as she'd planned this meeting; yet whenever she focused intently on one of Anderson's cases, her brain began to fog up with confusion.

The book was filled with case studies, children in Thailand and Lebanon and India and Myanmar and Sri Lanka who had made statements about other mothers and other homes. These children behaved in a way that was at odds with their family or village cultures and sometimes had intense attachments to strangers, who lived hours away from them, whom they seemed to remember from previous lifetimes. They often had phobias. The cases were compelling and strangely familiar. . . . Yet how could they be true?

She found herself going over the same cases without finding any clarity of belief or disbelief. In the end she couldn't read them at all but absorbed, like a clammy mist, the impression of something deeply unsettling. Children who seemed to remember lives spent selling jasmine or growing rice in a village somewhere in Asia until they were hit by a motorcycle, or burned by a kerosene lamp — lives that had nothing (or everything) to do with Noah.

Janie ran her fingers through her son's soft hair, grateful for once for the television affixed to the wall above their heads. (When had restaurants joined airports in assuming their customers needed to be endlessly glued to the tube?) She pulled out the computer printout she'd tucked in the binder and looked again at the doctor's qualifications:

Jerome Anderson

M.D.: Harvard Medical School

B.A.: Yale University, English Literature

Psychiatry Residency at Columbia Presbyterian Hospital, New York, NY

Professor of Psychiatry, University of Connecticut School of Medicine

Robert B. Angsley Professor of Psychiatry and Neurobehavioral Sciences at The Institute for the Study of Previous Personalities, University of Connecticut School of Medicine

The meaning of these words was clear enough, and she clung to it: an educated man. She was simply getting another expert's opinion. That's all it was. And it didn't really matter what his methods were, as long as he got results. Maybe this doctor had some sort of especially soothing approach with children, the way some people could placate horses. It was an experimental procedure. You read about things like that all the time. It didn't matter what Noah *had,* or what Anderson thought he had, so long as he was *cured.*

She flipped through the binder she'd put together for him. It was the same type of binder she used when courting new clients, except instead of town houses and apart-

126

ments, each section was marked by a colored tab signifying a year in Noah's life. The binder had all of Noah's information, the odd things he'd said and done: everything, except the crucial thing. She hadn't mentioned Dr. Remson or his possible diagnosis, worried that Anderson might balk at working with a child who might be mentally ill.

It was odd to be meeting him at a busy diner. Dr. Anderson had suggested meeting at her home — it was his usual protocol, it makes the children more comfortable, he'd said — but she needed to get a sense of the man first, do a quick kook check, so they'd compromised on the place at the corner. Still, what kind of a doctor made home visits? Maybe he was a quack, after all —

"Ms. Zimmerman?"

A man stood over her: a tall, lean figure wearing an oversize navy blue wool sweater and khaki pants.

"*You're* Dr. Anderson?"

"Jerry." He smiled briefly, a flash of teeth in the crowded room, and extended his hand to her, then Noah, who glanced away from the TV just long enough to brush Anderson's huge hand with his tiny one.

Whatever she'd been expecting (someone professional, maybe a bit geeky, with the sharp profile and dark, curly hair she'd glimpsed in the video), it wasn't this man. This was a person pared down to his essence, with the high cheekbones and glittering eyes of an Egyptian cat deity and the weathered skin of a fisherman. He must have been handsome once (the face had a fierce, elemental beauty) but was now somehow too austere for that, as if he had left handsome by the side of the road many years back, as something for which he had no use.

"I'm sorry if that sounded rude. It's just on the video you seemed —"

"Younger?" He bent slightly in her direction, and a whiff of something came off of him: she had a sense of something unruly running beneath the elegant, contained surface. "Time does that."

Just pretend it's a client, she told herself. She shifted modes, smiled professionally. "I'm a little nervous," she said. "This isn't exactly my sort of thing."

He settled himself across from her in the booth. "That's good."

"It is?"

His gray eyes really were unnaturally bright. "It usually means the case is stronger. Otherwise you would not be here." He spoke crisply, enunciating each word.

"I see." She was not used to thinking of Noah's illness as a "case" that might be "strong." She might have objected but the waitress (purple-haired; harried) was handing out menus. When she turned back toward the kitchen, a YOLO tattoo in Gothic letters stood out against the pale skin of her shoulders.

YOLO. A slogan, a rallying cry, carpe diem for the skateboarder set: *You only live once.*

But was it true?

That was the problem, wasn't it? She had never thought about it in any deep way. She hadn't had the time or inclination to speculate about other lives: this one was hard enough to manage. It was all she could do to pay for their food and rent and clothes, to try to give Noah love and an education and get him to brush his teeth. And lately she had barely been managing any of it. This *had* to work. She didn't have another option, aside from medicating her four-year-old. But what had she been thinking about?

Oh, right. Other lives. Which she wasn't sure she believed in.

And yet: here she was.

Anderson was looking at her expectantly across the table. Noah was watching the television, doodling away on his place mat. The waitress who only lived once came and took their orders and left again like a purple cloud of surliness.

Janie reached out and lightly touched her son's shoulder, as if to protect him from the man's quiet intensity. "Listen, Noey, why don't you go stand by the counter for a minute and watch the game from there? It's much closer."

"Okay." He squirmed out of his seat, as if happy to be released.

With Noah out of earshot, her body seemed to wilt into the booth.

On the television near the counter, someone hit a home run; Noah joined the regulars in cheering.

"He likes baseball, I see," Anderson said.

"When he was a baby it was the only thing that could calm him down. I used to call it baby Ambien."

"Do you watch as well?"

"Not on purpose."

He pulled a yellow pad out of his briefcase and scribbled a note.

"I don't see how that's uncommon, though," Janie added. "Lots of little boys like baseball, don't they?"

"Sure they do." Anderson cleared his throat. "Before we begin. I'm sure you have questions for me?"

She looked down at her binder with all

the colored tabs. The binder that was Noah. "How does it work?"

"The protocol? Well, I ask you some questions and then I ask your son —"

"No, I mean — reincarnation." She flinched at the word. "How does it work? I don't understand. You're saying all these kids are — reincarnated and they remember these things from their other lives, right?"

"In some cases that seems to be the most likely explanation."

"The most likely? But I thought —"

"I'm a scientific researcher. I take down statements from children and I verify them and suggest explanations. I don't jump to conclusions."

But conclusions were exactly what she had been hoping for. She picked up the binder and held it against her chest, comforted by its physicality.

"You're skeptical," he said. She opened her mouth to respond, and he silenced her with an upraised hand. "That's okay. My wife was skeptical, too, at first. Luckily, I'm not in the belief business." His lips twisted wryly. "I collect data."

Data. She clung to the word, as to a wet rock in a raging river. "So she's not skeptical anymore?"

"Hmmm?" He looked confused.

"You said — your wife was skeptical at first. So she believes in your work now?"

"Now?" He glanced up at her face. "She's —"

He didn't finish his thought. His mouth hung open for a moment that seemed to go on, embarrassing them both, and then he snapped it shut. Yet the moment had happened, and there was no taking it back; it was as if his defenses, that ordinary force field shielding one's basic human nature, had inexplicably shattered.

"She's gone. Six years ago," he said at last. "I mean — she's not alive anymore."

He was grief stricken, that's what was wrong. He was lonely; he had been dealt a blow. Janie knew what that was like. She looked around the ordinary room at the children munching on their French toast, their dads fondly wiping away dribbles of syrup; those people were on the other shore, and she was on the side of the aggrieved with this pained-looking man who was patiently waiting for whatever she was about to say.

She kept her voice soft. "Shall we continue?"

"Of course," he said, more vigorously than she'd expected. He pulled himself together quickly, the elegant planes of his face realigning. He held his sharpened pencil aloft over his yellow pad.

"When was the first time you remember Noah doing something that seemed out of the ordinary?"

"I suppose . . . it was the lizards."

"The lizards?" He was scratching away.

"Noah was two. We were at the Museum of Natural History. We went to see the lizard and snake exhibit. And he was . . . just . . ." She paused. "The only word for it is transfixed, I guess. He stood right in front of the first tank and starting yelping. I thought something was wrong, and then he said, 'Look, a bearded dragon!'"

She glanced at Anderson and saw how intensely he was listening to her. The other psychologists had never been interested in the lizards. He bent to write a note, and she noticed that his blue sweater, which looked so soft and expensive, had a conspicuous hole in the sleeve. It was probably as old as she was.

"I was pretty surprised, because his vocabulary was limited at that point, he had just turned two, it was all 'I want Mom-Mom and water and duck and milk.'"

"Mom-Mom?"

"He usually calls me that, or Mommy-Mom. I guess he likes to have his own name

133

for me. Anyway, I thought he was making it up."

"Making what up?"

"The name. Bearded dragon. It sounded fanciful to me, like something a child would dream up, a dragon with a beard. So I laughed at him, thinking it was cute. And I said, 'Actually, sweetie, it's a —' and looked over, you know, at the card. And, sure enough, it was called a bearded dragon.

"And so I asked him, 'Noah, how do you know about bearded dragons?' And he said —" She looked again at Anderson. "He said, ' 'Cause I had one.' "

" 'Cause I had one?"

"I thought . . . I don't know what I thought. He was being a kid, making things up."

"And you never owned a lizard?"

"God, no." He laughed, and she felt an uncoiling, a relief at talking freely about Noah's differences. "And it wasn't only bearded dragons. He knew all the lizards."

"He knew their names," Anderson murmured.

"Every lizard in the place. At the age of two."

She had been so startled, so proud of his obvious intelligence, of his — why not say it? — giftedness. He knew the names of all

134

the lizards — something she had never known. It thrilled her, watching him stare into each miniature rain forest, so cunning and mossy, its inhabitants barely moving except for the flick of a tongue or a jerky journey across a log, while his high pure voice exclaimed, "Mommy-Mom, it's a monitor! It's a gecko! It's a water dragon!" She had thought with relief that his way in life would be clear: scholarships to the best schools and universities, his formidable intelligence greasing the way to a successful life.

And then, gradually, her pride had turned into confusion. How did he know this stuff? Was there some kind of book or video he'd memorized? But why hadn't he mentioned it before? Had someone taught him? The matter had never been clarified; she had merely accepted it as part of his specialness.

"Was there a book or video at a friend's house, maybe?" Anderson asked now, as if reading her mind, his quiet voice bringing her back to the clatter of the diner. "Or his nursery school? Something he might have seen somewhere?"

"That's the strange thing. I asked around — I was pretty thorough. There was nothing."

He nodded. "Would you mind if I asked

135

around a bit myself? At his school and with his friends and sitters?"

"I guess not." She looked at him sideways. "It sounds like you're trying to explain it away. Don't you believe me?"

"We have to think like the skeptics think. Or it's all —" He shrugged. "Now: did you notice any change in his behavior, after the episode with the lizard?"

"His nightmares got worse, I guess."

"Tell me about those," he said, his head bent over his pad. But it was too much, suddenly, to tell.

"You might want to look at this." She placed the binder that was Noah on the table and slid it across to him.

Anderson turned the pages slowly, poring over the details. The case was not as strong as he'd hoped — the nightmares and water phobia were commonplace, if unusually intense, the rifle and Harry Potter references were interesting but inconclusive, and the knowledge of lizards was promising, but only if he could prove that there was no clear source for the child's expertise. Most important, there was nothing concrete that might lead him to a previous personality — guns and Harry Potter books were as widespread as air in this culture, and a bearded dragon pet was nothing much to go on. The child had mentioned a lake house to his teachers, but it was useless to him without a name for the lake.

He glanced up at the woman, who was building a structure out of sugar cubes. She was, like most people, a contradiction: steady blue eyes, fidgety hands. When she looked at Anderson her eyes were evaluating, cautious, but when she turned to her son a palpable warmth shone from her features. Still, he wished she had trusted him enough to invite him home. The diner was loud, and it would be difficult to get anything from a child in this setting.

He watched her nimble fingers finishing the little white brick house. "Nice . . ."

What was it called? The word dropped down suddenly from the gods of language, like sugar to his lips. ". . . igloo," he continued. Being back on a case was good for his vocabulary, at least. The child in him was sorry when she dismantled it quickly, piling the cubes neatly back in the dish.

He took a sip of tea. He had forgotten to take out the tea bag. The liquid felt dense against his lips. He tapped the binder. "You're very thorough."

"But — what do you think?"

"I think his case has promise."

She glanced at her son, engrossed in the baseball game at the counter, and leaned across the table. "But can you *help* him?" she whispered.

He could smell the coffee on her breath; it had been a long time since he had felt the warmth of a woman's breath on his face. He took another sip of tea. He had managed mothers before, of course. Decades of mothers: skeptical, angry, sorrowful, dismissive, helpful, hopeful, or desperate, like this one. The main thing was to remain composed and in control.

He was saved from answering by the waitress, who, hoarding the smiles afforded her for her one and only life (Why did people tattoo that on their bodies? Did they really find it inspiring to live only once?) set down a steaming plate of pancakes with a scowl.

He watched the mother fetch the boy.

Now he could get a good look at him. He was lovely, of course, but it was the watchfulness in his eyes that drew Anderson. There was occasionally another dimension in the awareness of children who remembered; not a knowledge so much as a wariness, a shadow consciousness like that of a stranger in a new country who can't help thinking of home.

138

Anderson smiled at the boy. How many thousands of cases had he handled? Two thousand, seven hundred and fifty-three, to be exact. There was no reason to be nervous. He would not let himself be nervous. "Who's winning the game?"

"Yankees."

"Are you a Yankees fan?"

The boy took a mouthful of pancake. "Naw."

"What team do you like?"

"Nationals."

"The Washington Nationals? Why do you like them?"

" 'Cause that's my team."

"Have you ever been to Washington, D.C.?"

His mother spoke up. "No, we haven't."

Anderson tried to keep his voice gentle. "I was asking Noah."

Noah picked up a spoon and stuck his tongue out at the distorted spoon-boy reflected in its bowl. "Mommy, can I go back and watch?"

"Not now, sweetie. When you're done eating."

"I am done."

"No, you are not. Besides, Dr. Anderson wants to speak to you."

"I'm sick of doctors."

"Just this one more."

"No!"

His voice was loud. Anderson noticed a couple of nearby women glancing in their direction, judging this other mother over their scrambled eggs, and felt a twinge of empathy for her.

"Noah, please —"

"It's okay." Anderson sighed. "I'm a stranger. We need to get to know each other better. It takes time."

"Please, Mommy-Mom? It's opening day."

"Oh, fine."

They watched him leap out of his seat.

"So." She looked at him forcefully, as if closing a deal. "You'll take him on?"

"On?"

"As a patient."

"It doesn't work quite like that."

"I thought you were a psychiatrist."

"I am. But this work — it's not a clinical practice. It's research."

"I see." She looked puzzled. "So, what are the next steps, then?"

"I need to keep talking to Noah. See if we can find something concrete that he remembers. A town, a name. Something we can track down."

"You mean, like a clue?"

"Exactly."

"So he can go to see . . . where he used to live in his previous lifetime? Is that it? And that will cure him?"

"I can't promise anything. But subjects do tend to calm down after we solve a case and find the previous personality. He may well forget on his own, you know. Most do, by the age of six or so."

She took this in warily. "But how can you find the — previous personality? Noah hasn't said anything that specific."

"Let's see how it goes. It takes time."

"That's what they all say, all the doctors. But the thing is —" Her voice quavered and she stopped abruptly. She tried again. "The thing is, I don't have time. I'm running out of money. And Noah's not getting better. I need to do something now. I need something to *work.*"

He felt her need across the table, taking hold of him.

Perhaps this was a mistake. Perhaps he should go back to his house in Connecticut . . . and do what? There was nothing to do but lie on the couch that was his bed now, under the paisley comforter that Sheila had bought twenty years ago and that still smelled very faintly of citrus and roses. Only, if he did that, he may as well be dead.

She frowned and looked away from him,

clearly trying to regain control of herself. He wouldn't comfort her with false promises. Who knew if he could help her son? Besides, the case was weak. There wasn't anything to go on, unless the child suddenly became a lot more talkative. He looked down at the table, at the remains of the brunch, the boy's half-eaten pancake, the dirty place mat. . . . "What's that?"

The woman was wiping her eyes with a napkin. "What?"

"That place mat. What's written on it?"

"This? It's a doodle. He was doodling."

"Can I see it?"

"Why?"

"Can I see it, please." He held his voice steady with great effort.

She shook her head, but she moved the plate and the orange juice glass and handed him the thin rectangle of paper. "Watch out, there's syrup on the edges."

Anderson picked up the place mat. It was sticky under his fingertips and smelled of syrup and orange juice. Yet even before he properly examined the marks on the paper, he felt the blood beginning to tingle in his veins.

"He wasn't doodling," Anderson said quietly. "He was scoring the game."

TEN

Janie stood in the middle of her living room. The room was dark, except for the head-lights from passing cars, there and gone, a flash on the wall. She could make out the familiar shapes in the dimness: couch, chair, lamp. Yet the objects looked different to her, slightly ajar, as if there had been a tremor in the earth.

She heard Anderson moving around in the kitchen. She cracked the window and the air came alive with the damp freshness of early spring. The gas lamp shimmied in the darkness, its flame always moving, here, then here, then here.

One thing had led to another. Noah had scored a baseball game without being taught how to do it, and so she had invited Anderson to come to her home to work with Noah in a quieter place, and they had spent the afternoon engaged in her son's favorite activity: Noah threw his bouncy ball against

143

his wall and caught it, while Anderson, standing by his side with his yellow pad, judged the accuracy of the pitch. ("Eight." "Only an eight?" "Well, maybe a nine." "A nine! Yesssss! A nine!") Noah's spirits rose under Anderson's attentions, as she had not seen him in months, and Anderson himself seemed a different man entirely. He laughed easily and seemed truly interested in Noah's skill at throwing and catching bouncy balls (amazing to Janie, who always found this game to be an unbelievable bore). He was so natural with the boy that she was surprised when he'd responded, in answer to her question, that he had no children of his own.

How could you not like a man who played so joyfully and with such obvious affection with one's son? When was the last time any man had done that?

But it didn't matter how many times Anderson asked him questions or in what manner. Noah was done talking to doctors about anything that didn't involve catching or throwing. Anderson's pad had acquired no new notes.

By late afternoon, it was clear to Janie that they weren't getting anywhere. Even Noah seemed to feel the dejection in the air and started throwing the ball around the room in a hyper, desultory way until it joined the two others in the lighting fixture on the ceiling and Janie put an end to the game. To relax him (and herself), she resorted to the mother's last trick: she put on his favorite movie, *Finding Nemo,* about the lost fish looking for his father, and they sat together, Janie and Noah and Anderson, side by side on the couch. Janie focused on the colorful fish and tried not to think about anything else, but the images couldn't hold her attention. Dread was dripping slowly through her, filling her with its paralyzing poison of what-now-what-now-what-now?

Anderson sat on the other side of Noah, his face inscrutable in profile, like the statue of a knight on a tomb. Before the movie was over, Noah had fallen asleep, his head drooping on Janie's shoulder, but they watched the movie to its end anyway, lost in their separate worlds. She felt a pang of misery when the father found the son, envy at all that fishy happiness. Afterward, she had carried Noah to bed, his legs dangling on either side of her like a huge baby, and tucked him in. It was only six.

When Janie returned, the tall man was pacing back and forth. It was strange to have him in her apartment without Noah in the room. It was as if the doctor had suddenly become a man — not someone she would have an interest in (he was far too old for her, too aloof) but someone who nevertheless charged the molecules of the air with a masculine difference.

She watched him pace for a few moments; he seemed entirely lost in his thoughts.

"So," she said at last. "What do we do now?"

He paused midstride; he looked surprised to see her there. "Well, we can try again tomorrow. If that's all right with you, that is?"

"Tomorrow?" She shook her head. "I've got a client meeting. . . ." But he wasn't listening.

"And in the meantime we need to corroborate the information we have. We'll check with the school about the lizards and the other behavior he exhibited there. It's too late now" — he glanced at his watch — "but I'll e-mail them in the morning. Can you give them a heads-up?"

"I guess so." She flinched inwardly at the idea of approaching Ms. Whittaker with this matter. Surely she would have no patience for it, and of course the preschool director would probably tell Anderson that Noah was already seeing a psychiatrist. . . .

146

"And a statement as well that they don't instruct children in the art of baseball scoring, of course." He chuckled to himself. "Though that would be highly unusual."

"Why do you need to corroborate, anyway?"

"It'll be a stronger case with multiple sources."

"A stronger case?" She wished he'd stop talking about Noah as a case.

"Yes."

"You mean — for an article or something?"

"Right."

"Well, I don't think I want any part of that."

"Hmmm?"

"I'm a private person. We're private people."

"Of course. We'd change all the names in the book."

The book. His excitement was suddenly becoming clear to her. She'd been wondering what kind of doctor he was, and now she knew: the kind that was writing a book.

"What book?"

"I'm writing up some cases. It won't be lost in academic obscurity, like the others. This one is for the public," he added eagerly, as if obscurity was the problem.

"I don't want Noah in a book."

He stared at her.

"Does it matter so much to you, Doctor?"

"I —" He didn't finish his thought. He turned a shade paler.

She couldn't trust him. He was writing a book. She remembered all those books her mother's friends had given her when she was dying: everyone trying to make a buck off the hopeless with their special diets and yoga poses. Even when her mother was only briefly conscious, the books kept on coming. In the end there was a closet full of them.

There was certainly no book that could help her now, and there was no mother, either. There was only this stranger with his agenda. She felt the weariness that was washing over her transform suddenly into something else — an emotion that startled her with its ferocity. For months people had been sitting coolly across desks telling her that something was wrong with her son, and she had taken it in, quieting the outward signs of panic as best she could. But this man, with his bright, questioning eyes and ashy complexion — this man had something to lose, too. She felt the anxiety in him as only the desperate can, and the knowledge of it was like a key opening the door on her vast frustration and fury.

"That's why you were so excited about the fact that he could score a baseball game, isn't it? It's not going to help us find any 'previous personality.' It's just a good detail for your precious *book*." He winced at the way she said the word. "Do you even care about helping Noah at all?"

"I —" He looked at her uncertainly. "I want to help all the children —"

"Right, by having their mothers buy your book?" She felt even as she said it that this man did not seem motivated by anything so coarse as making money, but she couldn't help herself.

"I —" he started to say again. And then stopped. "What is that?"

They both heard it, then: from the bedroom down the hall. A whimpering.

"I think we woke Noah," Anderson murmured.

The whimpering became a whooshing, like the wind wailing up a chimney.

"No. He's not awake."

The noise gathered power until it blew through the room: a hurricane, a force of nature, and then slowly the howl took form, became a word. "Mamaaaa! Mamaa!"

Always, it surprised her: that torrent of emotion that seemed beyond what a small

149

boy would be able to summon. Janie stood wearily, on shaky feet. She looked at Anderson. She didn't trust him, but he was the only one here. "Aren't you coming?"

And they headed together toward Noah's bedroom.

Chanai Choomalaiwong was born in central Thailand in 1967 with two birthmarks, one on the back of his head and one above his left eye. When he was born, his family did not think that his birthmarks were particularly significant, but when he was three years old, he began talking about a previous life. He said that he had been a schoolteacher named Bua Kai and that he had been shot and killed while on the way to school. He gave the names of his parents, his wife, and two of his children from that life, and he persistently begged his grandmother, with whom he lived, to take him to the previous parents' home in a place called Khao Phra.

Eventually, when he was still three years old, his grandmother did just that. She and Chanai took a bus to a town near Khao Phra, which was fifteen miles from their home village. After the two of them got off

151

the bus, Chanai led the way to a house where he said his parents lived. The house belonged to an elderly couple whose son, Bua Kai Lawnak, had been a teacher who was murdered five years before Chanai was born. . . . Once there, Chanai identified Bua Kai's parents, who were there with a number of other family members, as his own. They were impressed enough by his statements and his birthmarks to invite him to return a short time later. When he did, they tested him by asking him to pick out Bua Kai's belongings from others, and he was able to do that. He recognized one of Bua Kai's daughters and asked for the other one by name. Bua Kai's family accepted that Chanai was Bua Kai reborn, and he visited them a number of times. He insisted that Bua Kai's daughters call him "Father," and if they did not, he refused to talk to them.

JIM B. TUCKER, M.D., *LIFE BEFORE LIFE*

ELEVEN

A door opened, and she fell through.

That's what happened, Janie thought afterward, standing in the dark living room. Yet there had been nothing so unusual about the sight of Noah yelling and thrashing about in his Ninja Turtle sheets. His mouth was open, his hair damp, plastered to his cheeks. She moved toward the bed to comfort and restrain him, but Anderson moved faster; he was beside Noah in an instant, leaning over him, holding down the feet kicking at the sheets.

A stranger was touching her son, who was calling out for her. Who was calling out —

"Mama!"

"Noah," she said, moving toward the bed, and Anderson looked up at her and held her back with his glance.

"Noah," Anderson said quietly. His voice was very firm. "Noah, can you hear me?"

"Lemme out!" Noah yelled. "Mama!

Lemme out! I can't get out!"

"Noah. It's okay. It's a nightmare," Anderson said. "You're having a nightmare."

"I can't breathe!"

"You can't breathe?"

"Can't breathe!"

Janie knew it was the dream, but she couldn't help saying, "Noah has asthma. We need to get his nebulizer — it's in the drawer —"

"He's breathing." Anderson's long body was poised over Noah's small struggling form, his hands still on his feet. Don't touch my son, she thought, but she didn't say it. She didn't say anything. She sent Anderson a silent message: One wrong move, bud, I'll boot you out of here so fast your head will spin.

"Noah," Anderson said firmly. "You can wake up now. It's all right."

Noah stopped moving. He opened his eyes wide. "Mama."

"Yes, honey," she called from the foot of the bed. But he was looking past her. She wasn't what he wanted.

"I want to go home."

"Noah," Anderson said again, and Noah turned his blue eyes on Anderson and kept them there. "Can you tell us what happened in your dream?"

"I can't breathe."

"Why can't you breathe?"

"I'm in the water."

"You're in — the ocean? A lake?"

"No." Noah took a few ragged, shallow breaths. Janie felt the struggle in her own lungs. If he stopped breathing, she would, too.

Noah squirmed into a sitting position. Anderson didn't need to hold on to his feet anymore. He was holding his attention. "He hurt me."

"In your dream?" Anderson spoke quickly. "Who's hurting you?"

"Not in my dream. In my real life."

"I see. Who hurt you?"

"Pauly. He hurt my body. Why'd he do that?"

"I don't know."

"Why'd he do it? Why?" Noah grabbed Anderson's hand, his eyes troubled. Janie herself had become invisible, a shadow at the foot of the bed.

Anderson looked back at him intently. "What did he do?"

"He hurt Tommy."

"Tommy? Was that your name?"

"Yes."

Janie was listening to her son, but the words echoed oddly in her mind, as if she

155

were hearing them from somewhere far away. And yet she was here, in this familiar room, with the glow-in-the-dark stars she'd pasted on the ceiling, one by one, and the bureau she'd hand-painted with elephants and tigers, and Noah, her Noah, and the door in her mind opening and closing and opening again.

"I see," Anderson said. "That's great. Do you remember your last name?"

"I don't know. I'm just Tommy."

"All right. Did you have a family, when you were Tommy?"

"Of course."

"Who's in your family?"

"There's my mama and papa and my little brother. And we have a lizard."

"And what are their names?"

"Horntail."

"Horntail?"

"He's a bearded dragon. Charlie and I named him that 'cause he looked like the Horntail Harry fought."

"I see. And who's Harry?"

Noah rolled his eyes. "You know, Harry Potter?"

At the foot of the bed, Janie heard herself inhale. She caught the breath in her chest, let it burn there. This familiar room, this unfamiliar tableau: the tall man leaning over

Noah, the round bright face almost grazing the angular one.

"And where do you live, with your family?"

"We live in the red house."

"The red house. And where's that?"

"It's in the field."

"And where's the field?"

"Ashvu?"

"Ashview?"

"That's it!"

"That's where you live?"

"That's my home!"

Janie felt herself exhale, a wisp of sound in the room.

"I want to go back there. Can I go back there?"

"That's what we're trying to do. Can we talk for a moment about what happened with Pauly? Can we do that?"

He nodded.

"Do you remember where you were when this happened? When he hurt you?"

He nodded.

"Were you by the water?"

"No. By Pauly's."

"You were in his house when he hurt you?"

"No. It was outside."

"Okay. It was outside. And what did he

157

do, Noah?"

"He — he *shot* me," he cried, looking up into Anderson's face.

"He shot you?"

"I'm bleeding. . . . Why'd he do that?"

"I don't know. Why do you think he did it?"

"I don't know! I don't know!" Noah was getting agitated. "I don't know why!"

"All right. It's all right. So what happened next? After he shot you?"

"Then I died."

"You died?"

"Yes. And then I came to —" His eyes searched the room. "Mommy-Mom?"

Somehow she must have slid down; she was squatting by the bed. She was breathing in and out. He was looking at her.

"Are you okay?"

She looked at the boy. Her boy. Her child. *Noah.* "Yes." She flicked at her wet eyes with a finger. "It's just my contacts."

"You should take them out."

"I will, in a moment."

"I'm tired, Mommy," Noah said.

"Of course you are, sweetie. Shall we go back to sleep?"

Noah nodded. Anderson moved away, and she sat down next to him on the bed. Noah put his sweet, sweaty Noah-hands on her shoulders and she leaned her forehead against his. They sunk down together like the single entity they once had been.

Anderson was in the kitchen when Janie emerged from Noah's bedroom for the second time that evening. She moved around the dark, quiet living room, looking at the objects that were not as they had been an hour earlier.

I'm Janie, she told herself. Noah is my son. We live on Twelfth Street.

A car passed, flashing white against the dark wall.

I'm Janie.

Noah is my son.

Noah is Tommy.

Noah was Tommy was shot.

She believed and she didn't believe at the same time. Noah was shot, and was bleeding — the words wounded her.

She wished suddenly that she'd never called this man, that she could go back to a time when it was merely Janie and Noah, making a life together. But there was no going back, was there? Wasn't that the lesson of adulthood, of motherhood? You had to be where you were. The life you're living, the moment you're in.

TWELVE

Anderson sat in the kitchen, Googling Ashviews.

It was all coming back to him now. The excitement. The energy. *The words.*

He'd found it at last, a strong American case. . . . Perhaps the case of his life, the one that would *connect.* If he found the previous personality (and he was optimistic that he would), perhaps he could even get the media interested. In any event it was the American case he needed to finish the book properly. He was sure he could convince Janie to let him publish it.

He had what he needed now. Ashview, Tommy, Charlie. A lizard, a baseball team. He'd put together bigger puzzles from less.

"You could have asked," Janie said. He hadn't noticed her coming into the kitchen.

"Hmmm?" There was a town called Ashview in Virginia, not far from Washington, D.C., where the Nationals baseball team was located.

Simple as that.

"To use my computer?"

He glanced up. She seemed annoyed with him.

"Oh! I'm so sorry. I wanted to get online —" He gestured at the computer, his attention catching on the town of Ashview's home page.

The Nationals were a D.C. team. There was an Ashview in suburban Virginia. All he needed were some death notices; a dead child would always make the papers. . . . He would have a name by the end of the week, maybe sooner; he was sure of it now. It was as if Tommy had wanted to be found.

"So I'm guessing it was helpful, then? Those things Noah said?"

He looked at her more closely. She was pale, her lips tightly compressed. He ought to sit down with her and help her process what had happened, but his urgency was so powerful. It was like trying to stop a wave. "It was very helpful," he said, trying to sound relaxed. "It was a good break. We'll find Tommy now, I feel it."

"Tommy. Right." She shook her head vigorously, as if she could shake off her thoughts. "So, Doctor, which is it? Drowned or shot?"

"Excuse me?"

She shook her head again, and he wondered for the first time if she was mentally sound. "You think Noah's this — other person, this Tommy, right? So I want to know: which is it? Was he drowned, or was he shot, or what?"

"It's not clear."

"Nothing's clear." She hurled the words at him.

Anderson sat back from the computer. "Science rarely is," he said carefully.

"Science? Is that what this is?" She choked out a laugh and cast her eyes around her kitchen, lingering on a dirty pot half-filled with water in the sink. "Perhaps it's unclear," she said, "because Noah is making it up."

"Why would he do that?"

She turned on the tap and began scrubbing the pot fiercely with her bare hands. "I'm sorry," she said, over the rushing water. "I'm not sure I can do this."

He looked at her back, groping for the approach that would work, the tone, the context, the possible benefits to her son. . . . He had employed it a thousand times. . . . How could he doubt himself now? He who had once been able to convince a Brahmin mother in India to let her daughter visit

162

untouchables in the previous personality's family. He could see it as if it had only just happened: her glistening orange sari gliding through the doorway of a hut made out of mud. At one point he had felt he could convince anyone at all through the sheer force of his will.

"Okay," he said coolly. "I'll leave, if you like. But what are you going to do?"

Her body went still. "Do? What do you mean?"

"You said you can't go on this way," he kept his voice soothing, reasonable. "That you're running out of money, that the doctors haven't helped. So — if I leave now, what is your plan for Noah?"

He felt a bit of chagrin; he was using her desperation against her. But it was in her best interest, wasn't it? And her son's? And his own best interest, and even Sheila's, for hadn't she wanted him to finish and publish this book? He wondered how much effort it was going to take to convince Janie to let him write about Noah. No matter.

"I'll —" But she couldn't get the words out of her throat. She turned to face him with raw, red, dripping hands, her fear written plainly on her face, and he felt sorry for her.

"Come here. Let me show you what I've

163

found. It's not much, but it might be a start."

He patted the seat near him. She wiped her hands on her jeans and sat down. He turned the computer screen toward her: pretty houses clustered around a shiny green golf course. *Welcome to Ashview!*

"Do you know anyone from a Virginia suburb called Ashview?"

She shook her head. "I've never heard of it."

"That's good. So we have someplace to begin. Of course, Thomas is a common name, and we don't know what year Noah is referring to, though we can use the Potter books as evidence that it's in the recent past. We'll scour the local papers for any obituaries of a shooting or a drowning related to a child named Thomas. It may take a little time before we locate him. But I think we are off to a decent start. You know the Nationals," he added, "are a D.C. team."

"Are they?" She squinted warily at the screen, the green expanse. She didn't trust him, he knew that; and yet he was necessary to her. They were necessary to each other.

Mahatma Gandhi appointed a committee of fifteen prominent people, including parliamentarians, national leaders, and members from the media, to study the case [of Shanti Devi, a young girl who, starting at the age of four, seemed to remember a previous lifetime as a woman named Lugdi from Mathura]. The committee persuaded her parents to allow her to accompany them to Mathura.

They left by rail with Shanti Devi on November 24, 1935. The committee's report describes some of what happened:

"As the train approached Mathura, she became flushed with joy and remarked that by the time they reach Mathura the doors of the temple of Dwarkadhish would be closed. Her exact language was, *'Mandir ke pat band ho jayenge,'* so typically used in Mathura.

"The first incident which attracted our attention on reaching Mathura happened on the platform itself. The girl was in L. Deshbandhu's arms. He had hardly gone fifteen paces when an older man, wearing a typical Mathura dress, whom she had never met before, came in front of her, mixed in the small crowd, and paused for a while. She was asked whether she could recognize him. His presence reacted so quickly on her that she at once came down and touched the stranger's feet with deep veneration and stood aside. On inquiring, she whispered in L. Deshbandhu's ear that the person was her 'Jeth' (older brother of her husband). All this was so spontaneous and natural that it left everybody stunned with surprise. The man was Babu Ram Chaubey, who was really the elder brother of Kedarnath Chaubey [Lugdi's husband]."

The committee members took her in a tonga, instructing the driver to follow her directions. On the way she described the changes that had taken place since her time, which were all correct. She recognized some of the important landmarks which she had mentioned earlier without having been there.

As they neared the house, she got down from the tonga and noticed an elderly person in the crowd. She immediately bowed to him and told others that he was her father-in-law, and truly it was so. When she reached the front of her house, she went in without any hesitation and was able to locate her bedroom. She also recognized many items of hers. She was tested by being asked where the *"jajroo"* (lavatory) was, and she told where it was. She was asked what was meant by *"katora."* She correctly said that it meant paratha (a type of fried pancake). Both words are prevalent only in the Chaubes of Mathura and no outsider would normally know of them.

Shanti then asked to be taken to her other house where she had lived with Kedarnath for several years. She guided the driver there without any difficulty. One of the committee members, Pandit Neki Ram Sharma, asked her about the well of which she had talked in Delhi. She ran in one direction; but, not finding a well there, she was confused. Even then she said with some conviction that there was a well there. Kedarnath removed a stone at that spot and, sure enough, they found a well. . . . Shanti Devi took the party to the second floor and showed them a spot where they found a flower pot but no money. The girl, however, insisted that the

167

money was there. Kedarnath later confessed that he had taken out the money after Lugdi's death.

When she was taken to her parents' home, where at first she identified her aunt as her mother, but soon corrected her mistake, she went to sit in her lap. She also recognized her father. The mother and daughter wept openly at their meeting. It was a scene which moved everybody there.

Shanti Devi was then taken to Dwarkadhish temple and to other places she had talked of earlier and almost all her statements were verified to be correct.

DR. K. S. RAWAT, "THE CASE OF SHANTI DEVI"

THIRTEEN

The Thomases of Ashview, Virginia, were not a lucky lot.

Ryan "Tommy" Thomas was killed at sixteen after his Honda Gold Wing motorcycle collided with a Dodge Avenger on Richmond Highway.

Tomas Fernandez was dead of unknown causes at six months.

Tom Hanson, eighteen, overdosed on heroin in an apartment outside of Alexandria.

Thomas "Junior" O'Riley, twenty-five, fell off a ladder while fixing his neighbor's roof.

Anderson sat at the desk in his empty office and clicked through another year of obituaries in the online *Ashview Gazette*. He started with the month of Noah's birth and went backward. Without a last name for Tommy, he knew the search would take a while, but he didn't mind — there was nothing like being back in the game, trying

169

to solve a case. And if he had to read the names a couple of times to make sure he wasn't missing anything, there was no one there to notice.

He'd hoped initially that by simply Googling Thomas, Tom, or Tommy, Ashview, Child, Shooting, Drowning, Death, he would hit something somewhere, but perhaps the name was too common or the time frame too long — if he could use the Potter books as a benchmark, it went back up to fifteen years. The Social Security Death Index, which was spotty when it came to kids anyway, was useless in this case.

Tom McInerney had an aneurism at twenty-two.

Tommy Bowlton died of smoke inhalation at twelve along with his two sisters during a house fire on Christmas Eve. (The age felt right, but since Noah had no fire or Christmas phobias, and had spoken of a brother, he'd put this one aside for now.)

Thomas Purcheck shot himself while cleaning his rifle, but he was living in California at the time and was a robust forty-three.

He had to admit it: he'd missed being engrossed in a case. He even missed the microfiche machines he'd had to use before everything went online, tucked invariably in a corner surrounded by shelves of dusty atlases and encyclopedias. The machines were like old friends to him, the way the knob fit firmly in his hand, the way the text scrolled horizontally across the screen.

They always reminded him of college, working in the stacks, where he'd first stumbled upon a slim book from 1936 called *An Inquiry into the Case of Shanti Devi,* and rushed back to Wright Hall to share it with his roommate Angsley. They'd spent hours at Mory's over the next few years poring over the implications between pints of beer, reading the reincarnation theories of Pythagoras and McTaggart, Benjamin Franklin and Voltaire.

It was Shanti Devi they kept coming back to, though. The little girl who astonishingly seemed to remember someone else's life.

If this case existed, and if it was real, they speculated, then there must be others. So for the rest of his undergraduate years, and throughout medical school, Anderson spent his spare time searching for them. He found many things that interested him — mentions of past lives from the Upanishads to third-century Christian theologians to Madame Blavatsky and the Theosophical Society, along with many fascinating studies of adult past-life regressions under hypnosis, though he wondered how much useful evidence they could provide. He absorbed the skeptics: the story of Virginia Tighe, the Colorado housewife whose past-life memories of being Bridey Murphy, recalled under hypnosis, bore a striking similarity to the life of a childhood neighbor, and the works of Flournoy, who diagnosed a past-life-remembering medium with multiple personality disorder.

But no matter how carefully Anderson had looked, he had been unable to find another case of a child who spontaneously remembered a previous lifetime.

There was no Internet back then, of course. For a researcher, that changed everything. . . .

Anderson swore silently to himself and turned back to his computer. He had to try harder. His concentration was not what it had been. He was always on the verge of a flight into the past. At Janie Zimmerman's his mind had been stimulated into competence by the excitement of being in the midst of a good case; when he was with the child, the right words had leaped to his lips, the way sometimes stutterers can sing. With Noah, he had sung.

Now, though, the words on his computer quivered before his eyes, and he steeled himself. He could not let his energy flag. He had often felt like an archaeologist, sifting through sand looking for shards of bone, fragments of a clay pot. You sat under the hot sun or the chill of the air conditioner and you simply waited for what was there all along to reveal itself. Patience was everything. You whittled yourself down to the words of type. If the words wavered, you sat still until they made sense again.

He was five years back from Noah's birth.

He glanced quickly through the obits of older Thomases succumbing to flu, pancreatic and prostate cancer, pneumonia, and encephalitis.

T. B. (Thomas) Mancerino, Jr., nineteen, died in a boat collision on Ashview Lake on Memorial Day.

Tom Granger, three, died of measles. (Measles! Why did people stop vaccinating when the data was so impeccable and the autism link so obviously unsubstantiated?)

Tommy Eugene Moran, eight, drowned — He looked at that one more closely.

Tommy Eugene Moran, eight, the son of John B. and Melissa Moran, of 128 Monarch Lane, died Tuesday in a tragic accident after drowning in his backyard pool. Neighbors say he was a cheerful child, passionate about reptiles and his beloved Nationals. . . .

He sat back in his chair.

You waited and then at last it happened: that moment when the sand shifted and you glimpsed something white, and the shard of bone was revealed.

FOURTEEN

In the Baltimore Greyhound station, Janie sat on a bench, buzzed out of her mind on bad bus station coffee, trying to pretend that the plan was a rational one. I can do this, she thought, so long as I don't focus on what the "this" really means.

Noah at least seemed to take it all in stride: this adventure, this bus station. He had exclaimed at the size of the Greyhound, amazed that a bus could have a toilet in it. "And we get to sit right next to it!"

Now he was thrilled with the video game machine, even though she hadn't given him any money for it. He didn't seem to care, happily jerking the handle this way and that, enjoying all the whizzing figures without realizing he wasn't controlling any of them. Which was pretty much how it was, wasn't it? You think you're in control, but really you're simply staring at the moving lights.

He ran up to her again. "Where are we

going, Mommy-Mom? Where are we go-ing?" They had been having this conversa-tion on and off for hours.

"We're taking another bus to Ashview."

"Really? We're really going?"

He hopped from one foot to the other, his face screwed up in an expression that wasn't entirely familiar to her. It was excitement and something else . . . anxiety? (That would be understandable.) Fear? Disbelief? She'd thought she'd known all his expres-sions by now.

"When we gonna get there?"

"In another couple of hours."

"Okay," he said.

"Is it okay? Do you want to go there?"

His blue eyes widened. "Are you *kidding me*? Of course I want to go! What about Jerry?"

The question startled her. "He's meeting us there."

"Can I watch *Nemo* again on the bus?"

"Sorry, honey, I told you, my computer is out of juice."

"Can I have some apple juice?"

"We're out of that kind of juice, too."

She couldn't wait for the second bus to arrive. So long as they were moving, she was all right. She was carried forward, leav-ing her thoughts behind her like a tangle of clothes on the shore.

Anderson had given her a sheaf of papers. She had them rolled up in her purse, a rubber-banded scroll. A news story about a little boy who drowned in Ashview, Virginia. The boy had drowned in his own pool. The pool boy had forgotten to latch the sliding doors to the backyard, and the mother had gone soon afterward to the basement to do the laundry, leaving her eight-year-old on his own watching television in the living room. A simple mistake, with terrible consequences.

Tommy Moran: a stranger's child.

She couldn't bring herself to look at the pages. She had the blank side facing out. The clean slate that Noah apparently wasn't given.

Tommy Moran, Tommy Moran.

"Look at the facts," Anderson had said on his second visit. They were sitting, again, in the kitchen. It was evening; Noah was asleep. Anderson seemed composed, but there was no mistaking the zeal in his eyes. He pulled the papers from his briefcase and placed them in front of her. "There are strong similarities."

She skimmed the page on top: a list of comments Noah had made and similarities between Noah and Tommy. Words leaped out at her. Ashview. Obsession with reptiles. A fan of the Nationals. A red house. Drowning.

And where was Noah's well-being in all this?

She set the page aside.

"How did you get this information?"

"Some of it is . . ." He gestured vaguely. "On the computer. Also, I've been in touch with the mother. She confirmed that her house was red and her other son is named Charles."

"You talked to Tommy Moran's *mother*?" She realized she was shouting and tried to contain her voice. She didn't want to wake up Noah. "Why didn't you ask me first?"

Anderson seemed unperturbed. "I wanted to make sure the case was solid. We e-mailed. I told her about my work, about the similarities. . . ."

"And she responded to this?"

He nodded.

"So — if I say yes — then what?"

"Then we take Noah to the home and find out if he can identify members of the previous personality's family, favorite places . . . that sort of thing. We take him around, see what he recognizes."

She considered everything he was telling her. The logical end of the road she'd embarked on.

She had heard stories of mothers who had worked tirelessly and reversed many of the symptoms of autism in their children; mothers who learned how to build ramps for disabled daughters, who taught themselves sign language to reach deaf sons. But when did you stop, when it was your child?

She knew the answer already. There was no stopping.

She got right to the point. "And this process will heal my son?"

"It might help him, yes. It often has a beneficial effect upon the child."

"And if I don't do this?"

He shrugged. His voice was restrained, but there was tension in it. "Then that's your choice. And the case is closed."

"And Noah will forget all about this?"

"It isn't uncommon for a child to forget by five or six."

"Noah is only four."

His eyes glinted. "Yes."

"I don't know if I can make it a year or two."

He faced her stoically across the kitchen table. She'd met him twice now, had shared intense hours in the same room with him, and she still didn't trust him. She couldn't figure out if the light in his eyes was that of

179

a genius or a crackpot. There was something stilted and hesitant about the way he talked to her, something that remained hidden, though it might simply have been the reticent nature of a scientist. . . . Still, he was good with Noah, gentle and patient, as if he cared about him, and he was a psychiatrist, and had handled many similar cases. Could she rely on that?

She felt again the current of fear that had been flowing inside of her for months now, like a river beneath a thin layer of ice. She heard it rushing through her dreams. When she woke up, she remembered nothing but the sickness of the feeling; she lay in bed and felt the power of it pulling at her and thought: my son is unhappy, and I can't help him.

"You still plan to write about this?"

He sat back in his chair and regarded her. He spoke so slowly it was maddening. She wanted to shake him. "I am interested in documenting the case. Yes."

"The case, the case. The *case* is a child, Jerry. Noah is a child."

He stood up, a flash of aggravation crossing his face. "I know that. You think I don't know that? I'm a psychiatrist —"

"But not a parent."

The anger dropped from his face as

quickly as it had arisen. He was impassive again. Resigned. He picked up his battered briefcase and glanced at her briefly, his eyes glittering with restraint. "Let me know what you decide."

She sat for a long time in her kitchen, looking over the documents he had assembled. Her questions were too numerous to count. What would Noah want with this other family? What could they do for him? Was it crazy to do this? Perhaps she was the sick one. Perhaps there was a rare syndrome that caused mothers to hurl their offspring into vortices of new age pseudoscience.

But no; she wasn't being neurotic. She was doing this for Noah. Not because he was wildly disrupting their lives and bankrupting them (though he was) but because the look on his face when she put him to bed, this night and every night ("I want to go home. Can I go home soon?"), was breaking her heart.

FIFTEEN

On the drive from his home in Connecticut to Ashview, Virginia, Anderson got two speeding tickets. He drove in a state of high excitement, barely catching his breath; he couldn't keep track of the speedometer, could hardly focus on the GPS. He looked out the windshield, thinking of his new American case, and felt like he was starting out all over again.

He remembered his first case as clearly as if it had happened the day before.

Thailand. 1977. The river.

It was early morning, and the day already warm. He was eating breakfast with his old friend Bobby Angsley on the veranda of his hotel. Up the river, toward the city, buttery sunlight bounced off the Temple of the Dawn, scattering color into the air like a jewel. In front of them, a dog struggled to cross the river, its matted head thrusting above the waves.

Anderson was jet-lagged and three days sober. His sunglasses gave everything a sickly yellow tint. He focused on his friend, who was flirting with the waitress as she arranged a saucer of clotted cream on the white muslin next to a plate of scones. Her face was perfectly symmetrical, like a face in a dream.

"Kap khun kap," Angsley said, placing his hands together in a parody of a polite Thai, or perhaps he had become one, Anderson didn't know. He'd seen him only twice since they'd graduated college ten years before, and each time had been a disappointment to both of them. They were on different paths: Anderson rising quickly within the university, en route to becoming chairman of the Psychiatric Department within a few years, and Angsley going in another direction, or rather (as far as Anderson could see) in no direction at all. Anderson had been surprised to find his friend settled anywhere; since college he had seemed perpetually on the move, briefly inhabiting the fine hotels and women of major cities from Nairobi to Istanbul, trying and failing to exhaust all that money born of generations of tobacco.

They watched the waitress go back through the open doors into the lobby bearing her silver tray. Nearby a string quartet was playing "The Surrey with the Fringe on Top."

"Look what I've brought." Angsley wagged his ginger eyebrows, reached into a paper bag at his feet, and pulled something out with a flourish, plopping it on the table. The thing slumped against the silver teapot, its legs splayed across the white linen: bright red yarn hair, striped legs, red circles for cheeks.

"You brought me a Raggedy Ann doll?" Anderson stared at it dumbfounded; gradually, it dawned on him. "It's for today. To give the girl."

"I was hoping for some kind of porcelain number but this is what they had. The stores here . . ." He shook his head.

"Are you out of your mind? You can't give a doll to the subject of an experiment." (Was that what this was? An experiment?)

"For god's sake, man, loosen up. Have a scone." Angsley took a bite out of a scone as large as a hand, sprinkling crumbs across the white cloth. His reddish hair was prematurely thinning across the expansive dome of his head, and his features had gone pink and blurry from too much sun and Thai whiskey, giving him a soft, pumpkinish look. Perhaps his brain had gone soft as well.

"It's bribery." Anderson frowned. "The girl will say whatever you want her to say."

"Consider it a gesture of good faith. She's not going to change her story for a Raggedy Ann doll, believe me. At least, I don't think so." Angsley peered at him. "You're hating me under those shades, aren't you?"

Anderson removed the sunglasses and blinked bare-eyed at his own white fingers. "It's just that I thought you wanted a scientific appraisal. I thought that was the point of bringing me here?"

"Well, we're kind of making it up as we go along, aren't we?" His friend smiled a broad, slightly manic smile with his crooked teeth, as deranged in its way as that of the doll.

A mistake, Anderson thought. This was all a mistake. A few days before he had been in Connecticut, trudging through the snow to his lab. He'd been studying the long- and short-term effects of electrical traumatic stimulus on a rat's central nervous system. He'd left the experiment at a crucial juncture.

"I thought this was a serious endeavor," he said slowly. The note of complaint rang in the air like a child's.

Angsley sounded hurt. "You didn't put up much of a fight, if I remember correctly, when I asked you to come."

Anderson looked away from him. The dog was still trying to cross the river. Would it make it to shore or drown? Two children exhorted it from the other bank, hopping in the mud. The rank river smell mingled in his nostrils with the floral scent of the tea.

What Angsley said was true. He had been eager to come. It had been a feeling, more than anything else, that had led him here, a wave of nostalgia that had overtaken him the moment he had heard his friend's excited voice in the midst of those bleak months after the baby had died and everything had fallen apart.

He and Sheila were in separate hells and hardly spoke to each other. He made it through his days, studied his rats, took down the results as he ought to, drank more than he ought to; yet felt much of himself, most days, to be no better than the vermin he studied. Actually, the rats had more spark.

Angsley's boyish enthusiasm had traveled the long distance between them like a memory of the interest he had once had in life and might find again, if he took the chance; and in any case it would be an escape, a respite, the thing he was looking for every night at the bottom of the glass.

186

"I've heard about the most extraordinary thing. It's Shanti Devi all over again," Angsley had said on the phone, and Anderson had laughed for the first time in months to hear the name. "I'll pay your way, of course, in the interests of science."

"Go," Sheila had said. Her eyes were red-rimmed, accusing.

So he had taken it, this chance, this respite. He was taking it. He'd been relieved to leave Connecticut, with its oncoming Christmas and its angry, devastated wife. He had told Angsley nothing of his circumstances, preferring not to discuss it.

"Shanti Devi," Anderson said now, aloud. It was probably nothing, he knew that. Still, the name was a tonic on his tongue, bringing him back a decade, to the taste of beer and youth. "It's pretty hard to believe."

Angsley brightened. "That's why we're going. So you don't have to."

Anderson glanced away from his eager face.

The mangy dog had made it across; he was scrambling up the muddy banks of the other side. He shook his fur, and the children screamed and scattered, avoiding the droplets of foul water that spun and sparkled in the light.

"No dolls," Anderson said.

187

Angsley patted Anderson on the hand. "Just meet the girl."

The girl lived a few hours north of Bangkok in a village in Uthai Thani province. The boat sputtered through the slums on the outskirts of the city, then moved past larger, more rural dwellings, wooden houses with piers at the ends adorned with tiny wooden temples, spirit houses for the dead. The harvested rice fields were golden brown on either side of them, dotted here and there with an ambling water buffalo or a small shack. Anderson felt the images taking the place of thoughts in his mind, soothing him, until he was nothing but a white hand skimming the surface of the water. The jet lag was catching up to him at last and he dozed sitting up, lulled by the hoarse, steady roar of the motor.

When he awoke a couple hours later the air had grown hot and thick in his lungs, and he was blanketed with sunlight. He realized he had dreamed of the baby. In the dream Owen was whole, a beautiful child with blue eyes like Sheila's that regarded him pensively. The baby sat up and reached out to him like the boy he might have been.

They approached a small wooden house on

stilts surrounded by lush foliage. How Angsley identified this particular house from the
identical ones that lined the road near the
pier was a mystery that Anderson didn't
bother solving. An older woman swept the
dirt floor in the shadows underneath the
house, chickens muttering around her
ankles. Angsley *wai*'d to her, his head bow-
ing over his hands, revealing the naked spot
of pink scalp at the center of his skull. The
two of them had a discussion.

"The father is working out in the fields,"
Angsley said. "He won't talk to us."

"Your Thai is pretty good, right?" Anderson asked. It occurred to him they ought to
have hired an interpreter.

"It's good enough."

It would have to be.

They climbed the stairs. A simple room,
well swept, slatted wooden windows looking
out onto cropped fields and blue sky. A
woman was placing an array of food on a
table in battered tin bowls. She was wearing
the same kind of brightly patterned cloth
the old lady wore, knotted right above her
breasts. She was lovely, Anderson thought,
or had been, not so long before; anxiety
seemed to have caught her beauty in its net.
When she smiled at them, worried lines
rippled from her dark eyes, and her crimson

lips parted to reveal bright red teeth.

"Betel nut," Angsley murmured. "They chew it here. Some kind of stimulant." He bowed his head respectfully, hands together: *"Sowatdii-Kap."*

"Sowatdii." Her eyes darted from one of them to the other.

Anderson looked for the child and discovered her crouched in the corner, watching the yellow lizards frisking in the ceiling dust. He was dismayed to see that she was wearing nothing. She was frail, almost emaciated, her face and concave belly painted with a white powder he surmised was used to keep away the heat: two round circles on her cheeks, a line down her nose.

The woman had laid out a villager's feast for them: white rice and fish curry, though it was only ten in the morning, and tin cups of water that Anderson was sure, as he sipped, would make him ill. He couldn't risk offending her, so he filled his roiling stomach, the taste of metal coating his mouth. Outside the window, a man shepherded a water buffalo across a field of golden stubble. The sun barreled through the slats in the windows.

Angsley walked over to the child. "Got something for you." He pulled the doll from his bag and she took it soberly. She held it

190

in her outstretched hands for a moment, then cradled it in her arms.

Angsley lifted his brows meaningfully at Anderson across the room, as if to say, "See? She loves it."

They set up at the wooden table, now cleared of breakfast. Two white men, a nervous woman, and a little naked girl who couldn't have been more than three holding a grotesque red-haired rag doll. She sat quietly next to her mother. She had an uneven birthmark to the left of her navel, like a splash of red wine. She clutched the doll tightly in her hands, watching her mother shave papaya into long, even strips with quick fingers.

They talked to the mother. Angsley spoke in Thai first, and then in English, for Anderson's benefit.

"Tell us about Gai."

She nodded. Her hands didn't stop moving. The strips fell away from the papaya into a tin bowl. Every time a sliver dropped from the knife, the little girl shuddered.

The mother spoke in such a low voice that Anderson was amazed Angsley could even hear her to translate.

"Gai's always been different." His voice, translating, was almost robotic. "She won't eat rice. We try to make her, sometimes, but she cries and spits it out." The mother made a face. "It's a problem." There was her tense, thin voice, and then Angsley's low flat one. The emotion, then the meaning. "I'm afraid she'll starve." As if reminded of this, she picked up a piece of the papaya from the battered tin bowl and handed it to her daughter. The girl clutched the doll in her left hand and reached for it, gripping it as if with pincers; Anderson saw that three of her fingers on this hand were deformed. It was as if these fingers had been drawn sloppily, in a hurry, without the refinements of nails and knuckles. The girl caught him looking at her fingers and she curled them into a fist. Anderson looked away, ashamed of himself for staring.

The mother stopped peeling papaya and let loose a stream of words. Angsley could barely keep up with her. "My daughter says that last time she lived in a bigger house in Phichit. The roof was made of metal. She says our house is no good. It's too little. It's true. We are poor."

She grimaced, lifting a hand to indicate the simple room. The girl stared at them, chewing papaya, and clutched the doll's floppy body more tightly in her hands.

"Also, she cries all the time. She says she misses her baby."

"Her baby?"

The girl was watching her mother talk. She was like a rabbit in a field, listening.

"Her little boy. She cries and cries. 'I want my baby,' she says."

Anderson felt his heart begin to beat a little faster. His mind, though, remained apart. "How long has she been saying this?"

"One year, maybe. We tell her to forget about it. My husband says it's bad luck to think of another life. But still, she talks." She smiled sadly, put down the knife, and stood up, as if wiping her hands of the matter.

The men stood, too. "Just a few more questions —"

But she was shaking her head, still smiling, retreating through a door in the rear of the room.

They watched her shadowy figure stirring something on a low charcoal stove.

The child sat at the table, stroking the doll's absurd hair, humming tunelessly. Anderson leaned across the table. "Gai. Your mother said you used to live in Phichit. Can you tell me about this?"

Angsley translated. Anderson held his breath. They waited. The girl ignored them, playing with her doll; its blank button eyes seemed to be mocking them.

Anderson walked over to Gai, squatting down next to her chair. She had her mother's high cheekbones under the circles of white powder and her mother's anxious eyes. He eased himself onto the floor and pulled his long legs into a cross-legged position. For a long time, fifteen minutes, he simply sat with her. Gai showed him the doll, and he smiled. They began to play silently. She fed the doll and gave it to him to feed.

"Nice baby," he said after a while. She tweaked the doll's painted nose affectionately.

"A really pretty baby." Anderson's voice was gentle, admiring. He followed Angsley's Thai tones floating up and down like paper airplanes borne haltingly up and then falling, missing their mark. Who knew if he was saying it correctly?

She giggled. "It's a boy."

"Does he have a name?"

"Nueng."

"Nice name." He paused. "What are you feeding him?"

"Milk."

"Doesn't he like rice?"

She shook her head. She was only a few inches away from him. He could smell the papaya on her breath and a chalky smell, possibly from the face paint.

"Why not?"

She grimaced. "Rice is bad."

"It doesn't taste good?"

"No, no, no, not good."

He waited a moment.

"Did something happen while you were eating rice?"

"A bad thing happened."

"Oh." He was aware of all the sounds in the room: Angsley's voice, the scratching of the lizards as they raced madly across the ceiling, the quick clicks of his heartbeat. "What happened?"

"Not now."

"I see. It happened in another time."

"When I was big."

Anderson looked at the sun sliding through the slats onto the wooden floor, the white circles glowing on the child's face.

"Oh. When you were big. Did you live in a different house?"

She nodded. "In Phichit."

"I see." He forced himself to breathe evenly. "What happened there?"

"Bad thing."

"A bad thing happened with the rice?"

She reached over the table to the papaya bowl, grabbed a piece of papaya, and shoved it into her mouth.

195

"What happened, Gai?"

She smiled at them with the fruit covering her teeth, the broad orange smile of a clown. She shook her head.

They waited for a long time, but she said nothing else. Out the window, the water buffalo was no longer in sight; the sun set the bright fields on fire. Down below, the chickens chuckled at them.

"I guess that's it, then," Angsley said.

"Wait."

The girl was reaching again into the bowl of papaya, and this time she took the paring knife her mother had left there. She picked it up with her imperfect hand. They were so rapt, these two grown men, watching her, they didn't react at first — they didn't take the knife away from the baby. They watched her pick up the doll, wrap its crude cloth fingers carefully around the knife, and with one, focused movement turn the knife toward her body, stopping just before it entered her abdomen, its point grazing the wine-colored birthmark.

It was only then that Anderson reached over, prying the knife from her tiny malformed fingers. She let him take it.

She said something else. She was looking up at him, her face urgent beneath the white powder. A ghost child, thought Anderson. A dream. And then he thought: No, she's real. This is reality.

There was a pause.

"Well? What is it? What did she say?"

Angsley frowned slightly. "I think she said 'The Postman.' "

It was late in the day by the time Anderson and Angsley headed back in the boat. The hired truck that had taken them to and from Phichit had let them off at the riverbank, and now they were returning silently to Bangkok. Anderson stood in the front. Next to him Angsley sat and smoked.

The boat glided past the shacks with jetties, little spirit houses perched on the ends, miniature temples built for the shelter and appeasement of ghosts; past the women bathing, the children swimming in the muddy river water.

Anderson unbuttoned his shirt. He took off his shoes and socks. He needed to feel the water sloshing his toes, splashing his ankles. He stood on the boat in his open shirt and T-shirt, the late-afternoon sun roaring on his head. Every hair on his body was standing on end.

He thought of Arjuna, begging the Hindu god Krishna to show him reality: "Reality, the fire of a thousand suns simultaneously blazing forth in the sky." He thought of Heraclitus: a man cannot step in the same river twice, for it is not the same river, and he is not the same man. He thought of the police and coroner's reports about the mailman from Phichit who had plunged a knife into the left side of his wife's abdomen, killing her and cutting through three of the protecting fingers of her right hand, because she had burned the rice.

The boat driver did something to the motor and the boat skittered forward, skipping over the river, dousing them with its cooling spray.

He remembered his college self, when he and Angsley had stayed up late discussing the case of Shanti Devi and the writings of Plato and anyone else who had taken a theory of reincarnation to heart, from Origen and Henry Ford to General Patton and the Buddha. He'd thought he'd given up all that. The survival of consciousness after death: it was a holy grail or a pipe dream, unfit work for a scientist of his caliber. Yet he had been searching since then in his own way, keeping track of what J. B. Rhine's people were doing with ESP at Duke, and exploring in his own work the connections between the mind and the body. Mental stress caused physical ailments: that much was certain; but why did some people emerge from trauma resiliently while others became plagued with night sweats and phobias? It was clear to him that genetics and environmental factors did not explain everything. He did not believe that it was a question of luck. He was searching for something else.

Something else.

Connection spawned connection in his mind, branching outward like glass shattering.

Not just nature or nurture, but *something else* that could cause personality quirks, phobias. Why some babies were born calm and others inconsolable. Why some children had innate attractions and abilities. Why others felt they should have been a member of the opposite sex. Why Chang, the irritable Siamese twin, who liked to drink and carouse, was so different in his nature from his easygoing, teetotaler brother, Eng. Surely the genetics and environmental factors in that case were the same. And birth defects, of course — the girl's deformed fingers provided a clear link between this life and another one, and might even explain —

Owen.

Anderson sat down. His throat was

parched; the sun had scalded him on the skin of his nose and cheeks and neck and he knew he would suffer badly later. When he closed his eyes he could see formless shapes moving quickly across a too-bright expanse of orange. The shapes coalesced into a face that was not a face, and he let himself see his child again.

Sheila had accused him of an inability to love Owen during his brief, tortured life, because he could not bring himself to hold and stroke the baby as she did. True, he couldn't look at his son, but it was because he loved him and was so powerless to help him; he was tormented by his ignorance. Why should this happen to *this* child, in *this* way?

In the hospital before Sheila had awakened he had stroked the tiny hand of his imperfect child and he had looked into that terrible, innocent face until he couldn't look at it any longer, or ever again. He had walked right out of the NICU and down the hallway into the maternity ward, to the window behind which the other babies slept and fussed, their bodies brightly pink with health.

Why? For no clear reason, one baby comes out the way Owen had, and others come out perfectly. What sense was there in

200

it: what science? Could it really be simple bad luck, an unfortunate turn of chromosomal roulette? Why was this child born this way, when there were no genetic indicators, no environmental factors at all?

Unless.

He opened his eyes.

Bobby Angsley was watching him, a faint smile playing at the corners of his lips.

"I've been tracking this phenomenon," Angsley said quietly. "In Nigeria. In Turkey. Alaska. Lebanon. You thought I was playing. Well, I was playing. But I was looking, too. I was listening."

"And you heard something?"

"Mostly whispers. Stories told late at night over raki or village moonshine with visiting anthropologists . . . some of the women are surprisingly comely, you know, in a sexy, Margaret Mead kind of way."

"Right." Anderson rolled his eyes and shifted his wet feet into the sunlight.

"No, listen," Angsley said quickly, and his intensity made Anderson look up. "Did you know there's an Igbo village in Nigeria in which they amputate the little finger of a deceased child, asking him to come back only if he'll live a longer life with them next time 'round? And when they subsequently *have* a child and that child *has* a deformed little finger, which apparently actually *happens* sometimes, they rejoice. And the Tlingit — the Tlingit of Alaska — their dying or dead appear to them in dreams, telling them which female relative's body will give birth to them. And don't get me started on the Druze. . . ." He jammed his cigarette between his lips, as if to restrain himself physically from continuing, and then took it out again. "Look, I know, it sounds like folklore. But there are cases."

"Cases?" Anderson tried to fathom what Angsley was telling him. There were layers beneath layers. "Verifiable cases?"

"Well, I'm no Charles Darwin. I'm not a very good scientist of any kind, as it turns out. I lack . . . rigor."

Anderson stared at him.

"You didn't bring me out here just for the girl."

Angsley looked back at him simply. "No." His eyes were glowing with fervor.

They rounded a bend in the river, and the city appeared before them like a gift: the golden stupas of the Royal Palace, the glinting red and green temple roofs.

If they could do it . . . if they had verifiable cases . . . then they would be able to do what nobody yet had done — not William James, not John Edgar Coover at

202

Stanford, not J. B. Rhine at Duke, who shut himself in the lab all those years with his ESP cards. They would have found evidence of the survival of consciousness after death.

"We'll need to go back tomorrow, first thing in the morning," Anderson said slowly. He was working it out as he spoke. "We'll get the girl and bring her to Phichit, see what she can identify. I'll meet you in the lobby at five thirty."

Angsley chuckled and swore softly. "All right."

There was a pause. Anderson could scarcely breathe. "Bobby," Anderson murmured. "There are really other cases like this one?"

Angsley smiled. He inhaled on his cigarette and let forth a long plume of smoke.

The light on the stupas was blinding in the setting sun, but Anderson couldn't stop looking. He could hardly wait until morning. There was so much work to be done.

"Recalculating."

How many times had the GPS said that? Where was he?

He'd taken a wrong turn somewhere.

Anderson pulled over to the side of the muddy road and got out of the car. Trucks zoomed by him on the highway, which stank of asphalt, exhaust, a false sense of importance: America. He looked around for road signs; last he'd noticed, he'd been somewhere outside of Philadelphia. How far had he gone astray?

He tried to shake the sights and sounds of Thailand out of his head. He felt his friend's presence near him, as if he had just left his side.

His best friend, gone now; it was all gone: the Institute, that fine edifice he and Angsley and Angsley's money had built. And what excitement they'd had in building it, when the field was theirs to discover and the cases flowed one after the other, sending them off: to Thailand, Sri Lanka, Lebanon, India, each case compelling and new. They'd had a good ride of it, too, until Angsley died suddenly, six months after Sheila, walking up a hillside on his property in Virginia, his heart seizing and stopping, just like that.

At the wake (Catholic, traditional — Anderson should have known right then that the widow would slowly drain the money from the foundation like the blood in her husband's veins) there was a look of surprise stamped on Angsley's face even the funeral director hadn't been able to erase. Oh, my friend, he had thought, looking at

204

that familiar body plumped with formaldehyde, rouge on its cheeks, headed for the family mausoleum — not the burial you'd imagined, your old bones bare on a cliff, gleaming in the sun.

Oh, my friend. You beat me to it. Now you know, and I don't.

Angsley was dead. The Institute was closed, its files shipped off. There was only one thing left to do, only one more case to investigate. All he had to do was finish it.

SIXTEEN

Ashview, Virginia, made Janie nervous. It was a suburb of D.C., full of the kind of Stepford McMansions she had always scorned: homes lacking any sense of history, taking up every inch of the space allotted with vast unwieldy garages. And yet . . . she had to admit there might be something enticing, for a child, in these new, oversize houses, the large bright green front yards, the oak trees that lined the streets too neatly, their green branches arching over the road.

They had driven down the main street a few times. They stopped by three different schools (one of which, apparently, was Tommy Moran's). Each was appealing in its own way, with its large ball field and playground.

"Do you recognize anything?" Anderson kept asking, but Noah said nothing. He seemed stunned, distracted, watching the buildings from the backseat, murmuring to himself every now and then in a singsong voice: "Ash-view, Ash-view."

"We've been through here already," Janie said to Anderson.

He had picked them up at the station and proceeded directly downtown.

"One more time. We'll take a different route."

He wheeled the car around and they headed back through the town's thorough-fare. Janie had it memorized by now. Star-bucks, pizza place, church, church, bank, gas station, hardware store, town hall, fire department: sliding by again and again like a town in a dream.

She glanced at Anderson. He drove stiffly, his jaw set with a stubborn resolve. He had twenty-four years on her and sixty-four on Noah, and there was no sign of fatigue in him. "I'm not sure he recognizes anything."

"That's not unusual. Some children are more attached to the actual house than the town. People remember different things."

At last he reached a gate. Anderson con-ferred with a guard who checked a list and then waved them through. They proceeded slowly down a street flanked by even larger, newer homes. A golf course gleamed in the hills beyond them. Anderson pulled up to a huge brick home that reminded Janie of a plain woman burdened with too many accessories. The only sign of human life was a plastic dump truck by the stone path to the front door, its wheels in the air like an upended beetle.

They sat silently in the car. Janie watched her son in the rearview mirror. His expression was unreadable to her.

"Well," Anderson said at last. "Here we are."

"They're rich," Janie said suddenly. "Tommy was rich." She felt it like a blow.

"It seems so." Anderson managed a tense smile.

Well, no wonder Noah wanted to come back here, she thought. Who wouldn't? So what if the house was poorly designed — who could be happy with a small two bedroom on the garden level when you'd had this?

Anderson turned toward Noah in the backseat and his face and voice softened. "Does anything seem familiar to you, Noah?"

Noah looked back at him. He seemed a bit glazed over. "I don't know."

Anderson nodded. "Why don't we go in and find out?"

Noah seemed to rouse himself. He unlatched his car seat himself and scrambled from the car and up the stone path.

A man in a polo shirt and crisp khaki slacks opened the door. He had a ruddy, exasperated face and limp red hair, and looked at them all with the dismay of a diabetic facing a troop of cookie-bearing Girl Scouts. Janie tried not to stare at him or at Noah, who was inspecting the man's boat shoes. She restrained herself from saying, "Sweetie, is this your daddy from another life?" and then almost started giggling from sheer nerves.

The man glowered at them. "I guess you all ought to come in," he said at last, stepping back and holding the door partially open so that they had to angle their bodies to enter. The foyer was the size of her living room in Brooklyn. "Just so you know, I'm not on board with any of this," he continued. "So if you're expecting any compensation, let me tell —"

"We don't want negotiations," Anderson said firmly. Janie realized that he must be nervous, too. He was gripping his briefcase tightly in his hand.

The man squinted. "Excuse me?"

"I meant — compensation."

"Right." He waved them into an expansive

great room. Janie tried to relax and simply breathe; there was the scent of something sweet baking in the air, and also something citrusy and antiseptic underneath that caught in her chest. From somewhere deep in the home a vacuum cleaner hummed.

The room was decorated in a tasteful, neutral way with luxurious beige furniture and framed prints of flowers on the walls. Through the sliding glass doors in the back of the room she could glimpse a large pool covered with a heavy gray tarp. It looked like a scab in the middle of the backyard.

"You're here!" A tiny blond woman smiled at them warmly from a balcony overlooking the room. She was balancing a hugely plump baby of about a year on her hip as if he were made of air. She was pretty, with a round face and fine, delicate features.

The woman joined the three of them standing awkwardly in front of the fireplace. She smiled graciously at Janie and Anderson, as if they had come for tea, and gave each of them in turn her soft hand. Her hair was held neatly at the nape of her neck with a cloisonné hair clip that, Janie noted, perfectly matched her silken, canary-yellow blouse.

"Thanks for coming all this way," she said. "I'm Melissa."

Melissa turned to Noah and extended her hand to him as well. He shook it solemnly. The whole room watched them without breathing, the skeptical husband from the doorway, the two anxious adults. Noah scuffed his feet shyly against the carpeting, and Janie noticed unhappily that his left sneaker was sprouting a little hole near the toe. Yet another thing she hadn't been able to stay on top of.

Melissa smiled sweetly at Noah. "Do you like oatmeal raisin cookies?" Her voice was light and high, like a preschool teacher. Noah nodded, looking up at her with wide eyes.

"I thought you would." She adjusted her grasp on the baby, jiggling him in her arms. "They'll be ready soon. I made mint lemonade, too, if you'd like some."

She was so appealing, with her bright blond hair and wide smile . . . like Noah. Any stranger would assume she was the boy's mother. She was the mom you'd pick from a catalog: I want that one. Anyone would want to go back to this big house and sweet-faced, cookie-making mom. Janie crossed her arms. The skin on the backs of her upper arms was slightly nubby, a medical condition that never quite went away. Noah had the same problem. She wanted to reach out and feel the familiar roughness on his upper arms. He's mine, she thought. There's the proof.

"Sit down, won't you?" Melissa implored, and they all sank as one into the curving couch. Melissa put the baby on the floor, and they watched him pull himself around the furniture on his pudgy, wobbly feet. Noah pressed himself against Janie, subdued, his head bent down, eyes unreadable beneath half-closed lids. She tried to soak in the warmth of his body against hers.

Anderson opened his briefcase and took out a piece of paper. "I have a list of statements that Noah made, if you wouldn't mind going over them to see what corresponds —"

Janie glimpsed the page:

Noah Zimmerman:
— unusual knowledge of reptiles
— can score a baseball game
— likes the baseball team the Washington Nationals
— speaks of a person named Pauly. . . .

Melissa picked it up and looked at it, blinking a few times.

"I must admit — I was skeptical when you e-mailed me. I'm still skeptical. But there are so many . . . similarities. . . . And, well, we try to remain open-minded, don't we, John?" John said nothing. "Or at least I do. I've done a lot of soul-searching since. . . ." Her voice trailed off. Janie felt her eyes moving automatically out the window, to the covered pool. When she looked at Melissa again, the woman was gazing at her with intense, misty eyes. "I'm glad you're here," she said. She flicked away a tear and leaped to her feet. "Hey. Why don't I go get those cookies? Keep an eye on Charlie, will you, hon?" John nodded curtly.

"Excuse me," Anderson said suddenly, standing as well. "May I use the —"

"That way." John nodded in the direction of the hall. Anderson excused himself again, and the room fell into silence. Noah looked at his sneakers. Janie watched the baby try to negotiate the tricky gulf between the couch and the armchair. The baby took a step, wobbled, and fell. He started to cry. John ambled over and picked him up. "Come on, now," he said, jiggling him in an automatic way. "Come on, now."

Anderson walked down the hallway, past a half-open door revealing a pastel yellow room filled with stuffed animals and a crib, and another door, closed, with a sign on it saying KEEP OUT in childish crayon letters. The letters looked cheerful, as if they were really only joking. He paused, glancing in either direction, and then cracked it open.

It was a boy's room. It looked like it might have been used yesterday, instead of five and a half years before. The bedspread, embroidered with baseballs and bats, was tucked neatly under the pillow; the baseball and soccer trophies on the bureau shone in all their fake gold splendor, as if they'd just been won; there was a bin with baseball gloves and another with balls, under a Nationals pennant and a framed poster of different kinds of snakes. A child's blue backpack sat in the corner, monogrammed TEM. It looked to be still filled with schoolbooks. On the bookshelf in the corner of the room there were a handful of Harry Potter books, along with a baseball encyclopedia and three reference books on snakes.

Anderson shut the door and hurried to the bathroom.

Inside, he locked the door, splashed water on his cheeks, and looked with alarm at the gray face in the mirror.

It wasn't them.

He had suspected it since the moment they entered the home, but he was sure now.

Charlie was a baby — far too young to

have been alive during the previous personality's lifetime — there was no way Noah could remember him. Tommy liked snakes, not lizards. And Noah seemed not to recognize any of it. It was the wrong family.

It was his fault, of course. His faculties were not fully operational. He couldn't find the word *lizards* and had written *reptiles* instead. He hadn't asked the age of the younger brother, Charlie. Small, crucial, uncharacteristic errors that led him in the wrong direction, to disastrous effect.

He had been too eager. The forward motion had been so pleasurable to him, he'd almost forgotten about everything that was happening to him in the desire to move and to keep on moving.

He ran his hand through his hair. The case was finished. He was finished. His faith in words was shaken at last, and with it all remaining confidence in his professional abilities.

What now? He'd erred, and now he'd go into the living room and make it right. And then he'd go home. Go back and resume? No resumption; he was done. That was clear. A fitting end to a long and ignoble career. Oh, but he had worked hard for his obscurity.

He leaned against the sink, steeling himself for the inevitable.

Seventeen

Janie could smell the cookies all the way across the room. "Hope you like 'em warm!" Melissa cried, holding the plate aloft like the cover of a book on entertaining. She had emerged from the kitchen cheerful and somehow brighter, her cheeks flushed and her lips newly slathered with pink lipstick. She handed a cookie to Noah and placed the rest of the plate on a side table. The sweet scent masked the citrus-and-ammonia odor of cleaning supplies and the sour Noah smell that traveled with him everywhere. Janie wondered if the other woman had noticed it.

John looked at Melissa over the baby's head. "Charlie's wet," he said, and made a face.

Melissa laughed sharply. "Well, change him, then." The couple's eyes met, and Janie got the distinct impression that more than one dispute had preceded this visit. John sighed; father and son left the room.

Noah sat still on the couch, his hands between his legs, his mouth full of cookie. He wouldn't lift his head.

"So." Melissa turned to Janie brightly. "I hear Noah's something of a Nationals fan."

"Yes."

"Who's your favorite player, Noah?"

"The Zimmernator," Noah said to the carpet, his mouth full.

"He likes Ryan Zimmerman. Because of the name, of course," Janie added.

But Melissa's eyes widened. "But he was Tommy's favorite, too!"

At the sound of the name, Noah jerked his head upward. It was impossible not to notice.

Melissa turned pale. She looked at Noah. She licked her lips nervously. "T-Tommy? Are you Tommy?"

He nodded hesitantly.

"Oh, god." She put her hand over her throat. Her pink smile seemed to float in her face, disembodied, as if it bore no relation to the wet, blinking blue eyes.

Was Janie dreaming? Was this actually happening?

"Tommy. Come here," the other mother was saying. Her white arms were wide. "Come to Mommy."

Noah gaped at her.

The woman crossed the small distance between them and pulled him up out of the chair, lifting his body into her arms like a rag doll.

But it couldn't be, Janie thought. He had the same rash on his arms that she had on hers. She had held him moments after his birth upon her breast and he had suckled instantly, "like an old pro," the nurse had said proudly.

"Oh, my baby boy." Melissa started to cry into Noah's hair. "I'm so sorry."

"Oh!" Noah said. His forehead was turning pink above her arms and the word emerged from him like a peep.

When he was pulled out of Janie's body, the doctor had held him high up so she could see him. He was still attached by the umbilical cord, smeared with blood and traces of white vernix. His face was deep red, contorted, beautiful.

"I am so, so sorry, baby. I made a mistake," Melissa said. Her voice was rough. The mascara started to roll down her face. "I know I messed up. I always check the latch. I thought I'd checked it. I messed up."

Janie could barely see the top of Noah's head. She couldn't see his face. "Oh!" he peeped again. "Oh!"

"I left the latch open! I never do that. Oh, I messed up." She clutched at his arms, which lay rigid on either side of him, and his skin mottled beneath her fingers, becoming as bright as his red Nationals T-shirt. "But why did you *drown*, baby? Why? You had swimming lessons!"

"Oh!" Noah said.

Only he wasn't saying "Oh," Janie realized suddenly. He was saying "No."

"No," Noah said again. He craned his neck to shake his head free, and she could see that his eyes were screwed tightly shut. He squirmed but could not get out of the other woman's embrace. "No, no, no!"

"I didn't know you'd go to the pool," Melissa was saying breathlessly. "I never knew you'd do that. But you could swim! You could swim. Oh, God, I messed up, Tommy. Mommy messed up!" She reached up to wipe her eyes with her hands and Noah wrenched himself loose.

He backed up across the living room. He was shaking so violently his teeth chattered. Janie moved toward him. "Noah, are you okay?"

"Tommy." Melissa reached out with her soft white arms.

He looked from one woman to the other. "Go away!" he screamed. "Go away!"

He moved as far away from both of them as he could, toppling the side table, spilling the cookies onto the floor. "Where's my *mama*?" he shouted, turning to Janie. "You said I was going to see my mama! You *said*!"

"Noah —" Janie said. "Sweetie, look —"

But he shut his eyes and put his hands over his ears and began to hum loudly to himself.

Anderson rushed into the room, followed by John, holding the baby, who was wearing only a diaper. John took in the scene, looking first at Noah, then his wife, the tears like tire tracks down the sides of her face. "What have you done?" he said.

In the kitchen, Noah sat at the table with his eyes closed and his hands over his ears. He was still humming. He wouldn't look at Janie, and when she put her hand on his shoulder he wriggled away. Another tray of cookies sat on the gleaming marble counter. Their smell permeated the room, powerful and nauseating, like a mistake it was too late to fix.

Anderson cleared his throat. Janie could hardly look at him.

"It was an error." He seemed to be addressing all of them or none of them. "It seems to be the wrong previous personal-

ity." Nobody answered him. "Let me explain
. . . ," he said, but didn't continue. He
seemed to have lost his bearings, if he had
ever truly had any.

Melissa was slumped at the other end of
the table. She had bitten her lip and now it
was bleeding. There was a smudge of blood
on the collar of her yellow blouse, a smear
on her white teeth. "I thought I was going
to get some answers," she mumbled. Janie
could see a streak of gray mixed in with the
blond sweep of her hair.

Her husband had a packet of baby wipes
in his hand and was cleaning her face, the
baby tucked under his arm like a giant
squirming football.

"There are no answers," John said. "It was
an accident."

He gently wiped the black marks from the
sides of her face and her chin. She let him,
her hands dangling loosely in her lap. As he
cleared the makeup she looked even
younger, like a child.

"You always say that," Melissa moaned.
"But it's my fault."

"The pool boy left the latch open." The
baby started to wail. "You know this. It
could have happened to anybody. It was a
fluke."

"But the lessons —"

"He wasn't a strong swimmer."

"But if I had checked the latch —"

"It's time to stop this, Mel."

Time to stop this.

The words woke Janie at last from her spell. This woman has lost her son, she thought. She *lost* her *son*. She let the words sink in. She saw, she couldn't help but see, a sweet-looking blond child struggling at the bottom of the pool. His small dead body floating in that crystal-blue water. A dead child: everything flowed from that fact, didn't it? Of all the bad things that could happen, that was the worst. And then they had come here and done this thing to her, this woman who had already suffered un-imaginably: they had gotten her hopes up and then had dashed them bitterly, and whether they had meant to or not was beside the point. *She* had done this thing; she couldn't blame Noah. And Anderson had followed the dictates of his own ethics in a way she couldn't truly fathom. But she was a mother and should have known bet-ter, and instead she had been cruel to this woman. It was unconscionable, what she had done, and all because she couldn't face the truth. Which was?

That Tommy Moran had died and wasn't coming back.

And Anderson's case was finished.

And Noah was sick.

It's time to stop this.

The baby was still wailing. "Mel." The husband was stroking her head like a puppy. "Charlie's hungry. He needs you."

Melissa took the baby from her husband mechanically. She pulled up her shirt and bra with a quick, deft gesture, and her round breast popped into view, its large, pink nipple as unexpected as a spaceship. Janie felt Anderson avert his gaze, but she couldn't look away. Melissa settled the hungry baby on her breast, and after a few moments her face took on a quieter expression.

Shame trickled down Janie's neck. She had put Noah through this, too, confusing him even further for no good reason. "I'm sorry," she said to Melissa.

Melissa closed her eyes, focusing on what was happening in her body, and Janie remembered the prickling sensation of breasts becoming heavy and alive with the flow of milk, the tug at the nipple with small sharp teeth, and then the deep inner sigh as the baby sucked the milk into his mouth.

"You people ought to leave now," John said, though it hardly needed saying. He led them silently through the house, Janie steer-

224

ing Noah with both hands on his back, his hands still covering his ears, Anderson following behind. John opened the front door. He wouldn't look at them.

The three of them stumbled down the steps and out into the pretty street. Trees waved in the breeze; the golf courses glowed in the distance. A boy on a bike whizzed by them on the sidewalk, ferociously focused, nearly hitting them. Janie watched him continue down the street, tires wobbling.

They drove away in silence. Janie sat in the back next to Noah's car seat. Noah wouldn't open his eyes or remove his hands from his ears. After a while his hands fell to his sides and she realized he had fallen asleep.

Noah is sick.

She tried the words out in her head. They lay there meaninglessly, like an innocent-looking chunk of plutonium.

Anderson turned down one street and then another, and the guard waved them out the gate. They were back in the world now, the confusing, hectic reality. They turned down Main Street, toward the motel. The GPS lady sang her indifferent tune. "Continue point two miles. Then turn left on Pleasant Street."

Pleasant, Janie thought. The word echoed

in her brain, transformed into *Psychosis*.

Out the window, the local high school was getting out for the day. Big kids slouching toward the parking lot, calling out to each other with loud, exuberant voices.

"Turn left on Psychosis Street. Recalculating."

Recalculating. *Medicating.*

"Continue point two miles on Psychosis Street. Medicating. Medicating."

They were going down a side street now, past a local bank, a sweet street with smaller houses, their porches adorned with American flags. Side street. *Side effects.*

"Continue point three miles. Turn left on Catherine Place." Catherine, *Catatonic.*

"Turn left on Catatonic Place. Medicating . . ."

Anderson was looking at her in the rearview mirror.

"Janie, I must apologize," he said quietly. "It clearly wasn't the right previous personality. I should have caught that. There were things I missed I should not have missed."

"Things?" Janie tried to shake her head clear.

"Yes, the younger son, Charlie — he is too young for Tommy to have known him. . . . I thought they had an older child named Charlie."

How do you stop trying when it is your son? But it has to stop *somewhere.*

It's time to stop this.

"Turn left on Denial Road. Medicating. Medicating."

The car seemed to be roaming the streets with a will of its own. Anderson was still speaking. "And I used the word *reptiles.* I should have said *lizards.* It is my mistake. It's not like me, but that's no excuse. I was not being precise. I didn't catch the difference between snakes and liz—"

"Jerry. Stop the car."

He pulled to the side of the road. He faced the front, beads of sweat glistening on the back of his neck. "Yes?"

"We're done here, Jerry."

"I agree, definitely, this was the wrong . . . home."

Was the man dense? "No, I mean . . . I'm done with schools and stores and houses. All of it. Please drive us to the motel."

"That's where we're going."

"The GPS said left. You turned right. Three times, actually."

He frowned. "No."

"Why do you think she keeps saying 'recalculating'?"

"Oh." His hands were white-knuckled on the steering wheel. "Oh." He looked through the windshield, as if lost at sea.

She tried to keep her own voice cool. "Jerry. Listen to me. There is no previous personality. Noah made it all up."

Anderson kept his gaze fixed in front of him, as if the answers lay there, on the asphalt road. "What do you mean?"

She looked at her sleeping boy. He was slumped in his car seat, his shining head tilted on one shoulder, pale lashes fluttering. She could see the seat belt making a mark where it crossed his cheek.

"He made it up. Because he has schizophrenia," she said.

She had said it, that word that sounded like every bodily function run amok at the same time.

She opened the car door and stepped out on the road. She leaned down, hands on her knees, sequestered behind a dense curtain of hair. The vertigo was too strong. She kneeled at the edge of the road. She felt it hard and firm beneath her, like reality.

"Are you all right?" He was shading his eyes and looked unsteady on his feet.

People like the two of them — desperate people — were dangerous, she thought suddenly. She saw the other mother, the black tear-tracks on her face. She felt sick again, this time with guilt. Yet some part of her, she realized, was also relieved. That door was closed. She was back in real life again, however terrible that might be.

Anderson wiped his face with his hand. "You've had a diagnosis," he said at last.

She looked around, as if wanting someone to contradict this: the grass, the asphalt, the cars whizzing by on their way to the supermarket or the mall. "Yes."

He shook his head. "Who?"

"Not exactly a diagnosis. A suggestion. By Dr. Remson. He's a child psychiatrist in New York. One of the best, apparently." This last she threw out to hurt him.

He took this in without reacting. "Why didn't you tell me?"

"I guess I was afraid you wouldn't want to work with us."

His eyes flashed. "Don't you know what my colleagues would say if —" He inhaled slowly and with an effort lowered his voice again. "You —" His lip trembled a little, then stilled. There was a cost, she thought, to calming that facade. "You should have told me."

I don't care about your colleagues, she thought. I don't care what happens after people die. I care about the boy in the car. That's all I've ever cared about. "Yes. I should have told you," she admitted dully. "When your son is very sick, you're not yourself, you don't behave in ordinary ways. You can't see clearly." She wiped her wet eyes with her hand. "It was irresponsible of me." She meant all of it.

He shook his head sharply. "Noah doesn't have schizophrenia," Anderson said.

She felt the hope begin to buzz up inside of her, and she smashed it fast before it could do any more damage.

"And you know this how?"

"It's my professional opinion."

She stood up and smiled thinly at him. "I'm sorry but that doesn't carry a lot of weight with me right now." She ignored his wince. "Besides, you saw Noah's behavior today."

"It was the wrong previous personality." Anderson bowed his head. "It was my fault. It's upsetting. But —"

"It's over. The case is finished, Jerry."

"Yes. Of course." He nodded slowly. "Of course. I just need a . . . ," he said. Then he walked a few feet away into the grass and looked around him, as if to find his way.

"Mom?"

Noah was waking up. He stretched and cast a shattering smile in her direction.

"How are you feeling, sweetie?" She

smoothed his hair, rubbed the red mark from the seat belt on his face. "Are you hungry? I have a granola bar in my purse."

He smiled sleepily. "Are we there yet?"

"We're almost to the motel."

"No, Mommy-Mom," he said patiently, as if she were daft. "When do we get to Asheville Road?"

Sujith Jayaratne, a boy from a suburb of the Sri Lankan capital, Colombo, began showing an intense fear of trucks and even the word *lorry,* a British word for truck that has become part of the Sinhalese language, when he was only eight months old. When he became old enough to talk, he said that he had lived in Gorakana, a village seven miles away, and that he had died after being hit by a truck.

He made numerous statements about that life. His great-uncle, a monk at a nearby temple, heard some of them and mentioned Sujith to a younger monk at the temple. The story interested this monk, so he talked with Sujith, who was a little more than two and a half years old at the time, about his memories, and then wrote up notes of the conversations before he attempted to verify any of the statements. His notes document that Sujith said that he was from Gorakana and lived in the section of Gorakawatte, that his father was named Jamis and had a bad right eye, that he had attended the kabal iskole, which means "dilapidated school," and had a teacher named Francis there, and that he gave money to a woman named Kusuma, who prepared string hoppers, a type of food, for him . . . he said that his house was whitewashed, that its lavatory was beside a fence, and that he bathed in cool water.

Sujith had also told his mother and grandmother a number of other things about the previous life that no one wrote down until after the previous personality had been identified. He said his name was Sammy, and he sometimes called himself "Gorakana Sammy" . . . he said that his wife's name was Maggie and their daughter's was Nandanie. He had worked for the railways and had once climbed Adam's Peak, a high mountain in central Sri Lanka . . . he said that on the day he died, he and Maggie had quarreled. She left the house, and he then went out to the store. While he was crossing the road, a truck ran over him, and he died.

The young monk went to Gorakana to look for a family who had a deceased member whose life matched Sujith's statements. After some effort, he discovered that a fifty-year-old man named Sammy Fernando, or "Gorakana Sammy" as he was sometimes called, had died after being hit by a truck six months before Sujith was born. All of Sujith's statements proved to be correct for Sammy Fernando, except for his statement that he had died immediately when the truck hit him. Sammy Fernando died one to two hours after being admitted to a hospital following the accident.

JIM B. TUCKER, M.D., *LIFE BEFORE LIFE*

EIGHTEEN

Denise woke up with the name on her lips.
The taste of it in her mouth, briny and bitter, like earth and sea at the same time. She
allowed herself ten seconds to lie there,
which was about seven seconds too long,
and then got herself up out of that bed. She
dressed carefully, making sure she did the
buttons the right way on her blouse and her
blazer, checking her stockings to be sure
that there were no runs, pulling and twisting her hair back into a bun and clipping it
so that it would stay put. The dress code at
the home was relaxed to the point of ludi-
crous (jeans and tracksuits, for goodness
sakes), but she had dressed professionally
all her life, even in those early years as a
student teacher, and she surely wasn't about
to stop now. Besides, it was important for
the patients and their families: it sent a message of respect.

She made the bed, collected her nightclothes, and put them in the hamper, and only then allowed herself to head to the bathroom. Hidden above the sink, behind the aspirin and tampons, was the bottle of pills Dr. Ferguson had given her. She took out a pill and cut it in fourths with the butter knife she kept on the shelf. Even a half gave her a loose, slightly dizzy feeling she didn't like, and a whole one made her foggy all day, but a quarter was usually enough. She gulped it dry and put the bottle back carefully, closing the cabinet until it clicked.

There. And there she was. That familiar blur of skin and wet brown eyes and black hair. Her hair was going back at the roots; she was way past due at the hair salon. She wished she could do what plenty of other black women did and just shave it close to her head and let it be. She couldn't help staring when she saw women with hair like that, marveling at the simplicity, the sleekness, the lack of fuss. She herself wouldn't have felt right with a look like that, though, would have felt — unprepared.

Downstairs, she started the coffee and turned on the radio, broke some eggs on the frying pan. She heard Charlie thumping around upstairs, doing whatever fifteen-year-olds did in the morning. Couldn't take him but a moment to throw on a T-shirt and some jeans.

"Charlie! Breakfast!"

She stood watching the eggs in the pan and listening to the news on the radio, leaning against the counter. Outside the kitchen window, Denise saw a layer of frost gleaming on the stubble of the newly planted cornfields. It had been a long winter and it kept on coming, continuing its victory laps halfway into spring. In their yard a lone bird tried and tried again to drink from the half-frozen birdbath.

Charlie pounded down the stairs. Always a shock to her, that this huge body with its bouncing dreads could have come from her slight frame, that he was hers, this hulking form that passed quickly in and out of her day. He sprawled onto a kitchen chair and started banging out a beat on the table with his knife and fork.

She placed a plate of steaming eggs in front of him and sat down. "Made you some eggs."

"Thanks, Mama." He jumped up to pour himself some juice.

"Charlie, sit, you're making my head spin."

"You sleep okay? That dog keep you up again?"

She paused; had she called out again in

237

her sleep? Is that why he was asking? "I slept fine."

"Good." He slammed down in his seat.

No, Charlie hadn't heard a thing. She exhaled quietly. This didn't mean she hadn't yelled out, of course.

She sat still, listening to the sound of the radio without focusing on the words. The pill was kicking in; she allowed herself to fall into the cadences of the voice, a man's voice oozing sanity and sameness, smoothing out the wars and the earthquakes and the hurricanes with its peaceful and predictable rhythms. The world could end, it did end, and you could count on that voice still being there to tell you how it all went down.

"Mama?"

"Hmmm?"

"I was asking if there's any bacon left?"

She made herself stand and felt dizzy; she opened the refrigerator door and stood there for a moment, holding on to it, looking inside at the bright, cool things. There it was, the shiny package. She took it out.

"Don't talk with your mouth full." She made her way to the stove, placed the bacon on the pan. It sizzled, spitting tiny droplets of oil on her good brown skirt. She knew the second the first waft of it hit her she wasn't going to be able to eat a bite herself.

She hadn't realized how unappetizing bacon could be.

The news finished and some classical music came on. She always put the radio on the classical station when Charlie was around. She thought it was good for him to hear it, the same way she watched the news programs or nature documentaries at night when he was home when what she really would have liked was one of those reality soap operas, the escape of watching rich, silly people behave badly. Dr. Ferguson thought that after everything that had happened she might loosen up about these kinds of things, but it had gone the other way.

She wrapped the bacon in a paper towel and carried the thing to Charlie's plate, dumping the glistening sticks on top of the eggs, and sank back into her chair.

"You're not eating, Mama?"

"Wait. Don't you have your civics test this morning? We didn't go over —"

"That was Friday. But I think I did pretty good."

"Charlie Crawford!"

"Did well. I think I did well."

"Is that how you talk in English class? Is that why she gave you a C plus?"

He ducked his head and began shoveling

the bacon into his mouth. "No."

" 'Cause you know you need to do better than that if you want to get into a good college. That's what the college counselor —"

"I got it under control." He glanced up at her, then down at his plate again, scraping up the rest of his food. Who knew what the truth was? Charlie had always been a pretty good student, but kids that age were unpredictable once the hormones started hitting; Maria Clifford's son, down the road, had gone from the honor roll to flunking out and working at the gas station as soon as you could bat an eye.

"Here, Mama, have some bacon. It's good." He dumped a morsel on the table in front of her and watched her until she picked it up.

"Why are you *at* me this morning?"

" 'Cause you don't eat."

"I eat. See?" Denise took the spike of bacon and put it on her tongue. Her mouth filled with the taste of something burned. She moved it to the inside of her cheek; she'd spit it out when he left. "Look. I'll try to get out on time today and we'll have a proper dinner together, okay?"

"Can't. Got practice."

"Practice."

"Yeah."

"Shouldn't you be studying instead of banging drums in someone's basement?"

"Garage."

"You know what I mean."

He shrugged, pushed himself away from the table. Grabbed his backpack from the floor. The neighbor's dog started barking again. You could hear it all the way down Asheville Road, probably as far away as the highway.

"Someone should kill that thing, do the world a favor," Charlie said. He was already moving toward the door.

"You be nice," she said.

He grinned at her through the dangling veil of his dreads. "I'm always nice."

And he was gone.

First thing she did was spit out the bacon. Second thing was shut off the radio. How she hated that music. They played it all day in the home, too, forcing the old people to take their music like their meds. Swallow it down, good for you, even if all it did was numb you through your day. At least the Hispanic people brought their own music, drumbeats and brassy melodies you could dance to, not that she'd ever do such a thing. Still, she knew she lingered too long in Mrs. Rodriguez's room, washing down those plump tan limbs with that music playing and the flowering plants on the table and the woman's daughter sitting there placid as you please doing crossword puzzles right next to the bed, though Mrs. Rodriguez hadn't recognized her own kin in at least two years. She liked the washing up. She'd inured herself by now to the smells, and Mrs. Rodriguez's flesh was less fragile than most; she didn't have to worry about every fingerprint leaving its mark the way she did with so many of the white people. There was something calming about being able to touch someone this way, without any hunger or discussion. Just skin on skin. A body and a washcloth and usefulness. So she lingered. It wasn't fair, she knew, to the other patients, who had no relatives, or plants, or music. She made a mental note to move faster today.

She stood now, relishing the silence, washing up the dishes, picturing Mrs. Rodriguez's room. Once she put the dishes away, she leaned against the counter and watched the clock, trying not to think of anything. 7:00. 7:30. She knew the name was still running loose somewhere in the back of her mind, but the pill muffled it enough so that she couldn't hear it. When the second hand at last hit 7:55, she finished her cup of coffee and exhaled with utter relief.

For it had begun. Her long, long day.

The Oxford Home for the Aged had once had aspirations. Anyone could see this from the tall fake plants and the columns and the pictures on the walls of mountain vistas — even from the name itself, which had no relationship to the institution of higher learning; someone had thought it sounded good. But somewhere along the line, something had gone terribly wrong. The linoleum floors were violently patterned by scuff marks from too many wheelchairs and stretchers and canes; the lobby smelled only a little like Lysol and the cigarettes the security guard smoked and a lot like the stale, slightly rank skin of the very old and the very sick. The ceiling directly above the elevator bank hung in strips from water damage, which had gone unrepaired for so long that the wound itself had turned black, like a skinned knee gone gangrenous.

A question of care, Denise thought. No one cared, so nothing happened. The management had changed so many times no one was sure who or where the current owner was, and the patients weren't with it enough to complain, and there weren't many family members that made it out there, though it was only fifteen miles from town. A vicious cycle: the place was so depressing that no one wanted to come, and because no one came and complained, the place got even more depressing. At another point in her life Denise would have taken it upon herself to get the place cleaned up, to start by talking to the janitors about what sort of cleaning solution they were using, if any, but she had no interest these days in taking on responsibilities that weren't hers.

She did her part; she kept a pleasant expression on her face and did her job the best she could despite the absolute storm of shit that sometimes came down on her (she didn't like to swear but some situations called for it). She kept on going despite the rotting ceiling and the rampant understaffing that left patients unobserved, sometimes for hours at a time, and the way the storeroom always seemed out of Dilaudid and morphine when it was needed the most. She was grateful for the job, grateful for the salary and that it took so much of her body and her attention and engaged so little of her actual mind. And yet: lately she was feeling her mind going off on its own a bit more than she was comfortable with. For instance, Mr. Costello, who was dying of lung cancer. Why did she ask him if he was scared? Where had that question come from?

Maybe his equanimity had gotten to her. He had tubes going through his nose to an oxygen tank right by his bed, couldn't eat much more than ice chips and scrambled eggs, slept fitfully most of the day, and yet his sleepy green eyes, overseeing the disintegration of his own body, seemed amused; content, even.

"So how'm I doing?"

She was checking the oxygen. "Still going strong."

"Damn. I was hoping to be dead by now."

"Come, now."

"You think I'm lying, but I'm not."

"You're not scared?" The words had blurted out of her before she even knew what she was saying.

"Naw. I'm the last of the Mohicans, you know. They've all gone." He waved a hand, as if his wife and friends had just now vacated the room.

"That's good, then," she'd said, adding, "I mean, that you're not scared."

He'd looked at her curiously. He was a smart old man. Had once been something — a chemist? An engineer? "Now why would I be scared?"

She smiled. "I didn't realize you were a believer, Mr. Costello."

"Oh, no, no, I'm not."

"But — you think there's something else. After this?"

"Not really. I think this is probably it."

"I see. All right." She could feel herself sweating. "And that doesn't — bother you? You don't find the thought of it unpleasant?"

"You trying to convert me now? Or the other way round?"

She wasn't sure what "the other way round" meant, exactly, but she didn't like it. "I'm sorry to intrude," she'd murmured, focusing again on the oxygen tank. It was half empty.

"You know what's really unpleasant, Mrs. Crawford? These tubes in my nostrils. They're goddamn aggravating. You think you can take 'em out for me?"

"You know I can't do that."

He smiled up at her stubbornly. "Why not, though? What difference does it make?"

"A little Vaseline might help."

"No, no. Don't bother."

He looked at his hands. His skin was fragile, she thought, like the kind of onion-skin paper used in letters from overseas. She wondered if they still used it, if anyone even wrote those kinds of letters anymore. Probably people just e-mailed now. The only letters like that she'd ever gotten were from

Henry, long ago. Those slim blue envelopes coming all the way from Luxembourg and Manchester and Munich to her little Millerton, Ohio, mailbox, the way she'd stand in the driveway, feeling them pulsing with heat in her hand. She'd spent long hours poring over the scrawl of his careless blue ink on the delicate surface, trying to make out the words, lingering on the tender throwaway lines — *& wishing you were here to hear it.* This was in their very early days, before she and Henry were married, when she was assistant teaching and he was playing the Dayton clubs and touring.

Now this is what I mean, she thought to herself. Why think about that now? What was wrong with her?

"My whole life, I thought, you die and you're kaput," Mr. Costello was saying. "You're done and you're done. Now, to be honest with you, I'm not always sure. I don't believe in God or anything. Don't get me wrong. I just don't have too bad a feeling about it, I guess."

"Glad to hear it," she said. She was still fussing with the oxygen cylinder. It didn't need to be replaced yet, she decided. Maybe it would outlast him.

At four, after finishing the bed pans and

turning Mr. Randolph and checking on Mrs. Rodriguez just because she liked to see the woman's zonked-out little half-smile at various points during her day, she called Henry. She stood at the nurses' station and heard the phone ring and ring and was about to hang up when his voice lurched into her ear.

"H'lo? H'lo?"

She didn't say anything. She could hear familiar music in the background. Thelonious Monk, *Pannonica*. It hit her hard, at the knees. She could still hang up —

"Denise? Is that you?"

"It's me."

He chuckled. "I'd know that silence anywhere."

"Well, then," she said. And gave him more of it.

"Charlie okay?"

"Yes, he's fine." How many months had it been since they'd talked? She'd lost count.

"Well, and how are you?"

"I'm just fine, Henry. You?"

"Ah, you know. They finally got rid of the principal with his head up his ass and now we got a new one, just as pigheaded. And don't get me started on the budget. Don't even have a room or a piano anymore, I go from room to room with a cart, like I'm sell-

ing doughnuts. Now how can you do anything with a cart?"

"I don't know." She didn't want to talk
about teaching. A vision of the classroom
came through to her anyway, the feeling of
chalk powder on her fingers, the
construction-paper-covered walls. Not that
anyone used chalk anymore. At Charlie's
high school it was all smart boards.

"I got them all singing a cappella. And let
me tell you, a second grade singing a cappella is a sorry thing. *This land is your
land . . .*" He sang, humorously off-key, the
sound lingering in her silence. He's trying,
she thought. He really is.

"What's Charlie up to, then?"

"Still nuts about that band of his. Practices
all the time."

"Practicing, hmm? He any good?"

"I don't know." She thought about it.
"Maybe."

"God help him, then."

"Oh, so you're a religious man, now?"

"Drummer needs all the help he can get."

They laughed, a tinge of the old complic-
ity that made her throat ache.

"You could call him up, you know. Hear
for yourself. I know he misses you. He won't
say it, but he does."

"Won't say it, huh."

She could feel the anger beginning to burn in him.

"He's just private. A teenager. That's all. It doesn't mean anything."

"Doesn't it?"

"Henry."

"Just tell me this. Do you ever say my name in that house? Do you ever think of me at all? Or is it like I've never even lived there? Because that's how it feels to me."

"Of course we talk about you, all the time," she lied. "It's been five years, Henry, I think we both need to —"

"Five years is nothing. Five years is shit."

She winced. He was speaking that way to provoke her. She must not be provoked.

"All right. Well, on that note, then, I'm going to —"

"Denise? You know what day it is?"

She said nothing.

"That's why you called me, isn't it? To talk about Tommy?"

The name caught her. She couldn't breathe for a moment.

"No," she said.

"I see him all the time. You know? In my dreams."

"Listen, Henry, I'm going to get off the phone now." But she stood there, holding on to it.

"He's standing at the edge of the bed, looking at me. You know. With that look he had. Like he wants you to help him but he's never gonna ask."

She was silent. This was why they hadn't made it: she moved and kept on moving, as if they could find Tommy that way and only that way, and he stayed stock-still, head bowed, letting it break over him again and again.

"You still think Tommy's coming back someday? You don't think that, do you? Denise?"

His voice had an urgency that reached all the way down . . . a voice that was a hand burrowing inside her, winding her guts around and around like a skein of yarn. She was aware suddenly that the name had never stopped repeating itself since she'd woken up with it that morning. Had been going on in the background all through the day. She was going to be sick. Going to be sick right now if she didn't get off the phone. Her hands started to shake.

"Denise?"

She readied herself to say something. But there was nothing to say.

She hung up the phone.

She was going to throw up.

No. She wasn't. (For one thing, she hadn't

eaten anything all day.)

Okay, then. She needed a pill.

No. She didn't.

She closed her eyes and counted to ten.

Then to twenty.

She always went the long way home, taking the highway to the exit and then doubling back, but today she got in the car and without telling herself what she was doing she drove out on the main road and turned right at the light. She drove straight through town, past the strip of doctors' offices, the dollar store and the liquor store and the Taco Bell, past the fire station and the boarded-up department store, heading out toward the cornfields where the turnoff to their house was, and McKinley.

McKinley Elementary was a low, concrete box pierced with vertical slits; it was built in the sixties, when they didn't believe in windows, and had that grim, prison aspect you found sometimes in churches and schools from that era. Inside had been a different story, the halls plastered with pictures and stories, the rooms vibrating with the bustling life force of young children being educated.

She had avoided this building for years, like a face that you tried to put out of your mind, and yet there it was, there it had always been, a mere five minutes from their house, and she realized now that during her days at the nursing home there was a part of her that knew what was happening, at every moment, at the school: that at 8:45 the bells were ringing and students were lining up for class; and at 12:40 they were eating lunch; and at 1:10 they had recess. Eleven years she'd taught there and its rhythms were ingrained in her bones.

She parked opposite the school, two doors down from the Sawyers' house, where Tommy used to go after school some days to play video games with Dylan. The video games at the Sawyers', she remembered now, were more violent than the ones she had let him play, and there had been some disagreements about that. She and Henry had argued about whether they should say something to Brenda Sawyer, or rather, she had gone back and forth, her disgust with the violent games battling with her natural reticence about telling other people how to raise their children, until Henry got sick of the whole issue and vowed to call Brenda up and tell her that there was no way any son of his was shooting anybody, even if it was only a game.

And in the end — in the end they had not

needed to resolve this issue. They didn't get the chance to figure it out, or to discover what kind of parents they would be to Tommy at nine and a half, or eleven, or fifteen. The Sawyers had been part of the crowd in those first few weeks plastering posters of Tommy all over Greene County, delivering doughnuts and coffee to the police officers with a subdued excitement, an intensity of purpose that she was initially grateful for but, as the days passed, couldn't help but resent. And Brenda and Dylan had been among the few who came calling a month after Tommy had disappeared, toting along a casserole and some flowers, as if they couldn't decide what to bring. She'd watched them from the bedroom window, the mother and son standing side by side on the doorstep with nervous faces, saw their bodies sag in relief when they realized that no one was going to let them in. They left the casserole and the flowers on the stoop, and when they had gone she tossed the flowers and scraped the disgusting noodley thing the woman had made into the garbage, washed and scrubbed out the glass pan, and had Henry deliver it back to them that very evening so she could be rid of them forever.

And there was the Sawyers' gray house

with the basketball hoop, same as ever, and there was McKinley. There were lights on in the office. Too late for afterschool and there weren't enough cars to suggest a meeting; probably it was the custodial staff. Or Dr. Ramos was working late.

If he was still the principal. Probably he had moved on. He had always been an ambitious man.

The light went off. She should go. But she sat in the car until the robust figure of Roberto Ramos exited the building, heading for his car in the parking lot. The same Subaru. He reached into his pocket, fumbling for his keys, and then out of some instinct he looked up and saw her car across the street. They looked at each other across that distance, a tall figure in a black coat; a battered minivan. She shivered in the cold air of the car, rubbing her arms. Maybe he'd just wave, get in his car, and go on. She hoped that was what he'd do.

And yet there he was, knocking on the window. She paused a millisecond and then unlocked the door. He slid in beside her in a rush of air and body heat, so vivid with his smooth pink cheeks and black hair and red scarf that it hurt her eyes to look at him. It was a mistake to have come here. So many mistakes today. She focused her attention on the steering wheel.

"Denise. It's so good to see you."

"I was just passing by on my way home. I work over at the Oxford Home now, you know, on Crescent Avenue."

"I'd heard that."

He rubbed his hands together. He was wearing winter gloves. "Some spring, huh. Hard to believe it's April."

"Yes."

"And how're they treating you over at the home?"

"Oh, fine, thanks. They're good people, most of 'em, anyway."

"Glad to hear that. It's so cold in here, can you — ?"

She turned on the car. The heater whirred to life.

They sat there, warming up. "That's better. Isn't it?"

She nodded.

"We've missed you, you know. I've missed you. Best first grade teacher we've ever had."

"I'm sure that's not true."

He put his gloved hand on top of her bare one and she let him, the muffled warmth of his flesh working its way slowly through the leather. Her principal; they'd worked well together for years. Just over six years ago now. No time at all, and yet she'd lived a hundred thousand lifetimes in between.

They had never talked about what had happened between them, and she'd been grateful for that. And yet it was one of the few memories she came back to — that she could stand coming back to — a half hour of time, six years ago, after the Valentine's Dance at the school. Eight months after Tommy had gone missing.

Those were the months, early on, when she thought maybe she could pick up where she left off, that it would be easier to go on with the life she'd had, taking care of Charlie, teaching her classes. She still checked findTommynow.com every night, of course, and put up fresh flyers in the library when the old ones became encroached upon, Tommy's chin covered by someone else's yoga lessons or baby and me classes. She no longer threw the offending flyers in the trash but simply moved them aside, tacking them a good few inches away from her boy's sweet face, and got herself out of there.

Dr. Ferguson thought going back to work might not be the worst thing for her — anything to ground her. The somberness never entirely left the other teachers' faces when they looked at her — laughter stopped when she entered the faculty room, though this had always been the case, actually. She was never sure why. Maybe they thought she was too proper for the kinds of jokes they told, when at one time she would have enjoyed hearing them. The parents, too, were uncomfortable with her, but she didn't mind. She was a robot, not a woman, but no one needed to know that. The kids were a little scared of the woman whose son went missing, and they knew something wasn't right with her, but they couldn't put it into words.

She was fine. Especially when there was work to do. That's why she had volunteered to chaperone the Valentine's Day Dance, and why she'd stayed late, cleaning up.

They'd been the last two left. Dr. Ramos had told the other teachers to go — she was the only one who resisted. They worked silently, swiping down the streamers like candy-colored cobwebs, sweeping the cupcake crumbs and the sparkles and paper hearts from the floor. "You really should go home, Denise," he'd said after a while. "I'll finish up here. I'm sure your husband's waiting for you."

"No," she said. She didn't really want to leave. She had nothing to do at home.

"Excuse me?"

"I just meant, Henry's away on tour and Charlie's on an overnight with his grandma.

258

Why don't you go, maybe you can pick up some flowers for your wife —"

"Cheryl and I are separated." He sat down heavily on the bleachers and tugged his hair with his hands. "I didn't mean to say that."

"I didn't realize. I'm sorry."

"Me, too. It just happened." His eyes watered suddenly. "Damn it all. I wasn't going to do this. I'm so sorry, Denise. I'm such an ass."

He had never called her Denise before. It was always Mrs. Crawford. She sat down next to him.

"What are you sorry for?"

"For sitting here feeling sorry for myself when you —"

"Don't do that." She cut him off fast. "You can't work it out with your wife?"

"She doesn't want to. I think there's —" He grimaced quickly. "Someone else." He shrugged, his eyes reddening. He pulled a flask from his jacket pocket and took a sip, shook his head. "Damn. I'm sorr—"

"Can I have some of that?"

"What?" He glanced at her, startled, and for the first time looked her in the eyes. "Of course."

She gripped the flask, took a sip, and then another. The liquor burned her lips, smooth and rough at the same time.

"What *is* that?"

He smiled at her reaction.

"Very good whiskey. You like?"

"I — it's interesting."

"Yes."

They sat there drinking for a while, the warmth of the whiskey sloshing through her. The room was silent and too bright, glittery piles of candy hearts and crushed carnations heaped here and there on the shiny wooden floor. A limp forest of half-cleared red streamers swayed from the ceiling. A too-familiar room enmeshed in strangeness. She took another sip and licked her lips. "It's good."

"Yes."

She watched a pink balloon become unmoored from the ceiling and drift slowly down.

"I don't know how you do it," he murmured. "Keep on going like you do. You're an amazing woman."

"No." She was weary of these sorts of conversations. As if she could choose what she could bear. She put her hand on his arm. Her vision was pleasantly blurry.

"You're a good man, and she's a stupid woman. Any woman should be happy to have you."

There were other things she meant to say

that she couldn't. Things that had to do with the way Henry was gone for weeks at a time now, the way he sounded on the phone when she called him on the road, a faraway quality in his voice as if wherever he was had too strong a pull on him for him to try to be there with her for even a few seconds. And she home with Charlie, night after night trying to be a mother to him, giving him dinner and a bath and books before bed when she was all emptiness inside. She didn't let herself say these things out loud, but maybe Roberto heard them anyway. He turned to her with a question on his face and she kissed him, or let him kiss her, or in any event their lips were pressed together and she felt her phantom heart unspool, turning rapidly round and round until there was nothing of it left . . . the old Denise would never do this, would never lie on the hard metal bleachers and kiss a man with such force she felt it throughout her whole body. She felt the nothingness inside her filling up with the stale air of the gym, the smell of basketballs and sweat and plastic mats and carnations and the taste of the whiskey, desire rising and filling every empty crevice, like smoke.

She didn't know what instinct made her pull back a little, placing her two hands against his chest with the tiniest bit of force, the tiniest push that she herself did not want or mean but which was enough to cause him to reel back, mortified, and flee the room, scattering apologies in his wake. It must have been the mother in her, still alive, even then, drawing her back from the oblivion she craved so very much. She stayed there in the gym for over an hour afterward, sweeping up, rubbing the carnation's ragged, slippery petals against her burning lips.

It wasn't something she could do again. The whiskey or the man. Not when the pull was so strong and Charlie still so young. She called in sick the next day and the day after that and then she didn't come back to the school anymore. She didn't answer any of Roberto's calls or messages. She submitted her paperwork and she stayed home. No one else questioned her about it; it was as if they'd been expecting it all along.

"If you ever wanted to come back," Roberto was saying now, fingering the edges of the glove compartment like a safe he might decide to crack, "we could find something — we could use another reading specialist."

She shook her head. "I can't go back."

He gave a resigned shrug. "All right."

"How're you doing, Roberto? You look —

tired. Your health okay?"

"I'm good, actually. I've — my wife had a baby."

"A baby?"

"Two months ago." He smiled in spite of himself, the pure blue light of his joy flaring through the tension in the car, as startling to her as if a bird had flown out of the glove compartment and circled around her head.

"I mean, I'm tired — you know how it is. But it's — it's good. Real good."

"You got back together with Cheryl, then?"

"You didn't hear? I married Anika. Anika Johnson? Anika Ramos now. She taught —"

"But she's —"

"Yes?"

He was watching her.

"She's lovely."

"Yes."

She's so ordinary, is what she meant to say. Plain Ms. Johnson with her straight mousy brown hair and her sallow face, her thin little lips set in a line. And you're — anything but. But she could keep her mouth shut. She could do that.

Ms. Johnson had been Tommy's teacher, had sent a predictable flower arrangement with the predictable note . . . *sorry for what you are going through. Tommy is such a nice boy. If there's anything I can do, blah-blah-blah.* Life continued to move faster than she could keep track of it. A new baby in the world. The world kept going on, and going on, how could it be, while she was — while she was —

"Are you doing all right, Denise? Can I help you in some way?" He glanced anxiously in her face, as if looking for some pain there he could brush away like an eyelash with his cool, gloved fingers.

She pulled back from him, arranging her features into the face she used day in and day out, the face that was her face now. "I'm just fine, thanks for asking."

Sitting alone in the cold car. She'd turned the heater off the second he'd left, the door yawning open to the freezing and fresh night air and closing back upon her, Roberto's broad back hurrying away into the darkness. She saw him burying his face in his baby's soft warm skin in gratitude and fear. She carried that everywhere with her now, that fear she sparked in other parents' eyes.

The cold kept her mind focused, alert. She was going to do it. She knew as she sat there she wasn't going to resist today. She was going to call.

She'd put it off all day, talking to Henry

and seeing Roberto and doing everything she always tried not to do, except for the real thing, the thing she stopped herself from doing every hour of every day, checking the day off on the calendar if she'd successfully resisted, months and years of black Xs until her weekly sessions with Dr. Ferguson were a thing of the past and she'd almost forgotten what it was she was marking. But now none of that mattered, it was the thing that needed to be done, so she picked up the phone and called that number which was carved jaggedly into her heart.

"Lieutenant Ludden speaking." He had picked up the phone in the middle of telling someone something, some story; his voice was light, joshing. She could hear voices in the background — brusque, workaday. She could almost smell the burned police station coffee.

"A lieutenant, now."

He knew her voice, of course, even though a few years had passed. You don't call someone at 11:00 PM and then again at 8:00 AM and then again at noon every day for years and not burn your voice into their consciousness. That had been the point. "Yeah." She felt the exhaustion bleeding into his voice at the sound of hers.

"So, when did that happen?"

"I was promoted last year."

"It's Denise Crawford."

"I know. Hello, Mrs. Crawford. How are you?"

"You know how I am." This was her true self, her true voice, hoarse and unwavering. Maybe that's why it had been so hard to stop herself from calling him.

"And what can I do for you this evening?"

"You know what you can do."

He exhaled.

"If there was news I'd call you, you know that, Mrs. Crawford."

"Well, I wanted to check in. On the investigation. On how it's going."

"How the investigation is going."

"Yes."

There was a long pause. "You know it's been seven years." His voice thin, almost pleading. She'd worn the man out. She considered this a kind of victory.

"Six years, ten months, eleven days, to be exact. Are you telling me you've closed the investigation? Is that what you're saying to me?"

"As far as I am concerned, Mrs. Crawford, this case will never be closed until — until we find your boy. But you must — you've got to realize that we have new cases every day. People keep on dying in Greene

County, Mrs. Crawford, and they have mothers, too, and those mothers, they call me, too, and I have to account for them."

"Tommy's not dead." The words were flat, automatic.

"I didn't say he was." His voice was heavy, despairing; this was how they talked to each other, the only true relationship she had in the world.

She looked out the window. All she could see was her own reflection, those eyes that were her real eyes all right, not fierce like the voice but tired, tired. Her mouth was full of that taste that had been in her mouth all day, the taste of something burned.

"I still keep my eyes peeled, though. I don't forget. All right? I don't forget any of 'em, but especially Tommy. All right?"

"Maybe you could search the files again. Maybe there's something you missed there that you'd only realize now, after all this time has passed. Or maybe something small has come up somewhere else that might have some bearing —"

There was a pause.

"There *is* something."

She felt her pulse quickening. Oh, she knew him. She could feel it in his silence. "What is it?"

"No. It's nothing."

"There's something."

"No."

"I know you found something. I can hear it in your voice. Tell me what it is."

"A boy disappeared a few months back in Florida. Maybe you heard about it?"

"I don't read the papers anymore. And they found him? They found the boy?" Her voice quivering with excitement while her guts twisted with envy. That word echoing in her ears: *found, found.*

"They found the body."

And then she was wrenched, again, with dismay. For herself, for the boy's parents, for all the parents in the world.

"You didn't hear about this?"

"How did the boy die?"

"He was murdered."

"How?"

"I can't tell you that."

"Detective. You know I can take it. You know that. Now you tell me. How. That. Boy. Was. Killed." She could barely keep her voice level.

"No, it's — it's part of the investigation. I don't know myself. It's not my case, they're keeping us apprised in case — there are any similarities."

"There are similarities?"

He sighed. "The boy was nine. African

American. There was a bike found."

"A bike? But — but — but there was a bike. We found Tommy's bike — by the road."

"I'm aware of the details of the case, Mrs. Crawford."

"And the man that did that — who murdered this Florida boy —"

"Has not been caught, no. They're working day and night on it, I can assure you."

"Day and night. Right." She'd seen how night and day went. Urgently enough for a day, a week, a month, and then it was an hour here, a few minutes there.

"Look, I'll keep you posted if we hear anything. Even if they find the perpetrator, there's no likelihood that there's a connection. You know that, right? It's more than likely it was someone who knew him, a relative, friend of the family —"

"Where was the body found?"

"Mrs. Crawford."

"Where was it found?"

"In a creek in back of the boy's school."

"But — we've got creeks all over the county. We need to get a crew together —"

"Mrs. Crawford. There's not an inch of this county I haven't covered myself. You know this. I will call you personally if there is anything relevant to the case. Look, even if there isn't, if they find this motherfucker in Florida — I will call you that day. All right?"

"Personally." She exhaled bitterly.

"Yes."

"It's his birthday today."

"What?"

"It's Tommy's birthday. He's sixteen years old."

A pause.

"You take care now. Okay? Mrs. Crawf—"

But she had hung up the phone.

NINETEEN

In the motel, Anderson stretched out on the bed, aching with dismay.

He had made a mistake. His faculties had not been fully operational. He hadn't found the word *lizards* and he had written *reptiles* instead. My god, he couldn't even follow a GPS anymore; the voice said one thing and his brain heard something else.

He had been too eager. A solid, well-documented, American case: he had thought that would make all the difference. He had been flying with possibility through the last few weeks, nodding off at night on dreams of validation, only to wake up to . . . mistake after mistake. And now he was finished.

He could hear the boy crying in the room next to his, the mother trying to calm him down. The cries fell on him like needles. Through the thin wall he could hear the words *Asheville Road.*

"When are we going to Asheville Road?" Noah had asked cheerfully when he awoke in the car. "When are we going?"

Even in his demoralized state, Anderson had felt the words bolting through him, the boy's excitement igniting his own. *Asheville Road!*

"We're in Ashview now, honey," Janie had answered.

"But it's the wrong one," the child said patiently.

"Maybe, sweetie." She looked pointedly at Anderson, as if she could see his raw exhilaration, and it pained her. "But we're done here."

"So are we going to the right one now?"

"I don't think so, baby. No."

Noah sat back in his car seat, glancing from one of them to the other with a look of incredulity. He turned to Anderson. "But you said you'd help me find my mama."

"I know I did." He gave a defeated nod. He had hurt them, the mother and the child. "I'm sorry, Noah."

"Noey," his mother said, "would you like some ice cream?"

The boy ignored his mother. His eyes, piercing Anderson's, were suffused with a despair that seemed too knowing for a child. "I'm *so disappointed.*"

272

And he had turned his head, blocking out both adults, put his hands over his face, and started to cry.

Anderson got out of bed. He opened the minibar, removed a tiny container of vodka, unscrewed the top, and put it to his mouth, experimenting. He hadn't drunk vodka in decades. He tipped a bit on his tongue, letting it tingle there, deciding, then gulped the rest of it down.

The vodka warmed his body nicely, like an invisible hand stroking him in places no one had touched in years. His mind shivered, sensing its coming annihilation. He wiped a hand across his face, brought it back smudged with rust. What now?

He looked in the mirror. A trickle of dark blood from nose to lips, his cheeks smeared with it. He could not meet his own eyes.

He shoved some tissues up his nostrils, staggered back to the bed. He was losing control; his roots were loosening under the power of the liquor like a tree in a windstorm, his mind veering suddenly, inexorably, toward the one thing he never let himself think about. The file he would shred to pieces, if it weren't evidence. His worst case.

Preeta.

He lay back in bed and tried to put her back where he had kept her all these years, away from his daily thoughts. Yet now he couldn't stop seeing her. A girl of five running through the courtyard with her brothers, chasing a ball, her shiny hair flying. He'd been happy to have such a delightful child for a subject, after a long stretch working with the timid, battered children of the mud flats.

Preeta Kapoor, slim and lovely, with large, serious eyes.

He had thought it would be one of his strongest cases.

The sunlight pouring through the small windows of the concrete house. The way the mother had stood up and closed the shutters, casting the room into shadow. The brass table glimmering in the dim room, his own hands sweating. The taste of the round, sweet dumplings on his lips — sugar and rose and milk.

A wooden Ganesh in the corner, removing obstacles. A TV against the wall, flickering with a Bollywood movie no one was watching.

"Preeta didn't speak very much the first few years," her father had said. "Until she was four, she was mainly silent."

"We thought perhaps she was . . ." The

274

mother grimaced.

"Mentally retarded," the father continued. "But then at four, she began to speak. She said, 'I need to go home.' "

" 'I need to go home and get my daughter,' that's what she'd say," the mother added. "She'd say, 'This is not my home, I have a daughter, I need to go get my daughter.' "

"And how did you respond?"

"We told her, this is your life now, perhaps you are remembering a different life. But she . . . persisted. And, also, she used unusual words."

"Words?" He took another sip of sweet tea. "What sorts of words?"

"Odd words," the mother said. "We thought she had made them up. Baby talk, you see."

"I see."

"So I looked into them, for the family," their friend, the lawyer, said. He took some notes from his briefcase. "I thought it was interesting, you see. The case interested me."

"And?"

The lawyer wagged a finger at Anderson. "You'll never guess what I found."

Anderson suppressed his impatience and smiled thinly at the lawyer, a plump-cheeked, cheerful man waving a sheaf of thin papers in his hand with a zealousness that Anderson knew well. "Yes?"

"The words are Khari Boli, a dialect from western Uttar Pradesh, over a hundred fifty kilometers from here."

"You're sure of this?"

"Absolutely positive!" His attitude rankled Anderson a bit; nobody deserved to be that certain.

"And you don't know this dialect?" He addressed the parents. They looked back at him placidly.

"Oh, no."

"Any relatives? Neighbors from that region who might know it? Any acquaintances at all?"

"I've asked," the lawyer said. "You can ask as well. The answer is no. They don't speak that dialect here. I wrote it all down."

He handed Anderson his notes. Anderson softened; they were not so unalike after all. The lawyer had documented everything, all the girl's earliest statements, with dates. "I wish I could continue this work myself, but — unfortunately I have responsibilities." He watched Anderson, his small eyes glowing. Another man entranced by the facts.

Anderson looked at the paper. All those Khari Boli words; utter gobbledygook to her family, and yet Preeta had known them as a tiny child.

The child understood words in a language she hadn't studied or heard before: his first case of xenoglossy. There had been others, but this had been the strongest.

Pretty Preeta, with her glossy hair and sober eyes.

They brought the girl inside, but she didn't speak. The father spoke, his elegant hands framing the words in the air as he explained, the mother passing another tray of roasted almonds and fruit custard and the round, rose-sugary dumplings he couldn't get enough of. . . .

"She always cries in the evening, cries and cries. She says she misses her daughter."

"She worries about her daughter. Who will take care of her? She says her husband is not a good man. Her in-laws are not good people. She says she wanted to go home to her parents, but they won't let her. She wants to go home and see her daughter."

The girl sitting at the table, listening silently to all this, her head bent down slightly like a penitent pupil, hands pressed in her lap.

"Did she give the name of the village in Uttar Pradesh?"

"Yes."

Of course they'd go. He couldn't wait, would have left that afternoon if possible. As it was, they had to wait until the morning. All five of them, crammed in Anderson's rented truck, traveled across the countryside. It was only a hundred miles as the crow flies, but this was India: the trip took nine hours.

The in-laws had turned them away at the door. He had spoken to them at the doorstep for a long time, his head bowed in the heat, murmuring in his most respectful and persuasive manner, but they stood there with closed faces and heard him out and shook their heads.

It wasn't that they didn't believe — that's what Anderson remembers thinking. Oh, they believed it was possible that this was their daughter-in-law, reborn, all right. They wanted nothing to do with her, in that life, or this. They wouldn't even give them the name of the previous personality's parents, the town she had lived in before coming here. The little girl stood silently. Her memory had encircled this place only, and no other. Who knew why?

"May we see the daughter?" Anderson had said as the door was closing. "Sucheta's daughter? Is she home?"

"There is no daughter."

The neighbors said otherwise. There had been a little girl, years ago. She had died. No one knew how.

Preeta had taken the news silently. She had thanked the neighbors (identifying two of them by name) and walked purposefully down a path to the bank of the river that flowed through the village, where the women were washing clothing. Anderson stood and took notes rapidly with his blue pen, the yellow pad ruffling in the wind, as in a hoarse child's voice she told them how her husband and her in-laws had treated her. How all alone in this village, so far from her parents, at the age of fourteen she had given birth to a girl and then, two years later, she had gotten pregnant and given birth to another girl. Her mother-in-law had been the midwife.

They took the second baby away from her instantly.

Stillborn, they had said later, but she had known better, she had heard the cries.

When she accused them of killing her baby daughter they had beaten her, kicking her in the face and stomach that very night, so soon after giving birth. When she felt the pain she thought maybe it hadn't happened and the baby was still inside her, but she gave birth this time to a black sorrowful thing made of blood and tissue.

Maybe she would have died, anyway. She might have been hemorrhaging.

In any case, they would never know; she threw herself in the Yamuna River the next morning.

The girl, Preeta, told them this story; it poured out of her in fluid sentences far beyond the scope of the child she was then, standing hoarse-voiced on the bank of that muddy rushing river while the women slapped their clothes clean on the stones at river's edge and the pages of his pad rose up and down like a fan, like breathing.

He had taken notes.

They had driven back the nine hours to her village in silence. Even the girl was silent.

He had told them he would come back next time he was in India, to follow up, to see how much she still remembered. He remembered how the father had shaken his hand with a good, strong handshake. How the girl had grabbed him about the legs, startling him, as he said good-bye.

Preeta, with her glossy hair and sober eyes, waving to him from across the court-yard . . .

Nothing to do but let the memory of it fill his mind like the scent of jasmine, like the scent of red mud.

He tried to follow up with his best cases every few years. But he was busy, at the prime of his life, pursuing cases in Sri Lanka, Thailand, Lebanon, building up the Institute, writing articles, writing his first book, then trying to get it reviewed in reputable places. All of this took time, and it was four years before he made it back to that part of India.

He wrote them a letter in advance of his visit but received no reply, so he did what he always did in those situations: he traveled across the country to see them.

The mother came to the door, distracted, a new baby on her hip. She flinched when she saw him.

They had gone back to the village without him. She explained this to him a short while later, in the same room he remembered with its shuttered window, its brass table glinting in the dimness, its ornately carved wooden Ganesh. This time the mother talked, while the father sat in the shadows, listening.

Preeta at nine. She showed him a picture. As lovely as ever, long-limbed and graceful, with a melancholy smile. She had been begging them to go back, to see the village again, and after a while the pleas were more than her doting parents could bear. Her father had business sometimes in that area, selling some textiles in a nearby town, so he took her with him. They had stayed in a small house in the village that sometimes served travelers.

By the time her father awoke the next morning, she was gone.

The same river, twice.

The villagers said she hadn't hesitated. She had walked purposefully to the river and had slid right down the side of the bank, red mud staining the back of her sari, the bright sea-green color waving like a flag in the gray waters. It happened quickly. Not one of the villagers setting up for the morning market said a word. They simply stood in shock and stared down at the dark, pretty head with its set face bobbing on the river's surface, the green fabric spreading out on the gray water and then sinking under its own weight, losing its brightness to the rush of the gray, as she went around the bend.

Nobody jumped in after her. They didn't know her. She was a strange girl in a small village. The river was dangerous. They never found the body.

Anderson had felt himself suffocating in that dark room. He thanked Preeta's parents, feebly, apologetically, for taking the time to tell him their story, and stumbled

282

outside, right into a monsoon. He stood there letting the skies fall down on his head. In a moment of confusion he thought that it was his child who had done this. His child that he had lost.

If he hadn't come to them, they would never have gone to the village, and the girl would have forgotten.

There was some follow-up to do in the village, taking down the villagers' accounts of the death. He did his research, he took it all down, every witness, his hand writing out the descriptions in careful blue ink on yellow paper while his inner eye was always trained on that muddy river, that bobbing head. He couldn't look at the river directly; he was afraid he might hurl himself in.

He went on a bender that night, seeking to bathe in oblivion, but the questions flew at him like crows that had been waiting only for him to open the door, crows flying at his face.

It was his fault.

His fault that the child's remains lay somewhere at the bottom of the river. His fault she would never have her own children, her own life.

His research was useless. Worse.

He had always believed in lucidity: in looking as clearly as possible at what was, despite the desire to veer off into comforting illusion and projection, and to follow the results rationally. So he couldn't protect himself now from the questions that followed: What did it signify, to be reborn only to relive the previous life's anguish? What was the sense in that? What was the meaning?

He could see, suddenly and for the first time, the appeal of escape, of nihilism. And yet some part of him, even then, the scientist in him, held him together, speaking clearly and steadily under the cacophony of blame and grief: Could the suicidal urge pour like a phobia or a personality characteristic from one life to the next? Could there be grief so unresolved and potent that it continued on, flowed into the next life as powerfully as a birth defect or a birthmark, where still it could not be shaken?

He was not a praying man, not at all, never, but he said a prayer anyway, standing on the bank of the river he couldn't bring himself to look at, that her next life would be far from here.

He had pulled himself out of his despair only with brute will. He had gone cold turkey on the long train ride back to Calcutta, the craving pecking at his nerves, hands trembling in evidence of an addiction he had only dimly realized.

When he emerged at last, shaken and sober, he had known that there were questions he couldn't ask himself. That there were attachments he couldn't make. It was the only way to continue. And he had continued in this way, steadily working.

Until now.

In the motel minibar, there were more tiny bottles — a whole row of them. Anderson turned the key and opened the door again and stared. It seemed only days earlier that he had stopped drinking, not decades. Oblivion had been waiting patiently for him all these years. All right then, he thought. He reached for another little vodka.

No.

He ran to the bathroom and spat and washed his mouth out, brushing his teeth twice. Not that way. Not after all this time. He threw the key to the fridge in the toilet and flushed, but it remained in the basin, glinting like treasure at the bottom of the sea.

He made his way back to the bed and stretched his body out, trying to revive the feeling of warmth the vodka had generated under his skin. He could taste the alcohol on his lips under the Crest. On the other side of the wall, the boy was still sobbing.

Damn.

He liked him. The boy. *Noah.*

Damn. Damn. Damn.

When Anderson dozed off at last, he dreamed of Owen. He dreamed that his son was whole. Owen was whole and Sheila was happy and there was no need to go to Thailand, no matter what Angsley had said on the telephone. He could stay in Connecticut with his family and his lab rats.

He awoke suddenly, to a feeling of loss so pure that at first he couldn't speak.

He sat up in bed. The room was still dark. His mind was clear.

I can help him, he thought. I can help this child. I got it wrong, but it's not too late to change that. So we had the wrong previous personality. Okay. That's happened before. I have the information I need now. I'll convince his mother. For Noah, I'll get it right.

But he had given up. Hadn't he?

He got up and opened the blinds, looking out the window at the dawn beginning to assert itself across the indifferent parking lot, pale light illuminating the street. Another day, whether anyone liked it or not. Yet he felt himself despite all his apprehensions hungry to begin it.

He walked over to his computer and

turned it on. He could hardly wait for it to boot up. He opened the search window and typed in *Tommy Asheville Road.*

TWENTY

Janie buckled in Noah and then herself with a feeling of grim determination.

In the event of a change in cabin pressure, the flight attendant on the video was saying, you put your oxygen mask on first, pulling the cord, and then you helped the others in your party who needed your assistance. The video showed a nice-looking dad tugging the oxygen mask over his own face, his placid daughter sitting quietly beside him, breathing bad air.

What kind of idiot came up with that rule? They didn't understand human nature at all.

She imagined the compartment filling slowly with smoke and Noah beside her, gasping. Did they really think that she could straighten the mask on her own face and breathe in clean air while her asthmatic son struggled to take a breath? The assumption was that she and her child were two entities with separate hearts and lungs and minds. They didn't realize that when your child was gasping for air, you felt your own breath trapped in your chest.

And meanwhile, she was lying to her own son, and this was making him howl in distress, disturbing the other passengers on the plane, disrupting their ability to hear how to fasten a seat belt, and seriously addling her already compromised good sense.

Noah wanted to go to Asheville Road, and they were going to Asheville Road, but he couldn't know that, not yet, not this time. Brooklyn by way of Dayton, that's what she'd said to him, grateful that he was still too young to make sense of a map. She was not about to make the same mistake twice. She'd make a new mistake instead, if need be.

"I want to see my mama!" Noah was yelling, and the other passengers looked at her as if she were lying to them, too.

The plane readied itself for takeoff and began wheeling forward, barreling down its runway. She had never been afraid of flying, but now she felt something like alarm at the plane's initial tremors as it rose.

When she was pregnant, she'd read studies that high levels of the stress hormone cortisol could cross through the placenta

and into the fetus, affecting fetal development and causing low birth weight. This
made sense to her: it wasn't just the carrots
she ate, the vitamins she took: what she felt,
her baby felt. She had tried to remain as
calm as possible, turning down a plum job
with a big corporate firm so as not to
adversely impact her developing baby with
long hours and maximum stress.

Now she felt the cortisol spiking through
her system and wondered if Noah could still
somehow feel it, if tiny particles of her stress
surrounded the air he breathed and made
everything worse. She couldn't help it,
though. The world was more dangerous
than it had been a few weeks ago. It was a
world that slipped and slid beneath you,
where children died because mothers forgot
to check the latch. How did you keep your
child safe in that kind of a world?

From the moment she'd stepped on the
Greyhound bus until the moment she'd
walked onto the plane with Noah and Jerry
at Dulles Airport, she'd had the feeling of
rolling down a steep hill. She couldn't stop.
If she put her hands out on either side to
slow the momentum, they would scrape
themselves raw.

The plane lifted into the sky. Noah's voice
rose to a high, keening wail. And she was

left with herself. What was she doing? How could she revisit this idea, after the fiasco they had so recently encountered? How could she risk hurting yet another mother?

How could she imagine that Noah was not hers and hers alone?

And yet, as if in response, the line came suddenly into her head:

Your children are not your children.

Where had she heard that? Who had said it?

Janie leaned her head briefly against the seat in front of her and patted her shrieking son's knee.

Your children are not your children.

She remembered now, as she listened to the cries overtaking her in waves of sound and saw the flight attendant frowning down the aisle in her direction: it was a song. A Sweet Honey in the Rock song she'd heard with Noah last summer at a free concert in Prospect Park.

It was an early July evening, the air mild and breezy. She had settled on a blanket with some friends and enough hummus and pita and carrots to feed a small city of preschoolers. The singers' voices had blended in perfect a cappella harmony *(Your children are not your children . . . though they are with you, they belong not to you),* and

291

Janie had taken off her shoes and wriggled her weary toes, listening to her friends' worries (private vs. public schools, thoughtless husbands). She herself couldn't afford private school and had no husband to complain of, but she was happy, because the song was wrong, and Noah *was* hers, and it was a beautiful evening, and she couldn't imagine having much love left inside of her for anybody else, anyway.

How could she have imagined then that she would be here, barreling faster than breath toward a woman who was not expecting them?

Only last summer, and yet it may as well have been another life.

"I WANT MY *MAMA*!" Noah shouted again, and the whole plane could hear him: as if she were kidnapping him, as if he hadn't always been entirely hers.

When the plane was safely aloft and Noah had finally exhausted himself, crashing into a fitful sleep, Janie reached under the seat in front of her and pulled out the pages that Anderson had printed out the night before. Copies of newspaper articles from the *Millerton Journal* and *Dayton Daily News* about Tommy Crawford, who lived on Asheville Road and was nine when he'd gone missing. He was a student at McKinley Elementary, where his mother was a schoolteacher.

The photograph in the newspaper article was from school picture day. American flag on one side, cheesy rainbow backdrop against a fake blue sky. You could almost hear the photographer urging: Smile wide, now. Smile big. Could be any boy, really. His skin was a light brown. He was African American. She didn't know why this should be surprising to her. He grinned up at her. He had a nice smile.

"AUTHORITIES CALL OFF SEARCH FOR MISSING BOY"

The Greene County police force called off the search today for Tommy Crawford, nine, of 81 Asheville Road, who disappeared from his Oak Heights neighborhood on June 14. Though the child is feared to be dead, Detective James Ludden, who had been leading the search effort, stated that "as far as I'm concerned, this case isn't over until we find the boy, one way or another."

Crawford, who attended McKinley Elementary School, is by all accounts a bright and popular boy. His parents describe a cheerful child who loves baseball and is a devoted older brother to Charles, eight.

"Charlie misses his big brother," his parents, Denise and Henry Crawford, said in a statement. "We miss our beloved boy. If you have Tommy with you or know where he is, please, please call —"

She looked away. There was too much pain in this piece of paper.

They were in the clouds now, on their way to a place she'd never been. She was flying on instinct, a mystery even to herself.

Janie believed in consistency. It was something she took pride in. She said, "No crackers before bedtime," and then she stuck with it. She had been even-tempered (mostly); she had been constant (as much as possible). Kids needed that.

She had tried to create order in Noah's life the way her mother had created order in her own, after the chaos of living with her father. She didn't remember much of the time before her father had left them. There was a memory of sitting high up on his shoulders at the state fair — but was that a real memory or something she made up from a picture she had? There was the time the two of them went to the mall on some errand and he had spontaneously bought a huge stuffed polar bear for her, far too big for any room but the living room, and her mother had objected but then laughed and let her keep it there beside the TV. There was the smell of his pipe and his scotch, and the sound of him banging on the door all night long when he drank and her mother wouldn't let him in. There was her mother holding a water glass filled with red wine (the first and only time Janie had seen her drink), telling her in the matter-of-fact voice she always had that she had asked him to leave and he wasn't ever coming back, and she was right; he didn't. Janie was ten then. She remembered that day perfectly, the startling sight of her mother drinking in the afternoon, the way the wine had splashed as her mother talked and Janie had been nervous it would spill over.

After that, her mother had gone back to work as a nurse and they got into a regular rhythm. She started working nights when Janie was thirteen, but she was home to oversee schoolwork, and always made sure there were healthful dinners in the house for her to warm in the microwave and clean pressed clothes for her to put on in the morning before school. And when those nights got a little lonely, Janie retreated to her room, where everything was exactly the way she wanted it to be. She opened the door and saw her framed posters of foggy

European castles and horses; her furniture hand-painted in cheerful primary colors; her closets organized by color scheme; her color-coded world.

A lifetime of creating orderly spaces had followed, and what good had it done? When the world was not orderly.

Even her mother had been, in the end, a mystery to her.

When she had gone through her mother's house that week after her death — those days when she was hardly conscious, her heart frozen over with grief, though words fought their way occasionally to the surface and cracked through (words like *why* and *orphan,* though as far as she knew her father was still alive somewhere, and *God,* whom she had never been taught to believe in but was furious at all the same) — she'd found in the drawer of her mother's bedside table the kind of book her mom had always made fun of. It even had a rainbow on its cover and a new-agey title: *You Can Change Your Life.* She flipped through the pages: it had chapters on meditation, karma, and reincarnation, ideas her atheistic mother had never seemed to give a second's thought — she'd roll her eyes and say, "Who has time to think about *that*? When you're gone, you're gone." Yet the book was well thumbed and heavily underlined, with passages marked with stars and exclamation points. One sentence, *Everything is a projection of mind,* had three stars next to it.

Had her mother wanted so desperately to keep life going that she'd lost her common sense? Or had she found something at the very end that changed the way she looked at everything? Or was it someone else's book, someone else's stars? Janie didn't know, and she would never know, so she'd put it out of her mind, permanently . . . or so she'd thought.

There are more things in heaven and earth, Horatio. That was one of the things her mother had loved to say. She was a practical woman who worked all day with surgical instruments, but she had always had a soft spot for Shakespeare. Janie had never thought much about the quote; it was something her mother said, usually with a huff of impatience, in moments when she was out of explanations — why her father had never called her, for instance, or, in the hospital, why she had refused to embark on yet another experimental treatment.

The last time Janie had thought of it was the night in Trinidad when Noah had been conceived. That night, after Jeff had left, she couldn't sleep, so she had walked by herself back to the beach. It was late, and she was conscious as always of her vulnerability, a woman alone, the vulnerability heightened by the nearness of sex, of being seen at one's most unguarded. That raw moment of closeness with Jeff had been there, she had been in it, and now it was gone, like a lit match flickering out in the humid darkness. She looked at the sky, which made a mockery of the night skies she had mostly known: this was the essence of sky, in its depths of darkness and of light. Its beauty, like a piece of music, stirred her loneliness into something beyond itself, made her look up and out instead of in. She had a message-in-a-bottle impulse to hurl her confusion out into the expanse, in the hope that something (God? her mother?) might be out there, listening.

"Helloooo," she'd called out, half-comically. "Anyone there?"

She knew she'd have no answer.

And yet, standing by the shore, the waves peeling back to expose the gleaming nakedness of sand pocked here and there with shells and stones and then pushing forward, drawing their eternal curtain over the rawness, a feeling of peace had washed through her. She'd felt something there. Was it God? Was it her mother?

There are more things in heaven and earth,

Horatio, she'd thought.

It had been Noah. Noah was her answer, the thing that was there. That had been enough for her.

So it was fitting, she thought, looking out now at a vast expanse of blue sky, that Noah would bring her right back here, to the most abstract of questions, which were now unbearably relevant. For either reincarnation was bunk, or it wasn't. Either Noah was sick, or he wasn't. And there was no way to know. There was no way to reason through it, or at least no way she knew, or could imagine.

Despite everything she knew or didn't know about living, despite the thousands of carefully analyzed, inexplicable cases, despite her moments of panic and her years of good sense, she would have to take a leap.

TWENTY-ONE

*"You're too serious for the beach," she was
saying. She was laughing at him.*

"Excuse me, sir?"

It wasn't Sheila; it was the flight attendant,
hovering over Anderson, offering him water
and pretzels. He shook himself awake and
took the tiny bag but refused the beverage,
even though he was parched, afraid to jostle
the sleeping child next to him by putting
down his tray.

The boy's mother sat beside her son, looking out the window.

What was her name?

It had fallen down the chute. It was gone.

His mind felt as clear as ever. It was
simply the word that eluded him. It was
there, right in front of him, taunting him,
and yet his brain balked, refusing utterly to
reach out even a finger to touch it. He felt
like Tantalus, parched and hungry, striving
fruitlessly for the cool water and the grapes

that were always just out of reach.

Tantalus, punished by the gods for telling humans their immortal secrets. Tantalus had high hopes for humans, and where did that leave him? Doomed, that's where. Banished to Tartarus. And how was it that he could remember the name and the story of Tantalus, but not the name he needed? Ah, the brain: who knew why it remembered what it remembered, or lost what it lost. And here he was: Jerome Anderson in Tartarus, the deepest region of hell.

Things were falling apart rapidly. The woman's name was in his folder, of course: on the yellow pad in his briefcase, which lay at his feet. He could bend down right now and retrieve it. This particular bit of information could be attained. Yet who knew when he would lose it again, or what else he would lose? He shouldn't be here at all, especially since the case was not proceeding according to protocol. Perhaps he should stop. The boy would forget, eventually. But Anderson didn't know how. He was the man who didn't stop, that's what he was, all he knew how to be, from the moment he had returned home from his first cases with Angsley in Thailand.

He had walked in the door two months later, electrified.

Sheila was waiting for him on the couch, her strong legs curled up beneath her. She looked the same: that moon face, as fine as ever, with its sprinkling of freckles across the nose, that heavy cloud of blond hair. He, on the other hand, was a different man.

She looked at him with a piercing, assessing gaze — he hadn't written her those two months except to cable her when he was coming home — and he was struck with tenderness for all of it: the old red couch with its stuffing showing at the seams and the young wife who was trying to figure out if she still had a husband, the concreteness and sheer flair that constituted life as you were living it, the vibrancy of the illusion. Before he kissed her or took off his jacket he was taking his files from his briefcase and laying them out on the coffee table.

The photographs weren't pretty, but he wanted her to *see*. He spread them before her, the dead and the living: the deformities and birthmarks and the coroners' reports of the previous personalities' death wounds. The girl with deformed fingers on one hand, the woman who had been killed when she had burned the rice. When he had finished with the last brutal and improbable detail he looked at Sheila and drew in his breath, wondering what she'd say. He felt

302

his whole life, his whole marriage, the only thing aside from his work that had ever meant anything to him, hanging in the balance.

"You certainly did surprise me, Jerry," she said.

She looked baffled and shocked and amused all at once. There it was, the thing he loved most in her, right there — that shadow of amusement that this was how her life was turning out. "For a moment there when you walked in I thought you were going to tell me you found another woman."

"This is what I want to do with my life. I want to go back, interview them all again in a year or two. Find more cases."

"You know that people are going to give you a hard time about this? That nobody is going to take you seriously?"

"I don't care about what other people think. I only care what you think." This wasn't, as it turned out, entirely true.

"You're giving up a very promising career."

"I'll make it work, somehow. For us," he added, the word dangling awkwardly between them. "So, what do you think?"

She paused, and he held his breath so long he felt light-headed from lack of oxygen. "I don't know, Jerry. How can I know? What you're telling me —" She shook her head. "How can it be possible?"

"But you see the data. I've shown it to you. What other explanation can there be? You think they're lying? But what reason would they have to lie? These families aren't getting any money from this, they're not looking for attention, believe me. . . . And, yes, it's possible that these kids have some kind of super ESP, I've thought of that, but these kids aren't just talking about other people's lives, they're saying they *are* these other people. And if you rule that out — I mean, what other explanation is there? And the birthmarks, the deformities, the way they match up to the modes of death, not always perfectly, no, but there is a connection, a visible connection, and I've only just started — there are too many instances for it to be random. It can't be random —"

"This is about Owen, isn't it?"

For the first time, he stopped talking. She always saw right through him.

She pored, perplexed, over the papers spread out across their coffee table. The notes, the faces, the bodies with the marks on them, the other bodies with deformities, though none as bad as Owen's. "You think that our son was born the way he was because of — something that happened in a previous lifetime? Is that what you think?"

"Can't you admit that it's likely? Or at least possible?" He was pushing her hard, but he couldn't help it. He needed this.

She frowned pensively. "You've always been a sane man, Jerry. A cautious man. It doesn't seem to me that that has changed, even if —" She shook her head. "So if you think it's possible, then I'll admit that it's possible. I'll give you that."

He grasped at her words. "That's all I ask."

"You're going to follow this anyway, until you're done with it."

He met her gaze. "I suppose that's true."

She sighed, glancing at him sideways with a weary, humorous, reproachful look. It was as if she knew right then and there that he would never be done with it, that they would never have any more children, that she'd spend the rest of her days living in the wake of this obsession until there was nothing more to do but join it.

And he was still at it, wasn't he?

Despite his compromised capacities, he was going forward. And now he was throwing protocol to the winds. The woman — the one whose name now eluded him — had insisted upon it.

■ ■ ■ ■

She had answered the door of her motel room instantly after his hesitant knock. She was wearing the clothes from the day before, and her face looked ashen in the morning light. "We had a bad night," she said flatly. He'd handed her the pages he'd printed out in the motel's office, filled with the research he'd gathered — research that indicated a missing child named Tommy Crawford who lived on Asheville Road. "You've got to be kidding me," she said when she realized what he was giving her. But she took the papers and looked at them while Noah slept soundly in the next bed.

"You think this is the previous personality," she said at last.

"I do."

She kept picking up the pages and putting them down again.

"It's not unheard of for people to reincarnate into a different race or culture." Anderson spoke in a low voice. He tried to keep his urgency in check. "There have been numerous cases in which children in India remembered lifetimes spent in a different caste. And some Burmese children have seemed to remember previous lives as

306

Japanese soldiers who were killed in Burma during World War II."

"So. If we do this —" She gave him a sober, warning look. "If we do go to Ohio —"

His heart leaped. He couldn't help it. "Yes?"

"We go now. Today."

"That's not how it works," Anderson had said reasonably. "We e-mail the family first. Or write a letter, if we can. We don't just show up on their doorstep." He had done this, as a matter of fact, in Asia, when the previous personality's family had no phone or method of contact. But in Asia the families were not like American families, and more likely than not they were at least curious to see him.

"That's exactly what we are doing," she had said. "I'm not going to approach some other grieving mother without being sure. Not again. If Noah doesn't recognize anything, we turn around and go home, and they are none the wiser."

His calm began to dissipate into the air. She couldn't be serious. "It's better to contact the family first."

"I'm going, with or without you. I'm going to take the next flight out."

"It's ill-advised."

"Then so be it. I am not going to take Noah home only to start this all up again. So I guess it's now or never. And if we do this . . ." She sat up straight on the bed. "You can't write about it. You understand? This is about my son, not your legacy."

He had tried to smile. He was so tired. "Fuck my legacy."

His legacy — oh, he had had high hopes for himself, but he hadn't gotten very far. There were so many things he still didn't know. Why were some children born with memories of past lives, their bodies marked with the imprints of past traumas? Was it related (it *had* to be) to the fact that 70 percent of the previous personalities these children remembered had died traumatic deaths? If consciousness survived death — and he had shown that it did — then how did this connect with what Max Planck and the quantum physicists realized: that events didn't occur unless they were observed, and therefore that consciousness was fundamental, and matter itself was derived from it? Did that therefore make this world like a dream, with each life, like each dream, flowing one after the other? And was it then possible that some of us — like these children — were awakened too abruptly from these dreams, and ached to return to them?

The blue sky through the window spread out before him, on and on. So many things he'd longed to explore further. He'd wanted to plumb the very nature of reality. He'd wanted to finish this book. But now his mind was shattered, and all he wanted was to help a single child.

He looked at the boy slumped against him, his body nestled on Anderson's arm. He could have been any child, sweetly sleeping. He was any child.

"He likes you," the woman said.

"And I like Tommy. Very much."

She drew in her breath sharply. "Noah."

"What?"

"His name is Noah."

Of course. "I'm so sorry. I don't know how that happened." Jerry. Jerry. Pull it together.

She had turned pale.

"I'm sorry. I'm a little tired —"

"It's all right," she said. But she looked away from him and bit her lip.

Noah. Tommy. Everything came down to names, didn't it? The evidence that one was this person and not that one. And if they got lost, the names — when they got lost — and all you had left was one long, blurry stretch of humanity, like a bank of clouds in the sky — what then?

He'd have to do better. He'd have to keep the names close. Noah, Tommy. He'd roll them up and fill the cracks in his mind with them the way people tucked scraps of paper wishes between the stones of the Wailing Wall.

They looked together at the sleeping boy.

"You know I can't promise anything," Anderson murmured.

"Of course."

She was lying, though. She thought he had promised her everything.

TWENTY-TWO

Denise perched at the end of her chair and surveyed the bowl of M&M's that always seemed untouched on the doctor's side table. Did anyone ever eat them? Were these the same M&M's she'd been staring at for almost seven years? Someone, she thought, should do an experiment. Put all the green ones on top and see what happens. Bust the good doctor cold.

"Denise?"

"I'm listening." She didn't feel like looking at him but decided he'd probably make a note of it if she didn't. His elegant, horsey face seemed even more elongated in worry.

"I said, everybody regresses sometimes," Dr. Ferguson was saying. "It happens."

She looked back at the M&M's bowl. "Not to me."

"You're too hard on yourself. You've done incredible work creating a life for yourself. Don't forget that."

"A life for myself." She said it the way she might say "A half-pound of salami, sliced thin, please," or: "Time for your meds, Mr. Randolph." But what she meant, which anyone could see if he was not a fool, was: my life is shit.

Dr. Ferguson was not a fool. She felt him regarding her. "You're disappointed in yourself."

She popped a green M&M in her mouth. The sugar turned to dust on her tongue. She couldn't taste a thing. "I'm done."

"And what does that mean?"

She might as well tell him the truth. Who else could she tell? "I'm done with it. I worked so hard all these years to pull it together for Charlie, and one phone call puts me right back there and it's as if it all happened yesterday. And I can't —" She took a breath. "I can't do it."

She felt him choosing his words cautiously. "I understand it must be extremely upsetting to feel that way again."

She shook her head. "I can't."

He crossed one long skinny leg over the other. "And what other choice do you have?" His Adam's apple bobbed visibly in his neck, like Ichabod Crane's in a movie she'd once seen. I guess this makes me the headless horseman, she thought. About right, too. She had no thoughts or feelings left. She was watching herself from a great height, the way the recent dead are said to watch their own bodies.

"Let's just say I'm considering my options."

"Are you telling me you're thinking of suicide?"

She took note of his concern. It was like a thought bubble hovering over his head, meaning nothing. She shrugged. A habit of Charlie's that always aggravated her, but she saw its usefulness now.

"Because if that's what you mean, if you're serious, I have to take some action. You know that."

That hospital. Those stained sofas, chipped floors, vacant faces watching mindless television. She shuddered.

Anyway, he would never give her a prescription if she seemed suicidal. And she needed the prescription. She didn't know why she had said it. "You know I would never do that. Never. I would never give him the satisfaction."

"Him?"

She gave the doctor a withering look. "The man who stole Tommy, of course." The minute she said it she knew it was the truth, that she couldn't do it. Damn it to

313

hell. And she'd been feeling so calm, too. "And of course I couldn't do that to Charlie."

Of course she couldn't. And wasn't there some tiny part of her that still wanted something from this life? To cast these fragments of herself to the winds, to see if they could take root somewhere?

"So what did Detective Ludden say, when you called him?"

"You mean, last night, or this morning?"

All right, Doctor, now you see where we're at, do you not?

A pause. "Either one."

"He said that the detectives in Florida were working hard on the case. That's what he always says, 'They're working hard, ma'am,' so polite, you know. And I know he thinks I'm crazy. All of them do."

"Who is 'all of them'?"

"Everybody. You think I'm paranoid? I'm not paranoid. Every time I run into people, they give me this look, even now, it's subtle but I see it, as if they're surprised, as if —"

"As if what?"

"As if something's wrong with me, and I shouldn't still be walking around, I should be —"

"Yes?"

"Dead. Because Tommy's dead."

It was the first time she'd said it and she wanted immediately to take it back. The words had fallen out of her mouth like marbles, rolling this way and that across the floor, irretrievable.

And people were right, she thought. Why should she keep breathing? All these years she'd kept it together not only for Charlie but also for Tommy: so that she would be intact when he came back to her.

But she couldn't pretend any longer: Tommy was dead and she was a — what? Not a widow, not an orphan. There was no word for what she was.

"I see," Dr. Ferguson said. He slid the tissue box closer to her across the side table.

They looked at each other. He was waiting, she realized, for her to cry. The square box gazed at her expectantly, its cardboard skin swimming with absurd pink and green bubbles, one tissue protruding obscenely from its slit, calling out for her tears, for her — what did the books call it? — catharsis. He wanted to see her break at last. Well, damned if he was going to get her to do that. What did it get you, catharsis? You still had to pick yourself up and go on with your life, your life that was a pile of shit. She stood.

"Where are you going?"

"Look. Are you going to give me the prescription or not?"

"It's not advisable —"

"Yes or no? 'Cause I'll go elsewhere. . . . You know someone else will give it to me if you don't."

He hesitated, but he gave her the slip of paper. "Come back soon, all right? Next week?"

You still had to pick yourself up and walk out that door and face the glare of the afternoon sun on the windshields of the cars in the parking lot.

You still had to find your car and put your key in the ignition and hear its full-throated cry as it came to life. You had to steer it onto the road with all the other living, moving things, all headed somewhere or other as if the rotation of the world depended on their trips to the dry cleaner's or the mall. You had to pull off the road into the parking lot of the CVS and get out of the car and stand waiting at the counter with all the other people seeking the potions that would buy them another hour or another day, whether they wanted it or not, and you had to put half a pill in your mouth, just half, and swallow it, hard and dry, feeling it scrape down your throat. And then, since you had no food in the house and you had a human being besides yourself to look after, you had to walk down the sidewalk to the Stop & Shop. You had to stand there inside blinking under those bright, bright lights, all those rows and colors leaping out at you, tomatoes so red they hurt your eyes, fiery orange bags of Doritos, neon green six-packs of 7-Up, everything chirping out to the living: Pick me! Pick me! Pick me!

And you couldn't stand there forever, as if you'd never seen a supermarket before. You needed, even then, especially then, when your momentum began to flag, to keep moving. You filled your cart with what your family needed. You put a dead, skinned chicken in there and a big box of cornflakes and a gallon of milk. You put broccoli in there for Charlie, the only vegetable he'd eat, and some Vidalia onions for Henry in case he came over someday and you also put in a bag of grape tomatoes. You knew that Charlie wouldn't eat them and you yourself preferred beefsteak but you grabbed them anyway, didn't you, their smooth red skins peeking out at you through the mesh of the bag, grabbed them because Tommy liked them, liked to hold them in his teeth and squirt them across the room, and you wanted to show yourself that you still remembered what Tommy liked, even if it did blast a hole in your heart.

Then you had to stand in line ignoring Mrs. Manzinotti staring at you from the dairy section, so you paged through the magazines filled with celebrities falling apart or falling in love or both, noticing that Mrs. Manzinotti was walking in your direction now and hoping that she still ignored you as she did the first few years, avoiding eye contact, flinching when you passed her in the market or downtown. But here she was, filled with determined good cheer, barreling toward you, as if all that was over with and we must go on as before, mustn't we? It doesn't matter if you're ready; you got ready, fast. So you talked about how nice it was that it was finally feeling like spring today (as if you had even noticed) and you asked after Mr. Manzinotti and Ethan and Carol Ann and when she said, 'And how's Charlie doing?' you said, 'We're just fine, thank you,' as if your own story were an article in a magazine someone could flip through and put back in the rack, as if your sweet boy wasn't (say it) somewhere in pieces under the dirt.

And while you paid the cashier, at that moment it occurs to you that there's a man in Florida stopping at a gas station somewhere right this minute. You can see him clear as day buying a big bag of Doritos and beef jerky and a Red Bull, then leaving the bag there on the counter with the clerk as he heads to the toilet to pee before he gets back on the road. And the eyes of that man standing there, those unrepentant eyes staring in the bathroom mirror, they were the last eyes Tommy ever saw before —

No.

No, because: Tommy was alive.

Alive on this earth right now in all his Tommyness: his love of tomatoes and marshmallows and butterscotch, his inexplicable hatred of strawberries, the way he'd grab her hand as she was leaving his bedside at night, asking her to stay for a few more minutes (Oh, why had she loosened herself from his grip and kissed him good night? Why hadn't she stayed for the few minutes he had craved?), the dimple in his cheek that came out when he gave that foolish and duplicitous grin after some piece of naughtiness, like that time he popped his brother's balloon on the way home from the carnival and pretended it was an accident.

Tommy was alive on this earth and no one could tell her otherwise.

Tommy was alive on this earth, and someday they would see each other again.

It happened sometimes. That girl out in Utah, for instance. The one with the friendly, open face and the yellow hair, who looked like she had stepped out of the goat stall at the 4-H instead of crawling on her hands and knees up from purgatory. There she was on the cover of the magazine, Denise still had that copy in the drawer of her bedside table, she knew it by heart: the girl had disappeared from her bedroom one night and then five years later she was home again and the monster who did it was going to jail for forever and a day. There were the pictures of her with her family, sitting on the couch with her mother's arm wrapped around her, her father's hand resting on her shoulder as naturally as you please. She was starting up school again, that's what the article said. Playing piano. A shy smile on her face, blue ribbons in her hair. The girl was intact. More or less. It could happen. Things happened. It wasn't any more or less unlikely than a child going for a bike ride to his best friend's house down the road one Saturday morning and falling off the edge of the earth.

But these thoughts, like the magazine's pages, were almost worn through from too much use. Which made her go back to the other thought. Which made her think again that she couldn't do it anymore.

I can't hold on to hope and I can't hold on without it, either, she thought.

She pulled out of the parking lot. When she reached the intersection, instead of heading right toward home she took a left and found herself driving out toward Dayton. She drove for a while past the even green fields, unsure as yet as to where she was going, until she saw the sign for the new Staples out beyond the mall. It was shining its big neon smile at her, as if it had been waiting for her, as if she was one of the devout who had found her way back home.

She felt a dim thrill when no one looked at her twice as she walked in the door. They kept doing what they were doing, a whole lot of nothing as far as she could tell. A girl with horrible fraying braids was paging through a magazine. A white boy with a knit cap on his head (why did they wear that indoors? unless they were bald, which this boy wasn't) was ringing something up. She heard his nervous scales of laughter echoing through the store. She wandered for a while down the long aisles filled with dangling supplies, each with its own clear sense of purpose, soaking in the chilled air. In aisle 10 she picked up a new gleaming staple gun and walked to the back where the copy center was, feeling its heft in her hand.

There was a line of people, clutching their papers. Selling cars, maybe, or looking for piano students. She stood on line, another person with the need to multiply her longing exponentially, holding in her other hand the flyer she kept in the glove compartment for this very reason. She waited her turn and then she handed her flyer to a boy in his early twenties, a boy with deep brown skin and a smooth, amiable, bored face.

Maybe Tommy will look like that someday, she thought. Maybe Tommy will get a job at Staples. He could do worse for himself. She was letting herself think it. She knew that. It was as if her conscious mind was still back in the parking lot of the Stop & Shop and she was letting this other part of herself take over again.

"Two hundred, please."

He took the paper from her and didn't look at it. Bless you, she thought. Bless you for not looking. The people in the stationery store in town had gotten used to her by now; the pity in their eyes was no longer fresh but had congealed over the years into something familiar, automatic, as if Denise were a stray mutt that wandered in every now and then for a crust of bread or a pat.

But Denise didn't need a pat, or any rewarmed pity. She needed her two hundred copies.

"Would you like that in different colors, ma'am? Or on white paper?"

"The face will be legible in different colors?"

"Sure. We can do that."

"Then maybe different colors, this time."

"All right. Which colors would you like?"

"You choose."

"I'll do yellow and green and red. How's that?"

"Great."

She smiled at him. She stood behind the counter, feeling its hard, sharp edge with her fingers. The feel of the pill gliding through her system. The staple gun heavy in her other hand. Henry had gotten rid of the other one. Twenty-nine dollars it had cost her and he'd thrown it right in the trash.

You've got to stop with the flyers, he had said.

The words flowed through her mind as coolly as the frigid air, as if they were words she was overhearing, spoken between strangers.

What right do you have to show up here and tell me what to do?

Charlie told me. That's what. Our son. He says you aren't even there for dinner half the time.

The boy eats. Look at him. He's not starving.

That's not the point. You are wearing yourself down and Charlie, too. And me, too.

What do you care?

You have to stop. Please.

I can't. What if —

Call the doctor then. Get some help.

What if it makes a difference, Henry? What if someone sees one of them and —

For god's sakes, Denise —

The boy was back. "Actually, the red's a little dark for a face. How about blue? The blue's real light."

"That'd be fine."

She waited. She had only to wait, her hands fingering the sharp edge of the countertop, Tommy's face multiplying in green and blue and yellow. She let her mind linger on each of the faces as they poured out of the machine, thinking, maybe this one. Maybe this will be the one that makes all the difference.

TWENTY-THREE

Charlie Crawford rode his bike home slowly from Harrison Johnson's house, his head percolating with riffs, his whole body pulsating with the thrill of victory and the first-class weed Harrison always had on hand from his brother's friend who worked at the pizza place.

Ba DA DA ba DA DA DA DA. The way he'd extended that last beat, rolling it and then holding it so it had resonated around the garage, he'd known right away: he hadn't fucked it up. He could see it in the way Harrison and Carson really stopped and listened for fucking once, in the grudging nods they aimed in his direction as he headed out the door at the end of rehearsal. He knew they'd been wanting to ditch him for that Mike kid at the community college, they never thought he was good enough, he'd always been the kid with a drum kit who lived nearby and could kinda sorta hold a beat. But today: he'd shown them but good. He'd killed that fucker, left it lying DEAD in the road.

Okay, okay, so maybe it wasn't the best drum solo ever of all time, maybe he wasn't, like, Lars Ulrich, but in his life this is what amounted to a major fucking victory and he was going to take that baby and ride it all the way home, the AMAZE-ing Harrison's brother's friend's weed flowing through him making everything all right, making every-thing so very, very all right that he did an extra loop around the block, down past the neighbor's vicious dog to the edge of the cornfields and back again, and didn't even particularly dread sailing back into his own driveway, where Thanks be to God his mother's car was out. Could it get any bet-ter? He could grab a carton of ice cream and go upstairs to his room and text Gret-chen. Or — even better — think about Gretchen without having the stress of actu-ally texting her, lying there on his bed while the high was still in him, thinking about Gretchen's breasts jiggling to the beat of his killing drum solo, her knees swaying open and shut in that jeans miniskirt she'd worn to school day before yesterday — or wait — even better — skip Gretchen entirely, too much work, and get right to it on the Internet, ready set go! Now that was a pleasant way to spend an afternoon.

He swung back down the block again, tingling with anticipation, his dreads flying like wings above his ears, then decided he'd better get on with it before the high faded. He never risked bringing any pot home — for one thing, his mom was all up in his ass about that shit and for all he knew would ship him out to a military academy if she found so much as a bud in his pocket, which was hard, actually, to keep on top of, to keep one's head in the game like that about every stray bud when you got stoned as often as he did. So far, though, she'd merely sniffed at him a few times after he came home, as though he were a rancid meat loaf in the fridge. She probably didn't know what the stuff smelled like, thought he had some funky-ass sweat. Luckily no one messed with his locker at school. He could have a drugstore in that thing and no one would be the wiser.

He dropped his bike in the yard and ran to the door. But there were people walking around the house, looking around. White people. A man and a woman, and a little kid, too. Uh-oh. Maybe some Jehovah's Witnesses, though most of the Jehovah's he'd seen around there had been black. He

327

didn't even know there were white Jehovah's. Did Mormons come this far out? Got to hand it to them, bringing the kid along, that was a nice touch. Hard to slam a door on a kid.

Funny little kid, too. He was hopping up and down like he was pretending to be a kangaroo, yelling, "This is it, this is it, this is it!" He kept patting the aluminum siding as if the whole house were a big red dog.

"Can I help you?" Charlie said. Summoning up his best this-fine-young-man-was-raised-right grin, which he could beam right through his stoner's haze. His specialty, actually. He could be sitting in the office of Principal Ranzetta herself right now and she'd have nary a clue. And had done so, in point of fact.

The three of them gaped at him.

The woman spoke up at last. "Is Mr. or Mrs. Crawford at home?"

Boy, they sure did their homework, these evangelical types.

"Mom isn't here right now. Maybe come back another time?" He looked up at them hopefully.

The lady and the old guy glanced at each other. They looked like they were having a disagreement without saying anything. Like the woman had an agenda and the old guy

328

wanted out of there.

Were they from the school? He didn't recognize them, but the old guy did have a school superintendent-y kind of vibe and the woman could be an administrator or maybe even a cop, she had that wired-up look. Maybe they'd found the pot in his locker and she was going to lock him up or throw him out or send him to rehab like that lame-ass in social studies who got caught with a bottle of peppermint schnapps in his desk. I mean, schnapps? That's what you get busted for? In your desk? Schnapps?

But why'd they bring a kid, though, if they were there to bust him? He couldn't wrap his head around that. The kid kind of creeped him out, too. He was staring up at Charlie with these weird, shiny eyes.

"So. What'd you want my mama for?" Charlie dropped the fine-young-man bit and stood squinting at the three of them.

"That's between us, I'm afraid," the woman said. She seemed tense.

Uh-oh.

He had a thought. It glowed with possibility in his brain, so he said it.

"Are you with the TV?"

"What?"

"You know, like *America's Most Wanted,* something like that?"

"No, we're not. Sorry."

"Oh." His mom was always talking about going on a show like that, keeping the word out there. They didn't do missing black kids, though, as far as he could tell. Only pretty white girls.

So who were they then? He fixed them with a long, pot-emboldened stare and watched them shift uncomfortably. Good, he thought. Go away, strange white people.

A pause. No one said anything except for the little kid, who was still bouncing on his toes and mumbling to himself, "This is it, this is it."

Go away, go away, go away, strange white people, he repeated silently.

"We'll come back later," the old guy said.

Hallelujah. You, mister, are a genuine psychic. (Maybe it wasn't too late for the porn, after all?)

"No!" The kid had this tiny little kid's voice, like he was on helium or something. "I want to stay!"

"We'll come back in just a bit, sweetie. Okay?" The lady ruffled his hair. She didn't seem like a cop anymore.

"NO!" The kid was getting on his nerves now.

"We're coming back, Noah. It's okay."

The kid started to cry. The man squatted

330

down beside him and asked him something in a low voice Charlie couldn't quite make out. The kid nodded. Then he pointed right at him.

"Sure. That's Charlie," he said.

The old guy and the lady looked at Charlie. He began to sweat, as if he'd done something wrong. "I didn't do anything to this kid," he said. "I don't even know him." Looking beseechingly at their staring eyes. He guessed this pot wasn't so good after all. It was making him paranoid.

"Is that your name? Charlie?" The old guy asked.

"Yeah."

They stood there, the four of them shifting on the little concrete doorstep, the blond kid still crying, giving him the heebie-jeebies.

Finally it occurred to him that maybe his mama knew these people. They knew his name, after all. She'd kill him if she found out he kept them waiting out on the stoop.

"Would you like to come in?"

"That would be nice, thank you," the old guy said. "We've been traveling for a long time."

What did you do with a grandpa and a woman and a sniffly little kid all standing in your living room? The old guy perched expectantly on the edge of the couch and began writing notes in this tiny spidery handwriting on a yellow pad.

"This is it," the kid said again. He sounded real excited. He started running around the room, the lady (he was pretty sure she was the kid's mom) following right behind him.

He knew there was something he ought to be doing. The idea came to him slowly, a shimmering density on the other side of the room that slowly took on weight and motion, wafting over to his brain like a helpful ghost. Food. When people are in the house you offer them food. "Would you guys like something to eat? A snack, or something?"

"That'd be nice," the old guy said. He looked really grateful, like he hadn't eaten all day.

When Charlie got back from the kitchen (empty-handed but for a few glasses of tap water — there was nothing in the fridge but some old pasta sauce and the ice cream in the freezer he was saving for himself) the kid was standing in front of the fireplace, pointing at the picture of the farm his Grandpa Joe had painted back when he was alive. "That was upstairs," the kid was saying. "In the attic."

"Yeah, we moved it down here after Pop

left —" and then he fell silent. "What'd you say?"

"Papa's not here?"

"My dad lives in Yellow Springs, now."

"Why'd he move there?"

"Well, he and my mama weren't getting along anymore, so they —"

The kid was looking up at him wide eyed. Man, this was one weird kid.

"My parents — they're separated."

"Separated?" The kid's face was moving around like he was taking it in.

"You know what *separated* means, honey?" the lady said. "That's when a mother and a father decide to live in separate places —"

The kid was walking over to the piano now, lifting the lid on the bench.

"Where's all the music?"

"We don't have any."

"There was music."

Charlie felt himself beginning to lose it. Freaking out. His grip on reality was slipping the grid. Maybe there was something else in Harrison's brother's friend's pot, like some peyote or something. He'd heard that sometimes people did that, spiked the stuff with something trippy that could send you to some crazy places, though why anyone would want to do that he couldn't figure,

333

since the whole point as far as he was concerned was to sand down the edges.

He looked at the kid. He was sitting on the piano bench. Try, Charlie, try. "You play piano?"

The kid just sat there.

"No, he doesn't play," the lady said.

Then the kid started to play the piano. It was the theme song from *The Pink Panther.* He could tell that right off, after the first couple of notes. He hadn't heard that melody in years, but back when he'd heard it, back when his brother played it, he'd heard it every day, sometimes every couple hours 'til their dad threatened to strangle him, and he knew beyond a shadow of a shadow of a doubt that He Was Fucked. He was Fucked-Up. He was Fucked-Up and he was going to freak out, right now, in front of all these white people.

"You gotta stop playing that," he said.

The kid kept on playing.

"You gotta stop playing that."

He heard the car coming into the driveway with its telltale hissing muffler.

Oh, Sweet Jesus, thank you. Mama's here.

"Hey, Kid."

Fucking Pink Panther.

The kid said: "Don't you know me, Charlie?"

334

The car door slammed shut. She was getting something out of the trunk. Come inside the house, Mama. Come inside and sort this shit out, take it out of my hands.

"No," Charlie said. "No, I don't know you."

The kid said: "I'm Tommy."

He tried to cling to the last shreds of the high but it wasn't there anymore, it was long gone.

TWENTY-FOUR

In retrospect, they'd done it all wrong.

Anderson stood in the Crawfords' kitchen, trying to detail for himself precisely how he'd let it all go awry.

Almost three thousand cases he'd worked on and he always did a postmortem and a follow-up, not only to track his subjects but also to learn how to do his work better. Now he was on his last case and he felt much as he did at the beginning, raw and un-schooled. His last case had been significant, he had been right about that: significant not because it was the American case that could stir the world at large to take note at last that there was evidence of reincarnation, but because it was the case that proved once and for all that he was finished.

He should have known better. What had he been thinking? They should not have talked to the teenager, should have left im-mediately to regroup. Almost three thousand cases and certainly fifty or sixty decent American ones: he *knew* this wasn't India, where the villagers would eagerly point out possible rebirths, sending him off to look at birthmarks he could barely see. In India they wanted him to succeed, were excited about the possibility of proving what they already knew. On American cases you were careful. You worked your way slowly, slowly, to the matter of what you did, in the gentlest possible terms, making it clear that all you were doing was asking questions.

They should have left before the mother got there.

He should have foreseen that the teenager might jump the gun like that. "Mama, this boy says he's Tommy," before the poor woman was even through the door.

He should have realized, most importantly, that since they had not found a body, the woman had not known that her son had died.

"Mama, this boy says he's Tommy," the teenager had said. And the woman still edging in the door, hip first, a bag of groceries clutched against her chest and a bundle of papers tucked under an arm.

"This boy says he's Tommy," and the boy inside playing the piano, and he himself paralyzed by goddamn verbal timidity and also the elation flooding the dopamine centers in his brain: the elation that always accompanied verification that a case was a match — for he was quite sure that the child had never played the piano before, and that the tune he was playing had meaning for the previous personality's family.

Music: was anything more powerful in summoning what was lost? Was it really so surprising that when the woman turned to the room there was hope in her eyes, that wild, hopeless hope you saw sometimes in the faces of terminally ill people discussing the newest treatments? Was it really so surprising that for a moment she thought that her lost son was there in the room somewhere, that he was alive and had made it back to her?

Or that when, instead, her eyes lit on the small white child who was Noah, who was now running toward her like a blond heat-seeking missile, throwing himself at her legs, she would be undone? She'd had to process all of it at once, the hope and the shock of disappointment and of Noah's life-force slamming against her body, all while stand-ing on the threshold of her home with her coat on and her keys still in her hand and a heavy bag of groceries in her arms.

He should have taken over right then and

there. Established a sense of order. Taken the bag from her arms. Mrs. Crawford, I'm Professor Anderson, please take a seat and we'll explain our presence here. That was the sentence in his head. He heard himself saying it in a soothing tone. But he hesitated, wanting to be sure he had the words right, and before he had a chance to speak, Janie rushed forward, grabbing Noah by his arm and trying to tug him off the woman's legs.

"Sweetie, let go."

"No."

"You have to let go of her. I'm so sorry," she said to Denise. She tried to pull Noah away, but he clung tighter, squeezing both her legs in his small arms.

"Is this some kind of sick joke?"

"Noah, you're bothering this woman, let go NOW."

"No!" he said. "This is my mama!"

"This is insanity," Denise Crawford said. She jiggled her leg in an effort to extricate herself from the child. She was still holding the heavy bag of groceries. No one had taken it from her. The teenager was standing there with his mouth ajar. Anderson was watching, forming the words in his mind. There was Noah pressing himself against Denise and Janie trying to pull him the other way, the two of them locked together in a battle of wills like the primal struggle of mother and child, until the stack of papers Denise had been carrying tucked under her arm began to slip, and in an effort to regain control she jiggled her leg again, or kicked, and Noah fell.

He fell backward, his head hitting the wooden floor with a loud crack.

Anderson felt the sound shudder through his body.

The boy didn't move. He lay still on the ground with his eyes closed. Anderson heard a gasp — that was Janie — then a splash as Denise's papers slid down, fanning out before all of them, Tommy Crawford smiling in green and yellow and blue.

Janie was by his side in an instant. "Noah?"

Then Anderson got hold of himself and crouched beside the boy. He took the boy's pulse, and the strong beats brought the room back to life again.

Noah's eyes opened. He blinked, looked up at the ceiling. His pupils seemed normal.

"Do you know who I am?" Anderson asked.

The boy's gaze glided from the ceiling to Anderson. He looked at him with a saddened expression, as if the question had disappointed him. "Of course I know who you are. I know everybody here."

Anderson stood up, brushed off his knees. "I think he's fine."

"You don't know that!" Janie cried. "What if he has a concussion?"

"We'll keep an eye out for symptoms. It's not likely."

"Really? How do you know?"

The question vibrated in the air between them. She doesn't trust me, he thought. Makes sense. Why should she?

"Oh!" Another thud — this time it was the bag of groceries falling as Denise finally lost her grip on it, the pinball whirr of onions rolling across the floor. Denise stared from Noah to the mess on the floor, shaking her head. "I'm sorry —"

Noah struggled to sit. His face contorted. "Mama?"

"So sorry," Denise repeated. Her knees seemed to buckle and Anderson was afraid for a moment that they were giving way, that she would fall, and the farce would be complete. Instead, she crouched down, collecting the papers, placing them neatly in a pile.

Janie gathered Noah in her arms. "Come on, sweetheart. Let's go get a — glass of water, shall we?" She didn't wait for his response; she stood up and walked out of the room.

"I didn't mean . . . to hurt anyone. . . ." Denise was hoarse, stunned, gathering the flyers one by one.

"Mama," the teenager said. "Leave them."

"No, I've got to . . ."

"Leave the flyers be."

"It's not your fault," Anderson said. "It's mine."

She looked up at him, but he couldn't meet her eyes.

Ten minutes later, Anderson sat up straight on the couch and let the full force of the woman's fury and confusion fall upon him. He knew he deserved it.

"What the hell are you talking about?"

"Maybe we should discuss this once you've recovered a bit more," Anderson answered slowly. "From the shock."

"Oh, I've recovered." The Crawford woman stood over him. She didn't seem entirely stable.

This simply proved that approaches always matter, Anderson thought. He should not have listened to Janie. He ought to have e-mailed the woman first. Given her some kind of warning.

She crossed her arms and he felt the rage

building inside of her, revealing itself in her shaky voice and the flash of her eyes. "So let me get this straight. You think my son is — reincarnated somewhere inside that child? That's what you think?"

"Ma'am, we try not to jump to . . ." He looked at her. Fuck it. "Yes. That's what I think."

"You people are out of your damn minds."

"Ma'am. I'm sorry you — came to that conclusion." He took a deep breath. He'd met resistance so many times. Why should it affect him so much now? He couldn't find the clarity inside of himself to explain what he needed to explain. "If you can just take a moment and let me explain some of the things Noah's been saying and you can either — agree with them or —"

"Some kind of crazy voodoo —"

"It's not voodoo," Janie said. She was standing in the doorway.

Anderson felt deeply relieved to see her there. "How's Noah?"

"Okay. For now. He won't talk to me. Charlie set him up in the kitchen watching cartoons on the computer." Janie turned to Denise. "Look," she said. "I know this all sounds crazy, and totally far-fetched . . . and the thing is, it *is* far-fetched, all of it, but maybe it's also —" She glanced at

Anderson, her eyes startled, flung open like a window. "It's also true."

Anderson was momentarily stricken with gratitude. Maybe it wasn't all gone to shit, after all.

"Look, we don't want to upset you. That's the last thing we want," Janie said nervously, and Denise laughed, a terrible sound.

"You can go ahead and believe whatever you like. That's your prerogative. But please leave me and my family out of it."

"Did Tommy have a lizard named Horntail?" Anderson asked suddenly.

Denise's face was unreadable over her crossed arms. "So what if he did?"

"Noah remembers being a boy named Tommy who had a lizard named Horntail and a brother named Charlie. He gave multiple references to Harry Potter books, and likes the Nationals baseball team." Anderson surprised himself with his newfound fluency with proper nouns, as if some other, intact part of his brain was retrieving the necessary information. This was some quirk of the aphasia, grist for someone's research paper, only it wasn't research, it was his life; it was this moment. "He talked about shooting a .54 caliber rifle."

Denise twisted her lips into a thin smile. "Well, then, you see? We never had guns in our home. I didn't even let the boys play with toy guns."

"He says he misses his mother. His other mother," Janie added quietly. "He cries about it all the time."

"Look, I don't know why your son says these things. If something is wrong with him, then I'm truly sorry. But this is non-sense, a bunch of half-baked coincidences, and you're telling all this to the wrong person, because to be honest, I don't care." Denise laughed again, if you could call it a laugh. Anderson could sense her pain behind that clear, furious facade, like lightning flashing in the distance. There was no way in. "Look, I'm not a minister and, far as I can see, neither are you. And I'm not going to stand here in my own living room and speculate about the hereafter, because none of it makes any difference. Because none of it brings my boy back to me. Tommy is —" Her voice caught. She shook her head and tried again. "My son is dead."

The words rang out in the room. She looked from one to the other, as if one of them might actually contradict her. He wished suddenly that he was a resident again, armed with his white coat, curing the sick; anything but who he was, where he was: in this room, agreeing with this mother that her son was dead.

"I'm so sorry," Janie said. Her voice was thick with tears.

Denise Crawford was not crying, though. She was continuing on, speaking in a voice so frozen Anderson felt its chill penetrating deep into his bones: that cold grief he knew so well. "He's dead. And he's not ever coming back. And you — you should be ashamed of yourselves."

"Mrs. Crawford —"

"I think you ought to go now. You've done enough. Just — go."

Janie tried to smile. "Mrs. Crawford — we'll leave, we're fine with leaving, if you could see Noah for a few minutes — you don't have to say anything, if you just sit with him and be . . . friendly —"

"You convinced this child that he's someone else. And you dragged him here all the way from god knows where —"

"New York."

"Why does that not surprise me? You brainwashed this poor child and carted him all the way from New York. And now you want me to play along like this is some kind of game." She shook her head. "It's not a game to me. Now get out of my house."

"It's not a game to us, either," Anderson said slowly, steadily. "Listen, Mrs. — I know

346

you've had a loss. A terrible loss. I under-stand how you feel."

"You understand? Why? Who did you lose?"

"I lost my — my —" He reached for the word but it broke beneath him like a step on a ladder, sending him tumbling into darkness. He saw his wife's face in his mind's eye. It was disappointed in him. "My others." It was all he could find. He'd lost the name of his own wife. His own son.

Denise Crawford stood up to her full height. She was almost as tall as Anderson. "I said, 'Get out.' "

This is why I spent so many years in Asia, he thought. This was what happened with American cases. He stood there. He couldn't think.

Janie looked at him, and he followed her down the hall.

I'm sorry, he thought. Sorry for pulling you into this. Sorry for making you believe in such a pathetic sack of bones.

"So what do we tell Noah?" she whispered fiercely. Her closeness in the hallway, the breath of her whisper in his face, hit him hard, and he recoiled instinctively from the intensity. "How can I make this right with him?"

"You'll figure it out."

"That's all you can say? That's it? I'll figure it out?"

From somewhere nearby, a drumbeat began, ominous, inexorable, as if leading his army to its defeat. He forced himself to lift his head and look into her eyes. "I'm sorry."

She turned away from him and opened the door of the kitchen. But it wasn't necessary for her to figure out anything, because Noah was gone.

TWENTY-FIVE

It was like a house of cards collapsing, Anderson thought. Everything that could go wrong had gone wrong. And he, watching the hysteria unfold, more helpless than any of them. He had reached for the words and they weren't there.

This never would have happened in India. In India they understood that life unfolded the way it unfolded, whether you liked it or not: the cow in the road, the swerve that saves or kills you. One life ended, a new one began, maybe it was better than the last one, maybe it wasn't. The Indians (and the Thais, and the Sri Lankans) accepted this the way they accepted the monsoons or the heat, with a resignation that was like simple good sense.

Damned Americans. Americans, unschooled in the burning dung heaps and the sudden swerves, Americans couldn't help but cling tightly to the life they were living like clutching a spindly branch that was sure to break . . . and when things didn't go quite as expected, Americans lost their shit.

Himself included.

Which was as good an explanation as any for what happened that afternoon.

But you couldn't really blame America, could you?

Because things in India went wrong, too, sometimes, didn't they?

Humans were so complex, how could you possibly predict how they would react in the face of the impossible?

You couldn't.

He stood in the center of the kitchen, trying to get his bearings. On the fridge, there was a picture of a grinning Little League team. He squinted at it closely, made out Tommy in the bottom left, holding a placard that read, LITTLE LEAGUE CHAMPIONS MILLERTON SOUTHERN DIVISION, "THE NATIONALS."

Ah, the Nationals. The missing piece. He'd forgotten they sometimes named the recreation league teams after the Major Leagues. A good piece of evidence, yet it held no satisfaction for him. What good was evidence now?

He walked out of the kitchen and began to look for the missing boy.

■ ■ ■ ■

Janie stood in the back door of Denise's house and looked out at an expanse of nothing.

She had let her vigilance flag for merely a minute, but it had been a minute too long, and now Noah was gone.

She'd done another sweep of the pantry, living room, and bathroom on the ground floor and the teenager was rechecking the other rooms in the house, but he wasn't there.

He must've slipped out the back door when she was talking to Denise and Charlie went off to practice his drums. He must have thought Denise had rejected him and that's why she had kicked him. Of course he would have thought that. Or maybe he thought that it was his own fault — his fault, when it was Janie's . . . well, no time for that now. There'd be plenty of time for regrets later.

She opened the back door: a stretch of muddy grass, yellow patched with new green coming up like an inversely graying head. A birdbath cradled a dark puddle of water, a leaf turning round and round in its center. The silhouette of a tree, buds at its fingertips. Then the yard stopped and the fields started, stretching as far as she could see.

"Noah?"

She'd forgotten how silent the country was. Somewhere, a dog barked.

"Noah!"

How far could a four-year-old get?

Fragments of consoling words flitted through her head: any minute now, don't worry, it'll be fine, it always has been, he's got to be here somewhere. Underneath them, panic rising like floodwaters, obliterating everything else in its path. The grass stretching out toward the low, green stalks of the newly planted cornfields.

"NOAH!"

She broke into a run.

Cornstalks prickled her ankles as she ran across the fields, searching for a blond head. She felt the tender stalks breaking beneath her feet as she ran. "No-ah!"

He could be anywhere. He could be curled up on the damp ground just beyond her field of vision, surrounded by green stalks. He could be in the trees beyond the fields, in the dark shadows of the woods.

Maybe it was the name. He was a stubborn boy. Maybe he was making a point and if she used the other name he'd acknowl-

352

edge her.

"Tommy?" The name tore itself from her throat, scratching at the air. "TOMMY!"

"Noah? Tommy? Noah!" The sound reverberated against the flat earth and the gray bowl of the sky.

"Tommy! Noah! Tommy!" Janie called, scouring the green and gray world. Was she looking for a blond head or a dark one? Was he to be lost a second time, was that his fate? To be lost and lost and lost again?

No. You're panicking. He's around somewhere. You'll find him any minute.

Or maybe you won't.

"Noah! Tommy!" She ran past the fields, into the woods, until she had lost all sense of direction. How could she help her boy when she herself was lost?

She thought then, couldn't help but think, of Denise Crawford. Denise, who must have stood in this same place not so very long ago, calling out this name, screaming it to the indifferent sky until her voice went hoarse, and in her panic and misery Janie knew that the distance between herself and this other woman had shrunk to nothing. They were mothers. They were the same.

TWENTY-SIX

Denise lay on the bed. She had wanted to help find the boy but her legs were unstable beneath her, and that doctor, or whatever he was, had taken one look at her and insisted she lie down. The pain in her head had been bad but was dulling fast, what with the two more pills she had taken. Looking at herself in the medicine cabinet she had been tempted to pour the whole damn bottle down her throat and put a stop to all of it once and for all, but she consoled herself with two more for now, popping them dry in her mouth and swallowing them without water, and put the rest in her pocket.

And now she was feeling no pain, no pain at all, thank you very much, and she was in a dream, an alternate reality, whereby everything had turned around upon itself and become something else entirely. Some demons had tried to deceive her, and she had injured an angel who had wanted something from her, but they were gone.

Shards of sharp voices, slicing through the air. Life was a glass that had dropped and shattered and they were the pieces. The people were the pieces.

Someone was calling for Tommy.

But Tommy was gone.

Tommy was missing. She could hear herself calling out for him. She'd been spun around and dropped back in that place, in that day she had never left.

She'd thought she'd put it away, thought she had moved past it, around it — not forgetting, never forgetting, but taking the long way around so she could get through, so she could make it through each day, but she was wrong because it had always been there, playing out on the screen of her soul. She had never left it. That day.

Tommy!

She'd woken up to the sound of the boys arguing. Henry had come back the night before bearing last-minute gifts he'd found in some airport, and as usual he'd messed it up and Tommy liked Charlie's better than his own. So the boys were fighting over it and she woke up to that, still half-asleep, and she'd thought, Damn. Not knowing. Not having the slightest idea what the day would bring. Just thinking, damn, because the kids were fighting and Henry was dead tired next to her, sleeping off all those late-night gigs yet another tour that had gone on and on, making her the single mother she'd never intended to be. They'd fought about it the night before, about him going back to teaching, making some steady money, being there for his family, fought about it in front of the boys as they had always tried not to do. "You're taking away what I love," Henry had shouted.

Taking away what I love.

And she'd awoken to the sound of the boys arguing and thought: damn, now I've got to go deal with this, no one else but me, so she stomped to the doorway and yelled out, "Work it out, boys, or you're going to wake your papa." And that's how she'd started that day.

And Tommy wanted to play at Oscar's and she said all right, you can go, because Henry was sleeping and the boys were fighting and she thought it might be better with him out of her hair for a while.

And so she had her day, her day with Tommy out of her hair. Charlie quiet, playing with his new toy. Henry sleeping. In the afternoon they'd had themselves a leisurely lunch and she decided to cook lasagna for dinner. While she cooked she'd looked out the window and the daffodils were blooming around the birdbath, and Henry was home, and the house was quiet, and she felt her own luck. There was Henry home and Charlie and Tommy and her house with the bird feeder and summer vacation soon and she felt her own luck at having this quiet moment, this life, this day.

Tommy!

But it was late afternoon, getting on toward evening, and she went to get Tommy to come home for dinner.

Walking leisurely down the road. There was no rush. It was Saturday. The green fields glowing in the dusk. Summer coming, and the air sweet with it.

She passed the barking dog next door and the mailboxes of the Cliffords and the McClures and turned into the cul-de-sac that Oscar lived in, a horseshoe of houses under tall trees swaying in the breeze. One of the trees must have been diseased; there was a man high up in it, sawing away at the branches. She stood and watched and thought what a shame it was, the limbs falling off that big old tree that had been around for centuries, while all around it spring was enveloping the world. In the cul-de-sac, the people were outside their houses, riding skateboards, listening to the radio, washing their cars. Oscar was shooting baskets on his driveway, his mom in her garden on the side of the house, watering the tomatoes. Denise could see the tomatoes as she walked up the steps of the house; they were small and round and green on the vine, like a promise.

She heard the basketball swishing through the hoop. The gush of water from one of the neighbors washing the soap off his car. The buzzing of the saw on the tree and then the slow cracking as a branch began to fall.

If you could go back — which you couldn't — if you could go back, she'd go back to that moment, she'd live right there, standing on the driveway in the springtime listening to Oscar's ball swish into the basket, waiting for Tommy. That moment before Oscar's mother looked up from her tomatoes and Denise read the surprise written plainly on the other mother's face, and her life cracked into two.

From then on there would always be the piece of life she was living and the other piece, the piece lived in darkness, in which something somewhere was happening to Tommy.

But it was happening all over again, had never stopped happening, that moment when Tommy had gone missing. She was locked inside it and there would never be any way out, no matter how many pills she took. She'd always be there, in that day, she had just imagined that she'd gone on, that she'd raised Charlie the best she could, that she'd kept on working.

Denise looked up at the ceiling, her head spinning. Things were rolling too fast now, fragments falling around her like bits of glass. The blue and white lights of the police car flashing in the window. The car she'd called too late, because he had been gone for hours, he'd never made it to Oscar's house.

She lay flat on the bed, fingering her pills in her pocket. She liked the feel of them, soft and crumbly around the edges. Friendly. She put another one in her mouth, it was dry and bitter, but another bitter pill was nothing to her.

She pulled them out of her pocket and looked at them.

Twelve little friends, winking at her, calling out her name.

TWENTY-SEVEN

Janie came in from the cornfields and sat down at the kitchen table next to Anderson. She put her head in her hands and tried to quiet the rush in her mind. Anderson was speaking to someone very slowly on the phone. She wondered how he could stay so composed when Noah was lost. But Noah wasn't his child, after all. This was a stranger; a researcher. Like Noah, this particular panic belonged to her alone.

He tried to steady her with his eyes. She avoided him, inspecting Denise's kitchen. The window overlooking the birdbath and the cornfields. The framed picture of peaches over the stove. The rooster clock, with its loud tick. She didn't like to think about the suffering that had gone on in this room.

Anderson hung up the phone. "Police are coming."

"Good." Her voice was raw from shouting. "Did you —"

"I checked the house."

"What about Mrs. Crawford?"

"Resting, but the child wasn't there."

"And the teenager?"

"Looking."

"Did you look in the basement?"

"And the attic. We'll look again soon. We'll find him," Anderson said. He looked exhausted, but also focused and awake. He was one of those people, she thought bitterly, who came to life in adversity. She had hoped she might be one of those people, too, but right now she didn't think so.

"I should drive around the neighborhood," Janie said. She stood up. "Give me the keys."

"Take a moment," Anderson said.

"I'm fine."

"One moment."

"No!"

"You can help more if you're calm."

She sat down again at the table. Her knees were shaking.

"How did this happen? How did I let this happen? He's four years old!"

"So he can't go far."

"Can't he?" She turned to Anderson. "I never should have come here. I never should have taken part in your crazy experiment.

What the hell was I thinking?"

"You were trying to help Noah."

"Well, it was a mistake."

"Look at me." His eyes were clear. "We'll find Noah."

Noah. The word caused an avalanche of longing. What she wouldn't give to have him in her arms again. His plump limbs and soft head. She'd never understood people calling their children delicious, but she got it now, she wanted to find him so she could eat him up, inhale him right back into her body so she would never lose him again.

Anderson stood up and poured her a glass of water.

"Here. Drink."

She took the glass of water and gulped it down.

"What if he has an asthma attack while he's out there? What if the man who took Tommy is still out there?"

Anderson filled the glass again and handed it to her and she drank it down.

"Now take a breath."

"But —"

"Take a breath."

She took a breath. The clock in Denise's kitchen kept on ticking; it hadn't stopped ticking all these years.

"I'm all right now. I can drive."

"You sure?"

"I'm sure."

He handed her the keys.

"Be careful, Janie."

"Okay." She clutched the keys in her hands and stood. At the kitchen door, she looked back at Anderson. He had filled a glass of water for himself as well and was sitting at the table, looking at it. He looked tired.

He hadn't meant for any of this to happen. She felt sorry she'd been harsh with him before.

"How did you do it?" she said quietly.

"Do what?"

"Lose someone? How did you bear it?"

"You take a breath," he said. He took a sip of water. "Then you take another."

She stood there, the keys rattling in her hand.

The doorbell rang.

Anderson looked up. "The police are here."

One case that involved several recognitions is the case of Nazih Al-Danaf in Lebanon. At a very early age, Nazih described a past life to his parents and his seven siblings, all of whom were available for interviews. Nazih described the life of a man that his family did not know. He said that the man carried pistols and grenades, that he had a pretty wife and young children, that he had a two-story house with trees around it and a cave nearby, that he had a mute friend, and that he had been shot by a group of men.

His father reported that Nazih demanded that his parents take him to his previous house in a small town ten miles away. They took him to that town, along with two of his sisters and a brother, when he was six years old. About a half mile from the town, Nazih asked them to stop at a dirt road running off the main road. He told them that the road came to a dead end where there was a cave, but they drove on without confirming this. When they got to the center of town, six roads converged, and Nazih's father asked him which way to go. Nazih pointed to one of the roads and said to go on it until they came to a road that forked off upward, where they would see his house. When they got to the first fork that went up, the family got out and began asking about anyone who had died in the way that Nazih had described.

They quickly discovered that a man named Fuad, who had a house on that road before dying ten years prior to Nazih's birth, seemed to fit Nazih's statements. Fuad's widow asked Nazih, "Who built the foundation of this gate at the entrance of the house?" and Nazih correctly answered, "A man from the Faraj family." The group then went into the house, where Nazih correctly described how Fuad had kept his weapons in a cupboard. The widow asked him if she had had an accident at their previous home, and Nazih gave accurate details of her accident. She also asked if he remembered what had made their young daughter seriously ill, and Nazih correctly responded that she had accidentally taken some of her father's pills. He also accurately described a couple of other incidents from the previous personality's life. The widow and her five children were all very impressed with the knowledge that Nazih demonstrated, and they were all convinced that he was the rebirth of Fuad.

Soon after that meeting, Nazih visited Fuad's brother, Sheikh Adeeb. When Nazih saw him, he ran up saying, "Here comes my brother Adeeb." Sheikh Adeeb asked Nazih for proof that he was his brother, and Nazih said, "I gave you a Checki 16." A Checki 16 is a type of pistol from Czechoslovakia that is not common in Lebanon, and Fuad had indeed given his brother one. Sheik Adeeb then asked Nazih where his original house was, and Nazih led him down the road until he said correctly, "This is the house of my father and this [the next house] is my first house." They went in the latter house, where Fuad's first wife still lived, and when Sheikh Adeeb later asked who she was, Nazih correctly gave her name.

JIM B. TUCKER, M.D., *LIFE BEFORE LIFE*

TWENTY-EIGHT

Paul Clifford woke up slowly and took stock of himself. Another day and he was intact — more or less. Maybe his nose was broken; it was sore as hell and he could feel dried blood itching like crazy on his upper lip. Probably not, though. He'd always been lucky that way. He'd get into some kinda deeply fucked-up mess and black out and then he'd wake up and find himself still alive on this shithole of a planet. A disappointing development, as his old AA sponsor had said to him once, when he called him in the middle of a particularly epic binge. Today he was lying facedown on concrete, not dirt or carpet. That meant he was in his mother's basement.

There was an ache near his balls and he realized it was a Ping-Pong paddle. He must have tripped against the table and fallen the night before and lay where he fell. His lip, too, felt funny, swollen; he moved his tongue around his mouth. It tasted like blood and dirt and bad breath and throw-up. There was a bit of vomit stuck to his hair, though he couldn't see how he'd had anything to vomit. He hadn't eaten anything solid in days.

He lifted his head. It was killing him, of course. He set it down gently on the cool concrete. It felt nice, like a pillow. Maybe he'd stay there a while. He couldn't remember what happened and who he'd fought with, but he had a feeling that it was well after noon and he'd royally screwed up again. No way Mr. Kim would take him back at the gas station now. That meant Jimmy would probably kick him out. He was behind on rent, though paying rent for somebody's couch never had sat right with him, anyway. He was getting ripped off, anyway, right? So who cares?

The job at the gas station wasn't too bad, though; the people coming and going kept his mind busy. When he was working his mom got on his case less about getting his GED or going back to AA. He'd tried to tell his mom he wasn't going back there, but she didn't understand and he couldn't explain it. She kept asking him, "Why?"

"Questions like that, that's why," he'd say.

At AA it was the same old business. They

368

wanted you to tell them a "story." Your "story." They wanted to get it out of you, your bad childhood, or whatever, and they never listened when he said he didn't have a story to tell. His dad was an asshole, and when Paul was fifteen he had divorced his mom and married the co-worker he was fucking, but lots of dads did shit like that. What difference did it make why he turned out this way? He was here now, wasn't he? But it wasn't enough for them. They wanted your blood, is what they wanted. This one counselor last time would not shut up about it. She kept looking at him and looking at him like she knew he was lying. His brain started to get that whirling feeling like it was a roulette wheel going around that might stop at any moment on the wrong number. And he had to leave that room right away. He left by the back door and walked straight to the grocery store and bought a beer. Just one beer. Happy now, bitch? he thought as he gulped it down. He went home to his mom's basement with that taste on his lips and in his mind like the smell of a girl he couldn't forget and then in the middle of the night he'd raided the house of all her brandy and NyQuil and elderberry wine and whatnot and for the next day or so he didn't think about anything and then she kicked him out.

He could hear his mom and brother moving around upstairs, doing whatever the hell they did all day. From down in the basement, he could smell the hot dogs she was cooking. He was hungover but he was also starving, so he was nauseated and hungry at the same time, something you might not have thought possible except he felt that way all the time. He would kill for a hot dog right now or even a peanut butter sandwich, but he didn't want to risk going up there because his mom would take one look at him and know what's what. She wasn't an idiot, even if she still let him sleep in the basement sometimes.

He lay there until he heard his mom and Aaron finish eating their lunch and the screen door slam when they went out. Maybe Aaron had a wrestling meet at school.

After they left he couldn't find the energy to get up for a long time and he lay on the floor of that basement where he'd spent so many hours as a little kid playing air hockey and Ping-Pong and video games. He thought about how hungry he was and how far into the shit he'd sunk.

Then his mind started to get that nervous feeling again, like he was going to blow up, and he felt around on the floor to see if there was anything there and came across a vodka bottle he must've bought the night before. There was a lick of it left but it wasn't enough.

He forced himself up the stairs to find some food. Maybe there was a bottle of Amaretto or something tucked away that he hadn't come across yet, though he seriously doubted it, after that last time.

Someone was outside; he could hear the crunching on the gravel. Maybe it was a guy delivering pizza who got the wrong address. He could eat a whole pizza right now, even if it had mushrooms on it. He'd find the cash somewhere. There had to be some change in the couch cushions or something. He flung open the door.

There was a boy standing there.

A little kid, yellow haired. He was standing in the driveway, staring at the house. The boy had a lizard on his shoulder. It was a pretty weird sight. He knew all the kids on the block and this boy wasn't one of them.

"Hey," Paul said.

The boy looked really nervous. Maybe some of the other kids had dared him to come by. All the moms on the block told the little kids not to talk to him; he could

tell by the way they looked scared sometimes when he said, "Hi." It hurt his head
to think of it. He wanted the boy to leave.

"Can I help you with something?"

He just stood there. He didn't say anything. He was a weird boy. Maybe there was
something wrong with him. Like he was a
mongoloid or something. What did they call
them now? Down's syndrome. He had a
friend who had a sister with it and she
stared at him sometimes, too, and didn't
mean anything by it. This boy had regular
eyes though, really big blue ones that were
looking at him like he stole his lollipop or
something.

Paul smiled. Tried to be nice. It was just a
little boy. He wasn't a complete asshole,
despite what everyone thought. "You need
something?"

"You don't know me?" the boy said. He
looked disappointed.

Somehow Paul had already said the wrong
thing. He felt a wave of exhaustion come
over him. It was too hard, sometimes, trying to be nice to people.

"I don't know any little kids."

"My brother's name is Charlie."

"Okay." Something occurred to him. "Are
you lost? You want to come inside and call
your mom or something?"

"No! No!" The boy started shrieking. "Leave me alone!"

"Okay, then. Okay. I got to, um, get going, then. Good luck getting home." If the boy was going to be a freak about it he wasn't going to get involved. He probably should call the police about the boy. Maybe one of the neighbors would, though. He started to shut the door.

"Wait —"

He turned around. "What?"

The boy's mouth was all twisted up. "Why'd you do that to me?"

"Do what?"

His eyes looked like they were going to pop out of his head. "Why'd you hurt me?"

Paul started to sweat. His sweat smelled like alcohol and made him thirsty for it. "I never met you before. How could I hurt you?"

"You hurt me bad, Pauly."

How the hell did the kid know that name? Nobody had called him Pauly in years. "I don't know what you're talking about."

"I was going to Oscar's and you stopped me. You were being nice and then you hurt me."

He started to shake. Maybe it was the dt's. How was that possible, though? "I don't know what you mean. I never met you

373

before. I never hurt you."

"Yeah, you did. With the gun."

He stood there. He couldn't believe it. "What'd you say?"

"Why'd you do it? I never did anything bad to you."

He was going nuts. That's what it was. It was like that scary shit he'd read in high school before he dropped out, the heart tick-ticking through the floorboards 'til you lost your fucking mind. The boy wasn't even here. Yet he saw him there, scuffling at the dirt, hands balled into fists, looking scared and furious all at the same time. Little yellow-haired kid. Nothing like that boy that was dead. Was somebody tricking him? But who could know?

"You never even let me try it," the boy said. "You said you would."

"How do you know about that? Nobody knows about that," he said. More likely he was still drunk. Maybe that was it. He didn't feel drunk at all, though.

The boy stood there with his fists, his whole body trembling. "Why'd you do it, though, Pauly? I don't know why."

He felt that feeling again in his mind, it was whirling and whirling like a goddamn roulette wheel, only this time there was no stopping it, this time it landed where it had been heading all along.

TWENTY-NINE

Janie drove on, wrapped in a world divided, a world of Noah and Not-Noah. The streetlights turning on one by one, the slight jolt of cracked asphalt beneath her wheels, the split-level houses with their basketball nets, their green lawns shading to gray in the falling dark, the night air itself, cooling rapidly, humming with evening: all of this was Not-Noah, and, therefore, useless.

The world was three feet tall, pale skinned, fair haired, its veins pulsing with life.

That's all her eyes would see. All they would recognize. She could see, but not register, the shapes in this Noahless world.

Her brain, though; her brain —

Her fault. That's what she couldn't stop herself from thinking. So many mistakes, so many places she could have gotten off this path, so many simple things she could have done. She could have not called Anderson. She could have decided that this trip was indeed a bad idea. She could have stayed with Noah in the kitchen while he was watching a video. She could have checked on him. She should have checked. Why hadn't she? He was only four.

Her fault.

She had thought that coming here might help him, when in fact she should have run hard and fast in the opposite direction. Remembering was not the answer. Forgetting was the answer. No other lives, no other worlds. Just this one, right here, this inexplicable, cracked-asphalt-filled life, with Noah in it. That's all she was asking for. That's all she wanted. She had made a mistake, though, and maybe lost him — for good?

No. Of course not. She'd see him any minute.

But it was getting darker now. Her child was wandering in it somewhere, lost and alone. Soon the darkness would swallow his red jacket, his bright blond hair. How would she find him then?

She rolled open the window and the night air filled the car with all its Noahless freshness and density: "NO-AH!"

Her eyes swept the landscape, finding nothing.

Anderson stumbled down the road away

from the Crawford house, the flashlight in his hand sending its futile trickle against the broad, smirking face of the early evening. Dusk was falling, and Noah was out in it somewhere, and the necessity of making it all right pulsed through him, pumping his body full of the harsh, spiking energy bequeathed by the hormones secreted by the adrenal medulla: adrenaline, increasing his heart rate, pulse rate, and blood pressure, raising the blood levels of his glucose and lipids, and sending his brain ricocheting from the wall of the present back, ten, twenty, thirty years.

Preeta Kapoor.

The same river, twice.

Who was he to play with lives, past and present, as if he were a god? When people are not meant to remember. That's why most of us don't. People are meant to forget. Lethe: the river of forgetfulness. Only some lost souls had forgotten to drink from its healing waters — forgotten to forget.

And here he was, walking these suburban streets that were more alien to him than any of the Indian villages ever were, loosing a lost child's name into the evening sky, tearing it out of his chest. His last child.

Noah, blond and buoyant, bouncing on the tips of his toes.

Walking and calling, a mouth, a pair of eyes; that's all he was good for anymore. Lethe rising up around him until soon he'd forget everything, even the names of the lost.

THIRTY

He had to get out of there.

Paul ran into the house. He could still hear the boy calling and crying outside.

He blew out the back door, straight through the yard, through the gap in the fence and out, running flat and hard across the field to the woods. When he passed the old well he gave it a wide berth, as if the bones inside might jump out and bat him around the face, that's how crazy the movie was that was playing in his head, only it wasn't a movie and it wasn't in his head. He tore through the woods, his gait unsteady, feet slipping wildly on the pine needles but propelling him forward, onward, as if he could outrun June 14 once and for all when he knew he would never get away, it would always be there, that boy still standing there back in the yard saying,

"Why'd you hurt me, Pauly?"

"Why'd you hurt me, Pauly?"

"Why'd you do it?"

And his own heart charging back *I don't know I don't know I don't know.*

THIRTY-ONE

He was sitting on the edge of her bed. His smooth, glowing skin. His radioactive smile.

Hi, Mama.

Denise opened her eyes.

It was dusk. She was alone in the room. Tommy wasn't there. She had heard his voice in a dream.

The word still buzzing in her ears. *Mama.*

The room was dark. Voices not far away, pinpoints of light rolling through the fields.

Tommy!

She sat up quickly, dizzily. Her mouth was coated with a bitter medicine taste and her eyes hurt when she blinked. She opened her hand and saw the pills in it. Through the window she could see the flashing of police lights in the fields and the woods beyond. She hiked the window open for some fresh air. People on the front step were talking. Fragments of conversations pierced her ears.

"— we've got a dozen men in the woods

now, Lieutenant —"

"Four years old, answers to Noah —"

She lay back down. All of it flooding back to her, swamping her mind: those people in her house, their words worming into her ears, talking about the hereafter.

That same old song. She'd heard it before, albeit with a different set of answers. She'd been born hearing it.

Seeing now the tent — that big tent in Oklahoma she hadn't thought of in thirty-odd years. Sitting with her granddaddy whom everyone thought had gone 'round the bend. Her mother said they were all a pack of snake charmers, but she didn't care, she was interested in seeing snake charmers and she'd wanted to go wherever her grand-daddy went. The tent was big and high like a circus. It was filled to the edges with more people than she'd ever seen at one time in her whole life, rows and rows of them. The minister stood in front and talked so loud the whole tent could hear him. He was a tall, thin man with very dark brown skin and he seemed angry to Denise, but the people didn't seem to mind much. Some of them sat still and listened to the minister and some of them laughed and sighed and called out.

She was sitting on the lap of her granddaddy, who loved her more than anyone.
She didn't know how she knew this, but she
knew. He had his big hand on her head and
every now and then he tugged on one of
her braids, as if to say hello.

She remembered that there were some
hymns that were pretty and then the minister started talking. He talked in that voice
people used when they quoted Scripture.

And the Israelites were weary from their
    journey, their hope waning in the desert.
And they spoke against God, they said:
    Can God set a table in the wilderness?
And God rained down on them manna to
    eat and gave them the grain of
    heaven. . . .

She remembered that she giggled, she
thought it was funny, the idea of setting up
a table in the middle of the woods. She
leaned back against her granddaddy's chest
with his hand on her head and his smell
of soap and grass and manure and she
dozed off right there in that din. Then the
minister's deep voice started yelling out,
"Who wants to enter the Kingdom of
Heaven? Who is here to testify? Who is here
to be healed by His power? Make your

presence known."

She opened her eyes and people were walking up the aisle. *Walking* is the wrong word. They were shuffling or hobbling or wheeling was more like it. There were people in wheelchairs and people holding children older than she was who couldn't walk by themselves. They came up to the front and they said their names and all of them were related to each other. I'm Sister Green. I'm Brother Morgan. Like that. One after the other. And all of them were sick. They were all part of the same sick family, with toothaches and stomach cancer and gout and clubfoot and blindness and palsy. She'd never seen so many different varieties of pain.

Maybe some of them had been healed that day, but she didn't think so. She didn't remember if they had. All she remembered was being shocked that the world had so much pain in it, and the unfairness that one family should take on so much of the suffering.

And her granddaddy was dead now. He'd gone to Tulsa to buy some tractor equipment and collapsed on the sidewalk with a heart attack, and since no one thought it strange to see a black man lying there or stopped to take him to the hospital, he died on the sidewalk under the hot sun. And her grandma died a few years later, from grief. And her mother a few years ago, from diabetes. And now Tommy, too, was dead.

And now it was her turn.

"I'm sorry —"

That was Charlie's voice. Faint, troubled, carried on the wind; she'd know her own child's voice anywhere.

Charlie was out there, somewhere, in trouble. Thinking it was his fault.

No, no, Charlie. Not your fault. My fault.

I should have checked on him sooner. I should have called the police. I was enjoying the quiet. I should have checked on him sooner and then I could have called the police because time was of the essence. Who didn't know that? When a child was missing you needed to get on it right away, that was rule number one, the golden rule of the Amber Alert Bible. You called the police. Right away.

But she didn't know he was missing and so it had been hours and hours by the time she had called.

Not your fault, Charlie.

She had to tell him. She had to tell him not to be sorry, that he had nothing to be sorry about.

I should have been a better mother to

Tommy. And to you. To you.

All this time he'd been waiting for her, her Charlie. Years had gone by, and she'd left him alone, she'd lost track of him, and yet there he was, still waiting for her somewhere, waiting for her to say: not your fault, baby. My fault. All mine.

Can God set a table in the wilderness?

She opened her palm and looked at the twelve half-crumbled pills that had been clenched so tightly in her fist. She considered them for a moment, and then she ran into the bathroom. Threw all the pills into the sink, sending the water rushing down over them, pushing the white residue down the drain with her fingers. She washed her hands well and dried them. She straightened herself in the mirror, smoothing down her hair, wiping her face with a wet towel. Nothing to do for those eyes.

Then she walked down the stairs and out into the night to find the place where Charlie was.

THIRTY-TWO

The lizard was gone. That's what Charlie had noticed first. Someone had taken Horntail from the tank in his room.

His high had faded now but for a jittery feeling that nothing was right and nothing would ever be right again. It was a familiar feeling. The feeling of not being stoned.

He was looking for the kid and he saw Horntail missing and then he knew. He just fucking knew where the kid was.

He slammed out the back door, through the yard, beyond the birdbath, until he reached the very edge of the woods. There was an old oak tree there that had wooden pegs pounded deep into its bark, and at the top of the pegs there were some planks of wood that his father had nailed together one day in an attempt to make a tree house. The tree house had never been completed — building the thing was more complicated structurally than his father had counted on.

He had sworn up and down about stability and bracing and never finished it, and their mother had forbidden them to go up there, since it was only a floor and nothing else, without any sort of railing or walls to keep them from tumbling down. But he and Tommy snuck up there anyway, sometimes, when they didn't want to be found. It was high up and in the summer you couldn't see it through the leaves.

They used to call it their fort. They kept stuff up there — the diary Tommy wrote in for a few months, Charlie's rock collection, gun and car magazines they had stolen from the dentist's office. Sometimes Tommy liked to take Horntail there and let him run around like it was the jungle. Until last year Charlie used to go up to get high.

Now he had to push his big body through the hole.

The kid sat there on the planks of wood in the dark with his hands around his knees, Horntail lolling on his arm. The kid was a mess. His eyes and nose were running up a storm.

Charlie squatted down next to him. "They're all looking for you, you know."

"Our room is different."

"What?"

"Our room. The stuff is gone."

"What stuff?"

"The lizard books. My glove and my bats and my championship trophy."

"Oh, you mean Tommy's stuff. Well, we had it there for a while."

He was afraid to look him in the eye. Did the kid have some kind of power like a weird kid in a movie? Maybe he saw dead people. Maybe the ghost of Tommy liked to hang around him. He didn't much care which it was; it was all spooky and he wanted no part of it. He wanted to get this kid down into the house and out of his life.

"How come you took my stuff away?"

"I didn't. Papa made Mama do it. He said it wasn't good for me once I came back here."

His face brightened. "You came back, too?"

"Well, I was staying at my grandma's, you know, for the first six months or so. While Mama and Daddy were out looking for — for Tommy."

Those long months at his grandma's. He hadn't thought of them in years. Kneeling on the shag carpet, Grandma's gospel music playing on her old record player, wondering what was happening back home, if they'd found his brother yet. They never talked about that. "If anything happens we'll be the first to know," she'd said, "so let's leave those folks alone to do what they have to do. All we can do is pray that he'll come home." She was bad off already by then, her feet swollen so much she could barely get down out of the armchair to kneel. He couldn't pray, though. He was too scared.

"Who took care of Horntail?" the kid said.

"I took him with me to Grandma's," he said, and started to laugh. "I let him loose on her carpet one time just to freak her out. She didn't like that one bit."

"Nah, she hates lizards."

"Yeah."

"And snakes."

"Yeah."

He looked down through the branches. He could see the lights from the police flashlights moving through the fields and the woods. They were looking for the kid, but the kid was floating high up above all that, the kid was somewhere else entirely.

"I'm sorry I broke your sub," the kid said.

"My sub?"

"Your submarine that Papa gave you."

"Oh."

The last time he'd seen Tommy. That last day. They'd had a big fight. His dad had come back from a long tour and he'd brought Charlie a shiny new submarine and

Tommy had gotten only a book and, boy, was he mad. Tommy wanted to play with his sub, just one turn, he kept saying, but Charlie never had anything Tommy wanted, it was always the other way around, and he loved his shiny new sub that Tommy wanted and he said, "No way." He said, "Get your own stinkin' sub."

"Just one turn," Tommy had said.

"No," Charlie said. "It's mine and you can't even touch it." And Tommy had grabbed it out of his hands, right then, breaking the periscope in two.

"Anyway, I'm sorry about it," the kid was saying now.

"That's okay. It was my fault. I should have let you try it," Charlie said. It occurred to him that he was talking to the kid as if he were Tommy. That was followed by another thought (the thoughts were hitting him like blows, one after the other, making him see stars) that only he and Tommy knew that Tommy had broken the periscope. He had meant to get his brother in trouble for it but he had disappeared before Charlie had the chance. He looked out in the dark through the rustling branches and felt overcome with vertigo; he sat himself down on his bottom and pushed his long legs out across the floating floor. Look: here was his body, his legs covered with goose bumps, his shiny shorts, his high-tops.

"I broke it 'cause I was mad. It was so nice," the kid said. "I never had a sub like that."

"That's okay."

Charlie was sitting there with his mouth open. It occurred to him he ought to close it. "You're him, aren't you?" he said, wondering at the words as they came out of his own mouth. "How can you be him?"

"I don't know how," the kid said.

They were silent. The kid ran his palm over the spikes on the lizard's back.

"Thanks for watching Horntail."

"It's nothing," Charlie said. He was proud of himself, all of a sudden, for keeping Tommy's lizard alive all these years. He felt his whole body flush with pride, like when he was a kid and he'd thrown a good pitch and Tommy had said, "Good pitch, Charlie!"

The kid stroked the lizard up and down his sides, Horntail looking back at him with its yellow eyes. He wondered if it had missed Tommy and recognized him now or if it was just another day for the lizard.

"I'm sorry about what happened to you," Charlie said finally.

"You didn't do it."

"I maybe coulda stopped it though."

"Nah, Charlie. You were a little kid."

Charlie gulped. His chest hurt. He could feel the words burning up through his throat and then he said them. "Mama told me to tell you to come home for lunch. To come home from Oscar's. She told me to tell you that. But I was mad at you for breaking my sub and I didn't want to talk to you and I didn't do it. And maybe if I had said that you would have come home early — maybe then —"

"Nah, Charlie. Anyway, I was dead already."

"You were?" Charlie said.

"Yeah. I was dead pretty fast."

"What happened?" Charlie said. He'd been waiting years to know. The kid didn't answer. His nose started running again. The lizard ambled down his arm to the floor, so Charlie picked him up and held the cool, breathing body in his hand. After a while he heard a rustling sound down below. Someone else was down there, breathing. The person didn't say anything.

"I saw him," the kid said at last.

"Who?

"Pauly."

"Pauly?"

"Pauly. Down the street?"

"You mean Paul Clifford?"

He nodded.

"He's the one . . . that killed me."

"Paul Clifford? Pauly down the street? He's the one who — he killed you?"

He nodded.

"Fuck. *Paul Clifford?* What'd he do?"

"I don't know. It happened so fast."

The kid took a deep breath.

"I was on my bike riding to Oscar's and I saw Aaron's brother Pauly was there. He said — he said he had this rifle and did I want to take a shot with it, it would only take a minute. So I said okay 'cause he said just a minute and you know Mama never let us touch guns."

"Yeah."

"So we went to the woods to do some shooting and he shot all these bottles and he wouldn't give me a turn at all. So I asked him if I could have a turn and then he shot me."

"He shot you? Because you wanted a turn?"

"I don't know why. I don't know. I was standing there and then I can't see anymore, it's all black. And when I wake up I'm falling."

"You're falling?"

"My whole body is falling and it's a long

way down, and the water's cold. It's real cold in there, Charlie, the water's way up over my head and cold and bad smelling. I try to keep my head up over the water and I yell and yell, but he doesn't get me out, Charlie, he won't let me out, and so I yell and yell and it hurts every time in my body, my body really hurts, but I keep on yelling and no one is coming and no one comes and I'm all alone in there, I'm all alone, and I can't do it. I try, Charlie, I try real hard, but I can't keep my head up anymore. It's cold under there and I can't breathe. I can see the sun shining down through the water, it's shining down really hard making the metal pail bright. It's really shiny. I can see it shining right through the water. And then I died."

"Man. Oh, man. Oh, man." He couldn't say anything else but that. He saw his brother Tommy drowning. They were all of them down there, Tommy and himself and their mama and his papa, too, all of them down there, drowning in the cold water.

"Fuck. Paul Clifford. Why'd he do a thing like that?"

"I don't know. I tried to ask him why'd he do that to me, but he wouldn't tell me. He ran away."

The kid didn't say anything else for a

minute. His nose was running down into his mouth and he wiped it on his sleeve. He mumbled something in a low voice.

"What?"

"She don't want me, Charlie."

"Who?"

"Mama. She don't want to see me. She forgot all about me. And I been trying to get back here since the day I was born."

He didn't know what to say. He put a hand on the kid's back and rubbed it in little circles. The kid's back was moving back and forth as he took big gulps of air. That's all right, Charlie thought. You go on breathing. You just breathe now. Breathe for all of us. You got some catching up to do on that score.

All his feelings for Tommy had been locked up in a room somewhere and now the door was open and they were running amok.

He looked at the kid. Little snot-nosed white kid who was and wasn't his brother. He couldn't take it in. He didn't even try.

THIRTY-THREE

"Tommy?"

Denise stood beneath the tree and heard the name come out of her own lips. It felt strange on her tongue and sounded strange to her ears, as if she was just trying it out, as if she'd never said that name before in her whole life.

She had stood there listening and felt her mind spinning in the dark and she wasn't grabbing hold of anything; there was nothing to grasp onto except those two voices that sounded just like her own two boys talking in that rickety pile of lumber they used to hide out in. Her own two boys, she'd know them anywhere, only it wasn't. She had heard and she hadn't. There was a thing she had to do but she didn't know what it was and she didn't know what was real anymore and then she heard a voice that was her own voice speaking the name.

"Tommy?"

She didn't want to look. She didn't want to see. It wasn't Tommy up there. She knew it wasn't Tommy. She heard and didn't hear. Tommy was dead and this was another boy.

But she grabbed hold anyway of the wooden steps nailed into the tree trunk and she climbed her way up through the hole, scraped her long body through.

The boy didn't look like her son. He was a small white child, his hair golden even at nighttime like a picture in a JCPenney catalog. Not like her sweet boy with his light brown skin that seemed lit from within and his grin that split your heart in two. Nothing like her boy that was lost.

This was a different child sitting there with Charlie's hand on his back.

The child looked up at her. He was all scratched up, his cheeks smeared with dirt and blood and tears, as if he'd crawled right up from the bowels of hell itself.

"Oh, baby." She held out her arms to him and he scrambled over and threw himself at her, pressing his small body against hers so tightly it made her draw in her breath and lean back against the bark, so real and rough and hard against her spine.

She didn't know if it was Tommy in there somewhere. She didn't know how it could be. She thought that probably in her confu-

sion she was making an honest mistake by
wishing so hard that it was so. But she had
known him by the look in his eyes that
matched the look in her own eyes; he was
one of the lost, one of her own.

THIRTY-FOUR

Paul woke up. It was dark. He felt cleaned out. Clean. He must've passed out. He lay flat on the pine needles, looking through the trees at the night sky. A clear night. He could see stars looking back at him. There were so many. He always liked the stars. They weren't coming down on him or judging him. They were just looking. None of it matters, that's what the stars said. Whatever it is, it doesn't matter.

He didn't want to move. If he moved his eyes from the sky, he didn't know what would happen to him.

Men were coming. He could hear them rustling. He could sense the flashlights invading the dark. They were moving through the woods. It was like a movie, only in the movie there'd be dogs. He'd be running in the movie, breathing hard. But he wasn't. He was lying calmly, facing the sky.

"What's that?"

"I thought I saw something!" He heard the real voices and the high, toy voices crackling from their walkie-talkies.

"Something's here!"

Not something. He thought. Someone.

He thought he should run. He should be running. The boy had known somehow and he had told them and they had come for him. But he felt his body settling in deeper into the pine needles and the dirt.

He was remembering that day, now. June 14. He realized he had never really left it, he had always been there, in that day, hearing the boy crying out from the bottom of the well.

It had started with the cat.

He had been aware of the cat for at least a couple of months, its skinny body and black and white spots as much a part of the scenery as the shit-brown grass or the cornfield behind it or the gray fence that separated their property from the Mc-Clures' and that the cat walked across every day. He watched it without thinking while he got ready for school, the way it walked down their fence one foot carefully after the other like it had a master plan it was following step by step, and he'd envied that mangy cat, that it could go wherever it wanted to go.

Then one day he was standing outside throwing a tennis ball against the shed and the cat was walking by on the fence and it looked at him. He felt it through his whole body, the cat looking right at him. Nobody looked at him like that lately. Not right in the eyes like that. The invisible man, that's what he felt like sometimes. The high school was three times as big as his middle school had been and nobody paid much attention to freshmen anyway and he had no friends there since they had sold their good house and moved across town to this crappy rental. All his friends were at the other high school. He wasn't picked on, but he found himself alone in the afternoons more often than not, doing his homework and playing his video games and throwing the ball over and over against the shed.

The next day he went out there to throw the ball again and the cat was there on the fence, and he brought it a bowl of milk and the cat came right over and lapped it up.

So he did it the next day and then the day after that, until the cat showed up when it saw him coming through the back door, like the cat was his. One time he was standing there and it rubbed right by him. He could

403

feel its body pressing against his leg. Its coat was matted and he was nervous about touching it. It might have fleas or something. It was making a little noise. Purring. The feeling went right up his calf through his whole body. It made his whole body hum.

Then that Saturday he woke up late and saw the cat out there and when he poured the milk in the bowl he heard a shout.

"What are you doing?"

He glanced up and saw his dad looking right at him. He was sitting there in the living room, one shoe in his hand, his face red.

Paul was so startled his hand shook and the milk spilled over the side of the bowl and spread across the table, falling off the wood, making a pond on the linoleum.

"I said, what are you doing?"

He looked up. It was the usual scene. His mom was reading on the sofa, his little brother arranging his baseball cards on the floor in front of the TV set, his dad watching the news from his chair — only he wasn't looking at the news. He was still looking at him.

It was like being in the dark and someone turns on the lights too bright. He watched the milk puddle grow on the floor.

"Cleaning up," he said.

He got a kitchen cloth and mopped it all up. He hoped his dad would leave him alone again. Paul licked his lips. His dad was still staring at him.

"You're drinking milk from a bowl now?"

"No."

"So why are you doing that?"

He looked at his dad's bare feet, resting on the ottoman. The ugliest feet he'd ever seen, the toes were all swollen from arthritis and having to stand every day in his good shoes. In the old days he used to make coffee for his mom and then leave in the morning whistling while they were eating breakfast, and he'd sleep in on the weekends and maybe watch a game on TV, but these days on Saturdays he was up before the rest of them with his feet up on the ottoman, shining his shoes. Now his dad's eyes were squinting out at him, two red slits in his heavy gray face, as if it was Paul's fault that his life had worked out this way and he had to stand there all day trying to sell stereos to people who only wanted speakers for their iPods.

"For the cat."

"We don't have a cat," his dad said.

"There's a cat out there."

His dad sat up now in the chair.

"You think it's your cat? That cat's got

nothing to do with you. That's not your cat. You think I'm gonna feed you and a cat, too? You can go get a job and pay for the milk yourself. Then you can get a goddamn cat."

"He's in school," his mom said from behind her book on the couch. "That's his job."

"Well, he ought to do better then."

"He's doing fine."

He could feel his dad starting up again. He looked at the wall. Lately it didn't take much to start him up. "How is a C in gym fine? How do you even get a C, if you show up, unless you're a total wuss?"

His mom glanced up, as if she was annoyed at having to interrupt her reading. She was always reading these true-crime books with terrible photos in the inserts. "It's only freshman year. Give him a break, Terrance. He's not like you."

His dad had been a wrestling champion when he was in high school. They had kept the trophies on a shelf in the old house. He didn't know where they were now, though. His mom had thrown most of that stuff out.

His father swiped at his shoe with the polish. "I'll say. He's a fucking disappointment."

Paul didn't say anything. At first he had

thought his dad was talking about the guy on the TV, some senator talking to the newscaster, but then he realized his dad was talking about him.

"Terrance . . . ," his mother said, but she said it really weakly. It was like that one word used up all her energy. She didn't have much to begin with. When she was home from working nights at Denny's she liked to do a lot of nothing.

His dad snorted. "Like we have money for a cat." He looked back over at the news.

Paul finished cleaning up the kitchen and went into his room and shut the door. He turned on his PlayStation and hunted down the peasants one by one, obliterated them with his tongues of fire.

After a while he reached the next level and still felt that jumpy feeling inside him. When he went outside his room they were all gone. His dad had gone to work and his mother must have taken Aaron out to a playground or something. He stood still for a moment, breathing in the empty house. He turned the TV on, looking for a baseball game or something to focus his mind, but there was nothing. He opened the fridge, but there were none of the yogurts he liked in there. He kept telling her to get them and she kept buying the other kind. There was no soda either.

"We've got to tighten our belts now," she'd said.

Fucking disappointment.

He drank one of his dad's beers. He thought maybe it'd make him happy and relaxed like it did sometimes for his dad, but instead it made him feel queasy and light-headed. He ambled into his parents' bedroom. He opened some drawers and looked at his mom's underwear and then he closed them fast. He squatted by the bed and pulled out the rifles from underneath. His dad kept them in their original boxes. They weren't supposed to touch them, but he liked to look at them sometimes when he was alone. When he was younger his dad used to take him out in the woods for target practice. "Nice one, Pauly!" he'd say when he hit a can, and he'd reach out and ruffle his hair. He'd do stuff like that with him all the time when he was a little kid.

His dad used to hunt, but he'd heard his mom say once that his dad was too hung-over these days to shoot anything.

Paul took the lids carefully off the boxes and he reached out and stroked the metal. They were beautiful.

He pulled one of them out of its box. He

408

wanted to feel it again in his hands, to remember what it felt like to hold that kind of power. He thought it would feel good to fire it. It might relieve all the pressure in his head and the weird beery feeling in his stomach. To shoot at the target on a tree and imagine his father's face. *Fucking disappointment.* When he had tried so hard in his new school and gotten mostly Bs and even an A in biology. He picked some bullets from the box under the bed and he tucked the rifle under his shirt and he headed out the back door.

He passed through the hole in the fence and into the cornfields. There was an old dirt road that snaked through them and eventually skirted the woods. It was a fine spring day and it felt good to walk along the road with the corn rising on either side of him, feeling the rifle against his stomach. His whole body began to tingle with excitement. He was thinking how it was a damn shame none of his friends was around to see him holding the rifle when he heard a squeak of wheels on dirt and saw a boy wobbling fast toward him on his Schwinn, his hands raised a foot above the handlebars, a crazy grin on his face, like he knew his mom would kill him if she saw him riding fast like that with no hands.

The boy slowed up when he saw him and put his hands back on to steer out of his way.

Paul had seen him around the neighborhood and had even played a pickup game of baseball with him once in Lincoln Park. He was Aaron's age but he was all right; he was a really good pitcher, for a nine-year-old. Aaron always talked about how he played up with the twelve-year-olds. He was black, like a lot of the kids around this neighborhood, which made Paul like him better, somehow, though he didn't know why. The boy rode right by him on the bike and nodded at him (why couldn't this kid have been his brother instead of Annoying Aaron?) and he thought, well, why not? It wasn't like showing a friend but it was better than nothing. He was tired of being alone all the time. Tommy was his name.

"Hey! Tommy," he called out.

Tommy had passed him; he put his feet down and looked back at him.

"Wanna see something?"

Tommy wheeled back a bit and looked at him over the handlebars like he thought it might be a trick. "What kind of thing?"

"It's really cool. Come here." Tommy got off the bike and walked over to Paul. "You can't tell Aaron. If you tell Aaron I'll know and you'll be sorry."

"I won't."

This wasn't such a good idea, Paul thought. If he told Aaron, his brother would rat on him for sure and he'd get in big trouble. But Tommy was waiting for him to make good on his promise. What kind of a loser would he be if he backed out now? He'd be the laughingstock of the whole neighborhood.

Paul edged the top of the rifle higher and higher until it poked up over his collar. "Look-ee here."

"Wow. That is cool." Tommy seemed suitably impressed. "That yours?"

He grinned. He liked this boy. He was a damn fine kid. "Yep. Genuine .54-caliber Renegade. I'm doing target practice. Want to take a shot?"

"I don't know." Tommy's face wavered. He grinned and then he grimaced like he couldn't decide. Paul could almost read his mind: my mom wouldn't like it, he was thinking. For some reason this made Paul want him to come even more.

"Come on. Onetime offer. Ends today."

"I'm going to Oscar's."

"Come on. Just for a minute. I won't tell anyone. I'll bet you've never tried it before."

Tommy's face turned up to him with this

weird look, like he wanted Paul to tell him the right thing to do. Like he really wanted to go to his friend's house but he also really wanted to try the gun and he couldn't decide which person to be.

"You're probably a good shot, too, what with your pitching and all."

He knew that would do it and it did. "Well . . . okay. Just one shot." And Tommy set his bike aside by the low wall of corn and they walked together down the road and into the woods.

His dad always used to bring a piece of cardboard with a bull's-eye on it when they went out to target practice, but he hadn't thought to bring that with him. They had gone shooting once at a place in the woods where there was an old well with a bucket swinging from the top and some trash around from when hippies and bikers used to hang out in that part of the woods.

"Hey, Tommy, watch this."

He grabbed a soda bottle and set it up on the well. He picked up the gun and felt its weight in his hands and looked through the viewfinder and without thinking took a shot. The recoil almost knocked him down but aiming it wasn't so different from one of his video games.

"Hey!" Tommy said. "Good one."

He looked on the ground and saw that he had hit the bottle right off that old well. The not thinking part was the part that had done it. Anytime he thought too much about anything he messed it up.

"Yeah. Thanks."

All the video games must have really helped with his hand-eye coordination. His dad was always giving him a hard time about playing them, but if he could see him now he wouldn't call him a wuss at all. Except that he would kill him for handling his gun.

"Can you set one up for me?" he asked Tommy.

"Okay." Tommy ran back out there and set up another bottle on the well. Really nice kid.

He aimed at the bottle and knocked that one over, too. It was amazing. Two for two.

The boy ran back to him breathlessly.

"You're good at this."

Tommy was looking up at him like he had just single-handedly won the marksman championship of the world.

"You think I can do it again?"

Tommy nodded. "Sure you can, Pauly. But can I have a turn next?" The boy was itching to get his hands on the rifle and show what he could do. Paul wondered if the boy would be a better marksman than he was. It was possible. "Just one more," Paul said.

Tommy put another bottle up on the stone well and stood back.

Paul aimed at the bottle and then moved his aim to the old half-rusted bucket glinting above it in the sun. He thought of his dad's face saying "fucking disappointment" as he squeezed the trigger. He heard a sharp ding of metal as the bullet hit and bounced off. Ha!

The bucket was swinging on its rope. Try that, kid, he thought.

"I did it!" He turned to the boy. He was excited. "Three for three," he was saying, but the boy wasn't there. He was lying flat in the dirt.

Tommy didn't move. There was a weird red splash on his back.

Paul looked around him. The forest was completely still. There was nobody there. There weren't even any birds singing. It was a warm, clear day. It was as if nothing had happened. He closed his eyes and wished that he could go back fifteen seconds to before he had aimed at the bucket, but when he opened them the boy was still lying on the ground.

Why couldn't he have aimed at the bottle and not the pail? Nothing would have ricocheted from the bottle. The bottle would have smashed.

He let the current of that thought carry his mind for a period of time he had no sense of (a minute, an hour?) as if by surrendering to it he could remain there, in the past. But the present asserted itself at last in his dry mouth and the heat beating down on his head. There was no taking it back. He was here. Tommy's body was there. His life was ruined. He was probably going to spend the rest of it in prison. There was nothing anymore to look forward to. He couldn't be a veterinarian, or anything at all.

It was unreal. His life was over because of the body lying there. But if the body wasn't there, then his life wouldn't be over, and would go on as before.

He closed his eyes and opened them and closed them again. But every time he opened his eyes the body was still lying there and he could hardly stand to look at it.

How could your whole life end so quickly? One moment it was there before you, not perfect, but yours, and the next it was gone. He put the gun down on the ground. He couldn't wrap his mind around it.

He hadn't meant to kill Tommy, but nobody would believe him. They'd probably think he was a racist 'cause Tommy was black. His dad was going to murder him. He'd strangle him with his bare hands. His mom would never talk to him again.

But what if he could make the body disappear? That boy's life was over. He hadn't meant to kill him, but he was dead now. But why should Paul's life be over, too? He didn't want to lose his life, he realized. It hadn't seemed very good to him an hour ago but right now he wanted it back more than anything.

He picked up Tommy's body and carried it to the well. It was lighter than he'd thought it would be and it was easy to tumble it over into the brackish water. He heard it splash. He looked at the dirt where the boy had been but there was no blood there at all or any sign that anything had happened. He stood there, next to the well, breathing heavily, trying to get his head on straight. It was done, he thought. It was over. It had never happened. He had never met up with the boy. He heard himself breathing and the barking of the dog way down the road and then he heard a splashing noise and something that sounded like a voice.

It was the boy. Tommy. Calling out. He wasn't dead. He was alive, in the well, at least some part of him was. Maybe he was dying in there. Probably he was almost dead. He'd die any second.

The voice was hoarse and feeble, calling out for help from at least twenty feet down. He could hear the splish-splash as he tread water in the well.

Paul couldn't bring himself to look down or to answer. The voice was wrapping itself tightly around his throat. He ran around, looking for a vine or a rope or something to pull him out with but there was nothing, no way to get someone out of something that deep, much less a person who was probably dying of a gunshot wound. He could run for help, but they were half a mile from any houses, and by the time help got there the boy would probably be dead already, and then how would he explain himself? Tommy shot himself and then threw himself down the well? He stood there, trying to figure out what he would say, what he should do, all these thoughts running through him, all the time listening to that voice that felt like it was coming from inside of his own body saying, "Help me, Pauly! Help me! Lemme out! Lemme out! Lemme out!" and then just "Mama! Mama! Mama!" and then, finally — nothing.

It was over. After a long time had passed he peered into the well and saw the same dark green dirty water that had always been there. The sun was still shining. He picked up his father's rifle and the bullets and ran back through the woods and down the road between the cornfields and kept running, past Tommy's bike, until he got to his own house. He put his dad's gun back in its box and slid it under the bed, drank another one of his dad's beers, and watched TV. It's over, he thought.

By night the police were knocking on every door in the neighborhood, and his mother went out with the others looking through the fields and the woods. By the next morning he was seeing Tommy's face grinning at him on every pole and storefront downtown. They drained the swimming pond on the other side of the fields. There was a sighting of Tommy in Kentucky, but it was nothing. They took the computer teacher at the elementary school in for questioning, but he came back to work. Paul waited for them to find Tommy in the well, but nothing happened.

Only nothing wasn't nothing. The nothing

had crawled inside of him like those para-
sites he'd read about in biology class, like
that worm in Africa that crawled into your
toe when you were swimming and before
you knew it had eaten you whole. Every
time he heard Tommy's name or saw his
face, every day at first and then less and less
as the months and years went on, he'd feel
that worm gnawing away at another piece
of him. It rotted his brain so that he couldn't
focus in school anymore. Once when he was
really fucked-up he saw Tommy's face on a
poster and thought it was his own dead face
smiling at him. That's what the nothing was
like.

Until today, when he had heard Tommy's
words coming out of the little white kid.

The people were moving closer now. He
could hear them rustling through the brush.
He should be running. He lay still, listening
to his own steady, easy breaths. Staring up
at all the stars. This must be what it feels
like to lose your mind, he thought, but he
felt clearer than he had been in a long time.
He had wanted to be a good person once,
or at least not a bad one, but then he had
shot Tommy Crawford and he had been so
afraid that he'd let him die in the well. He
hadn't wanted to do it, but he had done it
just the same.

419

The flashlights' beams crossed the dirt and the tree roots and moved up to his face. He blinked into the blinding lights. It was the police. He'd know their flat robot voices anywhere.

He closed his eyes and saw the stars again. All the pressure in his mind was loosening; he breathed it out into the sky. He had held on to the words for so long (*it was me; I did it*) and now he could release them. All he had to do was speak.

THIRTY-FIVE

Janie saw the flashlight first, swooping across the road. When she drew up next to Anderson he looked at her through the car window without recognition, his shirt untucked, his eyes wild. The sight of him shocked her. She hadn't realized he'd cared so much for her son. She opened the door and he blinked and then got in without a word.

"I'm going to check the house again," she said. She would not let herself stop moving, or think.

"Right." He nodded. They drove on to the house in silence.

A detective in a brown suit was standing by a car in the driveway as Janie pulled up. He was pacing with his back to her, yelling on the phone. Janie stepped out of the car and his words flung themselves at her. "We need to drain it right now, goddamn it. I don't care how deep it is, if he says the

421

child's body is in there —"

The phrases echoed in Janie's mind, chopped in pieces. Jumbled.

Drain it —

The child's body —

She felt herself slipping away. This wasn't real. She wouldn't let it be real. She would go far away from wherever it was that this was happening.

"Come into the house." She heard Anderson's voice, but the words didn't mean anything to her.

"Come on."

It was good not to understand words. If you let yourself understand words, then you would feel them and there was no telling what might happen.

Anderson was taking her hand and trying to lead her forward but she had no feeling in her feet. That's what flesh was like in the unreal world. Like shadows. The man next to her was a shadow, and the detective was a shadow, and the figures moving slowly toward her across the yard, two tall shadows, one short, like a child, like —

Noah! Janie's heart exploded. She hurled herself forward.

He was clinging to Denise Crawford's waist and looking up at her. Beautiful, dirty Noah, swirls of snot across his cheeks. Janie was standing right in front of him now, but he didn't move his eyes from the other woman's face.

"Noah?"

He wouldn't look at her. Why wouldn't Noah look at her? How could that be possible? She felt her knees buckling. She was falling, only something was behind her, holding her arms, keeping her up. It was Anderson. She let him hold her up.

"Noah! It's me! It's Mommy!"

Noah turned, then. He took her in quizzically, from very far away, the way a bird deep in the forest might look down at a passing human.

They all watched as he looked, and sought a breath, and couldn't find it.

Breathe, Noah, breathe.

It had never been this bad. Janie held him in her lap in the car, the inhaler pressed against his mouth. Didn't even bother with the car seat.

Blue and red lights flashing through the windshield, leading the way. If Noah was alert right now he would have loved that. His own police escort, complete with siren and flashing lights.

Breathe. His head lolling back against her as if he were an infant. Even through the new worry she felt the relief of having him in her arms again, when she'd thought she might never have another chance. *Breathe.*

"He's going to be okay, right?" the Crawford boy asked.

He'd insisted on coming and was sitting next to her, tapping his fingers on his knees in a frenzy of percussive nervousness. Janie wished his mother would tell him to stop, but Denise seemed oblivious. She was sitting up front in the passenger seat, giving Anderson directions in a dazed voice.

"He'll be fine," Janie said, speaking to herself as much as anybody. "He could use some more powerful albuterol, but he'll get that at the hospital."

"This happened before?" the teenager said.

"Yes. He has asthma."

"Really?"

"Yes, really."

"So it's the asthma?"

"Yes."

"Wow, that's a relief. I thought maybe he was having some kind of flashback about what happened last time and he was, you know . . . drowning all over again."

Janie didn't say anything for a moment. She held on to her baby boy, who was struggling to breathe and had nothing to do with that story or any story. Anderson piped up from the driver's seat, "It doesn't work like that. Though there is sometimes a connection between the mode of death and . . . abnormalities. Sometimes subjects who have asthma had a previous personality who drowned or was somehow asphyxiated."

Shut up, Jerry, Janie thought.

"Good to know," Charlie said at last.

Anderson glanced at him in the rearview mirror. "He talked to you about drowning?"

"Yeah. In the well. He got himself pretty worked up."

"I don't understand." Janie turned on Charlie. "He told you he drowned in a well? Why'd he tell *you* that?"

"Maybe 'cause he thinks I'm his brother?"

She looked at him: a teenager wearing a sleeveless Cleveland Indians T-shirt and shorts, his long, wiry body radiating youth. "Do you believe him?"

"You don't really have any choice, if you listen to him, do you?"

She clung to Noah. He was leaning against her chest, his hand tightly clutching her arm. She could feel each of his breaths scraping itself together inside of him. "I guess not."

"You don't believe him?" Charlie was looking at her.

"No, I do," she said. It was true.

"Oh, you don't want to, though?" He was more perceptive than he seemed.

"I guess — I wanted him to be all mine."

He laughed.

"You think that's funny?"

He had a smile that took up his whole face. Like Noah's smile. Like Tommy's.

"Lady, no offense, but you don't know anything," Charlie said. "He was never all yours."

THIRTY-SIX

Janie thought she'd have that image in her mind forever: Noah lying on the hospital bed, pale but breathing, one hand holding the albuterol mask to his mouth, the other clutching what he had reached for first, which was Denise's hand. Denise was sitting next to him, holding the small hand in her own.

Janie sat in the chair next to Denise. She'd thought about asking to take the other woman's seat by her son, but she couldn't risk upsetting Noah. At one point, Denise had loosened her hand a bit from Noah's and shifted, as if to offer Janie her rightful place by Noah's side, but Noah had grabbed her wrist, his eyes meeting hers over the mask. They regarded each other for a moment like two horses recognizing each other across a field, and then Denise shrugged slightly and settled back again, placing her other hand over his.

After fifteen minutes or so of this, Janie couldn't bear it any longer.

"Noah? I'm going to be right outside. Just for a little while. Right outside that door," she'd said, and the two of them had turned their heads and looked at her as if they hadn't known she was in the room.

Janie didn't want to leave him there like that, but she had to get out. She needed air. She started to back slowly out of the room.

"Mom?"

Janie and Denise both turned to him. He took the mask off.

He looked at Janie. "You coming back?"

Never had she thought that the sudden spark of fear in her own child's eyes would be something she could savor. But everything had been turned on its head this day.

"Of course, sweetie. I'll be back in a minute. I'll be right outside that door."

"Okeydoke." He cast her a sleepy, contented grin. "See you soon, Mommy-Mom."

"Put the mask back on, sweetie."

He settled the mask back on his face with the hand that wasn't holding on tightly to Denise. Then he gave her a thumbs-up.

Janie pulled the curtain and closed the door gently and left her palms there, resting her forehead against the door. One breath, then the next. That was how it was done.

One breath, then the next.

"He's fine, you know."

She turned. A gaunt old man was sitting on a chair in the hallway. It was Anderson. When had he become so frail?

"They'll let him out soon," he added.

"Yes."

She sat down next to him, blinking up at the ceiling, at the small dark bodies of dead bugs trapped on the bottom of the bright bowl of light. One breath, then the next.

"Quite a day," Anderson said.

"I should go back in there. I don't even know that woman."

"Noah does."

Silence.

"Most of them forget with time, you know," Anderson said. "Present life takes over."

"Is it bad to hope for that?"

Anderson's rigid body seemed to soften. He patted her hand. "It's understandable."

When she closed her eyes, the bright oval of light shone inside her lids. She opened them. Her brain was roiling. "That man . . . the one the police have. He's the one who killed Tommy?"

"Possibly."

"Will Noah have to be there? At the trial?"

Anderson shook his head, a wry smile

playing at the corners of his mouth. "A previous personality isn't much of a witness."

"I guess you're right," she said. "I still don't understand how they found him."

"I expect . . . it had to do with Noah."

She would ask later. She would find out later. There was only so much information a body could handle at one time. One breath, then the next. Anderson's back was straight as a rail, his hands in his lap. At attention, still.

"You don't have to wait here, you know," she said. "You can go to the hotel. Take a cab. Get some rest."

"It's all right. We'll rest . . . on the day after today."

"Tomorrow."

"Right. Tomorrow."

The word lingered in the air.

"And tomorrow," he murmured.

"And tomorrow," she said. *"Creeps in this petty pace from day to day."*

He glanced at her, startled. *"To the last syllable of recorded time. And all our yesterdays have lighted fools the way to dusty death."*

"You know your Shakespeare," she said. Perhaps he also had a Shakespeare-quoting mother. She felt all of a sudden as if her mother was in the room with them. Maybe she was. Could people be reborn and also be here, as spirits? But that was a question for another hour.

Anderson smiled ruefully. "Some words I remember."

"Everybody forgets words sometimes." She thought back to the way he seemed to substitute some words for others. The way the GPS had flummoxed him. "But it's not just that, is it?"

He was silent a moment.

"It's degenerative. Aphasia." He smiled dryly. "That word I can't forget."

"Oh." She felt it like the blow it was. "I'm so sorry, Jerry."

"There's more to life than memory. So they tell me."

"There's the present moment."

"Yes."

"Memory can be a curse," she said. She was thinking of herself, of Noah.

"It is what it is."

Silence.

"Maybe I will go, then." He put his hands on his knees, as if willing himself to stand.

"Actually . . . Can you stay a few more minutes?" There was no way to keep the need from leaping out of her voice.

His eyes seemed silver in the bright fluorescent light. "All right."

"Thanks."

"Can I get you something?" he said. "A cup of coffee?"

She shook her head.

"Or if you're hungry, I could go to the — I could —"

"Jerry?"

"Yes?" He looked — what was it he looked? For the first time, with her own desperation finally waning, she saw him as he was: how hard he had worked in his life, and with what courage; how tired he was now, and how deeply he felt he had failed.

"Thank you," she said.

"For what?"

"For . . . what you did for Noah."

He nodded faintly. His eyes shimmered briefly and he closed them. He settled deeper into the chair, stretching his long legs out and to the side, so as not to block traffic in the hallway. She felt the tension flowing out of him, leaving his body and moving out into the air. He leaned his head back against the wall, next to hers, their hair almost but not quite brushing against each other's.

He let out a soft exhalation. "You're welcome."

John McConnell, a retired New York City policeman working as a security guard, stopped at an electronics store after work one night in 1992. He saw two men robbing the store and pulled out his pistol. Another thief behind a counter began shooting at him. John tried to shoot back, and even after he fell, he got up and shot again. He was hit six times. One of the bullets entered his back and sliced through his left lung, his heart, and the main pulmonary artery, the blood vessel that takes blood from the right side of the heart to the lungs to receive oxygen. He was rushed to the hospital but did not survive.

John had been close to his family and had frequently told one of his daughters, Doreen, "No matter what, I'm always going to take care of you." Five years after John died, Doreen gave birth to a son named William. William began passing out soon after he was born. Doctors diagnosed him with a condition called pulmonary valve atresia, in which the valve of the pulmonary artery has not adequately formed, so blood cannot travel through it to the lungs. In addition, one of the chambers of his heart, the right ventricle, had not formed properly as a result of the problem with the valve. He underwent several surgeries. Although he will need to take medication indefinitely, he has done quite well.

William had birth defects that were very similar to the fatal wounds suffered by his grandfather. In addition, when he became old enough to talk, he began talking about his grandfather's life. One day when he was three years old, his mother was at home trying to work in her study when William kept acting up. Finally, she told him, "Sit down, or I'm going to spank you." William replied, "Mom, when you were a little girl and I was your daddy, you were bad a lot of times, and I never hit you!" . . .

William talked about being his grandfather a number of times and discussed his death. He told his mother that several people were shooting during the incident when he was killed, and he asked a lot of questions about it.

One time, he said to his mother, "When you were a little girl and I was your daddy, what was my cat's name?"

She responded, "You mean Maniac?"

"No, not that one," William answered. "The white one."

"Boston?" his mom asked.

"Yeah," William responded. "I used to call him Boss, right?" That was correct. The family had two cats, named Maniac and Boston, and only John referred to the white one as Boss.

JIM B. TUCKER, M.D., LIFE BEFORE LIFE

THIRTY-SEVEN

Bones don't lie. That's what the archaeologists say, and they're right.

Bones don't make up stories because they want to believe them. They don't repeat something they overheard somewhere. They don't have ESP. They are verifiable, carrying in their fissures the truth of our flawed materiality and our uniqueness. The crack in the femur, the holes in the teeth. So there could be no greater evidence, to Anderson's way of thinking, than the bones positively identified as belonging to Tommy Crawford, which were discovered in an abandoned well in the woods not far from the Clifford residence.

Anderson stood next to Janie, Noah, and Tommy's family, looking down at the hole in the earth into which they had lowered an expensive box covered with expensive flowers already wilting in the heat. He thought he ought to be observing the reactions of the subjects to these proceedings, but he wasn't: instead he was thinking that when his own time came, he wanted none of that for himself. Let them leave his hacked-up body on a mountaintop to disintegrate and feed the vultures, as the Tibetan monks did, until the corporeal part of Jerry Anderson was nothing but bones on a ledge. He was thinking it wouldn't be so very long now, that he would never let his body outlive his mind.

The boy's father, Henry, was standing next to the hole, the shovel in his hands. He filled the spade and threw the dirt high over the coffin, the earth seeming to pause in midair and fall with a scattering thud, and then he scooped another shovelful without pausing, until it seemed like one long continuous movement, the shoveling and falling earth and shoveling, his face slick with sweat.

They all watched him. Noah, subdued, stood between Denise and Janie, holding Janie's hand. Charlie had an arm around his mother's shoulder.

Of course, no amount of data could convince someone who wasn't open to being convinced. People came up with the answers they wanted. Always did. Always would. Anderson had tried to guard against this in his own work, hired researchers to check and recheck his data and colleagues to review his articles, urging the highest standards of skepticism, but it was inevitable there would be some bias. His colleagues were his colleagues; they had wanted to trust him. He had believed for so long that if he rid his work of even the slightest tinge of subjectivity it was only a matter of time before his data was accepted; it was part of the battle he'd been fighting, only now it was late morning and the air was warm and the scent of the soil was rich and fresh and he felt the fight beginning to lift out of him. Let people believe what they wanted to believe.

Detective Ludden, for instance: the answer that made the most sense to Detective Ludden was ESP. It never ceased to amaze Anderson. Here was this rational professional man with his razor-sharp intellect and world-weary outlook, grasping at some idea of Noah's super extrasensory perception as inherently more likely than that some fragment of Tommy's consciousness might continue in some fashion after his death. A samosa vendor on the streets of New Delhi, a taxi driver in Bangkok, would laugh themselves silly at such naïveté. But psychic powers were a phenomenon the police departments in America had at least had some experience with — they had all heard stories of clues being generated this way; some had even employed psychics themselves from time to time. So little Noah Zimmerman was an amazingly powerful psychic intuiting the last moments of Tommy Crawford's life. Whatever floats your boat, Detective.

And he had to admit, once he had made his peace with that aspect of the case, the detective was surprisingly game. Before they had even positively identified the remains, he had interviewed Noah. Taken careful notes and used them to fill in the blanks, to elicit a more comprehensive confession, not that the killer was holding back. But the detective wanted the facts presented as fully and clearly as possible, Anderson understood this, he wanted to know what happened, and isn't that what we all want?

Everything squared, more or less, with the evidence. The bones, the bullet-shattered ribs.

The father wanted the killer dead, but the mother felt that there wasn't much point in that. And the prosecutors had taken the death penalty off the table, since he had confessed, and had been a young teenager when the crime had occurred. And, after all, he may as well work through his guilt in this life. No point in bleeding it on into the next. So Anderson had agreed with Denise on the uselessness of the death penalty, although she still refused to use the word *reincarnation.*

Tommy's spirit, that's how she put it.

Whatever floats your boat, my friend. Whatever floats your boat.

He had been thinking more seriously about karma lately. He had never focused on it in his work — it was hard enough to find verification that consciousness continued, without getting mixed up in the complexity of ethical ramifications across time — but occasionally he had run searches of the data, trying to see if there was a connection between the kinds of lives people led and their next lives. There was nothing conclusive, although a small fraction of those in peaceful or affluent conditions remembered previous lives in which they'd meditated or behaved in a saintly way. He'd had his own thoughts lately, though, that ignorance and fear and anger, like trauma, could perhaps be transferred from one life to the next, and that it might take multiple lifetimes to overcome them. And if anger and fear could persist — then also, of course, stronger emotions could as well, such as love. Was that what drew some people back to reincarnate within their own families? Was that what caused some children to remember their past connections? And if so, then perhaps this phenomenon, these children's memories he had studied so carefully, was not against the laws of nature, after all. Perhaps it was the foundational law of nature that they were proving, what he'd been documenting and analyzing for over thirty years without knowing it: the force of love. He shook his head. His brain was going soft, maybe.

Or maybe not. He'd kept so many of these questions at bay all these years, and now they whirled around him, touching him with something like awe, on their way to someplace else.

THIRTY-EIGHT

Denise would never get over it. She knew that.

Tommy's bones at the bottom of the well.

She and Henry had spent some time with those bones. When the police had finished testing and tagging and photographing them, the funeral parlor had given them time before the burial. She'd clutched them to her chest, run her fingertips along the smooth sockets that had held his shining eyes. There, but not there. Some part of her wanted those bones, wanted to put the femurs under her pillow at night when she went to sleep, to carry his skull around in her purse so she'd be with him always; she understood now how people went crazy and did crazy things. But another part of her knew that it wasn't Tommy. He wasn't there.

Tommy's bones, where Noah had said he'd drowned; she supposed that was proof, if that's what you were looking for, but she wasn't looking. Somehow it had ceased to matter to her.

Yet how could it not matter whether this boy carried some little piece of Tommy deep inside of him? Some fragments of his love. Tommy's love for her, surviving, inside of Noah. That was something, wasn't it?

But surely we all carried some little piece of each other inside of us. So what did it matter, whether the memories belonging to her boy existed inside this other one? Why were we all hoarding love, stockpiling it, when it was all around us, moving in and out of us like the air, if only we could feel it?

She knew that most people couldn't follow her where she'd gone. Would think, like Henry, that she'd gone off the deep end. How could anyone understand what she herself didn't understand?

Her heart — something had happened to it. That's what she would say, if she thought he could listen. She'd known it had been cracked for good. Shattered beyond repair. But she hadn't counted on it cracking open.

She would never get over losing Tommy. She knew that.

Neither could she go back to the person she'd been. There was no resistance left, nothing held back, after a lifetime of hold-

443

ing back. She could feel every stray breeze penetrating to her core. It was terrifying, but there was nothing to be done. Her heart was cracked open now and the whole world could come on through.

Henry pulled her aside after the burial. The others were standing by their cars in the heat, giving the two of them a moment to grieve alone. They stood by the turned earth and scattered flowers, that surreal yet familiar tableau which called out, *Believe it.* Denise squinted her eyes in the sun at all the graves running in orderly rows and the trees arching over them. Trees and stones and earth and sky, as far as she could see.

Henry took her hand in his and she felt her skin jump with the relief of feeling his flesh against hers again. He squeezed her fingers and said, "I'm not coming to the house." Everyone was gathering at her house for the reception after the funeral. She had hired a caterer. She felt too over-whelmed at the moment to handle Henry's resistance. He had to come.

"Just for a little while, Henry. Please."

He was holding her hand, but he was glowering. "I can't stand to be in the same room with those people."

She knew which people he meant. "They

won't bother you. It doesn't matter, Henry."

He let go of her hand. "What do you mean, 'It doesn't matter'?" He raised his voice. "And it doesn't matter that they're crazy, that doesn't matter, either, I suppose?"

She had hoped that if he could spend a few moments with Noah, it might be good for both of them: Henry might see what was there to be seen and take it whatever way he wished. And she knew Henry's coldness hurt Noah. During the funeral service she'd noticed the boy glancing up at him with wounded eyes.

"It might help you, to talk to him. And I think it would help the child. . . ."

"I cannot believe that you, of all people, Denise . . ." Henry's voice was raspy. He bent his head down, and she wanted to touch that familiar haze of black and gray she knew so well, but stopped herself. His eyes, when he looked up again, were beseeching. "I know it's hard, it's brutal," he said. "But I never thought you'd fall for something like this. Maybe I should've known, the way you thought Tommy'd still come back to us. And now you found yourself a way to continue to believe that, didn't you? In the face of everything."

"You think it's all a fantasy."

"I think you're doing everything you can to believe Tommy is still alive. You think I don't want that, too? You think I don't look for him everywhere, you think that I haven't been seeing my son in every child's face in a crowd? But we need to hang on to reality."

Reality. The word stung her like a slap. "You think I don't know Tommy's dead? We're standing at my son's grave. I know he's dead. I know he's not coming back."

"*Do* you?"

"Not as Tommy. But —" She groped for the words. "There's some piece of him here. Oh, Henry. I don't know how to say it, and even if I did you wouldn't believe me. But, I swear, if you spent some time with him. The doctor —"

Henry snorted.

"Dr. Anderson says the boy can score baseball games. Nobody taught him that. You taught him that, Henry."

Henry was shaking his head.

"Otherwise how could he know something like that, without being taught?" It was not the argument she meant to have, but the real argument wasn't made up of facts, no matter how many Dr. Anderson collected. The facts were important, she knew that, but she also knew no long list of traits or statements was going to sway this man. She didn't know what would.

"I don't know," Henry said. She could tell from the heaviness in his voice that she was losing him, that his stamina for the conversation was running out. If only she could find the right words. She felt keenly that her marriage, what was left of it, was hanging in the balance.

Henry turned to her, the lines of his face sagging, as if grief had increased the pull of gravity. "I know my son is dead. I know it because I've held his bones in my hands. And I know it in my soul, if there is such a thing, which I highly doubt. To be honest, Denise, I'm disappointed in you. You always were one of the most reasonable people I knew. And now you're leaving me alone with it. Our son is dead, and you're leaving me alone with it to go listen to some crazy little white boy."

"He's not crazy. If you could only —"

"You're killing me with this shit. You know that? You're murdering me right here where I'm standing. You've lost your damn mind."

She looked at the man who was still her husband. He was suffering, and she couldn't help him. She was making it worse. She put her hand on his shoulder and felt his muscles tense beneath her fingers, the pain running from his body to hers like water find-

447

ing a new vessel.

"Maybe so." Her thoughts were not her thoughts; that much was true.

Henry's eyes softened. Denise felt the relief rising in her chest.

"We can get you some help, 'Nise." He put his big arm around her waist. They were holding each other now, swaying slightly. "Makes sense with all this —" He motioned at the grave, the cemetery. "It's understandable. I see that now. We'll find you a new doctor, if necessary. I never did like that Ferguson."

A breeze took up, whipped around them. She leaned back into her husband's strong arms and let herself fall into that familiar comfort. She'd missed it. She'd missed him. The lilies on Tommy's grave moved to and fro in the wind, as if they were shaking their heads. The too-sweet smell of flowers fought in her nostrils with the heavy smell of upturned earth. Underneath the earth, the box, the bones. Tommy's bones. Not Tommy, though. He was everywhere, connected to everything, including the wind, including Noah. She didn't know how that could be, but she couldn't pretend otherwise. Not even for Henry. She released herself from his grasp and squatted down, letting some of the dirt fall through her fingers.

"I'm sorry, Henry. I don't want to leave you alone with it, I truly don't. I miss him, too, every second of every day." She scooped up another handful and let it trickle down, a dry rain beneath her fingers. She thought of Tommy's face. She concentrated on his smile. She couldn't look at Henry. "But Noah's not crazy. He has some of Tommy in him. Some of Tommy's memories, and some of his — love. For you, too —" she started to say, turning, but Henry's wide, receding back was already moving away from her.

THIRTY-NINE

Every funeral reception was different, Janie supposed. She hadn't been to many of them. The Jews also sat shiva, a different sort of party, albeit with the same theme.

And some people, like Tommy Crawford, had a wake. That event had taken place the night before, in a hushed, crowded room in the funeral home. She and Noah had lasted only a few moments in that room, staring at that shiny wooden box covered with flowers. The casket holding Tommy's bones, the photograph of the child propped right next to it.

Noah had stared at the picture. The smooth brown skin, the mischievous grin. "That's me!" Noah had yelped. "That's me!"

She'd had to hurry him out of there. Heads were turning in their direction, muttering. She caught sight of Tommy's father glowering at them as she pulled him from the room and down the corridor and out into the night.

That was a wake. But why did they call it that? Wake, like the rocking waters after a passing boat, the instability that followed some major event? Wake like that?

Or wake, the imperative?

Wake up, Janie.

She speared some cubes of turkey with a toothpick and put them on a plate with some potato salad and a pickle for her and some cheese and pineapple for Noah, balancing the plate on her open palm. The room was filled with people she didn't know wearing dark suits and dresses. People who had known Tommy. Everyone chatting, catching up. Tommy had been dead for years now, and the freshness of shock and sorrow had transformed, turned inward.

A group of teenagers clustered together by the food table, awkward in their suits. They didn't know what to do with their plates, either. They held them shakily in their hands, shoveling unwieldy spoonfuls of potato salad into their mouths.

Denise passed by, calling out, *Thanks for coming, thanks for coming.* She was on fire. There were no other words for it. Janie would say it was probably grief if she had to call it something. But you couldn't look away from her.

The room seemed to slow. The clink of cutlery, the murmurs: over now, at rest. A river of sound flowing through the room. Noah was standing across the room from her, next to Charlie, the lizard on his shoulder, the big teen's head angled downward. The sun sharp in the living room windows, glancing off Noah's hair. A warm day, the heat glistening on their relaxed faces, a sickly sheen on the surface of the potato salad on Charlie's plate.

Noah talking to Charlie, telling Charlie something, one more thing she'd never know. A droplet in that ocean.

Wake up, Janie.

A line from an Emily Dickinson poem floated back to her.

As Lightning to the Children eased
With explanation kind
The Truth must dazzle gradually
Or every man be blind —

The heat of the bodies in the room. Noah standing in the sunlight. There was nowhere to sit, the room was sliding before her, the walls shooting up into the sky —

She squatted on the carpet. Her plate in her lap.

So many strangers: old people hugging, shaking their heads. The glum, embarrassed teenagers. Anderson, standing by the wall, watching. Denise. Charlie. Noah.

She was the only one here who hadn't known Tommy, except for Anderson.

And Noah, of course, who you really . . . couldn't . . . count.

The giggles came scrabbling up her throat like hungry mice. Up and out. She covered her face with her hands.

But it was okay, actually, because she wasn't really laughing. She was crying. She had the tears to prove it, right there on the Styrofoam plate, dripping onto the cheese squares. And that was okay at a funeral reception. Maybe preferable. Hopefully the people there thought she had known Tommy. Maybe they thought she was his piano teacher. She looked like a piano teacher. Didn't she? Though she couldn't play a note. Maybe she should learn. Noah could teach her the theme to *The Pink Panther*. . . .

Her nose running against her fingers, the slickness of snot, the salty splash of tears.

"You all right?"

Denise stood there with a plate in each hand.

She looked up. "I —"

"Come with me."

Denise's bedroom was sunny. The curtains were pulled all the way back, and Janie had to shade her eyes from the glare. She sat on the bed. She was hiccupping, and her eyes were tearing. Denise brought her a box of tissues.

"I could give you a pill, but it might knock you out."

"I think I'm already knocked out."

Denise nodded curtly. She seemed efficient now, a brisk nurse. "Do you want some ibuprofen?"

It wasn't what she needed, but she'd take it. "That'd be good."

She lay down on the bed and tried to quiet herself as Denise bustled around in the bathroom. Then she bolted to her feet.

"Oh! Noah. I need to get back —"

"Charlie's looking after him." She was back in the room with a pill in her hand and a glass of water in the other. "And that doctor is there."

"Yes, but —"

"He's fine. Sit."

She sat. The light in the room was blinding. She took the pill she didn't need and swallowed it. It was not pain that was causing her lightheadedness. It was reality. She was sitting on this too-busy flowered bed-spread in this other woman's room — that was real; and the sunlight in her eyes was real; and here was this other woman, who was also real. And the reality of the situation was also bigger than that . . . but what did she do with it? Even the thought of it made her head spin.

"I'm sorry." The words emerged without thought.

"For what?" Denise's face revealed nothing.

"To take you out of the — party." The word hovered between them painfully. Janie winced. "I mean, the wake . . . no, that's not right. I mean . . ." *Wake up.*

Denise took the glass back from her. "Charlie's good with kids," she went on, as if trying to draw her back to normalcy with her patter. "I've been trying forever to get him to do some babysitting around here. Make a little money instead of siphoning off my wallet for god knows what. Comic books and junk food and video games, mostly. And that's only the stuff I know about."

"Wow." Janie tried to pull her mind around to what this woman was saying. "Having a teenager, that must be tough. . . . I'm just trying to make it through preschool

455

at this point."

"Charlie's a good kid. But he hates to study. And he's dyslexic on top of it. So . . ." She shook her head ruefully.

"Dyslexia . . . when do you know if they have that?" She hadn't thought about that one. Yet another thing to worry about.

Denise handed her a tissue and watched while Janie blew her nose. "Usually around first grade — when they start to read — that's when the learning disabilities start to become evident."

"Oh. I see." She tried to remember if Noah had any issues recognizing letters. He seemed pretty good at that. "Was Tommy also —"

"Just Charlie." Her voice was abrupt.

Janie brooded on it for a moment. There was a hereditary connection, wasn't there? But could you inherit things from the family of your previous incarnation? Her head began to swirl again. She took a deep breath. Where did Tommy end and Noah begin? What did Henry and Denise have to do with it? She wanted to ask Denise but didn't have the courage. "I suppose by the time they are teenagers you know them pretty well inside and out."

For the first time, Denise cracked a smile. "Are you kidding me? I don't know half of

456

what's in Charlie's head most of the time. He just — disappeared on me." The words pricked the air. Her face closed up again. Janie wanted to fill up the space between them but couldn't find the right thing to say.

She cast her eyes around the room. There was not much to look at except pictures: school pictures of Charlie and Tommy on the wall (she recognized the one from the newspaper article), others on the bedside table. A framed snapshot of a toddler lurching across the floor toward a beautiful young woman with gold hoop earrings and open arms.

"That was the day Charlie learned to walk," Denise said simply. She was standing right next to her, looking over her shoulder. "He went from one or two steps to walking clear across the room. It looks like he's walking to me, but he was really walking to his brother, right behind me. He idolized that boy."

Janie looked again at the picture. She hadn't realized that the woman in the photo was Denise. She picked up the one next to it.

A picture of Tommy jumping from a wooden raft. It was a snapshot, but the camera had captured the sun sparkling on the water, the rough-hewed wood of the raft. Tommy was caught in midair, legs splayed; she recognized the pure elation on his face. She *knew* that expression. She couldn't look away.

Denise glanced at the photograph. "That was by the lake house. We used to go there every summer." Her voice was wistful. "Tommy loved that place."

"I know," Janie said. "Noah talked about it."

"Did he? Really?"

"He told his teachers it was his favorite vacation," Janie said. The words hovered in her mind a moment, and she waited for the jealousy to follow. But she didn't feel any jealousy, looking at that picture that seemed to contain the distillation of Noah's joy. She felt something else flooding through her: gratitude. He had had a good life here, with Denise; for the first time, she realized that she couldn't separate that from the loving, exuberant boy who had been born to her.

Denise gently took the picture from her hands and placed it back on the bedside table.

"He used to cry and cry when we had to go home," she mused. " 'When we going back there, Mama? When we going back?' In the car all the way back. Drove us all plumb nuts."

"I can imagine," Janie said. "He gets very attached. He's always been that way." But what did *always* mean? When did *always* begin?

"We haven't been there in years." Denise's eyes clouded. "Maybe . . ."

The idea shimmered there in the room with them, a mirage of a lake with a blond boy jumping into it. Janie averted her eyes from the child in the photo; it was too much to contemplate. The fantasy faded before either one of them had dared to name it.

"You seem pretty calm about all this stuff," Janie said.

"Calm." Denise chuckled. "Well. We don't know each other, do we?"

"No. We don't."

There was a burst of laughter in the living room.

"I guess I should go back in there," Denise said. "There's a lot of people in my house. And they are having too much fun. This is a funeral, after all." The smile holding up the edges of her lips seemed fixed there by sheer will. She smoothed her hair back toward its bun, though nothing had gone astray.

"Okay. But — Just one more thing . . ."

The woman stood there, waiting. Janie felt

all her questions bubbling up within her; she couldn't hold them back any longer. "What if Noah doesn't get over this? What if he wants to be here all the time, just like he wanted to be at the lake?"

Denise pressed her lips together. "Your son will be all right. His mama loves him like crazy."

"Mommy-Mom," she said.

"What?"

"I'm Mommy-Mom. You were Mama. That's what he called you." Denise frowned at her warily. I shouldn't have said that, Janie thought. But it was too late now. "And what about your son?" she said.

"Charlie will be all right, too," Denise said, but she didn't sound certain. She sounded like she wanted to get out of there.

"I meant your other son." It wasn't the right way to say it; she didn't know if there was a right way. What do you think of it all? is what she wanted to say. What does it mean?

It was as if Janie had stepped on a broken toe. Denise's eyes flared. "Tommy's gone."

"I know. I know. But —"

"No."

"But, Noah —"

"Is someone else," she said fiercely. Her eyes shone. "*Your* son."

"Yes. Yes, he is, but . . . but you yourself saw, didn't you see, you said you did, that his memories — seemed real. They were real. Weren't they? And the bones were —" There was no way to articulate what she wanted to say. She shook her head.

Denise stood wincing in the sunlight that sliced across her face.

"So —" Janie continued miserably — she couldn't stop now. "Is it some comfort? Does it help?"

Denise said nothing. She was standing in a ray of sunlight filled with whirling dust. She seemed both transfixed and utterly at sea and Janie was suddenly ashamed of herself for asking.

"I don't know," Denise said slowly.

"It's just that . . . you seem like you know something."

"Really?" Denise started laughing. " 'Cause I was kind of hoping you did."

And then they were both laughing — the kind of hard, helpless laughter that made Janie's stomach ache, cracking up at this joke the universe had played on both of them. The moment lasted longer than Janie had thought possible, until finally they both stepped back, gasping. Denise had tears running down the corners of her eyes and she ran her fingers over her cheeks.

"Oh, my. They'll think I've been sobbing my eyes out in here," she said. The words fell like a shadow across the room.

"I won't tell them."

"Better not."

They glanced at each other. They were connected and yet they were each on their own with this.

"I guess I better get going," Janie said reluctantly. "Before Noah eats all the brownies."

Denise wiped her eyes with a tissue. "Ah, let him enjoy himself."

"You've forgotten what a four-year-old on a sugar rush is like. They turn into tiny maniacs."

"No, I haven't forgotten." Her face was cool and dry. It was hard to imagine she'd been crying with laughter a moment before. Janie opened the door and let the human sound engulf them.

"That's good," Janie said. It was something to say. Janie lingered at the open door and listened to the noisy room where Noah was sitting. For some reason she felt nervous about going back to him. "I don't know who he is anymore," she said. "Or maybe it's myself I don't know." She thought perhaps it wasn't right to say these things, especially to Denise, but she didn't know who else she could say them to, or what was right anymore.

Denise wiped her dry face with a new tissue, tossed it into the wastepaper basket, and looked up. "You're here," she said quietly. "And Noah's in my living room, waiting for you. Isn't that enough?"

Janie nodded, pierced by the truth of it. Of course it was enough. She stepped toward the room where her son was.

"It does help," Denise said abruptly. Janie turned; Denise's eyes were full of emotion. "It does. Not with missing him, not with that part, but . . ." Her voice trailed off.

They stood together in silence, the air between them alive with the wonder of everything they didn't know.

Noah looked up when Janie came back into the room. He was sitting on the sofa. Always those blue eyes tore right through her, touched some part of her nothing else got near. She settled down next to him.

They watched the teenagers standing around the dining room table picking at their potato salad and muttering to each other, their bodies moving jerkily in ill-fitting suits.

"Can we go now, Mommy-Mom?" Noah said.

"Don't you want to spend some time with Tommy's friends?"

He shook his head. "They're all so . . . old."

"Oh."

"That's sick," one of the teenagers said, and they burst into laughter that stopped abruptly, as if remembering where they were.

She wished she could do something to ease the tension and sadness on Noah's face, but what could she do? She'd thought she could fix him, but that had always been beyond her power.

"Everything's different," he said.

"Yes, I guess it is."

His mouth twisted.

"Oh, honey. I'm sorry. Did you think it would be the same?"

Noah nodded. "Are we going home soon?"

"You mean, to Brooklyn? Yes."

"Oh."

He blinked a few times, looking around the room. She followed his gaze.

She hadn't taken the room in fully before; she had been too shocked to see it properly. It was nice enough, this interior of a small suburban ranch house. Someone had filled it with comfy brown furniture, piled with pillows in complementary blue. An upright piano stood under the stairs; it was a bit banged up at the edges, but the wood glowed. The rectangular picture window looked out on a leafy street. The mantel on the brick fireplace was populated with mementos and figurines: a curled stone cat, some candles, a small wooden angel holding a wire butterfly, a baseball trophy. It was nothing so extraordinary, this house of Noah's dreams and her nightmares. It was just a house. He had felt loved here.

"We can't stay here, Noah."

"I want to go home, but I want to stay here, too."

She pictured their own apartment, his cozy bedroom, the tigers on the bureau, the stars. "I know."

"Why can't I have both?"

"I don't know. We just have to do the best we can with what we have. We're in this life now. Together."

He nodded again, as if he had already known this, and crawled into her lap. He leaned his head back against her chin.

"I'm so glad I came to you."

She turned him around so she could see his face. She thought she had known all the different phases of Noah — the moody and bereaved Noah, the freaked-out Noah, the boisterous, affectionate child she knew best

465

— but this was something new. She kept her voice level. "What do you mean?"

"After I left the other place."

"What place?"

"The place where I went after I died." He said it simply. His eyes were pensive and unusually bright, as if he'd caught a fish unexpectedly and was admiring the silver scales shining in the sun.

"And what was that like?"

A simple question; yet the answer held worlds inside of it. She held her breath, waiting for his answer.

He shook his head. "Mom, you can't describe that place."

"And you were there for a while?"

He thought about it. "I don't know how long. Then I saw you and I came here."

"You saw me. Where did you see me?"

"On the beach."

"You saw me on the beach?"

"Yes. You were standing there. I saw you and then I came to you."

Even when she thought the limits of her mind had been pushed as far as they could go, there was always another level to the vastness.

He pressed his forehead against hers. "I'm so glad you're my mom this time," Noah said.

"Me, too," Janie said. It was all she needed.

"Hey, Mommy-Mom," he whispered. "Guess what time it is?"

"I don't know, bug. What time is it?"

"It's time for another brownie!" He pulled his head back, his eyes brimming with his customary, mischievous joy, and she knew that the other child was gone for now; he'd thrown the fish back into the ocean.

FORTY

After the guests had left, and Janie and Anderson had helped Denise and Charlie put away the leftover food, and Janie had wiped the table down while Denise vacuumed up the brownie crumbs; when the place at last was neat again, the subjects of Anderson's last case sat on the couch, side by side, Charlie and Denise and Noah and Janie.

Anderson settled into the armchair across from them. He felt the chair holding his body. He let himself sink into it.

It was dusk. The five of them were silent, strangers bound with strangeness.

"So you're leaving tomorrow?" Denise said at last.

"We are." There was a note of apology in Janie's voice. "Our flights are in the afternoon."

They had had their visit; they had been interviewed by the police; they had attended the funeral. Now there was life to be resumed, jobs, responsibilities. For all but him, Anderson thought. Oddly, the thought didn't trouble him. He wondered why.

"What do we do now?" Janie asked Anderson.

Everyone looked at him.

There was some more paperwork to be done. The paperwork had once mattered to him greatly but didn't anymore.

Anderson shrugged.

"We just leave here, then? That's it? We don't" — she looked at Denise — "keep in touch?"

"There can be visits. If you like." He smiled. "It's up to you."

"Oh." Janie looked around the living room. "Do you think that's a good idea?"

"It's up to you," Anderson said again. It sounded flippant, even to his own ears. He was experiencing an emotion that was unusual for him. Was this what relaxation felt like?

"I could visit you," Denise said suddenly to Janie. "I could come to Brooklyn."

Janie looked relieved. "Oh. That would be nice. Wouldn't it, Noah?"

"Not right away, of course," Denise added quickly. "I mean, I think we all need a little time . . . but I'd like to come and see where you live someday," she said to Noah. "To see your room. Could I do that?"

He nodded shyly.

"So. It's settled then," Janie said.

Anderson watched them. Everything was settled, and nothing was, he knew that. Things would change. Noah would change. Anderson would need to follow up, of course. Yet he had no hunger for it. Maybe the connections would hold and maybe they wouldn't, or they would transform into other ways of being. He hadn't realized how much he missed silence. They sat for a long time this way, the sunlight shifting into a deeper, heavier light, Noah quiet between Denise and Janie. Anderson lifted his face to soak in the last rays of sun like a sleepy animal.

"I think we need to get back to the hotel now, honey," Janie said to Noah at last, stirring all of them. "It's getting late."

Noah stretched. "I want to take my bath here," he said drowsily.

Janie started in her seat. "You *want* to take a bath?"

He pushed out his lower lip. "I want a bath *here*. In the pink bathtub. With her."

He pointed at Denise, who shrugged a little and looked to Janie for direction.

"Oh."

470

Anderson watched the resistance rise in Janie, and then he felt her let it go. "All right," Janie said.

"And you can give me a bath next time, okay, Mommy-Mom?"

She hesitated only briefly and then she grinned right back at him. "Sure, Noey. Whatever you want."

FORTY-ONE

Noah wanted a bath, so Denise was giving him one.

That was the task, the last of this long day, and then she could rest. She had buried one child today, what was left of his body, and now she was going to bathe another.

Another child. That was how she thought about it to herself at that moment, and how it seemed to her as she smiled at the boy and set him on the lid of the toilet with one of Charlie's old *Garfield* comic books while she rummaged around in the bathroom closet for some bubble bath.

There was a Mr. Bubble bottle in the back — she had used it when her boys were little and there was a bit left, so she had kept it, years past the time of her children's baths, the way people keep such things — because some part of her thought that maybe she could also keep some piece of Tommy's childhood intact, as if it was bottled, too, in the bright pink container.

When the truth was, it was already gone. Gone where?

Mr. Bubble grinned at her, an insane smile.

She turned on the water. It thundered in her ears. Her mind flashed back to Tommy, gasping for air, calling out for her in the watery blackness. Mama!

Focus on the water. You'll be all right.

She put her hand under the stream to ground herself and poured the remains of the Mr. Bubble into the water, the bubbles proliferating in the tub, bursting to life.

"Is that — bubbles?" Noah jumped off the toilet and leaned over the side of the bathtub.

"Yep."

"Oooh. Can I get in?"

"Sure."

He stripped off the rest of his clothes and then seemed to hesitate. He perched on the edge of the tub. "It's not too cold, is it?"

"No, honey, it's nice and warm."

"Oh. Okay." He nodded to himself, as if making a decision, then lowered himself into the tub and began swatting at the bubbles. "When I was Tommy we always did bubbles."

It never ceased to amaze her when he said

things like that.

"Yes. You two boys always made a big old mess."

He laughed. "We did."

Focus on the love. You'll be all right.

She closed her eyes for a moment and remembered Charlie and Tommy going at each other in the tub with the bubbles, the soapy water oozing onto the floor. She held on to that feeling until the whole room seemed to vibrate with the force of her love for them. How much there was.

The water was still pouring down over and through her fingers, changing moment by moment. As a child, she'd seen a movie about Helen Keller, how she had felt water running from a pump and had finally connected the name to the source of the name — but now she was going in the opposite direction, and names were losing their sense. What was Noah or Tommy, and who was she? Her head roared with a bright confusion.

"Hey, look!" He was calling for her. Whatever she was to him, she wasn't a stranger. There were no strangers.

"Look," Noah said. "Look at this bubble!"

The shine of the faucet pierced her eyes. Denise looked over, a beat too late.

"Oh! Popped. Sorry," Noah said.

"Okay."

"Look! Bubble!" This time she looked over quickly.

"I see it," Denise said. "That's a big one."

It *was* a big one. It spanned the distance between his knees, growing bigger and bigger as he moved his legs apart, shimmering like crazy for its split second of existence.

"Look!"

The bubble grew larger still. In the ever-changing map of its colors, someone was drowning and someone was being born.

"Oh! Popped."

"Yes."

There was nothing to hold on to anymore. Only everything.

Noah looked down, then, and put his whole face in the water. He lifted his head. He had a bubble beard and a bubble mustache and he was grinning away like a demonic baby Santa Claus. "Guess who?" he said.

Denise smiled. "I don't know," she said. "Who?"

"Me!"

FORTY-TWO

It was late by the time they got home from the airport. Charlie sat next to his mom as they pulled into the driveway. Another night on Asheville Road; same old sounds of crickets and the Johnsons' TV playing an Indians game. Crazy that it seemed the same when what was in his head had changed so much. He guessed that was how life was. Who knew what was in anybody's mind? And meanwhile people died and had whole new lives, like the fireflies that arrived in June, flashing here, then gone, then here again. It was like some kind of batshit magic trick.

Charlie had spent hours catching fireflies with his brother when they were little. Tommy would run around the yard with a jar, Charlie right at his heels. Once they'd caught a few, they'd put the jar on the steps and sit, watching them buzz and spark. They always pitched a fit when it was time to let them go. They wanted to keep them as pets, even though their mom explained that they'd die that way, that they belonged in the wild. One night Tommy and Charlie couldn't take it anymore — they lied and hid the jar under Tommy's bed, and the next morning they had woken up to find themselves the owners of three dead bugs in a jar: dry, ugly, black-winged things that looked like ordinary beetles, as if someone had come in the night and drained the mystery right out of them.

Now Charlie wondered if the kid, Noah, ever saw fireflies in the city. Or if he remembered them. Even though he wasn't Tommy. Not really.

He looked sideways at his mom. What was she thinking? He knew it was probably about his brother, but sometimes, lately, she surprised him. She'd ask his opinions about things, like what kind of food they should serve at the reception or whether they should ask his dad over for dinner. Why so curious what I think all of a sudden, he wanted to say, when you haven't given a rat's ass for the last seven years? And it was a problem, too, because it meant he couldn't get stoned as much. He'd had a quick toke or two in the garage the day before the burial and she'd noticed in, like, half a second. Not even. She'd looked him right in the eyeballs and he was grounded before he even knew what hit him.

Denise stared out the windshield into the darkness, pondering gradations of loss.

She would always miss Tommy — there was no stray piece of her that wasn't always missing him. But this other child, this child who was not Tommy, had brought a sweet taste to a mouth that had been filled with bitterness. They had been through it, the two of them, and there was that bond that she knew would always be between them.

When they'd said good-bye at the airport he had held on to her for a long time, and she was surprised to realize she couldn't speak for a minute. Finally she'd said, "I'll see you in Brooklyn."

"Okay."

"Will you show me your room?"

He nodded. "I've got stars in my room."

"Stars? Really?"

"They're glow-in-the-dark stickers. On the ceiling. All the constellations. My mom put them up there."

"Well, I can't wait to see them."

She made herself smile. She was still holding Noah by the shoulders and he had his hands on her waist, as if they were dancing.

She didn't want to let go of him. She wasn't sure she could. Around her the other figures were insubstantial, blurry: she saw Janie glancing at her watch and Dr. Anderson speaking softly to Charlie. Then Charlie put his heavy hand on her back and said, "C'mon, Mama, they've got to get to their gate," and she knew she had to do it (*Let go*) and she let him go.

The three of them walked away from her and stood at the end of the security line: Dr. Anderson, a stiff man like her father had been, of that same breed — farmers and doctors who took their jobs seriously, who had kindness in them under all that proper bearing; and Janie, another mother who was doing her best with the job she was given; and that little boy with the yellow hair for whom she had some love in her heart, no use denying it. (*Let go.*)

For goodness' sake, Denise. She'd kept her shit together while the winds of hell were blowing fiery sparks into her mouth, she could certainly keep it together now. She forced herself to watch as they joined the line of people carrying whatever they were allowed to bring with them on their way from this place to the next. Beside her Charlie stood up tall like a man and she was grateful for his steadying hand.

Now she glanced at him in the car. He was looking out the window, having his Charlie thoughts — what did that boy think about? She'd have to find out. She'd have to ask him. He was drumming a beat with his fingers on the windowpane.

Maybe he was thinking about Henry. All these years he'd been the one insisting that she had to face it, that Tommy was dead and never coming back, and yet the discovery of Tommy's bones had completely undone him. He'd never believed in the death penalty, thought it was unfairly applied and racially skewed, but now he was bitter that the prosecution wasn't talking about it for Tommy's murderer, who had been so young at the time. Death consumed him. Still, maybe she'd call him and ask him to come over for dinner. And if he said no, she'd keep trying, and one of these days he might do it.

What she had said to Henry at the graveside was true: she did miss Tommy every second of every day. She missed him and yet she felt his presence at the same time, not in the other child but all around, and she couldn't hold on to it or make sense of it, any more than she could hold on to Tommy, any more than she could understand why she opened her heart so instantly to Noah or why her love for Henry was an ache she couldn't get rid of.

"You okay, Mama?"

He'd been watching her. He was always watching her, her Charlie. She turned around to face him. "I'm fine, honey. I truly am. I just need another minute."

"All right."

She turned off the engine and they sat in the driveway in the dark.

FORTY-THREE

Only the good-byes to get through, Anderson thought, as he passed into the busy throng of humanity waiting for loved ones at the baggage claim. All around them families craned their necks eagerly, or fell upon their relatives with cries and hugs and handfuls of balloons. Fathers lifted daughters high up in their arms.

People used to reunite at the gates, but that was a different era. Now people claimed each other and their luggage in this grim, cavernous space, calling out "Mine." This is mine, the blue one. You're mine. A young beauty in cutoff blue jeans searched the crowd; an older, heavyset woman stepped forward and enveloped her in her arms.

Only the good-byes to get through — and then —

"All set?" Janie put a hand on his shoulder. They knew each other better now, had achieved that intimacy, whether he liked it or not. She was worried about him. He looked away.

"My car is in the parking lot." He gestured with his chin. "Do you want a lift?"

"We'll just take a taxi," she said, and he nodded, his mind crowing with relief. He would not have to speak then, not after the next few minutes. In his mind he was already on the road in his car, moving through the quiet night. "It's the wrong way for you," she added. "Or, if you want, it's so late to drive, you can stay the night with us until morning. We have a pull-out couch —"

"I'll be fine." He avoided her eyes. There was too much warmth there. He didn't want her to care about him. He was already gone.

He squatted down next to Noah. "I'm going to say good-bye now, my friend."

"I don't like good-byes," Noah said.

"Me neither," said Anderson. "But sometimes they are . . . good." He'd meant another word, but no matter.

"We'll see him again soon, though, bug," Janie said, attempting a reassuring briskness. "Won't we, Jerry?"

"It's possible."

"Possible?" Janie's voice was higher than usual. He kept his focus on Noah. Noah seemed to be managing this separation better than his mom. Maybe by now he was used to it. "You mean, probable, right?"

No, Janie, he thought. This time I said the word I meant to say.

"I think you'll be so busy having fun you'll forget all about me," he said to Noah.

"No, I won't forget. Will you forget me?" The boy looked anxious.

He put his hand on Noah's head. His hair was soft beneath his fingers. "I won't. But it's okay to forget, sometimes," he said gently.

The boy took this in. "Will I forget about Tommy, too?"

"Do you want to?"

Noah considered. "Some things I want to. Some things I don't." His small clear voice was barely audible among the people milling around them. "Can I choose which ones to remember?"

He'd miss this child.

"We can try," Anderson said. "But we can't forget about now, Noah. The moment we're in. The life we're in. That's more important. We can't forget that."

Noah laughed incredulously. "How could you forget that?"

"I don't know."

Anderson was still squatting, and it was hurting his knees. The boy touched his forehead to his and seemed to peer right into him. He smelled like the lollipop the flight attendant had given him on the plane. "You don't know a lot."

"That's true." He looked at Noah. The case was almost complete. There was only one thing left. How fascinating that he had not asked about it before.

"Can you do something for me? I know it's odd, but can I see your — chest and your back? Just for a second? Would you mind? Is it okay?" He turned now to Janie, who had been listening to their conversation. She nodded. He stood up, pulled Noah away from the people, against a dormant carousel, out of view.

An adult would have asked why, but Noah simply lifted his T-shirt.

Anderson turned the child around carefully, looking at his pale chest and back. Two birthmarks, faintly visible: a faint round circle on the back, slightly reddish, and a ragged star of raised skin in the front. The path of a bullet, written plain on the flesh.

At another moment, he would have taken a picture of it, but now he simply let the T-shirt fall. The evidence was there.

A large family at the next carousel was counting baggage. Two boys in soccer shirts were running gleefully around the carousel.

His good-bye over, Noah ran and joined them in an impromptu game of airport tag.

"You can use it," Janie said in a low voice.

There was a certainty in her voice he hadn't noticed before; she had seen the marks on her son's skin. "For your book. You can write about Noah. You can use his first name."

"Can I?" It was a question for himself.

"I'm sorry I doubted you before. You have my permission," she said formally, "to use his story any way you like."

He tilted his head in thanks. Perhaps there was enough juice left in him to finish this chapter, if he did it quickly. He owed that much to the man he had been. The man he was now, though . . . who was that?

"Do you think Noah is — getting better?" Janie asked haltingly. The trust in her eyes as she looked at him both touched and alarmed him.

"Do you?"

She thought about it. "Maybe. I think so."

Noah and the soccer boys were doubled over with laughter.

"Why did Tommy decide to come back in the States, do you think?" she said, her eyes on her son. "Why wasn't he reborn in China or India or England? You said once that people often reincarnate in the same area.

But *why*?" She was puzzling over it earnestly, and he felt a kind of bemusement, as if all the questions that had buzzed about him for so much of his life had found a fresh new field to swarm.

"There does seem to be a correlation." He spoke slowly, picking each word with care. "Some children speak of spending time in the areas in which they died, picking their parents from the people that pass by. Others are born into their own families, as their own grandchildren or nieces or nephews. We have speculated that may be due to . . . to love." There was a different word he wanted, a more clinical one, but it was out of reach. "Perhaps personalities love their countries, the way they love their families." He shrugged. "How a consciousness migrates is not a question I've been able to answer. I've been stuck on establishing its existence." He shifted his feet impatiently. "Listen," he said. "It's been —"

"But I'm not sure what to do now." She touched his sleeve, and the gesture startled him. "How do I go back and raise Noah now?"

"You rely on your intellect and your . . ." Again, the word eluded him. ". . . feelings. Your feelings are good." He was whittled down now, either to banalities or simple truths. Either way, they would have to do. "We have to say good-bye now," he murmured.

"You'll need to follow up with Noah's case, though? Right?"

I don't know, he thought, but he said, "Sure."

"So I can e-mail you sometimes? If I have more questions?"

He nodded, but barely.

"Okay." They eyed each other, at a loss for how to part. A hug seemed out of the question, but a handshake seemed too formal. At last she held out her hand to him awkwardly, and he held it briefly in his own large one and then on impulse raised it to his lips and kissed it. The skin was soft beneath his lips. It was the kiss of a father at a wedding, releasing his daughter from his care. He felt a pang of some obscure loss, either for her companionship or for womankind, so far behind him now.

"Be well," he said, releasing her hand. He grabbed his battered bag and headed out the doors into the warm night.

He was free.

That's who he was.

Free. The cars and taxis slowed, pulling over to pick up relatives and customers, and he passed by them as he headed for the parking lot, enjoying his momentum, the way his legs swung smoothly, efficiently, his mind stretching out gratefully in the dark.

He cared about Janie and Noah, but they were receding from him rapidly. His last case, and it was done.

They were back there on the ground and he was — buoyed up.

He had fought with everything he had to hang on to his life as he had once known it, and now it was gone, and he floated on the lightness of his defeat. He had applied the full force of his mind to his attempt to understand the unfathomable, and maybe he'd been able to extract one or two teeth from the maw of infinity, and now he had only to write out this last case.

He had thought that as he grew nearer to his own death the unanswerable questions would pierce him unbearably, and now he found to his shock and delight that he had no need for questions. What would happen — would happen.

How 'bout them apples?

He would finish his book now and then he could do what he liked. And when one day he could no longer read the Bard . . . then he'd go over the parts he had committed to memory, remembering the depth and cadence if not the lines themselves. He could babble Shakespeare to himself under the oaks all day like a crazy man.

Or he could go back to Asia. It'd feel good to be on Asian soil again. And what was stopping him? Nothing. He could go now if he liked. He could take the next flight out.

Thailand. The dense, humid air, the chaos of its streets.

Why not go? He felt the excitement beginning to pulse through him as he thought about it. He could visit the enormous Reclining Buddha, with its 108 auspicious signs carved in mother-of-pearl on the soles of his feet. He could start to meditate. He'd always been too nervous that a spiritual practice might undermine or influence his scientific objectivity, but that was irrelevant now. And if the Tibetans were right, then meditation could lead to a more peaceful death, which might positively influence his next life (though his own data was inconclusive on that score).

Maybe he'd even stop at a beach. The Phi Phi islands were supposed to be something to see. White sand like silk between your toes, blue water clear as glass. The present moment. Surrendering to that. He'd heard you could take a boat ride and see the strange limestone outcroppings rising out of the mist like something in a Chinese scroll painting: those scenes of painted mountains twisting up into the coiled, unseen sky, while one lone human lingered in a boat down below, so tiny as to be almost invisible.

He'd have to buy a bathing suit. He couldn't wait.

FORTY-FOUR

Janie leaned her head against the taxicab window, her arm around her dozing son, taking in the familiar sights. There was the broad expanse of Eastern Parkway, its apartment buildings and yeshivas and stately trees; the Met Foods where she bought groceries, and the dark swath of Prospect Park. The sameness surprised her, as if she had expected to find the world at home transformed. They passed the diner in which she'd met Anderson for the first time, where the waitress had YOLO tattooed across the back of her shoulders.

You Only Live Once. That's what people said, as if life really mattered because it happened only one time. But what if it was the other way around? What if what you did mattered *more* because life happened again and again, consequences unfolding across centuries and continents? What if you had chances upon chances to love the people you loved, to fix what you screwed up, to get it right?

They were outside her brownstone now. The gas lamp flickered in the night like a friend happy to see her. She paid the driver and hauled her heavy, sleeping boy in her arms and out of the cab, feeling stung with gratitude that they were home, and lived on the ground floor.

In their apartment, Janie carried Noah straight into the bedroom and put him down on his bed without turning the lights on. She curled up beside him, facing him in the narrow bed, and pulled the comforter over them both. He stirred and rubbed his eyes, yawning.

"Hey, we're home." He sighed, and nestled up against her. He threw his foot over her hip, placed his forehead against hers. He put his hand on her shoulder in the dark.

"What part of the body is this?" he whispered.

"That's my shoulder."

"This?"

"That's my neck."

"And this is your noggin, noggin, noggin. . . ."

"Yes."

"Mmmm."

Silence. Then a sound from deep beneath

493

the bedcovers. A sleepy grin. "I farted."

And, like that, he was asleep again.

Janie slowly got out of the bed. She moved quietly across the room and paused in the doorway.

Noah shifted; he was on his back, now, sleeping under the stars. They glowed above him, all the man-made constellations, that map that was all most of us could handle of the universe that went on and on without end. Years ago, she had placed the plastic decals up there, creating Noah's own big dipper, his own Orion, thinking that for the rest of his life when he saw the stars he'd feel at home. She tried to remember herself as she had been then, but she couldn't go back, any more than she could mistake the pasted-up stars for the real.

Noah's lips slid upward, as if he was having a very pleasant dream.

She stood in the doorway for a long time and watched him sleep.

EPILOGUE

Nothing about the trip to New York was what Denise had expected.

For instance, the fact that Henry decided to come with her: that had floored her.

You never knew what you'd get lately with Henry. There were days when he woke up whistling "Straight No Chaser" and made blueberry pancakes on Sunday mornings for Charlie and her. Other times he stayed up all night, drinking beer in the living room, the TV on loud on any dumb show, and if she got up to check on him or ask him to turn it down, he growled at her to go back to sleep. She always made an effort the next morning to wake early and get herself together and go over her lesson plans for the day, because she knew it would take a while, pushing him out of bed and making sure he got himself dressed and on his way. Sometimes it felt like she had two surly teenagers in the house. It was amazing the three of them ever got to school on time.

"This is me now. You want me, fine, this is what you get. You don't, that's fine, too," he'd said when he offered to move back home. His face was hard and he'd shrugged as he said it, as if it didn't matter much to him either way, but she'd seen right through him, as if he were one of her own children, saw plain as anything how much he wanted her to take him back. And how much she wanted it, too.

She was happy to have him back. He had that heaviness in him from Tommy's death, she didn't expect that would ever go away, but he could savor a plate of good food, and she found herself loving again the simple pleasure of cooking, putting a little of this in with some of that and having it come out of the oven steaming, the whole house smelling delicious, and then eating every bite of it. "You're putting meat on your bones again," that's what Henry kept saying, poking her in the new soft layer over her ribs. And it was good for Charlie. That was clear. The boy was a clown, always had been, and she could see now how much artfulness there was in it. There was nothing she liked better at the end of a long day than seeing Henry throw his head back and send that belly laugh of his out over the dinner table after Charlie had said something funny, and the flush of pleasure stealing over Charlie's face as he ducked his head shyly, taking it in. Sometimes after dinner they played together in the garage, Charlie on drums and Henry on bass, the sounds vibrating through the walls and out into the neighborhood, drowning out even the neighbor's dog, and she felt that everything was probably going to be all right.

They didn't talk about Noah. Neither of them wanted that fight; there was no winning it and no end to it. When spring rolled around and the idea of visiting Noah intruded into her thoughts as she went about her day, she'd pushed it aside at first, afraid to upset the new and delicate balance at home. She'd sent Noah a gift instead, on Tommy's birthday, though she hadn't mentioned that in the card.

She had talked to Noah a few times on the phone those first few months, but it was usually a disaster; whether that was due to the boy's youth and natural impatience with the telephone or the oddness of the circumstances, she wasn't sure. He'd been eager to talk to her for the first five seconds, often pestering his mother to make the call. Yet he answered her questions about kindergarten in a shy, monosyllabic way and (after reviving briefly to ask about Horntail) was clearly relieved to get off the phone a few moments later. It always took her the rest of the afternoon to recover from the intense feelings that followed. After a while, the calls had tapered off.

By summer she was determined to see Noah in person. She thought she could handle it now. Janie had agreed to it, though she sounded cautious: "He doesn't really talk about Tommy very much," she'd said, and Denise thought that was just as well.

She booked the ticket before telling Henry. Charlie had a job at the Stop & Shop bagging groceries and another as a lifeguard at the pool, so he couldn't come. When she told Henry she was going to New York to see Noah, he stood there wincing at the name, and she wondered if the risk was too great.

"I'll go with you, then," he'd said at last, as if he'd suddenly become somebody else's husband. "If that's all right? Got a couple old friends I want to look up."

He had spent a few years there, when he was young and a promising bass player.

She let him come. She didn't ask any questions. She didn't want to know, maybe, what his real motives were, and she wanted his company. She had never been to New York.

Another thing she hadn't expected: to have so much fun with him.

Their first night in the city they went to the Blue Note and got a seat right by the stage. They drank glowing blue drinks and listened to Henry's old friend Lou tearing it up with his sax and then afterward they went out somewhere else with the band, laughing and drinking and eating cheap, good food 'til the early morning, listening to the musicians' easy banter and their stories about staying in somebody's cousin's house on the road with the smell of chitlins blasting from the kitchen, their tales of tightwad band leaders and musicians who stumbled out of the bathroom with their noses dusted white and their pants down, and that time Lou's Seattle girlfriend flew out to see him play in San Francisco and ran into both his Oakland and Los Angeles girlfriends that same night.

Back at the hotel she and Henry hungered for each other like the old days. The force of it surprised her. It was nice to find out that was still possible, after everything that had happened.

She hadn't expected Henry to come with her to Janie's apartment the next day, or that Janie's apartment would be so small and old-fashioned — she'd imagined a big modern loft, like those New York apartments on television, not this quaint place with its ornate woodwork like something in her mother's house.

It was a hot day. When the two of them straggled in, Janie took one look at them and said, "Let me get you some water. Or would you like ice coffee?"

Denise shook her head. "Wish I could. If I drank coffee now, I'd be up 'til dawn."

While Janie went to get their drinks, Denise stepped into the living room, where Noah was.

He was almost six, that tender age when the baby plumpness starts to melt away from children's bodies and you can see, in their newly angular faces, the people they might become. He was absorbed in a book, sitting cross-legged on the couch, his hair bright and wild on his head. (Why didn't she ever take that boy in for a haircut?) He didn't seem to notice them.

"Noah, look who's here," Janie said when she came back with the waters, and he looked up.

Denise stood in the middle of the room, clutching the gift she'd brought, feeling her mouth go dry as Noah met her gaze with cheerful, unrecognizing eyes.

She hadn't known until that moment how deeply she had cared. She hadn't expected that at all.

"This is your Aunt Denise, don't you remember?" Janie said, stepping forward.

"Oh. Hi, Aunt Denise." He smiled politely, accepting her present and her presence in his life the way a child did, not questioning where she'd come from.

She sat down and cradled the icy water in her two hands as somewhere far away from her Henry introduced himself to Noah, and the child ripped the wrapping from the box in two quick strokes. Inside was Tommy's old baseball glove.

He pulled it out with a cry — "Hey, a new glove!" — and she took pleasure and pain in his open, uncomplicated glee.

They walked to the park. It was a bright day, the air kicking with a bit of wind.

"So. I've got one question for you," Henry said to Noah, as they walked. He turned to the boy with his gravest expression.

"Yeah?" Noah looked up worriedly.

"Mets or Yankees?"

"Mets, all the way!" Noah said.

Henry grinned. "That's what I wanna hear!" He high-fived the boy. "What do you think about Grandy? Think he can bring it?"

That was all it took, apparently. They talked animatedly about baseball for the rest of the way to the park while Janie and Denise walked quietly side by side. Denise was mute with disappointment.

"I'm sorry," Janie said, her voice low. "I didn't know what he would do when he saw you. He doesn't talk about it anymore, but I didn't know. . . . I guess he's just Noah now."

They walked on a bit in silence.

"He still likes the things he likes, though," she continued. "Lizards and baseball and new things, too. You should see what he can make out of Legos. These beautiful buildings."

"He's like his mom," Denise said at last.

Janie blushed, shrugged. "He's happy."

They got to the park and found an open stretch, a meadow. An elderly couple walked by arm in arm. A large Hasidic family moved down a path, corralling their children, keeping them from veering too close to the pond at the meadow's edge. People were feeding the ducks, a frenzy of beaks and crumbs. A girl stood in the grass twirling a Hula-Hoop around and around like someone from another time.

Janie and Denise settled on a blanket under the protective limbs of a large tree and took out containers of oily mozzarella balls and hummus, grapes and carrots and pita chips, weighing down the napkins with the thermoses so they didn't fly away. They had brought a baseball with them and the glove, and while they set up the picnic Henry and Noah crossed over into the open grass and tossed the baseball back and forth, Henry catching the ball in his bare hand, like he used to do.

Denise watched them. Noah *was* happy. Denise could see that. It was nice to see him happy, like any child. It was for the best that he had forgotten her, Denise knew that, though knowing didn't make it hurt any less. She was grateful that nature had righted itself but couldn't shake off the feeling that something had been taken away from her that might have been precious, if only she'd been able to find a way to make it so.

She leaned back on her elbows under the fluttering green leaves. Henry threw the ball in a steady, relaxed rhythm, his face as friendly and neutral as Noah's. She realized what she had already known: Henry didn't believe any more than he ever had but was doing this for her. Because he loved her.

The sound of that love was in the thwack of the ball in Tommy's old mitt, and the sound of her love — for Henry and Tommy and Charlie and Noah — was in the clicking of the wind in the leaves overhead, all of it making a web of sound that caught her and held her in this moment, right here, right now.

She sat back and watched Henry and Noah toss the ball back and forth, back and forth, like fathers and sons and men and boys anywhere, anytime.

"Now let's see you try a pop-up," Henry said, and he threw the ball straight up into the sky.

Janie wrote to Anderson. She thought it might be useful for him to keep track of what was happening with Noah, in case they did a new edition of his book. Now that normality reigned in her land in all its hectic glory, she liked to remind herself sometimes of where they had been. She and Jerry hadn't been friends, but they had shared a deeper connection: they were allies. She wrote about Denise and Henry's visit, giving him all the pertinent data: how much Noah had enjoyed it without recognizing either one of them. She sent the e-mail, and then another one, but he didn't write her back.

She hoped he was all right. She had seen him only once, when he had stopped by to visit and give her a copy of his book, a few months before he left the country again for good. The reviews of his book had been mixed; some critics had responded to his research by attacking him playfully, as if it was all a misunderstood game of telephone or fraudulence, nothing to take seriously; and others had been interested in his findings but hadn't known what to make of them. Anderson hadn't seemed to care, though. He'd been much quieter, and also somehow looser, as if some tight string had been snapped. He was wearing a white shirt with pockets, the kind of thing island people wore. She had mentioned that and he had actually laughed. "That's true. I'm an island person now," he'd said.

Janie didn't want to forget everything that had happened, but she couldn't help herself. Daily life was too insistent. She was busy with work, the pleasure of creating harmonious spaces, the headache of quibbling clients. To her great surprise and delight, Bob, her erstwhile texting fling, had entered her life, responding to her sheepish text "If you still want to get together, let me know?"

with enthusiasm; they had been seeing each other once or twice a week for six months now, long enough for her to begin to believe that it might actually be happening, and to think about (maybe, someday) introducing him to Noah. And, of course, there was Noah to look after: monitoring his homework, handling his dinner and bubble bath (how much pleasure she took now in ordinary life!), keeping up with all the needs of his ever-evolving self. He was getting older. Sometimes, when they were riding their bikes in the park, she let him pull a little bit ahead of her on the path, and as she watched his blond head and narrow back and small pumping legs cycling away from her and around the bend she felt a pang of loss that she knew was only ordinary motherhood.

One night she woke up in a panic, sure she was losing something precious, and she went to Noah's room and watched him sleep (the nightmares, thank goodness, had stopped long ago). Once she was content on that score, she turned on her computer and checked her e-mail.

There it was, at last: Jerry Anderson's name in her in-box. No subject heading. She opened it quickly. BEACH, he had written. All caps. Nothing else. The word resonated through the silence of the apartment, causing ripples of alarm and relief. "Are you all right?" she wrote. The screen cast a strange, pale light in the darkness, and she felt his presence rise up at that moment as if he were right there with her. "Jerry?"

I'm fine. She imagined him saying this, though he'd written nothing back. It was a feeling she had, though whether it was true or made up, she didn't know. Still, it calmed her to think she could feel him there, across that vast space.

The next day, Janie was on her way to get Noah from afterschool, thinking a million thoughts at once, when suddenly she stopped. She looked around.

She was standing in a subway car, feeling the motion beneath her feet. The train pulled up from underground, up and out over the Manhattan Bridge, the early evening light shining on the river, on a boat carting its cargo from here to there, on the people in the subway car, every detail leaping forward with a heightened, tender clarity. The Band-Aid on the knee of the teenager across from her. The spiky hair of the woman reading next to him. The Rastafarian's lips moving beneath his beard as he chewed gum.

Inside the subway car, advertisements for beer, storage space, mattresses: "Wake up and Rejuvenate your life."

I've been wrong, she thought suddenly.

What had happened to Noah had seemed to separate her from other people who didn't know the story — or, when she tried to explain it to her closest friends, "couldn't believe in that stuff." So she had put it away, kept it to herself, as if it was yet another thing keeping her subtly apart, when in fact . . . in fact, the implications suggested otherwise.

What *were* the implications?

So many lifetimes. So many people loved and lost and found again. Relatives you didn't know you had.

Maybe she'd been related to someone in this very subway car. Maybe that guy with the suit and the iPad. Or the Rasta chewing gum. Or the blond man with the polka-dot shirt and the fern sticking out of his bag. Or the woman with the bristly hair. Perhaps one of them had been her mother. Or her lover. Or her son, the dearest of the dear. Or would be, next time around. So many lifetimes, it stands to reason that they were all related. They'd forgotten, that's all. It wasn't a hippy dippy campfire song. (Well, okay, it was, but it wasn't *just* that.) It was real.

But how was that possible?

It didn't matter *how*. It *was*. She looked around the car. The olive-skinned man next to her was reading a newspaper ad for a matchmaker. The kid across from her was jiggling a skateboard on his banged-up knees. The dearest of the dear, she thought. She was feeling punchy.

It would be hard to live that way. To look at other people that way. But you could try, couldn't you?

The doors between the cars flung apart and a man emerged, homeless, shuffling into the subway car on grimy bare feet. His hair was matted into a coarse helmet, and his clothes — she couldn't look too closely at his clothes. He lumbered unsteadily through the car. His smell was like a force field, repelling everything in its path; when the subway finally stopped and the doors opened, new people stepped in with one foot and turned right back around to go to another car. Most of the people already in the car left in droves.

Some stayed put, though. Decided to bear it out. They were too tired to get up or too distracted by their handheld devices or they didn't want to give up their seats. Their stops were coming up soon. And anyway, that was the car they'd picked, the hand they'd been dealt, this time around. They looked carefully away from him; they were afraid to draw his attention.

She was the only one looking in his general direction, so he walked right up to her. He stood there, swaying in front of her, his smell making her eyes water. He didn't have a jar or anything. He held out a dirty palm.

She pulled three quarters from her pocket and placed them on his palm, and as she did so, her fingers brushed against his hand, and she looked up. His eyes were a caramel color, bright around the pupils and darker at the edges, and peering into them was like looking into a double eclipse. He had thick lashes, brushed with soot. He blinked.

"Hey, thanks, sister," he said.

"You're welcome." His face seemed to spring forward, his needs and hopes etched clearly there, as if he had been waiting all this time for her to notice him.

Paul lost twenty pounds that first year. He got shuffled around the prison as if he was a piece of paper on the ground being stepped on with muddy boots. He couldn't sleep; he'd lie there in the top bunk breathing in the smell of urine from the toilet in the corner and listening to the prison sounds of dripping and snoring and yelling. He didn't know if the yelling was the other inmates screaming in their sleep or if they were pushed into wakefulness by their own misery, as he was. And underneath it all, the never-ending echo of Tommy Crawford calling him from the bottom of the well. He had long ago stopped trying not to think of Tommy Crawford; what he'd done was in the threads of his prison clothes and the grout between the cement bricks and the cat piss smell that permeated everything. Sometimes he still wished he could go back and do it all differently, but he couldn't. Other times he wondered why life was like that: you did stupid things and couldn't take them back no matter how much you wanted to; there were no second chances. He had said that to his lawyer once and the woman had pursed her lips, looking at him across the table like somebody's sad mother. She was a woman in her fifties, thin, with bushy gray-blond hair tied back with a rubber band and blue eyes that always looked as if she'd been up all night worrying about him. He didn't know why she would do a thing like that, when he wasn't even related to her, but he was grateful for her services, and that he would get out of prison someday, though he would be almost thirty by then.

One day after a year or so had passed, they told him that he had a visitor.

He thought it must be his lawyer or his mom.

The guard brought him down the long hallway and into the room where the tables were.

When he saw who it was, he wanted to back up out of the room, but it was too late. She was sitting there, waiting for him. Her hair was grayer now than it had been in the hearing, but her face was the same, and her eyes turning to him looked like Tommy Crawford's eyes when he was trying to decide whether or not he should go with him into the woods to practice shooting.

He wished he could hide under the table.

She picked up the phone on the other side of the heavy scuffed glass, so he did, too. "I got your letter," she said.

He looked at her. He couldn't think of any words to say.

He had written a letter about how sorry he was about what happened to Tommy. How he had liked Tommy and wished that Tommy was alive and he was dead. Everything he wrote was true. His lawyer had thought it might help if they went to court, but then they had plea-bargained, and he had sent the letter anyway, thinking the parents would never respond. Why would they?

"You said in the letter that you're an alcoholic." Her voice was low. She didn't meet his gaze through the glass. "Is this true?"

"Mmm," he mumbled. Then forced himself to say it. "Yes." He was used to admitting it now, after all those AA meetings in prison.

"But you're sober now?"

He nodded, then realized there was no way she could see him with her head bent down like that. "Yes."

"Is that why it happened? Because you were drunk?" She was looking at her hands on the table in front of her.

He swallowed. His throat was dry. There was no water here. "No."

"Then why?" She glanced up. Her eyes were sad, but they had no anger in them.

"It was an accident," he said and saw that shadow of skepticism, that downward twitch of the lips, that had crossed so many faces since he had confessed. "But that's not why," he added. "It was because I was a coward. A coward and an idiot." He bent his head, too. He looked down at their hands, the two long brown ones, the two stubby white ones with the nails half-chewed off.

She made a noise on the other end of the phone. He couldn't tell what kind of noise it was.

"I'm sorry I killed your son," he said into the phone. The words were garbled because his throat was so thick and so dry. He put his head down on his arms and hoped the guards didn't think he was crying. He was, a little bit, but that was beside the point.

He felt she was waiting for him to say something else. He wasn't sure what, and then he knew. He took the phone into the cradle of his arms and said the rest: "I know you can't forgive me."

Forgive. It wasn't a word he had ever used before recently. Wanting forgiveness was a part of him now; he craved it like he craved alcohol.

There was a long silence.

"It's funny," she said at last, though there was nothing funny in the whole world, as far as Paul could tell. He looked up and her face was calm. "I've been thinking about that." She spoke like a teacher, someone who knew something. "The Bible says 'Forgive and you will be forgiven,' . . . and the Buddhists, of course, believe that hatred

514

only leads to further hatred and suffering. As for me — I don't know. I know I don't want to hold on to hatred anymore. I can't."

Her eyes lingered on his face, as if she was deciding whether or not he was hideous. It occurred to him that wanting forgiveness meant you had to give it, too. He knew he hadn't forgiven his dad for some things. He couldn't imagine doing that.

"Tommy's teaching me, every day," she continued, and he nearly fell right off his seat. How could Tommy be teaching her anything? "He's forcing me to let go of him," she said, "to surrender to the moment at hand. There's joy there. If you can do it."

He couldn't believe she was sitting there talking about learning something from her dead son, talking about joy, to him. *To him!* Maybe he'd driven her crazy and he'd have that on his conscience, too.

"How is it here?" she asked quietly. "Is it bad?"

He couldn't tell whether she wanted to hear that it was or it wasn't.

"It's what I deserve, I guess," he said simply.

She didn't dispute it, but she didn't seem happy about it, either. "I'd like you to write me," she said. "Will you do that? I want to know what it's like in here and how you're getting on. I want to know the truth."

"Okay." He thought that he would tell her, too, even if she *was* crazy. He could tell her all the things he'd been through here that he didn't want his own mom to know about.

"So we've got ourselves a deal?" she said. He nodded. She stood up. She belted her coat tightly across her waist — she was thin, like something that could break in two seconds, and at the same time he felt that she was probably tougher than he could ever hope to be. She lifted her hand up to him and waved good-bye, a smile passing across her face, there and gone, so quick he wasn't sure if he'd imagined it.

After the visit, he stabilized a bit. He stopped hating the feel of the scratchy uniform on his skin, and the way one moment slammed into the next moment with no room for wriggling free except for the novels he got out from the prison library and the GED class he was taking and the visits from his mom to see how he was doing. He wrote letters to Mrs. Crawford, telling her the truth. He woke every morning from a heavy, dreamless slumber, still surprised to find himself there.

The people in the novels he was reading lived in peat and stone dwellings in hilly lands covered in mist, and they raised dragons and learned magic. They passed on their secrets from mother to son.

Anderson felt the warm water licking at his feet.

He walked in slowly, aware at every moment that he could turn back, the water encompassing his calves and his sore knees, his thighs and his chest. He was unsure of what he was going to do until the last moment the sandy ground slid beneath his feet and he was swimming, and even then he glanced back and saw the shore so close and his sandals and his book right there, waiting for him.

The beach was empty. It was too early for tourists and there were no fishermen on this side of the island. It was as if he was the only one in the whole world who was awake. There were a few palm trees scattered here and there, the craggy mountains cradling the water, the sign about the water's current planted in the middle of the beach. He couldn't read it anymore, not in any of the languages they had posted, but he knew what it meant.

The water, a transparent green, took on a deeper, bluer hue as he swam. He swam out until his sandals were two specks on the sand, his book a blur of blue. He enjoyed the feeling of his body exerting itself, helped on by the current. Words floated out to him and he clung to them. Silence. Ocean. Enough.

He should have told someone. He could have told that woman who had e-mailed him, for instance. The one with the son. The thought of his last case was like a strand of hair tethering him to land — all that was left between himself and the open sea. He could go back and try again to e-mail her. He had meant to write "Good-bye" and the word had come out wrong, a different word. He hoped she understood what he meant.

If he stopped thinking of it, if he let the current carry him, the strand would break easily of its own accord.

Think about something else, he thought. He closed his eyes. The sun created dark spots on the pulsing orange inside his eyelids.

Sheila.

The day he met Sheila.

A Saturday. He'd left the lab early and had taken the first train he saw until the end and walked the rest of the way to the beach. Sitting on the damp sand, brooding. A whole universe out there, so many things unknown. Why was he stuck in cages with the rats?

Two girls were sitting next to him on a beach blanket. A blonde, a redhead. Two silly girls eating ice-cream cones and laughing at him.

The blonde was the bold one. She walked up to him.

"Are you religious?"

"Not at all. Why?"

He glanced at her. Her cheeks were pink from the sun, or maybe she was blushing. Her hair was tied back in a band but coming loose around her face in bright fluttery pieces.

"We were thinking you must be religious to be wearing that. Don't you have a bathing suit?"

He looked down at himself. He was in his usual graduate student attire, long-sleeved white oxford shirt, black pants.

"No."

"Oh, I see. You're *far too serious* for the beach." She said it lightly, teasingly. She had a strong white body. It hurt his eyes to look at it. Silly polka-dot bathing suit.

He scowled at her. "You're making fun of me."

"Yes."

"Why?"

"Because you're far too serious for the beach." Her blue eyes were both affectionate and mocking. He couldn't make sense of that. She was making him dizzy.

The ice cream was dripping down the cone in the hot sun over her fingers. He had the strangest urge to lick them.

Why not, polka dots?

"Your ice cream is melting," he said.

She licked the cone, then her fingers, one after the other, laughing at herself. He had taken her for a giggler, but her laugh came from someplace deeper, it rolled out into the air, taking up space. Ice cream, he thought, giddiness rising up his body from the white soles of his feet. The secret to life is ice cream. Her laugh rang in his ears and kept on ringing.

He had hoped it would never stop.

He was getting tired now. This treading water business was more exhausting than he had anticipated. There was more resistance in him than he'd thought there would be. Just stop moving, he thought. *Let go.*

He opened his eyes. The current had worked fast. The sandals and book were gone now, blended into the shore.

He felt his heart pounding. He calculated how far he was from the beach. He could probably make it back if he wanted to. And then what? Back to that small, increasingly circumscribed existence of seafood and short walks. Not a terrible life. But winding down . . .

He didn't miss language anymore. He liked the concreteness of this new way of living: the briny taste of the crab he was eating, the shy, curious face of the girl serving it, the sand slipping through the toes of his sandals as he walked back to his bungalow, the feel of his breath tickling his nostrils as he meditated. It was as if the earth was holding him in its gaze, cupping his face in its hands. He felt it whispering to him in a wordless language he had forgotten his whole life and only now remembered, speaking to him of a reality so vast he couldn't impart it to another human even if he had the ability to do so. He barely recognized himself in the mirror: the brown, careless, leathery face, the wild, much-too-bright eyes — who was this man? He had accepted the simplicity of this life gratefully but knew that soon he would not be able to understand even the most basic transactions. He would be forced to succumb to the only thing he feared: helplessness.

The shore was a pale smudge in the distance. His book was out there, on the sand. He felt bereft without it; he had carried it with him through these last days. At first it was to forestall conversation — dipping his face into those pages he had written and could no longer read — but lately it had become like a friend to him. When he awoke in the night disoriented and afraid, he turned on the light and through the thick bodies of the circling moths sought out its blue cover on his bedside table. It spoke to him without words, assuring him that he had lived.

Perhaps a tourist would find it while out collecting shells. Perhaps it would change everything for her.

His legs ached. He stared in the sunlight at the retreating wisp of shore until it seemed merely a trick of the eyes, an imagined oasis. Here, then gone. Of course the body would resist its demise. Of course; this was how life was. How could he have thought otherwise? It was a lesson he'd learned again and again: no matter how carefully you planned or did your research, the unknowable things would rise up out of the deep and overturn everything. But that was what had drawn him in, wasn't it? The depths of what we *don't* know?

Maybe he'd see Sheila again. Her face. Or some glimmer of her in another.

Maybe he wouldn't.

He looked around him at the wide sky, at the ocean that continued now as far as he

could see. The water sparkled in the sunlight, dazzling his eyes. Every molecule
glistening in the radiant, polka-dotted
world. He felt his limbs relax, his body melting beneath the beauty of it.

Blue sky, blue water, and nothing else.

The undiscovered country.

Look at it this way, Jer, he heard Sheila saying. *Now you're going to get some answers.*
He felt the curiosity beating through him at
the thought of it, stronger than his heart.

ACKNOWLEDGMENTS

This book was inspired by the work of the late Dr. Ian Stevenson and Dr. Jim Tucker at the Division of Perceptual Studies at the University of Virginia School of Medicine.

I am particularly indebted to Dr. Tucker for consulting with me and for allowing me to include parts of his excellent book of nonfiction *Life Before Life: Children's Memories of Previous Lives,* within this made-up tale. Anderson's thinking on why children might remember previous lifetimes owes a great deal to a chapter in Dr. Tucker's fascinating book *Return to Life: Extraordinary Cases of Children Who Remember Past Lives.*

For those who'd like to read more about Dr. Ian Stevenson, *Old Souls,* by Tom Shroder, is a riveting account of the man and his work; *Children Who Remember Previous Lives,* by Dr. Stevenson, gives an overview of his approach.

I'd also like to give thanks:

To my brilliant editor, Amy Einhorn, whose vision guided this novel through many drafts and made it an incomparably better book. To the amazing team at Flatiron Books, including Liz Keenan, Marlena Bittner, and Caroline Bleeke.

To my agent, Geri Thoma, who went above and beyond and whose wise counsel I can always rely on. To Simon Lipskar and Andrea Morrison at Writer's House for all their help. To Jerry Kalajian at the Intellectual Property Group for working to give this story another life.

To my advisers: Rebecca Dreyfus, for endless patience, love, and confidence in me, and for good ideas both large and small; Bryan Goluboff, who always found time to help me untangle the plot; and Matt Bialer, for incredible generosity that made a huge difference.

To Bliss Broyard, Rita Zoey Chin, Ken Chen, Meakin Armstrong, Youmna Chlala, Sascha Alper, Nell Mermin, and Julia Strohm for reading drafts of this novel and giving great advice. To Catherine Chung, who helped me focus this book at a crucial moment.

To the Virginia Center for the Creative Arts and Wellspring House, for perfect working environments.

To the late Jerome Badanes, whose encouragement still matters.

To the dear friends who have advised and supported me through the many incarnations of this book, especially Liz Ludden, Sue Epstein, Martha Southgate, Tami Ephross, Lisa Mann, Stephanie Rose, Shari Motro, Rahti Gorfien, Susannah Ludwig, Edie Meidav, Carol Volk, and Carla Drysdale.

To my teachers, especially the late Peter Matthiessen, who lit the spark, and Kadam Morten Clausen, whose meditation classes and extraordinary teachings helped me stay calm through the ups and downs of this process and eventually changed my life.

To my parents, Alan and Judy Guskin, who always believed in me; my wonderful sisters, Andrea Guskin and Carrie LaShell; my stepmother Lois LaShell, whose faith in my abilities never flagged; and my stepfather, Martin Rosenthal, a true original. To my incredible Cuomo in-laws, Sylvia, George and June, and the Cuomo sibs: I'm so proud to be part of your family.

To my husband, Doug Cuomo, for limitless love and support; and my children, Eli and Ben, for being so kind and so fun.

Words can't express how lucky I feel to
share this life with the three of you.

Reading Group Guide available at:
us.macmillan.com/reading-group-gold

ABOUT THE AUTHOR

Sharon Guskin lives in Brooklyn with her husband and two sons. She has been a fellow at Yaddo, Virginia Center for the Creative Arts, Blue Mountain Center, and Ragdale, and has degrees from Yale University and the Columbia University School of the Arts. *The Forgetting Time* is her first novel.

The employees of Thorndike Press hope you have enjoyed this Large Print book. All our Thorndike, Wheeler, and Kennebec Large Print titles are designed for easy reading, and all our books are made to last. Other Thorndike Press Large Print books are available at your library, through selected bookstores, or directly from us.

For information about titles, please call:
  (800) 223-1244

or visit our Web site at:
  http://gale.cengage.com/thorndike

To share your comments, please write:
  Publisher
  Thorndike Press
  10 Water St., Suite 310
  Waterville, ME 04901